To Alyssa — Finding deep friends, in whatever places, is a joy. Thank you for listening. Thank you for making sure I'm not messing up!

Courting Witchcraft

Monarchy of America: Book 2

Thomas Gondolfi

TANSTAAFL PRESS

TANSTAAFL Press
891 PH 10
Castle Rock, WA 98611

Visit us at www.TANSTAAFLPress.com

Courting Witchcraft

First printing—TANSTAAFL Press
Copyright © 2021 by Thomas Gondolfi
Cover art: Kristin Bryant at www.kristindesigns.com

Printed in the USA
ISBN: 978-1-938124-63-1

Book layout by Hydra House Books

Monarchy
of America

with Duchies defined

1—Thursday, May 3, 1888

"Stella, watch the tail, damn it all!" the barrel-chested Carlos barks. Blood runs down his forehead before taking a radical right turn at his eyebrow ridge and dripping down his sideburns. The cut is at the center of a palm-shaped bruise that covers most of the right side of his face. A hellfighter gets these kinds of injuries almost every time we struggle to put a demon back in place, which lately has been almost a daily event.

"Which one," I snap back, using my earth magic to reshape the stone wall to give me a half roof of protection against a flailing appendage as big around as a hogshead. The demon we are fighting reminds me of a monstrous beaver with four prehensile tails in place of the wide, flat one. But then a beaver usually tops out at three feet. With tusks instead of the classic rodent overbite, this one stands twelve feet high without getting off its forelegs.

"Raquel, tighten your hedgerow," Carlos orders. Carlos de Aldana is the leader of our team. His heavily pockmarked face should be called ugly, but I find it reassuring when the chips are down.

Raquel Ruiz is a nature witch who most everyone calls Menaj or Menagerie because she always has one or more critters hanging around her, often nesting in her long, wild hair. Now, her wall of vines and bushes closes in on the arse end of the hellspawn, limiting the movement of its tails.

Maxwell Parker comes over and lays his hands on Carlos's back. A glow from his white witch powers at least seals the boss's cut.

"Thanks, Max."

"You're welcome, *jefe*." Even though he is aged twenty-eight years, Maxwell Parker has the cracking voice of an adolescent teen boy. He once mentioned he'd lost a consistent tone in his voice as a child when chicken pox covered him so severely he nearly died. His vocal cords had been permanently damaged, for when he talks, it squeaks and breaks.

"I WILL SUP ON YOUR HEART AND DRINK BLOOD FROM YOUR SKULL," the monster says. It really isn't like talking; rather, it puts the thoughts directly into your head. Even in the loudest steam plant, you can't not hear a demon who isn't interned.

Steam. Power. That is what brings us to summon demons to our world. Their bodies produce massive quantities of heat to boil water. While not as prevalent as the use of coal, demons are becoming more and more common. The initial costs are higher, but their upkeep is nil. What we hellfighters do is deal with the ones that get free, like this *joda* in front of us.

The beast moves to my left. I'm playing right wall so I co-opt my stonework to move left to match its stride. As my stone wall slides along with the massive demon, I catch sight of a pair of stubby, almost vestigial wings on its back. Everyone else must have missed them.

"Bloody demon has wings!" I shout. With the tiny stubs it has on its back, it probably can't fly fast, but any ability to just float off into the sky matters as we enter the final phase to reinter it. We must make sure it just doesn't flap off to find a new place to wreak havoc.

Without missing a beat, Carlos switches our team around the way a conductor gets more from an orchestra by his baton movements. "Maxwell, take Donny's place as bait. Donny, you have the sky." Donny O'Sullivan, with hair as red as his name implies, slides behind Raquel's hedgerow. With water powers, his typical role is as one of the two people that take turns taunting the demon. Because we need another side to our box, he has to change up. I think Carlos would have rather used our other baiter to keep the demon from flying away, but Bea Media is just too new to our team to understand such a shift easily. She is an ice witch just over from Spain.

Maxwell says, taking up his new duties, "'Love does not delight in evil, but rejoices with the truth.'" The scripture sends a flare of goodness hitting the beast just in the right nostril.

"AND MAY SATAN LUNCH ON YOUR TESTICLES, SCUM!" it roars back as it lunges away from Bea toward him. It takes four ponderous steps before Bea, bless her, follows through with a cone of snow and ice that strikes the beast's ear.

"GOAT CONCUBINE!" it screams, turning to lumber toward her again.

Demons are notorious for their inability to look beyond the present. Whoever is hurting them at that precise moment receives their attentions. By using this fact, a team of hellfighters has an easy task, relatively speaking, to allow the beast to go exactly where we want it to with judicious prods. My team, the *Dos Campanas*, or Two Bells, is the best, at least in the Boston area. We take our name from the two differently toned bells of the Mission Church that we use to message the team on the location of any loosed demons.

"We only have another ten feet. Can you guys hold him while I set up the pentagram?" I ask.

"We got it, Stella," Carlos says to me after catching the eye of each of the other team members. Despite the cry of the earth that it does not belong in a curl like a tsunami, I leave my twelve-foot cobblestone and brick wall in place.

In the failing evening light, I look at the exploded basement beneath with a certain amount of dread. For nearly a month after the demise of Baron Snowdonia and the end of his plot to release hellspawn to cause chaos and destruction in Boston, we had no demon escapes. Then they restarted in earnest but with one deadly difference.

"Please, Lord, make this a clean one. I pray not just for my own personal preference but for the life of some poor soul."

As I get closer to the dark hole, I smell that my prayers have not been answered. Issuing forth from the orifice is the odor from holding a penny tight in your hand during the summer. The bitter tang of an overripe privy follows quickly on its heels.

I pull a metal lamp from my carpetbag. I've taken to carrying the oversized tote instead of a purse so I could bring a change of clothes. Many a dress had been burned, ripped, or torn asunder in this vocation. With all the callouts the last few weeks, I need to be able to cover myself in case of an accident.

Using a match, the oil-impregnated cord catches and provides a modicum of light. The reek of spilled intestines is overbearing in the murky cellar. Slithering into the hole, I urge the rock into a smoother shape to minimize at least the physical damage to my outer dress. It won't save me from the red stains that are sure to follow. Blood drips from the ceiling joists, and bits of flesh peel off the walls to land in the greater puree that had been a human. The majority of the body, sans legs or much in the way of a gut, lies propped up against the remnants of a wooden staircase. It is much more intact than we've found in any other such case.

Morbidly curious, I move closer, only to see not the macabre grimace of death on the victim's face but a beatific smile. That frightens me more than the gore that drips on my neck and down the back of my dress. He holds a strand of metal wire in his right hand that leads two feet away to its broken end. His fingertips have some odd, black calluses on them that weren't done by any demon.

"Stella, how is it going down there? *El diablo* is a handful, and we're getting tired," calls down Carlos. I'll have time for morbid curiosity later. I have a demon to imprison.

"Hold on, Carlos, it's a mess down here."

I rip the remnants of the man's peasant blouse off his chest and use it as a rag to wipe down the ceiling. Holding a demon on ground that has blood, flesh, or even a grave is like using your arm to put meat into the mouth of a lion. Confident that no more drips will happen, I urge the flesh-impregnated soil to pile up into the lowest corner of the basement to be removed later.

Witchcraft is quite a lot like true love. Two people join their lives together, and somehow they become more than one. Neither is demanding. Neither dominates the other. It is a partnership. That is what it feels like to share with the earth. I ask, and it willingly gives, as that is the nature of our collaboration.

Before I can set a pentagram in place, I find a smashed bit of tin and metal bits. My first thought is a lantern, but there is a spring and wind-up key. I scoop the bits into my bag for later examination. I scuff a flat, smooth area on the clay-rich ground. Extending my senses through my hand, I no longer feel the weakness of blood within feet of the point I intend to temporarily seal the creature.

Holding the lamp in one hand, I draw with the other. "He who dwells in the shelter of the Most High will rest in the shadow of the Almighty. I will say of the Lord, He is my refuge and my fortress, my God, in whom I trust. Surely he will save you from the fowler's snare and from the deadly pestilence. He will cover you with his feathers, and under his wings you will find refuge; his faithfulness will be your shield and rampart..." I've had a great deal of practice lately so it only takes the one single recitation of the scriptures of Psalms 91:1–4 to draw the five-pointed star and its protecting circle on the dirt. As I do, I urge minerals in the earth to collect to each trace line of the star and fuse with the goodness of our Lord and savior. A faint glow shows my handiwork in the shadowy environment. There are no gaps so the prison is ready.

"Bring him in!" I call to my comrades.

A roar of defiance answers my team moving into the most dangerous phase of our work. Up until now, it has been getting the demon to make the choices we want. Now we physically have to move this mass of chaos the last few yards.

I let my wave of stone relax and form a shepherd's crook twenty feet long and over a foot through. I put the hook in the middle of its back and pull, using the earth's strength. I hear grunts of my team pushing.

"LEAVE ME, OR I WILL HANG YOU ALL BY YOUR ENTRAILS! AWAY!"

Earth may be slow, but it possesses a great deal of raw power. My physical strength might squash a cockroach on a good day, but augmented through the earth, I am something of a strongwoman. No matter how much the hellspawn backpedals or digs its claws into the cobblestone for purchase, our team inexorably pulls it back to its jail, inch by inch. I mentally will the earth to shorten my improvised hook with each successive movement toward me.

The hellspawn changes its tactics. No longer is it spending its energies trying to kill us but instead in finding an escape. "RELEASE ME, MORTALS, OR I WILL HAVE YOU CLEAN MY BUNGHOLE WITH YOUR TONGUE AS YOUR ONLY NOURISHMENT FOR ALL ETERNITY!"

Between the six of us, we give it no opportunity to find a way beyond us. The beaver shrinks as the magic in the soil sucks him toward my pentagram. I hear a low, throaty howl that reminds me of a windy day blowing over a chimney followed by a short pop and then silence.

The chaos that we had battled against is chained, leaving us with nothing to do. As always, that break from desperate activity to nothingness leaves us numb.

"*Joder*," Raquel says with about as much vehemence as one might have walking into a spider's web. A squirrel takes that moment to emerge from Raquel's mussed hair onto her shoulder. It chatters something I assume to be a rebuke. Raquel, on the other hand, leans against the cleanest of the basement walls.

Carlos drops down to the floor against the same wall, his face a pale white, accentuating the pitting there. Maxwell collapses to the ground and rolls onto his back, panting. Donny, sweat trickling like from some mountain spring out of his hair, opens a canteen and chugs the entire thing dry. I can empathize. My dress is soaked through and bears the red pox and other smears of blood splatter.

I offer weakly, "Can we not have another released demon for a few months?"

# # #

A milk bath at the O'Shaughadain Bathhouse is a necessary cleansing experience. It removes the feeling and appearance that I'm Sweeney Todd wandering the streets looking for another human victim.

Clean and in fresh clothing, I leave the steaming warmth as dusk trades places with night. The streets are nearly empty, and the bareness reminds me of how tired I am. The tub bath may have been an error as it relaxed me too much. I bite my lip and push forward, only a few blocks from my flat. Despite my willpower, I stagger over a cobblestone that might be a tiny fraction of an inch above the others around it.

"Ma'am, you don't look very well. Maybe you had one too many at your local pub?" says a man striding down the boardwalk. He is in the traditional bobby's blue uniform with the white acorn device of the king's seal across his chest. His diminutive height is more than made up for by the breadth of his shoulders. The man looks like a short ape. I detect just the hint of a guttural German accent from the squat guardsman.

I wonder what happened to our regular beat policeman, Paterna. It must be his night off or some kind of transfer. "No, sir. On Mary's grave, I've not had a drop. I'm a hellfighter, and I just spent the evening battling with a demon. I'm more tired than…" I trail off. "Well, more tired than anything I can think to compare myself to."

The beat cop says, "Another demon? By his son, Jesus Christ, but can't those beasts be held in place for once and for all?"

"I'll be honest, Guardsman, no one expected people to start sacrificing themselves to release one."

"I guess that is nothing but the truth. Do you want me to help you the rest of the way home?"

"No, thank you, sir. It's just over there. I can manage another pair of blocks."

"Yes, ma'am. Then you have a nice night. Get some rest."

"Top of my list, sir."

I should be in my poderabile, the air-powered vehicle Viscount Henry Helms gave me for helping to save his business. But the problem with owning a buggy, trap, or cart is that it needs to be someplace when it isn't being used. There is nowhere near Chapman's Boarding House that I can stable it, horses or no. So, more often than not, I spend my time walking, like now, or taking the trolley.

The door to my home is in sight. I'll be on time for dinner before my landlady locks the door tonight. I'm certain the widow Chapman has some sterling qualities, but if so, the Lord has failed to show them to me in the nearly five years I've lived as her boarder. That being said, cooking is one of the lesser of her skills. I rent a home here only because the room and board are cheap, period. Between the poor food, my landlady's snooping, and her faux moral superiority, I have sworn on more than one occasion to find new living arrangements. I just never seem to find the time. And with demons being loosed almost every second day, I don't have the time or gumption to do so now.

Between the crown's survivor pension of my husband, who died in the liberation of Ireland, and the salary paid to me by the Coal Syndicate for spelling coal dust out of the air, I get by. I don't live lavishly, but I have a roof over my head and food in my belly. Moving anywhere likely would upset that balance.

Some might ask me to use the monies I make from being a hellfighter to pay for home and provender. Instead, everything I make being a hellfighter gets saved for that rainy day that is old age. I will be able to take care of myself in my dotage. I won't be a burden on anyone.

"Emperor of Spain Plans State Visit!" calls an enterprising young girl hawking the evening edition of the *Boston Herald* only a block from home. I don't know who she could be calling to except me as the streets are empty. I stumble up to her stand like someone just about in her cups. Maybe I should have taken that officer's offer of his arm. "Young Amanda, if I remember correctly. I'll take one."

"Yes'm, I be called 'Manda. Thanks for 'membering. That's a penny, Widow Ochoa," she says, handing me over the paper. I unsnap my purse and offer her two but pull them away at the last moment. Amanda's eyes go wide in lust for the extra tiny coin.

"If you would be so kind, Amanda, let the others know I prefer not to be called a widow."

"Yes, ma'am, I will!" As I drop the coins in her hand, one bounces off and falls to the ground. I bend over to pick it up. Something slams into my shoulder like the fiery sword of the devil himself. A loud bang reports and echoes off the buildings and back to me like a badly stuttering young man.

I fall backward. Amanda falls forward atop of me with a scream. Another bark shatters the evening's silence as I feel the pain pierce through my gut like a fireplace poker being shoved through me. The young girl in my arms grunts and spits blood onto my face.

I don't know what is happening. It is too blurry, but I know I need to protect the young miss. The earth and cobblestones come to my aid, rolling the pair of us up into a protective cocoon. The three more repeated explosions of what I now recognize as gunshots are followed by bullets deflecting off our stone and mortar security blanket.

Constabulary whistles fill the night air, most at a distance. That one guardsman should be very close. Several more whistles sound as bootsteps come running up toward us. My energy seeps out of me like milk from a leaky churn.

"Ma'am! Are you OK? Help me get the stones off of her and the girl!" No German accent.

"Stella?" I recognize this voice as Paterna.

"Get Maxwell," I manage to whisper. "Bell in Hand. Healer." I feel someone pressing on my side and what had been a dull ache erupts into full-fledged agony. "AAAAA!"

"You, Kennedy. Go to the Bell in Hand and get Maxwell here now. Hurry."

Extreme pain dilates time. It seems to go on forever. In other ways, the world goes on around you at a speed that rivals the fastest locomotive or dirigible. It flies by, and while I focus on my body's cry for help, I can't follow everything that transpires.

Eons go by before I hear Maxwell's screechy voice.

"The girl first," I hear someone bark. Nothing exists for me except for pain. Bits and pieces of the conversations around me soak in.

"Last rites will have to wait. Stella needs me," Max says. I need last rites? I wish I'd been able to...

"Stella? Stella, can you hear me?"

"Max. Oh, fuck, I've made a mess of things."

"Stella, this is going to hurt."

"Sure it is."

# # #

"Through this holy anointing, may the Lord in his love and mercy help you with the grace of the Holy Spirit. May the Lord who frees you from sin save you and raise you up." Max's voice causes my mind to lumber into existence. I sit up with a start, clawing at my middle. My dress has a hole the size of a dinner plate ripped out of it. I see an angry, round puckered scar, very similar to a belly button just inches to its right. In sitting up, I sway, uneasy if not downright dizzy.

"Careful, Stella. Take it easy. Those wounds are going to take a day or so to fully heal."

I can feel just a mild throbbing where there had once been agony. "Wounds? Plural?"

He touches my shoulder, where I find a similar tenderness within the mass of old scarring I bear from my lesson in how not to summon a demon.

I must be slow, thinking about myself first. "What about Amanda?"

Inspector First Antonio Guizzetti kneels down next to me. "The newsgirl is dead. A shot went right through the middle of her chest."

This isn't the first time I'd survived a disaster where others perished. I look at the sheet covering what had been a promising young life. "Did you at least get the scum?"

"No, Stella. What can you tell me about what happened?"

"I was coming home from a demon hunt. Tired." A tear leaks down my cheek. I try to wipe it but find that lifting one of the arms that is supporting me starts me tipping. "I was buying a paper when I heard the first shot. It knocked me over. I just tried to protect us."

"First shot?"

"Five shots total, I think," I say, my focus wavering. My eyes are spending as much time closed as open.

"Five?"

"Did you see who shot at you or where from?"

"No. Wrapped us up," I mumble. My head lolls to my shoulder.

"Inspector...Antonio, enough," squeaks Maxwell. "Can't you see she can barely sit up, much less answer questions? A serious healing like this saps the will from the patient."

"*Lo siento*. You're right. Can you take her home, or do you want one of my men to help?"

"I can handle it."

If it weren't for Maxwell's broken voice, I wouldn't know who was speaking. "Stella. Stella, can you stand up with my help?"

"Sure, I'm not that tired—I think."

"Take my arm."

Another voice intruded. "Inspector. We found where he fired from—an attic storeroom on the third floor of Schafer's Dry Goods."

Squeaky voice. "Stella? Stella. Listen to me. We need to go to your rooming house."

My attention fails to keep up with what's going on. I hear Chapman's querulous voice. "No. Men are not allowed in the rooms."

"Do you want to carry her up the stairs? Then by the love of God, please observe some silence and let me do this. She isn't light."

That isn't nice, or fair.

2—Friday, May 4, 1888

My alarm clock goes off. Flailing an arm in that direction, I manage to knock it onto the floor with another clang, but not silence its caterwauling. From beneath my covers, I lean out and turn off the disturber of the peace. I can't remember the last time I had to be woken up by the alarm. Climbing out of bed fifteen minutes or more before it rattles the whole house is my norm. I must have had such a good time last night that I can't dredge up the memory.

As I stir, my left arm aches, as does my right side. My eyes are nearly glued shut with sleep. It's warm in the room so I climb out of bed, finding myself wearing the tatters of my work dress.

SHOT! I grab at my middle. A perfect circle with puckered edges the size of a blackberry mars my skin. The skin that covers it is warm and the color of salmon. While I can't see it, I wince as I touch a matching hole on my back. I follow the bloody rips in the fabric of my bodice, where I find another mostly healed wound. It hides in the decade-old burn scarring of my left bicep. One day I'll have to properly thank my mother for her lack of skill at protecting me.

I test my injuries to find movement only causes a bit of stretchy hurt. Nothing that would keep me from working, not that Mark Carlton, my supervisor at the Coal Syndicate, would care if I were in the last stages of consumption. He'd insist on my attendance and a full day's soot removal.

I realize that I'm still thinking in terms of normalcy. Two bullet holes perforate my tender personage. The assassin targeted either a papermonger, at least a year away from her first sparking, or little ole me. So, while I have no idea why I might have angered someone enough to shoot at me, it would behoove me to take precautions.

I should amend that latter comment. There are two people who might be so bothered. First would be John Quarrels, whom I am about to testify against in the Monarch's Court of High Crimes for murder and attempted murder. I'm sure he would like me dead. But as he is behind bars, I don't see how he could arrange for me to be shot. The second might be Bruce Jasperson, the leader of the Coal Syndicate. I've theorized that he pulled Lord Snowdonia's strings to get witches to taint their demon installations. I have no proof against him, only a good, solid hunch. But that and seven cents will get you eggs, bacon, and toast at Cindy's Restaurant.

As someone once said, *Señor* Jasperson could kill a virgin on stage in the middle of the Boston Market and not be prosecuted. He has too much influence, too much power. But that is why I don't feel it can be that fat little toad. Why bother over me? It doesn't make sense. I'm a nobody to him.

That brings me to exactly zero people that have a reason to come after me. I mean, a mugger would have attacked me at close range, and why a gun? No, I'm confused. But I have work, and that takes precedence at the moment.

I find an envelope under my door. I pick it up, turning it to find that it hasn't been through the Royal Post, for it has no stamp, nor does it have a return address. It has only my name in block letters on the outside. Frowning, I prize it open. There is a single slip of paper on the inside.

The missive has simple block letters saying, "Leave Boston today. Don't come back. We are watching—NPP."

I catch a bitter whiff of burnt tobacco from the paper. Taking the message out of my mouth, I sniff it more closely—wintergreen. And it is a cigar, not a pipe or a cigarette. Yes, as a woman, I know too much about tobacco. My mother's butler, Ozias, likes just about all forms of the evil leaf. As I didn't care for my mother, I spent a good deal of time below stairs, where I got more positive feedback and friendship from the servants than I did from my own flesh and blood. Ozias's favorite is smoking a pipe with an aromatic maple blend.

I'm not worried about the implied threat that the paper shares. I have to assume the NPP has decided I need a reminder that they exist. The NPP—*Non Patiatur Phythonissam*—Latin for "Suffer not a witch." As you can surmise, it advocates for the removal of all witches everywhere with as little compassion as possible. While quasi-illegal, the NPP has a number of high-ranking lords that sympathize with their aims. These covert allies keep the organization's shadowy adherents from being in the crosshairs of the Royal Dragoons. This isn't the first warning I've received or curse I've endured. Likely it won't be my last, either.

This makes me wonder if they were behind the attack last night. Wouldn't their purposes have been better served with a threat like "More to come," or "That was just a taste"? Get out of town seems too mild after the severity of the attack. I have to think they aren't connected.

I dress in my last work skirt. I still have a few blouses, but I'm down to just this one and my two best outfits. I absolutely need to get to my seamstress for more clothes. Being a hellfighter is celebrated work that pays well, but it is hard on the wardrobe.

Now presentable, including the *peineta* holding my hair in a snug roll, I traipse down the three flights of stairs. I'm trying to come up with a way I might be able to protect myself against any further bullets. I'm not worried about the second bullet and beyond. Guns and ammunition are made out of metals, and I am more than adequate as an earth witch. But that won't matter if the first shot kills me.

I do have an idea, but I can do nothing about it now due to a lack of time.

"Widow Ochoa, if I may have a word with you?" Alice Chapman's tone is one of a nagging wife. I doubt she will take no for an answer. She knows I disparage the term widow as I'm not a withered-up hag who is unlovable. On the other hand, Alice reminds me of the stereotype of a widow, with her pruned face, liver spots, and crow's feet. A stiff wind would blow the woman's slender frame away.

"Certainly, Widow Chapman, if it is brief. I am on my way to work in order to pay the rent."

"Men are not allowed in the rooms at any time. There is such a stipulation that you agreed to when I allowed you to move in here."

"And I have never brought a man to my room."

"What do you call last night?" the harridan screeches, like fingernails on a chalkboard. "That man was in your room for at least an hour! I run a respectable home for women. I'll not have my home used as a bawdy house."

"Mrs. Chapman, I don't know if you were aware, but I wasn't in my right mind last night. I don't know what happened."

"Oh, being drunk doesn't make that filth any better! And with a boy-man whose voice hasn't even settled."

I don't know what possesses me. Maybe it is the fatigue of battling five escaped demons in just the last eleven days. Perhaps it is the way she disparaged Maxwell, my friend and comrade. Could it be the bodies we've found in basements turned into little more than human hamburger? Or the death of a girl who hadn't gotten a chance to live her life, to feel a man between her thighs, to raise her own children, all because someone dislikes me. But more than likely, I've just had enough of this old crone's holier-than-thou attitude over the last years. I get right up into her face before answering. "Mrs. Chapman, my private life is not for your discussion or rumination. If I chose to take the entirety of his majesty's fleet into my vagina on the altar before the Virgin Mary herself, then it is my business, not yours."

"I'll only have ladies living under my roof," she hisses at me between clenched teeth.

"When did you become one?" I offer back with the calm of a saint but the malice of Lucifer himself. My blood stokes up again in my already abused body.

"You will keep a civil tongue in your head, missy!"

"Why? You never have had one the entire time I've lived here." I must keep anger from coming forward, knowing the ramifications if I don't. Witches have a way of causing catastrophic damage if they don't reign in their temper. It is actually one of the key things we are taught.

"That's quite enough, Mrs. Ochoa. You will vacate these premises by the end of this coming week. I will not have someone so flagrantly disabuse my authority."

I shrug. "As you have no authority, you have to invent some. But, I wouldn't dream of staying where I am not wanted." I notice two of the other women who live under Chapman's auspices pull their heads back from around the corner where they'd been eavesdropping.

I march right up to my lodgings. With my mind in a whirl, I just stuff random items from tabletops and bureau drawers into a second satchel. With a quick glance around, I see nothing else of immediate need.

I come down with my two bags to find a whispering event in the dining room by the other ladies living at Chapman's House of Morality and Abuse. Alice herself waits by the door with a broom clutched tightly in her arms like a quarterstaff.

I open my purse and hand the harridan twelve dollars and four bits. "There is my rent for next week. I will send for the rest of my things. I offer you the courtesy of a good day only as a matter of form." Picking back up my bags, I stride out the door.

"Ungrateful bitch!" she screams out as I trundle away.

It is fortunate that I have work to focus my attention on. The thought of what that dowager would look like entombed in a bubble of rock, eighty feet below the earth's surface, crosses my mind in the most pleasant way. However, the crown takes a dim view of witches abusing their powers. The penalties are harsh enough for even the slightest of infractions.

I look up when the first snowflake lands on my nose. A fine mist of white is covering the sky like lace. You have to love these late spring snows. It reminds me that my winter coat is still back at the boardinghouse. I shiver. After the confrontation with the sow, I must hustle in order to make it to work on time.

# # #

My bags won't fit into my wooden locker in the employee room. I settle for putting them on the ground and enticing the earth to wrap a band of stone around them. I manage to punch in a full minute before the timeclock turns over to eight AM. As is his norm, Mark Carlton stands sentinel over the device.

"Made it on time, did you, Mrs. Ochoa?" He has a smile on his face rather than his usual glower for me. Weeks ago, I'd humiliated him by forcing an apology when he had no choice. His smile is out of context.

"Yes, sir. And you look like you are having a wonderful morning."

His smile grows wider. "Better than you can know, Mrs. Ochoa. If you would take your position and begin ridding us of the pestilence of the soot in the air, I'd appreciate it."

I already have the unease of needing to find a new home, but to have Carlton smiling and being polite instead of barking has me concerned.

Spelling soot out of the air is not dangerous or onerous for an earth witch. I entice the coal byproducts that float around the sky as smog, soot, and cinders to come back down and join their brethren on the ground where they belong. As they want nothing more than that, it is an easy sale. But I'm the only earth witch in Carlton's cadre. The others are all air witches who must force the air to shove the tiny bits down. This is much harder and more difficult. Earth is tenacious and stubborn. Coercing it to do anything takes eons; just ask the rivers how long it takes to carve out canyons.

While the job is easy, it is tedious. Just standing there as a ring of black-gray forms a volcanic-style cone around me means I must use my prodigious imagination elsewhere. I spend the time worrying about my need to find a place to live. Luckily, tomorrow is Saturday, and other than a couple of appointments, I'll have time to investigate options. Unluckily, the cost will almost certainly be more than I can defray from this job and my widow's pension. That may not be important now with money being flung at me from every direction because of the mass of demon escapes, but when they stop, I'll be forced to drain my savings. My mind reminds me that I always have the option of doing what my mother does—land reclamation. You convince a piece of earth that it belongs to someone new who really has no rights to it at all. I'll not mince words. It is stealing property by right or custom from one person to another. This proves quite the quandary for an independent woman—destitution or immorality.

A commotion breaks my mental downward spiral. I see Mark Carlton trying to block Inspector First Antonio Guizzetti's progress as the constable walks in my direction.

"I'm sorry, but she is working. You can talk to her on her break or after normal business hours."

"I'm of the Royal Constabulary. I have the right and power to interview any witness at my bidding, not yours, sir."

"I'm not denying you that right, sir," Carlton adds that last word almost as an afterthought, "I am only asking that you not interrupt her work."

Antonio perches his hands at his hips, one wrapped around the baton a guardsman carries to enforce his authority. "Mr. Carlton, are you not aware of Royal Edict Seven about interfering with a constable in the pursuit of his duties?"

The pair are just close enough that I can see Carlton's adam's apple bob. "In general, yes."

"Paraphrased, it says that I can do my job how and when I see fit. And, any pretentious busybody that gets in my way, I can beat into submission. Then, I'll arrest him or her for the high crime of breaking R.E. Seven.

"Now, before I pull my nightstick from its loop, do you wish to accede to my very reasonable request for a few moments of Mrs. Ochoa's time, or do you want me to send for the police surgeon?"

"Then I will just dock her pay for the missing time."

"I've been polite to this point, Mr. Carlton," Antonio says, drawing his baton. "Docking her pay will be seen as an attempt to sway my investigation."

Tension hangs in the air for several seconds. I hope my boss will be so stupid. I know at confession on Sunday, I will have to add this to my list of sins. In a rare, wise move, Mark didn't continue his bluster.

"As you will, Officer," Mark says, walking away.

Antonio walks up to me, sliding his stick back into place. "That man is more pugnacious than just about any person I've met."

"Just about."

"I really thought I was going to have to thrash him. I wouldn't have enjoyed it, but a threat must be followed through or your next threat is meaningless."

"I think my ex-landlady is worse. You probably would have had to beat her skinny arse."

"Ex?"

The inspector's voice, not to mention his broad shoulders, sends a shiver down my spine and right into my lady parts. I feel a familiar slickness forming. Inspector Antonio Guizzetti's smooth, caramel-colored skin shows above the high collar of his police uniform. If I wasn't afraid of becoming someone's property, I'd make a beeline to place a passel of sweet kisses on his prominent cheekbones and hope that I could get my hands on his taut backside.

I'm lucky that I have my confessor, Father Juan, and my playmate, Karie. Together they keep me from just being a floozy that lifts her skirts for anyone and spending more time on my back than a whore on Friday night. Father Juan guides my soul, and Karie keeps my prurient fires banked and not blazing. I give a swallow before answering.

"Yes, I threw myself out this morning because...Never mind. It isn't important. What can I do for you on this glorious morning, Constable?"

"Glorious? You were shot last night."

"True, and God has seen fit to let me live for another day. I can't avoid the term glorious, can I?"

"I'm sorry, I thought I was talking to the cynical Stella Ochoa, fastest sarcasm slinger in all the kingdom. Can you point her out to me?" Antonio does a fake scan around the soot bins.

"OK, normally I'm a bit skeptical, true. But maybe this is that event that makes me turn over a new leaf."

"Never. Anyway, I need to find out what you remember from last night." He pulls out a pad and starts taking notes.

"It's kinda fuzzy. There was a bloody mess when we interned the demon. By the way, did you get that corpse with the smile?"

"Corpse?"

"Yeah, the one that remained after the demon plowed his way out."

"There wasn't enough of a body to call it a corpse, just some bloody goo. You know I always feel funny talking to you, a woman, about this stuff. It doesn't faze you when other women will go into a faint."

"Wilting flowers. But be that as it may, there was a body. The torso was almost intact, minus its guts. The face seemed untouched. It had a funny smile on it as if the owner hadn't even noticed his arms and legs being ripped off."

"Interesting. We found nothing like that. I'll log that information but go ahead and move forward."

"My team broke up, and I wanted a bath. Swanned over to O'Shaughadain's. On my way home, I got rousted by some midget policeman I'd never met. Oh, I don't blame him—"

"I'm sorry, midget policeman?"

"Yeah. Must have had the beat last night instead of Guardsman Paterna."

"But Paterna was on the beat. Can you describe the officer?"

"About five foot, maybe five-two. Massive shoulders. Reminded me of a short gorilla."

"How unusual. You say that he rousted you."

"Yeah, I must have been staggering a bit from being too tired. He probably thought I was in my cups...*borracha*," I say, pointing at myself.

"Got it. Then what?"

"After I allayed his fears about being drunk, he offered me help to my home. I declined. He walked on. That's it."

"OK."

"I walked over to the paper stand to get the evening edition."

"Be as detailed as you can remember here, Stella."

"I offered Amanda, I don't know her last name—you did notify her family, didn't you?"

"Yes, Stella. It is one of the most important duties of a King's policeman. It doesn't make it my favorite," he says with a sigh. "Yolanda Simmons is a gracious woman. She had a passel of young ones. But they all died in one way or another. I'd be surprised if we didn't find her in the river by week's end."

"Give me her address," I say flatly.

"That's not a good idea, Stella."

"I can find it myself if I have to. Save me the time and give me the address."

"I'm going to regret this, but..." He opens his book to another page and writes something down before tearing it out. As he hands it to me, he says, "Go easy, Stella."

"I will, Antonio," I say, softening my tone.

Releasing the paper, he says, "Now continue with what happened at the newsstand."

I recount the events of the previous night in more detail than I thought I'd possessed. Antonio makes me stomp out the cadence of the shots. It doesn't take a witch to figure out that the weapon is cartridge, not muzzle loading, and that it is likely a revolver rather than a carbine.

"We found the location where the man kneeled to shoot, three floors up and fifty yards or so down the lane. At that range, you could only hit the broad side of a barn with a handgun. So we suspect that he was actually using a Colt 1880 revolver rifle. It was a popular sniper weapon in the Irish Independence."

"All fine and good, Inspector, but I'm not sure that gets us any closer to who or even why."

"True. Do you have any thoughts?"

"Only one other remote possibility. I received a threatening note from the NPP this morning."

"The NPP, eh? Threatening, how?"

"I have the note in my purse and will get it for you. Yes, a little bit of paper that basically said for me to get out of Boston. They promised they would be watching."

"NPP?" he asks again with a raised eyebrow.

"It was marked that way."

"Go on, Stella."

"But why try to drive me out of Boston when they tried to kill me the night before. It doesn't make much sense."

"True. I personally believe that somehow Quarrels is orchestrating the event from prison. You did hear that he pleaded innocent?"

"Yeah, the idiot," I say.

"Well, look at it from his point of view. Snowdonia is dead. If he can eliminate you as the star witness for the bench, he may be able to lay the entire thing on Franklin Cardiff's decaying corpse. I think he is wrong, as the evidence is too strong against him, but it gives him a chance to stay out of prison."

"And a chance to get hung, too. Besides, if Quarrels were the one targeting me, I don't know how he'd arrange it."

"Nor do I, but it seems to be the most logical assumption. Whether it is him or not, we'd like to keep you sequestered for the five days until you testify."

"What? Hide me away? What about my job? What about finding a new home?"

"Yes, hide you away from harm. And those other things we could help with."

"Well, there is one thing hiding won't allow me to do, and it is the one thing you can't help with. What if there is a demon escape? I won't sacrifice the lives of Bostonians because of some risk to mine. No, Antonio. I will not do that."

"Then let me give you a guardsman to be with you until the trial."

I laugh without mirth. "And if the man is a trained sniper, what good would that do? Pop! Stella is dead. Pop! Gendarme is dead. Assassin fades into the night. No thanks, Inspector. I'll pass."

He stares hard at me with his hazel, rimmed in black, eyes. His jaw clenches. I think he'd like to take a switch to me, but as I'm not his woman, he doesn't have the option. "Remember when I said you were stubborn? I want to up that to blamed pig-headed."

"Oh, are you going to arrest me for that, sir?" I say with some flirt in my voice while batting my eyelashes. I even put my wrists out for him to cuff. Part of me wonders how it would be to be paddled by the man. I have a feeling that, knowing my own mind and body, it would probably end up with Stella being disgracefully noisy in the best possible way. Instead, he shakes his head before giving me a brotherly hug. "You are still going to testify, right?"

"Absolutely, Inspector. It is my duty to king and country. I'll add, it will give me quite a good deal of pleasure putting that murderer at the end of a rope. If you want someone to pull the trap door, I volunteer."

"Stand in line, Stella," he says, turning away.

I don't know how men put just the right amount of jiggle in their buttocks and sway to their shoulders as they walk. It has to be natural, for they aren't conscious of it. "Karie. Karie. Karie. You are in for a very randy visit," I mutter to myself. I need to keep in mind my lover's touch and her skin against mine slithering amongst the silk sheets of the Blue Room to reign in my impulse to grab the inspector's derriere.

This brings my attention back to the fact that I'm without a bed for the night. "So, where do I go tonight?"

As lunchtime approaches, I notice a familiar figure out the front gates. The ragamuffin boy I had taken in a scant three months ago is blossoming into quite a man of the rakish variety. Tommy's sandy mop of hair probably hasn't seen a brush in a *semana* or more. He wears sturdy work clothes but proudly displays his livery blouse as a stableman to the Helmses. He gives me a short wave and sits to wait.

The lunch whistle blows. As disturbing as Mark's smiling face was this morning, that he isn't there to caution us that we only have a twenty-minute meal break is worse. I grab my lunch out of one of my bags, noting that no one has tried to defeat my stone burglar deterrent. Punching out on the time clock, I end up on the brickwork next to Tommy. Maybe I'm not as ladylike as I might be on a bench, but it's a relief to sit down after four hours of standing.

Tommy executes something like a formal bow. "Hello, Mrs. Ochoa. I have a message for you."

"Mrs. Ochoa? Really. It's Stella to you now that you don't work for me any longer. And sit your arse down."

He plops back down next to me and hands me an envelope. If I didn't already know the source, the musky scent wafting up from the note would have identified its sender as the Viscountess Adrianna Helms.

"I don't know why them upstairs folks like that falderal," Tommy says as I pull out the pink paper. Adrianna's hand is smooth and flowing like a gentle stream through foothills. She would have made an excellent royal scribe.

Mrs. Ochoa,

It would please me if you would honor me with your presence this Saturday at eleven in the morning for *merienda* and a consultation on the state of demons as a power source.

I apologize for failing to get an invitation to you in the post earlier in the week.

Please RSVP with the bearer of this missive.

Viscountess Helms

As if she needed to invite me. We have spent every Saturday afternoon since my recovery together. She nursed me to health after Gazzunreep exploded the earth beneath my feet in the ill-fated attempt to arrest Baron Franklin Cardiff. Since then we've developed a friendship, at least in the mutual interest of keeping demon power from being scuttled by bad press.

"You can tell Lady—"

"Stella? I'm right sorry for interrupting, but you see that copper over there?"

Inside the main gate of the Coal Syndicate, Mark Carlton talks convivially with a group of five German ladies. Their provincial dress gives them away. With them is a short policeman with broad shoulders, making him look like an ape. He looks like the patrolman I met just before I was shot.

"Yes," I say with not a certain amount of interest.

"He's the one I done seen talking to Baron Cardiff before he done run off."

My head snaps around to face Tommy. "Are you absolutely certain?"

"Honest. I swear on the Virgin Mary."

The baron had escaped in such a timely manner that it had been suspected he'd been tipped off. Tommy told the constabulary what he'd seen, but nothing came of it. No policeman was identified explicitly until now.

"You too rich now to want to earn a bit more?" I ask him.

"I ain't rich, but I wanna be. Whatcha want me to do, Stella?"

"Follow that guardsman you just pointed out. Follow him all day and then come meet me at the Bell in Hand tonight at eight bells to let me know what he did. If you can learn his name without exposing yourself, do so."

"Lady Helms will box my ears if'n I'm gone that long, Stella."

"I'll smooth over your absence with the Lady Helms."

"Alright, Stella. I trust you."

"Better hurry. He is leaving. Oh, and if he sees you, it's better if the Helmses' coat of arms isn't seen."

I have never seen a man take his shirt off so fast, even my Aaron before we would tumble into bed. Tommy tucked the entire blouse into his overalls. With this look, he could blend into any group of day-laborers in the city.

"Good boy." With one problem being worked, I turn to another. What was Carlton up to with those five ladies?

# # #

The rest of the workday goes by without a single additional sighting of Carlton. While this is good in that none of us filter women gets verbally abused, it is ominous. He has never left us unsupervised or without worthless suggestions for so long.

I punch out with half a smile and half a frown on my face. I guess it is a wash, all in all. Collecting my duffels, I head for the nearest newspaper stand. A boy hawks papers from six different cities and three editions from Boston. I spend three pennies for one each of the *Boston Evening Journal*, the *Boston Globe*, and the *Herald*. I tuck them into my bags and make a beeline for the Bell in Hand.

The bright lights and the cheery singing from the Bell in Hand spur me on in. My favorite pub is little more than a fisherman's bar. We get whalers and tuna men right off the boats and smelling like it. There are mechanics, gaffers, sailmen, and every other sort that gather here to unwind from the heavy, dangerous work they do day-in and day-out. That all being said, it is a sight more friendly than the more upscale establishments further south and west. I might have to dodge a swat on my fundamentals from time to time, but I also know that if I were to fall down drunk that the patrons would find a place for me to sleep and not take advantage of my state. You can't say that of any other pub attended by so-called gentlemen.

Four boisterous roughs sit at the table reserved for my team, the *Dos Campanas*. My team is nowhere to be seen this early in the evening.

"Aye, if it ain't the lady of the city," a local fisherman, Bill Mattingsly, says over his ale. "Ya still got your key?"

It seems barely possible that less than two months ago, I had the entire town of Boston bowing at my feet. I had been presented the key to the city, given an experimental horseless carriage, a fair bit of coin, and a useless country estate, all for bringing a couple of people to justice who had contrived the release of demons. Now, I'm still knee-deep in the hellspawn, trying to understand why people would sacrifice their lives to release the creatures.

"That was weeks ago, Bill," I say back. "I'm not even newsworthy anymore."

"Hi, Stella!" Michaeleen O'Flynn, the owner of the Bell in Hand, says, putting down cases that, by the rattle, contain full bottles of liquor. "Want me to throw those dock maggots out of your spot?"

"Let 'em be, Michaeleen. It's just me tonight. My bustle isn't too big for a bar stool. How about a pint of bitter and an extra-large helping of whatever's on the stove?"

"Lamb stew. I'll fetch the stew while you pull yourself a mug. You know where the taps are."

I pull in my skirts to move behind the bar. On second thought, I decide I don't need alcohol tonight. I need my wits about me. I pop the cork on a jug of cider and fill up a glass. I barely get back to my seat when my host slaps down a trencher with a meaty mound of stew in front of me. He rushes off to do the same for several other guests. The stew is mostly root vegetables, they keep the longest, but there is plenty enough lamb to make a tasty gravy. On the corner, I see that Mick has added a splash of cranberry sauce. The thick slab of sourdough, the heavy, rich taste of the meaty juice, and the tart bite of the red berries satisfy like nothing that *la perra* Chapman has ever served. I may have to pay for this one, but I darn well enjoy it.

I pull out the first of my three papers and separate out the classified ads. "For let," I mumble around a mouthful of stew.

"Ya ain't gonna leave us, are you, sweetie?" Bill asks with just the tiniest bit of a slur.

"No chance, Bill," I reply after I clear my mouth with a swig of cider.

"T'en why 'r ya talkin' 'bout fer let?"

"I was talking about where I'm going to sleep tonight and every other night, Bill. I got run out of my boardinghouse."

"Ya cun share my bed."

I peel his fingers off my hand. Bill is good folk, but when he gets a few beers in him, he thinks he is the reincarnation of Don Juan. "I think your wife might object, Bill. If you're smart, you'll head home right about now and spend some of this attention on your woman."

"Naw. Tha' cow woulda know wha' ta do with it. You shore would."

I'm not a newspaper's agony aunt or a priest to help Bill's marriage so I drop it. "Sorry, Bill, but I don't sleep with married men."

"Well, tha' ain't no fair."

I forget about Bill and return my thoughts to my situation for the night. It wouldn't be the first time I've slept rough, but I'd rather not if I don't have to, especially with the cold lately. I mean, there is the carriage house I store my poderabile in. Still, without heat, it will be as comfortable as lying on gravel. Karie's is out. Not too long ago, we had a close brush where our loose, in more ways than one, relationship almost became permanent. I don't want to chance her getting the wrong idea. Loving is one thing. Sleeping is another. I don't want to push my luck.

I would have asked for floor space from one of my teammates, but they aren't here. I don't have the kind of relationship with the Viscount and Viscountess Helms to go begging a bed. That really leaves my mother or renting a room. I'd rather sleep in the fish offal bin at the docks than ask my social-climbing mother for my old room back. As Hobson's choice, I'm going to have to spend some of my coin to find a place to put my head. As I don't have a good deal of funds on me, it probably won't be much more than bed-space in some fleabag hotel.

"Steeeeeeeela?" Mick says as he pulls a beer on tap. He drains some foam off the top.

"Huh?"

"You must have been woolgathering. I called your name three times."

"Sorry, Michaeleen. I seem to have put myself into a bit of a jam."

"I heard. Kinda hard not to hear Bill when he's had one too many. What would you say to the cot in my basement? It ain't the Parker House, but it's warm."

"Michaeleen, you are a godsend. I'll just be here one night."

"Stay as long as you need. You've helped me more than once. Hell, I make my rent just on the tourists coming in to gawk at your *Dos Campanas*. Using the cot in my basement is simple and obvious, Stella."

"Thanks, Mick."

"Head down whenever you feel like it. I'm stocked up here so I won't be down again. You know where the privy is."

"Well, if'n it ain't the lad," Bill slurs to one side of me.

"Evenin', Bill," I hear Tommy say. It's such a pleasure to hear the confidence in his voice, compared to the temerity of just months ago.

"You are early, my friend," I say, stuffing another spoonful of stew into my mouth. Hunger has overtaken my manners.

"Well, it were obvious that copper weren't moving no more tonight so I done come here to tell you what you wanted."

"Go on," I manage around my meal. My mother would have rapped my head with a spoon for such poor etiquette, but I'm in a pub.

"His name be Heinrick Meier. He left the coal yards and walked to the coal offices. He went inside and up a granite staircase. He didn't stop at the gal they got working out front, but she nodded at him like she knowed him."

"'Curiouser and curiouser!'" I quote Alice.

"Sure is. Then he come out and walked into the slums in the Black Sea...you know, where—"

"Yes, we've had this conversation before, Tommy. I've heard of a whorehouse before, and just because the Black Sea has more than one doesn't make any difference. I'm not a fainting society lady."

"Yes, Stella. Well, he done gone into the red light district. I'm thinking he might be going to one of the bawdy houses, but he walked right past 'em. Went up to one of those tenements 'tween Broad and India."

"That's a rank place to live, what with the cesspit just north of there."

"Yes, miss. I feel like washin', and I just walked through there."

"I don't doubt it. Anything else?"

"He went up to a fifth-floor walk-up. I asked around. That's how I be gettin' his name. They are all proud of Copper Meier. Not so much crime there now as before him and his invalid mama moved in."

Something isn't sitting exactly right with me. This Meier is a hero who lives in the slums but deals with Carlton and someone else in the Coal Syndicate. Add to that he may have taken a bribe for information from Baron Snowdonia? All thoughts for later.

I pull out the invitation from Lady Helms and write a note on the back accepting her gracious hospitality on Saturday. I also claim responsibility for Tommy's late return, promising an explanation to her on the morrow.

"Good...no, GREAT job, Tommy. I have one more request before you head home."

"Yes, Stella?"

"You still have lots of your steelyard friends sleeping rough?"

"'Course. I wouldn't leave them just 'cause I have a bed t'sleep in and coin in my pocket."

"Excellent. Any chance you can get three of them to come help me move my stuff out of my boardinghouse? I'll pay, of course. Say three bits apiece?"

"Stella, you spend that kind of coin around, and I can have a hundred of them waiting in line to help," Tommy says, flashing me that bright smile of his again.

"They can't be squeamish about moving girl things."

"No problem, ma'am. Most of them wouldn't know no girl thing from a doily on the table. 'Sides, I'll have Mikey pick a pair to come with her."

"Great. Have them at Chapman's Boarding House at half-past five bells on Monday night."

"You got it, ma'am."

"Here is a dollar for your work today."

"Stella, it weren't worth no dollar. 'Sides, if it weren't for you, I'd still be huddling in three-day-old newspaper next to the iron furnace buildings."

"OK then, will you take two quarters?"

He grins. "Now that I'll take, Stella."

I give him that and three more bits. "Give one to each of the folks coming to help me."

"Yes, Miss Stella." Tommy skedaddles like a racehorse leaving the gate.

I turn back to my paper and start circling ads that might lead to a new place to live. All of the ones that aren't in the Black Sea or other obvious tenements are considerably more expensive than I was paying at Chapman's. I resign myself to the rent costing an extra two dollars a week or more. The concept of that, along with the excitement of the last two days, has me tuckered out. My body is giving up after a full day of spelling soot out of the air and other strenuous activities. My mind is fogging over after a confrontation with my landlady. With my stomach full, I'm flagging even before the eight o'clock bells.

I slip away to the basement before Bill decides I need company.

3—Saturday Morning, May 5, 1888

"I have an eight thirty appointment with Professor Xavier," I say to a secretary. Her desk is wedged into a small anteroom used as a reception room in the Applied Sciences Building of the University of Boston. My voice echoes against the bare stonework.

I wrestle with the discomfort of my clothes this morning. I'm wearing a corset of sorts. In the Bell in Hand's basement, I found some discarded wrought iron. Over my chemise and bloomers but under my blouse and petticoats, I've wrapped a layer of it around me like someone might lead foil but as thick as corset stays. It covers me from my waist up over my bosoms in a spiral of bands. They are just far enough apart to allow me to bend and twist. Yes, I've armored myself. It isn't comfortable, but if shot, it should grant me a second chance. I fear it may be a permanent part of my wardrobe until they capture the shooter that seems to want me dead.

And as chance would have it, it itches and pulls in all the wrong places. On the plus column, it does keep my breasts from jiggling around when I move.

The older woman peers down her long, narrow nose and through a pair of horn-rimmed glasses at me. Sleeping on a cot in a dirty basement isn't ideal. I appreciate the gesture by Michaeleen, but I need better lodgings. I admit I'm not as well turned out as I'd like in my spare clothes but I don't think I warrant such a searching look even as I fidget.

"If you have a seat there, Professor Xavier will be with you in a moment," she says in a nasal tone with so much buzz in it I wonder if she has a beehive up her aquiline nose. I sit on one of the hard, straight-backed chairs bearing the hand-painted university's crest. Much money went into the embellishment and none at all to the comfort. My bottom is sore before I can say "Rumpelstiltskin." How much of this is because of my new undergarment, or the chair, I sayeth not.

I take this appointment rather than seek out new lodgings, as

Professor Xavier's calendar is difficult to get onto. From what I understand, she takes many professional trips to Egypt and other parts of Europe to collect information and artifacts related to ancient witchcraft. So I take what is available and ignore the urge to reschedule. Worst comes, I get a hotel room for a night or two or avail myself of that cot.

Some moments later, the secretary gets up from her desk and knocks on one of the two doors behind her. She pokes her head through. Turning to me, she says, "Professor Xavier will see you now."

With a name like Xena Xavier and being a professor at the liberal University of Boston as well, I expect the unusual. I'm not disappointed. Her hair is the white of a new pair of bloomers and stands straight up four inches like porcupine quills. She wears blue denim overalls with a three-foot hood hanging back off her blouse, signifying her Ph.D. rank. While breeches aren't unbecoming on her, they aren't acceptable most anywhere by women except, by coincidence, here. Boston University is well known for its acceptance of the loosest of community standards. Some say they actively work to lower society's morals. I reserve my opinion.

Xena darts from behind a desk cluttered with a mound of unsorted papers, manuscripts, and souvenirs. She offers me her hand and a smile that says I'm the answer to all her prayers. When I put out my hand, she gives it a hearty male-style handshake. "Mrs. Ochoa! I'm so pleased to meet you."

"And I, you, Miss Xavier."

"Oh, call me Xena. I even let the students call me Professor Xena."

"Well then, call me Stella."

"That will be all, Carmen," Xena says to the secretary, who is eavesdropping at the door. I hear it close with a resounding thump. "Excellent, Stella. What are you here to talk about? I've heard of your exploits and just couldn't turn down your request for an interview. Are you here to earn a degree to back up your famous tales of derring-do?" With a wave, she offers me a very comfortable, overstuffed chair. "Tea?" she asks before I even get my petticoats pulled in beneath me to sit or answer her first question.

"Yes, please," I respond when I don't see a coffee service. "Black."

Xena pours the brew into a pair of cheap pottery mugs that I think are supposed to portray the face of Admiral William B. Cushing. She hands me mine and then adds six or so cubes of sugar to her own. While the container isn't anything to boast about, the tea is Darjeeling. With the English monopoly on its colony, India, I've only had this beverage one other time.

"This is delicious. Where did you manage to get it?"

"You can find it now and again if you are willing to do business with pirates."

"Excuse me…pirates? Surely you're joking. There aren't pirates in this day and age."

Xena leans back in her chair and looks at me over her cup. "Whenever there are countries, there will always be folks doing things across imaginary lines that aren't sanctioned by law. Call them pirates, smugglers, brigands, or something else. I prefer the more colorful term."

"Fair enough, Professor," I say, taking another sip.

"It's like the flamboyant term witchcraft. Magic itself is still an art form. I can foresee a day in the future when it will be codified and turned into pure science. Now tell me, what fun will that be?" I've never thought of witchcraft as fun. It is a vocation like many others. It takes skill and the right parents.

"I never thought of it that way, Xena."

She sits back up with a jerk. She reminds me of a broken wind-up toy as she will sit there passively for some time and then lurch into action when you least expect it. "You still haven't told me why you wanted to see me today. We'd love the prestige of having you as a student. Heck, if I were the dean, I'd give you an honorary degree just for the publicity alone."

"Thank you, no, Xena. I have to earn a living and don't have the luxury of time to get a degree. I'm here about demonology. You may have read about my recent run-in with a reigning prince from hell, Gazzunreep?"

"Yes. That's what started all of the interest in you. I wouldn't mind spending some time with you just picking your brains, Stella."

"I'd enjoy that, as long as you mean it figuratively and not literally," I chuckle. The professor points at me and guffaws like a braying donkey. After she settles down, I continue. "I want to know why Gazzunreep didn't kill me with his fire beam eyes. I was told that if anyone knew, it would be you."

Xena skews her mouth to one side of her face. "I'll make a bargain with you, Stella. You let me spend a couple of evenings getting your thoughts and letting me decide how to use it in my work, and I'll share my own skill and knowledge with you."

"Deal," I say without even a second thought.

"First, tell me about yourself and your powers."

I regale her with tales of my youth, developing earth powers at the tender age of six. I share my mother's schooling, my magical talent up through secondary school, and my eventual proctoring of my failed exam.

"Tell me more about that. Gazzunreep must have been an implacable foe."

"More than that," I say, pulling the hair back from the left side of my face to show the scars he left. "These go all the way down my body. Xena, please don't tell me that he somehow imbued me with some of his powers by scarring me."

"Perish the thought, Stella. In all recorded history, even back before the great pharaohs of Egypt, there has never been such a case. What you suggest is a myth, like making a deal with a demon."

"Good. Well, my mother dismissed Gazzunreep before he could totally consume me." I decided Xena didn't need to know about my mother letting the demon burn me just to teach a lesson.

I share something that I'd not told anyone. "Most of my life, I could feel God's power in church on the Sabbath but didn't recognize it as something to be manipulated or controlled. I thought everyone felt that warm, syrup-like sensation in church. It wasn't until I'd started hanging out with the *Dos Campanas* that I discovered I could feel God's powers, especially around my teammate Maxwell, the white witch. I toyed around with my skills in my spare time until I could draw on the white powers to some extent. I still have much to learn and honestly don't have the time to take it up, not with the new rash of demon releases, work, and the clockworks of staying alive."

"You say that your mother wields the powers of an earth witch. What about your father? Is he a white warlock?" Xena asks, draining the last of her tea and refilling her cup. I swear she puts in even more sugar this time.

"Honestly, I don't know. My mother says he was a Spaniard who left because she could bear no more children, when she speaks of it at all. Normally, she avoids the subject entirely. She won't even tell me his name."

"What about grandparents?"

"Never knew anything about my father's side of the family. My mother's parents died before I was old enough to know them. Mother says that Grandma Priscilla was an earth witch, and Grandpa Martin could feel the earth's powers but not use them. As their only child, her parents doted on her and gave her the training she needed to blossom."

"Did they want more progeny?"

"Yes. Mom told me once that Grandma Priscilla bemoaned that she wanted ten more, enough for a soccer team, but it never happened to catch."

"More tea, Stella?"

"I'm good, thank you."

"Then how about you give me chapter and verse about what happened at the Snowdonia Estate."

"Well, the papers did get it pretty well, between Antonio and me telling it to them."

"Humor me."

I have told the story so many times I can do it in my sleep. I parrot out again how Inspector Guizzetti and I went to the Baron Cardiff's home to arrest him. How the baron, an ice witch, twisted the planes and disabled me with dizziness. When the inspector managed a shot to injure the baron, the blackard lord called Gazzunreep up from its fiery home. Antonio raced after Cardiff. I was left to confront a reigning prince of hell itself. After ducking and weaving the beams of fire from the demon's eyes, it pins me with one right in the middle of my chest.

"So what did the flames from its eyes do to other objects?" Xena asks.

"That beam of light, no bigger around than the shaft of a ten-penny nail, sliced through everything as neatly as a butcher's knife might a tub of lard. It ignited its target into flames and left a black scorch mark on either side of the cleft."

"And what did it do to you?"

"Other than turning my clothes to ash, nothing."

"No pain?"

"No pain—a bit of warmth, which was quite refreshing after the day of freezing in the poderabile—the self-propelled carriage."

"What about the explosions the papers mentioned in lurid detail?"

"After hitting me with multiple beams with no tangible effect, Gazzunreep fired at the ground under my feet, causing the frozen water in it to explode outward in steam. The shrapnel of rock, dirt, twigs, and even grass embedded into my legs." I take the improper act of lifting my dress and rolling down one of my stockings to show the scars.

"Excellent," is all she says. Xena closes her eyes and kicks back her head in thought. Not ten seconds go by before the second door of her office bursts open. In storms a skinny, young Englishman whose weathered skin has seen much more of the desert than our cold Boston winters. "Bloody board of regents couldn't find their arse with—" He trails off when he sees me with my stocking rolled down. I drop my skirts as fast as a rattlesnake might strike. He weakly says, "My apologies for my language and intrusion, miss."

Xena jumps up and hugs the man. "Stella, this is my husband, Rupert." Without a trace of gray, his dark hair and the lack of any wrinkles or sags seem to put him only a lustrum, or maybe a decade my senior, much younger than his wife.

"No apology necessary, Mr. Xavier. I come from a rough part of town. I would take it as a kindness if you'd wipe your mind of my lewd display."

"I will do that, ma'am. And your background doesn't excuse my poor form, Miss Stella.

"I thought you were alone, m'love."

She gives him a quick squeeze and a peck on the cheek. "I'll hear your bellyaching after I'm done with this lovely child. Now get off with you," she says, shoeing him out like one might a naughty child. For that matter, the age difference between them magnifies that image, but who am I to judge. *John 8:7—So when they continued asking him, he lifted up himself, and said unto them, "He that is without sin among you, let him first cast a stone at her."* I ofttimes share a bed with a woman out of wedlock. Who is to criticize how these two find love? I won't pick up a rock.

There is a rap at the outer door. "Come in," bellows Xena in a way that belies her slender form and her female countenance and accentuates her irritation at a second interruption.

"Professor Xavier. Your nine o'clock is here."

"Grief, have we been talking that long?" Xena replies more to me than anyone. She directs her next remarks to her secretary. "Tell Professor Anthony that I'll talk to him about the fundraiser tomorrow. This has precedence."

"Yes, ma'am."

"Xena, I can come back if—"

"Nonsense. I don't get opportunities like this very often. Think about what it would be like to be able to sit down with a friendly demon and chat the afternoon away. Wouldn't you take the happenstance?"

A friendly demon is a contradiction in terms, but I think I see her point. "I get it. What next?"

"I'm sorry for the disruptions, Stella. I was about to give you the sum of my accumulated wisdom—not much, that is," she deprecates herself. "I see three possibilities. First and least likely is that there was another witch in the area that somehow shielded you. I don't see how that is possible, given your description of the feeling when you were struck. You'd likely feel a cold sensation against your skin, not warm, if there were some form of shielding. And I'm not sure there is an ice witch that could counter a demon bolt like that, even the late and unlamented Baron Snowdonia."

I want to be sarcastic and say that I'm here for what is possible, not what isn't, but I remember the old saw about flies and honey. Instead, I smile as my hostess stands to poke at the hearth with an ash pan.

"Hold out your hand, Stella."

Puzzled, I comply. Xena whips around and drops a red-hot coal into my hand from the ash pan.

I react as anyone might, I yank my hand away with a twist to dislodge the burning ember from my grasp. "Fuck!"

The coal falls to the floor and starts the heavily worn rug on fire. Xena moves the carpet with her feet and stomps out the blaze. She then scoops the fiery bit back into the hearth.

"WHAT THE HELL?" I shout, preparing for a battle.

"Show me your hand," the professor says with a broad smile.

I turn it over again to find it reveals no red mark nor blister, only some sooty gray. Come to think of it, it didn't hurt then or now.

"What the hell?" I say in a more ladylike tone. I just keep looking at my hand in disbelief.

"Yup, that just eliminates the first possibility entirely."

I stand up and move over to the fireplace. With some trepidation, I reach down and touch the grating. I feel intense warmth but nothing much else from the metal that would raise blisters nor turn an average person's hand black. I pull my blouse sleeve up my arm and reach into the cheery red coals themselves. I pull out one that is the color of an orange.

"*¡Vete al demonio!*"

"Nope," Xena says. "So it looks like one of two remaining possibilities," she says as I stand there gaping at the rapidly cooling coal in my hand. I toss it back into the fire before I turn around and drop into my seat, with my mind racing a million miles an hour. "The second option is that you are a latent fire witch. But oddly, I find that about as likely as the first option because of some things you've said. I can put that to the test in a much less dramatic way." She walks over to the door her husband had come through and opens it. "Honey, could you come here for a second?"

The weathered man comes back into the room. "What can I do for you, my dove?"

"Could you please come demonstrate your fire juggling for our guest?"

"Sure." He comes into the middle of the room and creates three balls of flame out of thin air, and begins to juggle them as if this were a side-show act.

"Stella," Xena says, "Do you feel anything? My husband is a fire witch. If you have any skill in that area, you should feel the power."

I don't feel anything. I open my mind to the same powers I can use both in earth and God's love but receive nothing from his display. I just shake my head. "No, ma'am. I don't feel it at all."

"That's good enough, Rupert," Xena says. "You can go back, or with Stella's permission, you can stay and listen. Just don't interrupt," she says, looking at him. Her husband opens his mouth. One by one, the balls of flame drop down his throat. He burps up a little bit of smoke. I nod my assent. As Hobson's choice, he takes his wife's desk chair.

"OK, the reason I'm sure that Gazzunreep didn't kill you with his flame blast is that, well, you are part demon yourself."

My brain overloads. "Now, just a freaking minute!" I bark, lurching to my feet.

"Yes?" Xena says sweetly, keeping her seat.

I start to pace with a level of agitation I've not experienced even being shot at. "How can someone be part demon? That's not possible. Any demon would kill a person. Besides, wouldn't it be like a human trying to breed with an ape? And even if—"

"Stella, if you will calm and sit down, I'll explain. It's not as bad nor as convoluted as you might think."

"I doubt that," I say, easing back into my seat as if it might wrap me up and devour me. This appointment is not going as I expected.

"There are demons among us," Xena says. Out of the corner of my eye, Rupert is quietly bobbing his head up and down in agreement with his wife's premise. "There aren't many, but they have learned civilized behavior and how to take shape as a human."

"How do they not burn down everything?"

"The very act of learning not to hate everything dampens their fire. These really can't be called demons any longer as they pose no more threat to humanity than other humans pose. I fear a bloody Brit, sorry my love," she says to her husband, "more than I do one of these demons. They have come down to us in lore as shape changers."

"So, how do they have offspring?"

"They can't. However, there are demons specifically created for carnal abuse of humans—succubi and incubi. Now succubi can't bear offspring. They have no womb nor the ability God gave Eve to merge a soul to a child she bears. But an incubus, on the other hand, can put its seed into any female he copulates with."

I shake my head. I'm about at my last straw. "My mother wasn't seduced by any incubi. She'd have told him that without a title or lands, he's unworthy."

"I didn't say your mother, Stella. It was at least one of your great-grandmothers. You said it yourself that your grandmother only had one child. The offspring of an incubus–human woman combination tends to mule out—to not be able to bear children. This usually happens in the next generation, but sometimes they can have one."

"This is beyond the pale," I say, staring at her. Rupert just shakes his head back and forth.

"There are some typical traits of the offspring of incubi. The males are usually irresistible to anyone who lusts after their gender. The female children generally carry the burden of a sex drive second to none. Both are immune to fires of all types and, if pressed, can understand the native language of the demons."

"So I'm some kind of gosh-blamed demon? When do I start killing and maiming those around me? Maybe I should just send myself to hell before someone else does it for me. Like maybe my own team?" I'm starting to get frantic. I came for answers and find despair.

"Calm down, Stella. Demon blood isn't chaos. It isn't evil. It is no different than carrying a trace of negroid, American native, Jewish, or even Chinese blood. Your soul controls your life and destiny, not some power from hell." Rupert is nodding up and down as he watches my tortured face. Xena continues, "So who cares? Does anyone care if some woman has slant eyes or a man a flat or bulbous nose?" Rupert changes to shaking his head sideways.

I take a baker's dozen deep breaths. "So, what do I need to know about this?"

"Not much, really. First, you will likely not be able to bear children, or if you do, it will be but a single child." I think a bit about that and realize that doesn't bother me. I'm a bit too selfish to be a mother, anyway.

"OK, I can live with that."

"Next, no fire, not even demon fire, can hurt you. That doesn't mean hellspawn can't tear you limb from limb, crush you, or find another way to deal damage to you, as Gazzunreep showed."

"That's not a detriment in my business. But wait a moment, how is it that Gazzzunreep could do this to me," I say, pointing at the scars he gave me in my youth.

"I guess that the powers only manifest after puberty. There are very few documented cases of this. Some of what I'm sharing is based purely on anecdotal word-of-mouth evidence. We have most of our evidence from the Egyptian hieroglyphics and stone tablets."

I twist my mouth at how not scientific this is. "What's the third thing?"

"Third, and probably most onerous, you will crave sex much more than the rest of humanity. No, I don't mean you will be a nymphomaniac. The demon blood drives the demon to have sex. The same will be true within you to a certain extent."

"I've already had to deal with that problem, Xena."

"And before I leave these points, I want you to be aware that you are human in every spiritual and loving way. Never doubt that. God can bless you. God can bring you to his bosom when you pass this mortal life.

"As far as I know, those are the only differences between you and any other person on the street. By the way, if I were you, I'd keep your heritage to yourself. Imagine the reaction a crowd might have that there is a demon in their midst."

"Wait a moment," I throw out there. "My mother doesn't have an extraordinary sex drive. I wouldn't know about any of the other items."

"Not all crossbreeds show all capabilities other than the inability to reproduce prodigiously, but those that do we've found have these commonalities."

I started this day with a very different view of the world. "*Dios mío*."

# # #

I park the poderabile in the Helmses' drive and turn the air tanks off. My magnificent machine is the brainchild of Viscount Henry Helms. Take a tradesman's box wagon, paint it a bright green, and name it *Lady Justice*. Now the most important part: take the tongue and the horses off the front. How does it go with no horses? Well, that's the genius of it. The wagon's box isn't empty but rather carries metal cylinders full of compressed air. By pushing or pulling the levers in the cab, it directs the air over some gears, which I've never seen, to move it forward or back—and it's mine. Lord Helms gave it to me for helping to save his business. I found the culprits making it possible for demons to escape. In fact, I am to testify against one of them Wednesday morning.

On the doorstep, I check myself in the reflection of one of the more prominent facets of the stained glass peacock inset in the door. The speed of the poderabile has messed up my respectability more than once. I comb the few stray hairs back into place and refasten them with my *peineta*. I wipe off a couple splotches of mud from my dress and one from my cheek with a kerchief. With a nod to myself, I pull on the bell pull.

I hear the familiar tinkle of bells inside. The door opens to the stoic face of Bastogne, the Helmses' butler. Over the past months, being a regular guest and confidante to Lord and Lady Helms, I've learned that despite Charles Bastogne's outward manner as a servant, he has a fierce but low sense of humor. Below stairs, he's told me a few jokes that would make a naval rank blush.

"Good morning, Mrs. Ochoa," he says in a deep voice that I believe belongs in the Boston Opera or at least a choir. I know better than to chide him about calling me anything but Stella. Viscountess Helms has firm beliefs on the proprieties of servants, and taking personal liberties is a definite offense.

"Good morning, Bastogne. And how is your day?"

"Exceptional, ma'am. I know you are expected. I'll show you in to—"

"Pshaw, Charles. I know her routine as well as anyone. My guess, she is waiting for me in the solarium. I know my way."

"As you wish, ma'am."

I drop my voice to a graveyard whisper and lean in to say, "Remind me to tell you the one about the vicar and the goat."

His stoic countenance cracks with a smile. He surreptitiously looks around before saying, "...but the goat needs confession, too."

"Damn. Thought I'd found one you hadn't heard."

"Unlikely, Miss Stella. I've been collecting them longer than you've been alive. But thank you for reminding me about that one. I've not shared that one with the rest of the staff."

I give him a brilliant smile and traipse back to Viscountess Helms's retreat. The solarium is overgrown with foreign plants, most blossoming here in the warmth, even in the cold of May outside. The air is warm and damp enough to cause my bloomers to stick to my thighs within moments of walking into the room.

"Stella!" Adrianna calls, getting up from her wicker chair, her blond hair flowing and loose like a cascade of honey. Her stylish lavender dress, with tiny white flowers, complements her pale skin.

"Thank you for coming!" She throws her arms around me and gives me a French-style kiss on each cheek as our petticoats and mutual bustlines vie for control of the space between our embrace. Both of us are...robust women. The viscountess is short and has enough bosom to endow three average women.

Sometimes, I think mine could suckle a calf. Yes, I'm comparing myself to a cow, but others have done it before, and it will happen again. Getting upset at my natural features only makes it worse. Hell, Karie often comments that they are my best assets. But then she says that about any of my body that she happens to be near at the time.

"We always get together Saturday afternoon and strategize on how to keep these chaotic escapes from impacting the demon power business as a whole."

"That doesn't mean I don't appreciate you being here. Come. I've got the *Tribune*, the *Record*, the *Ledger*, and the *Royal* from Philadelphia, the *New Murcia Times*, *Daily Eagle*, and the local *Post*, *Globe*, and *Herald* for us to rummage through." I can hear her starched taffeta petticoats rustle under her dress as she turns away.

"Not the *Chicago Tribune* or *Charleston Leader*?"

"Despite its size, Chicago isn't in our immediate concern, and I've decided that Charleston just follows where the palace leads."

"OK, but if we are going to do our usual paper reading, I'm going to need coffee to fortify me."

Adrianna smiles as she leads me to the service cart. "I know better than to invite you without having coffee." She pours some steaming black gold into a demitasse cup without adulterating it before giving herself some tea with milk and sugar.

Picking up the cups, we drink. I let out a very unladylike sigh. My hostess's pink lip-salve stains just the very edge of her cup as she takes a very dainty sip. *Why are simple marks on a glass exciting me?* I wonder as my middle melts somewhat. I empty my cup in three more swallows. "I needed that, Adrianna. Thank you."

"Trying day?"

I think about being shot, the threatening note, my homeless status, and the revelation of my tainted blood before replying, "Just a little. But let's not talk about me. You and your husband have enough troubles without borrowing more. How goes refitting all of the demon installations with locking enclosures?"

"Henry has crews working double shifts. He'd be working at night too, but people object to workmen making noises in their homes while they are trying to sleep." She shakes her head from side to side. I'm not sure if it is because she thinks they should be allowing it or if her husband is working too hard.

"What keeps someone from just picking the lock?" With a long practice of helping myself, I discourteously pour myself another cup of coffee.

Adrianna wrinkles her pert little nose at me before answering, "They have a new type of lock that can't be picked or jimmied. Certain to goodness, I don't have a molly about how to pick a lock. Henry showed me one of these new locks and the key that goes in it while assuring me that he's hired burglars to try and open it. They failed. If you are interested, I'm sure he'd be more than happy to show you one and explain it."

"No. I'd probably not understand it. Just as long as it makes things very difficult for anyone trying to kill themselves by rubbing out a pentagram, I'm happy," I say. Now that the first cup is working its magic on me, I take a more ladylike sip of the second.

"It's going to be at least a month before every single Forever Power demon installation is secured."

"What about the other installation companies?"

"Henry did convince them to do the same, but they haven't moved with the same dispatch."

"Bloody," I curse.

"Yes, Stella. But Henry has some ideas there as well. He is considering buying out two of the three remaining demon power companies and has put out feelers in that regard. If successful, he can force the issue.

"Right now, Henry is using our break-in-proof enclosures as a competitive advantage. But as busy as he has been retrofitting, at our expense, I might add, he hasn't done but a handful of actual installations in over two weeks."

"Maybe you ought to advertise his new feature?"

"Way ahead of you, Stella. Full-page ads in every news service that has more than a hundred subscribers from the duchy of New Andora in the north all the way to Florida in the south. Will be in the dailies as well as the Sunday edition."

"Impressive."

"And downright expensive, but necessary."

"Well then, shall we get to work on these papers," I say, emptying my cup again.

"Well, grab one and give it a read," she says as she takes another sip. The rose against the ivory of the china sends chills right down to my nether regions. I know that Lord and Lady Helms are not intimate, at least in a sexual way. I also know that Lady Helms entertains a number of women in her bedchambers, and Lord Helms frequents my best friend, and Boston's grand dame of whores, Karie Taylor. The viscount's marriage had been one of wealth and power, not love. Given all of that, they care deeply for one another. I wouldn't ever want to come between man and wife for any reason. I shake off my prurient thoughts to come back to the mound of newspapers.

The truth is, we don't read every page of these periodicals. That would take days. We scan for articles that could impact the demon business. Those are the ones we spend time on. Weeks ago, I volunteered to help the Helmses protect the use of demons as a power source beyond the blasted Snowdonia affair. I'm torn about why I agreed to do so.

I may be just trying to spite that midget-souled Jasperson, the leader of the Coal Syndicate, the one I think has been behind the demon escapes all along. Or perhaps I'm doing it to protect the concepts of demons as an excellent alternative source of power. Mayhap, I just enjoy the comradery of Lord and Lady Helms. There is too much of myself intertwined in each possible answer so it is probably a combination of all three.

"Uh-oh," the viscountess says, breaking the silence. "Listen to this, by Edward M. Johnson." Mr. Johnson is one of the most respected editorialists of all the American Monarchy. Rumor has it that HRM Frederick II reads Johnson's piece before he has even broken his morning fast and sometimes before his morning ablutions.

Adrianna starts reading aloud, and without noticing, she crosses her legs—exposing her curvaceous calf above some stylish black boots. My blood, and other liquids, simmer just below boiling. My paramour, Karie, is due for a raunchy visit tomorrow. I have to work hard to keep my mind off carnal thoughts, Adrianna's gams, and the mental image of Karie's nude body so I can really listen to what my hostess is reading.

"There is no question that Forever Power has held up its end of the social contract to keep the public safe in its dealings with the dark powers of hell itself. There is no questioning the bravery of the hellfighters in battling and returning escaped demons to the service of mankind. Together, the diligence of both groups in tracking down the evil men involved in the release of the caged chaos which ravaged our fair cities puts them in the ranks of heroes. But this hasn't stopped the carnage. It hasn't eliminated the physical disaster wreaked by evil incarnate. Can any benefit be so great as to warrant the potential damage that demons pose to life, limb, and property?

"Demons have often been touted as the power source of the future. True, they do not produce the health and environmental damage that coal byproducts do. They don't have the onus of the deaths of dozens, if not hundreds, of coal miners every year. There will never be a shortage of fiends.

"Yet, even with the conscientiousness of the demon power industry and hellfighters across the globe, hellspawn are a source of chaos and destruction. They remain a focus for anyone wishing mayhem. Within each imprisoned beast is the potential for apocalyptic damage to the fabric of our very existence through carelessness or malice.

"Over the last weeks, we have seen an increasing number of demon releases, seemingly by a cult or organization willing to endlessly sacrifice themselves in order to cause damage to our cities, death to our people, and maybe even wreck our monarchy. We don't know precisely what motivates each of these madmen as they are always destroyed by the very pandemonium they unleash. Is not having demons in many homes the moral equivalent of giving an idiot child a revolver and telling them to behave?

"We believe that the crown has been too long silent on this issue. We applaud his willingness to let moral capitalism solve its own issues under normal circumstances, but how many demon escapes are required before the king acts? How many fires like those in '72 must we endure? How many graves do we have to dig before enough is enough?"

"Sounds like we have our work cut out for us," I say.

"And then some, Miss Ochoa.

"Bastogne!"

"Yes, Lady Helms?" he says, coming around the corner as if he'd been there all along listening for her call. I personally think he is part mentalist.

"Has Lord Helms returned from Forever Power yet?"

"No, ma'am. You know he tends to use Saturday to work on his inventions. That may not be the case today with his added burdens of late, but it is his norm."

"Very well. Bring him to us the moment he does arrive."

"Very good, ma'am. Will there be anything else?"

"Not right now. Thank you, Bastogne." The butler fades into the background like a ghost might with the dawn. "So how can we counter Johnson's article? Not only are the people going to read that, but so will the king."

Thankfully, she sets both her feet on the ground, letting her dress cover up her legs. This allows me to potentially use my brain as something more than a sizeable erogenous zone and focus on our dilemma. My mind doesn't come up with anything immediately as the afterimage of

Adrianna's lower calf remains burned there.

"How about we show how dangerous coal is by putting someone in a large glass room with a burning fireplace? No, that has many issues, doesn't it."

I tactfully keep my mouth closed on that. Who would be silly enough to sit inside, for one? The mental photograph of Adrianna's petticoats over her limbs sparks an idea inside me.

"At first, I was thinking charts and graphs, but people won't stop— *no les importará*. We need something flashier. So, I think the best way to fight *fuego* is with *fuego*, pun intended."

Adrianna smiles, but my joke doesn't quite earn one of her girlish chuckles. "How so?"

"Well, Mr. Johnson has called demons dangerous at any time and coal, no matter its byproducts, safe. Why don't we disabuse that notion? Imagine setting up a demon capture in a big gathering. That would be impressive by itself, but then put something against it to show that once sealed, the beast is safe. I'm thinking dancing girls all around the pentagram."

"Oh, that's good. Dancers will get men's attention, especially if we go to something like those French floozies that show their petticoats and legs for everyone to see. I think they are called can-can dancers," she says, eagerly picking up on the idea and going right where my mental image had been.

The energy is infectious. "Maybe have the demon power a steam calliope that they dance to."

My fear of loose demons rears its head enough to put conditions, "We'd have to make sure it is one hundred percent safe. Maybe a glass barrier around the pentagram to prevent accidental or intentional mischief."

"And as absolute security, how about hiring a team of hellfighters to mingle in the crowd without being seen. That way, if something happens, they can stop it before it goes anywhere."

"I like that, Adrianna. It won't be cheap."

"None of this will be inexpensive. But it's big. It's flashy. It's positive," she says.

"We could go one better if we could get a playwright to pen a production. Maybe about a group of hellfighters that have nothing to do."

"You know, that may be the best idea yet. And I have some contacts in the theatre."

"Good, because I wouldn't know where to start."

"It's quite simple, Stella. Wave money in front of someone, and they get quite excited about the prospect. Hell, if things go well, we might even get the chance to perform for the king," she says as she brings out stationary. "Just a quick note to Miss Cartwright, and I should have a handful of writers' names by the evening."

I try not to frown. I remember Ruby Cartwright, one of Adrianna's paramours, from a few weeks back. I didn't know she was involved in the theatre, but that would make some sense. Actresses are somewhat known for their loose interpretation of what most people call morals and standards of decency. Please don't get me wrong—I am not running down her character in any way. *Matthew 7:2—For in the same way you judge others, you will be judged, and with the measure you use, it will be measured to you.* I am definitely not what most anyone would call a moral woman, either.

"Assuming Henry agrees—"

"Assuming Henry agrees with what?" Lord Helms asks, walking into the solarium. As usual, he looks just a bit unkempt, and his suit hangs on his skinny form like he is a scarecrow with a dearth of hay.

"Dear, thank you for showing up in such a timely fashion. Stella and I have a perfectly wonderful idea to help bolster the industry." With a great deal of excitement, she shares our ideas with her husband while I realize I still haven't solved the problem of where I'm sleeping tonight.

I know Michaeleen would put me up again, but I need to find something more permanent. The problem is that Saturday evening is not an ideal time for one to be looking for lodging. And no one does business on the Sabbath. There is no way my boss would give me time off on Monday. I'd sleep rough rather than give that cow, Chapman, any satisfaction by returning to my own room. *Proverbs 16:18— Pride goeth before destruction, and a haughty spirit before a fall.* It is either eat crow or rent a room in a hotel.

"...Oh, Mrs. Ochoa?"

"Huh, what?" I realize I've tuned out my hosts.

"I was saying that I love your plan of attack, but you looked like you just ate a slug. What's wrong?" Henry asks.

"Oh, nothing at all, Lord Helms."

"And if that isn't the biggest load of succotash I've ever heard," Henry says, putting his white-gloved hands on his waist. Beneath the bleached fabric of his gloves are burn scars similar to those down my left side. He got those in our mutual fight with the demon lord Gazzunreep. In order to save my life, he permanently damaged his already demon-burned hands by wrangling the poderabile to get me to a doctor. I've never forgotten the debt I owe him, one of many reasons I help with his public image fight.

"I agree, husband. What are you keeping from us, Stella?"

"I'm not going to burden you with my problems!" I bark back as fiercely as I can.

"And why not? You regularly come and help us with ours."

"That's different," I say with all the intelligence of a six-year-old arguing her case for one more cookie than her brother got.

"Either you 'fess up, friend Stella, or I'm going to have to tell your mother on you."

Damned, but Adrianna plays rough. My mother and I don't get along well since she let a demon burn me during my witchcraft testing. Ostensibly she did it to teach me a lesson. It worked insomuch that I haven't made the same mistakes again, but it alienated us even more than we had already been. And Adrianna met her at my so-called hero's celebration after defeating Gazzunreep. Little did I know that the gathering would have the pair of them becoming friends.

"¡Mierda!" I curse.

"I usually only hear that kind of language when I go back to the loading docks," Viscount Helms says.

"Yes, and if you tell my mother about it, she will threaten to wash out my mouth with soap."

"So what is it you aren't telling us, *amiga*?" Adrianna asks.

I cup my face in my palm, knowing exactly what is going to happen. "Where do you want me to start? Where I got shot or where I got thrown out of my boardinghouse?"

My hosts barrage me with questions faster than the repeating shots of the assassin.

"Wait, you got shot?"

"Are you alright? Do you need to lie down?"

"Why didn't you tell me?"

"BASTOGNE! Fetch the doctor."

"Who did it? Why?"

I take a deep breath. "Bastogne, don't get the doctor," I call out at the retreating butler. He stops and turns. "Maxwell from my hellfighter team, you remember him from the parties, healed me. I am quite well enough to tackle anything short of a demon lord."

"When did this happen? Why hasn't it been in the papers?"

I take the time to go over the events of last night and what the police have said, avoiding the mention of constabulary protection. "I'm quite safe now that I'm on my guard. Don't forget that bullets and most weapons are of the earth," I temporize to put them at ease. They both look at one another and communicate in the way only a married couple can. I read care and concern.

"So, if you are really sure that you are in good health—"

"I could wrestle an ox. I'd lose, but I feel well enough to give it a go."

The pair chuckle. "Then tell us about your landlady evicting you."

"Well, more precisely, I threw myself out of my own home by calling the *gilipollas puta* on her hypocrisy and her lack of authority over me. As a result, I'm no better than a hobo without a place to put my head except where I park the poderabile. I haven't had the chance to find new lodgings."

"You poor thing," Adrianna says with her hand over her mouth.

"So let me see if I understand this right," Lord Helms says, in a voice I've come to learn is the beginning of some pontification. "Instead of finding yourself a home, you came here to help protect my business?"

I twist my mouth to one side in embarrassment. "Something like that."

"Henry?" Adrianna says with a look to her husband. That mental shorthand flashes between them again. I can even see where this is going, and I'll not have it.

"Quite right, m'lady. Stella, you must move in with us."

"Oh, no, you don't," I say, standing up and moving backward as if a bear is advancing on me.

"Oh, yes, Stella, we do!" Adrianna says as if butter won't melt in her mouth.

"You trapped me here in this gilded cage once before under the guise of nursing me back to health. I won't let you do it again."

Henry takes one of the seats next to the mass of newsprint. "And while we are on the topic of lodging, what do you think you will be looking for? A single house or—"

"Heavens, I couldn't afford to rent a house by myself."

"Rent?" Henry retorts. "Who said anything about renting? I was talking about buying."

"Ahhhhh." My mouth can probably catch flies at the moment. "If I can't afford to rent one, how can I possibly buy one?"

"Henry, we have to teach this poor little chick. It's the least we can do."

"No question, my dear," Henry says, picking up a cup of coffee his wife poured him. He sips. "Stella, before I start your lessons, do you have any plans other than looking for lodging? This may take a while."

"I should meet my hellfighter team, the *Dos Campanas*, at the bar to get my cut. But if I don't show up, Carlos will hold it for me. I could also use some time to see my seamstress about some more work clothes."

"Good. Then quit looking like a cat cornered by a dog and pull up a chair. We are going to introduce you to the world of high finance. And before you object, I know you have the funds to make this work."

"But that money is for my dotage."

"And wouldn't owning your own home, free and clear, save you money in retirement?"

"Well, yes."

Henry just rolls over me like a trolley without its front sweeper. "Then let's start with what you want. Then I'll prove to you that you can afford it and have still more money for your dotage or retirement, not that I can imagine you that way. I imagine you fighting demons with long gray hair, in a wheelchair, yelling dockside curses as you do."

The image is amusing, but I'm serious about not being beholden to anyone. "I'll listen—"

"Out of politeness, I'm sure," Adrianna interjects.

"Indeed," Henry says. "So, do you want a home on your own? Plenty of alone time. No one to bother you when you come and go. No one to say 'boo' if you have a male friend over."

I shudder. As much as I value my independence, loneliness scares me. "I've never lived alone. Closest I came was when Aaron went off to war. But that was a tiny apartment where you could tell what the neighbors had for dinner just by sniffing in my own parlor."

"OK, maybe an apartment building?" Adrianna offers.

"A whole building? *Joder!* Surely I can't afford that."

Henry continues his line with, "Stella, with the money I know you have saved away, I could get the next thing to a mansion if you want. Besides, a building with tenants pays you money; it doesn't cost."

"Huh? Oh, like the Widow Chapman, curse her heart. I don't want to be a *puta* like her."

"Being a landlord is like anything else. There are the good and the bad."

My mind winds up. "Could I bring along the other girls from Chapman's?"

"Not only that, you could make money doing so."

I collapse into a chair, finally giving in to my friends and their guileless offer of help. I am beginning to regret telling them my problems.

4—Saturday Afternoon, May 5, 1888

Three hours later, I give up. Both Henry and Adrianna are quite knowledgeable about money. They seem intent on making me drink from the bottom of the Niagara Falls of their wisdom. "OK. OK. Let me think it over. I'm up to my ears in interest rates, depreciation, amortization, rents, and other things I've never even heard of before. Let me at least sleep on it."

"Of course, Stella. We are just offering you advice and ways you can make your money make more money for you. And it also solves your current problem at the same time," Henry says.

"Speaking of sleeping," Adrianna says, "I know you objected to staying with us as a guest, but I think you'd better take the guest room, or I might just have to telegram your mother about how you are a tramp and need to be taken in."

"Oh, you bitch. You wouldn't."

Adrianna doesn't answer, just gives me her dimples and a twinkle in the eye.

As wet as my bloomers are over her, living under her roof might be putting the cat a little too close to the canary cage. "You fight dirty. Alright, but only for a night."

Lady Helms doesn't answer again, only gives me that look of victory that she does so well.

"Just give in, Stella. You've lost," Henry says, handing me over the ten pages of notes, graphs, and figures he'd used in his explanations.

"*Miedra!* OK. You win, but I do have a couple of errands I'd like to run before dinnertime."

"Promptly at eight, Stella."

"Thank you both. I may never be the same, but thank you."

# # #

"As you know, Mrs. Ochoa, there is a door in the back of the guest room, which is yours," Bastogne says, handing me the key. "Their lord and ladyship feel you would be more comfortable if you didn't have to ring the bell just to get in and out."

I look at him dubiously from the doorway. I didn't think Lord or Lady Helms had any such idea. "And who might have put that bug in their ear?"

Bastogne gives one of his wry smiles. "I don't know what you may be alluding to, madam."

"I'm sure you don't. I should be back well before suppertime."

"Yes, Mrs. Ochoa."

I turn and walk over to the poderabile while Bastogne closes the door behind me. I find a stowaway in the cab.

"Tommy! You scamp. What are you doing here?"

"I heared that you are moving in. Thought I'd come down if'n you needed me to move the poderabile into the stable."

"How did you hear that I was moving in?"

He smiles, showing the gap between his two front teeth. "News travels faster below stairs than one of them telegraphs and its magic wires."

"Well, don't be getting any ideas. I'm only here until I find a new place to live."

"They says that Lord Helms is buying you a house," he says with glee.

"Nonsense, Tommy. He thinks *I* should buy a house. Gossip may be faster than the newspaper, but it isn't always right. Remember that."

"Yes, Stella."

"Did you get in touch with your friends about helping me move?"

"Yes, ma'am. Mikey will be at your old boardinghouse just like you asked. She gots two big friends to help her."

"You are a treasure, Tommy."

"I tries, Stella."

"Now give me a hug and get off with you. I'm sure you're shirking your duty to the Lady Helms, and I have places to be."

#

With some finicky lever adjustments, I manage to get the poderabile into the narrow alley behind the Bell in Hand. I won't be here long, and the afternoon is not a time for deliveries. It shouldn't inconvenience anyone.

The bright lights and cheery song draw me in as usual. The entire bar is rattling with the refrain of, "Away, away with rum by gum, with rum by gum, with rum by gum." The satire of it makes me smile. My people shout down the growing number of damned teetotalers with the ironic song. A guitar player is strumming and belting out the verses before the rest of the bar picks up the chorus, all the while banging their steins of bitter and glasses of harder liquor on the table.

The entire *Dos Campanas* team is at our usual table, singing along with as much gusto as the rest of the bar. Donny has his arm around his girl and her matching red hair. She is a decorative thing that makes pies for a living and is trying her damnedest to get him to slip a ring on her finger. Manaj is bottle-feeding what looks like a rather large kitten until I get close enough to realize that it is a lynx cub. Maxwell is mostly in his cups already, roaring out the song rather than being melodious. His voice breaks from time to time like an adolescent. Usually, it would embarrass him, but instead, he just sings louder. Likewise, Carlos adds little but bass to the tune. He seems to ignore the melody as he bellows out the words. He isn't drunk. This is just his way of letting loose the stresses of risking his life so much lately.

The only one I don't know much about is Bea Media, the ice witch from Spain. She came over to the American Monarchy specifically because we have embraced demon power. Spain has avoided it to this point. There is little call for an ice witch in their kingdom other than keeping the food chilled, a job just one notch above me spelling soot out of the air. Her innocent look hides the fact that she is competent and has learned quickly from Carlos about how to do this job. Right now, she looks lost amongst the revelry our bar exhibits. Spain, from my understanding, is much more staid than us rowdy Americans.

Carlos notices me as I slide in and pick up the tune. He reaches into his breeches and tugs out a rather massive pouch. He tosses it toward me to land on the table. Even over the song, I can hear the jingle of coins as well as feel the joy of the gold and silver metals within. I don't think I've seen such a fat take from our exploits. But then it has been several days, and more than a few demon escapes combined to produce that purse. Without missing a beat, I pick it up and push it down the front of my blouse between my breasts. It's almost as good as a pocket, for no one thinks a woman should have pockets on her skirts, even my seamstress. I never understand why.

I catch the eye of Helga, the waitress that comes in on Friday and Saturday nights to help with the crush. She is thirty or more feet away, and nothing short of a steam whistle would cut through the noise so I make my hand like it is wrapped around a beer stein. She nods and has Michaeleen pump another bitter from his taps.

Helga is a great gal. Her presence reminds me that compared to some, I am petite. She towers over most men, putting her gigantic German breasts at eye level to most of them. It is probably what gets her at least half of the big tips she earns most weekends. She is a sweetheart. She comes toward me carrying a tray with no fewer than seven big pints of ale. Like she has a mechanical adding machine in her head, she hands them off one at a time to those who have ordered them. I'm the last one on her service, just about the time the drinking chanty ends. The guitarist brings down the tempo to a romantic love song that he sings in a high, furry voice.

Helga plops down into the chair next to me with a heavy sigh, both from her and the chair. I offer her the cost of the beer and a tip at least as generous as that of the menfolk. "At least ya don' go pattin' my bottom fer da extra," she says. "Sometimes, I am thinkin' I should just join a bawdy house and be done with it."

"I won't say you are wrong," I offer, taking a long draw on the pint of black beer, one of the Bell in Hand's biggest attractions.

"Aww, Stella, I know they be not thinking its anythin' more than a feel, but it does get old sometimes. I goes home some nights with more bruises on my bum than I'd get fallin' down two flights of stairs."

I can't think of anything to say to refute her argument so I settle for another gulp of beer. "You know about arnica?" I offer in consolation.

"Yup. Got the jar right next to my bed. Don't bother with it Friday nights, but Saturday, I go to bed with the inside of my bloomers greasy with the stuff."

"So, I heared that ya is lookin' for a place to room," she says, changing the subject radically.

"I was—am?" I say, adding the last like it is more a question. I know I said I'd stay with the Helmses, but I am not yet convinced.

"Wells, my house got a room if ya are interested. Ten dollars a week, but no food, and ya got to find your own place for laundry. That last part is the killer for me. I cook up quite a schnitzel, but havin' to lug my unmentionables all over town to clean them is right embarrassing."

"I'll think about it, Helga, but I think I have another situation already."

"Ya think about it. Michaeleen knows where I live if you be changin' ya mind." She looks back at the bar where a number of steins and glasses are piling up. "I'd better be gettin' back to my work now."

"Thank you, Helga."

The topic at the rest of the table seems to be the upcoming Kentucky Derby. The news has listed all of the horses. The *Dos Campanas* seem to be deciding which one to bet on. The discussion flags mainly because the majority of us are so tired we can barely lift our drinks.

"I have good news, and I have bad news," Carlos says to us.

"By God, give us the good news first. I don't think I have enough energy for bad news right now," I say.

"I know we are all worn down to the nub trying to cover all of Boston and Charleston so I made some inquiries. I've made a deal with *Los Lobos*, the hellfighters to our southwest, to pick up responsibility for more of Boston proper. I also talked with the Minute Men, the coven in East Boston, to cover a chunk of the area that was covered by Baron Snowdonia's Cannons."

"You mean I might get a night's sleep without worrying about a callout?" Raquel says, taking the bottle away from the snoring wildcat.

"I wouldn't go that far, but it should cut our work by about a third."

"I'll take a third. Anything to get half a bit of rest," Max says, his voice breaking midway through.

"I agree," I add. "I don't have the energy to keep up this pace. How long are these agreements good for?"

"At least until the Cannons reconstitute. My understanding is that the constabulary and the Coven of Massachusetts are both looking very closely at their membership. So, it may be a while before they are stable again."

"And damned well they should," Raquel says, rocking her furry friend like an infant. "When their leader nearly kills Stella, a prominent lord, AND a member of the law enforcement establishment, they deserve a little 'looking into.'"

I interject. "I really don't believe any of those other witches knew what he was up to. Snowdonia didn't trust anyone, even those he risked his life with. The man was a narcissist."

"A what?" Donny asks.

"He loved nothing but himself," Carlos says. "After the Greek man Narcissus who fell in love with his own reflection."

Carlos surprises me with his knowledge of mythology. It doesn't happen often.

"You can say that again, the pompous peacock. You should have seen him walking down the street like women should genuflect for his glance," Raquel shares.

"That sounds like the baron, alright," I confirm.

"Enough baron bashing. He was a waste of space and our time. What's the bad news?" Donny manages even with his girl whispering in his ear and some mostly unnoticed groping of his thigh under the table.

"Well, we won't be making quite the flood of *doubloons* we have been in the past few weeks. A third less work means a third less income," Carlos says, leaning back with his mug, his job of town crier done for the evening.

"Well, maybe I should cancel my mansion," Donny says with a smirk. The pout on his girlfriend's face speaks volumes about her. *Little gold-digging bitch*, I think in a rare unchristian thought. *I've warned him about her more than once. It's his problem.*

"Thanks for that, Carlos. I hate to break up the party, but I've got two more stops before I climb into a bed."

"'Night, Stella."

"May your night be restful," Maxwell offers.

# # #

I choose to walk to my destination, only a block and a half away. The windowless shop is only thrice as wide as the doorway. Its only signage is a hanging wooden carving of a thimble, a bobbin of thread, and a needle, each sized for a giant's hands. I open the door, triggering a calliope in the rear of the shop to toot out a happy tune. Paula Simpson's front room is smaller than my ex-bedroom by at least half. It sports some well-worn but comfortable living room furniture. Pale blue walls light up from the waning sunlight trickling in from the skylight overhead.

"Be with you in half a shake," I hear from a room curtained off with heavy black velvet.

"No rush, Paula."

"Is that you, Stella?"

"Yes. It's me again."

"You go through more clothes than a regiment of society women," she says, her voice carrying over the sound of the mechanical monstrosity she uses to sew with. I'd seen it once. It is seven times the size of a proper treadle machine. With that much steam and gears, I wonder how she keeps the fabrics clear of grease.

"That's the truth, Paula."

The chuffing of steam from the other room reminds me of the poderabile at high speeds. It stops. Moments later, Paula parts the black curtains. She wears a cloth measuring tape around her neck like a man's tie and carries a notepad. Take a frail woman that might be able to squash a bug and remove half of her flesh. Worse, she isn't short, standing as tall as I am. Oddly, I think Lord Helms and her might make a good match, at least physically. "So, what is it today, Stella?"

"Well, with all of the demon escapes lately, my clothes have taken a beating. They likely will be abused until either we find out why people are stupid enough to let a demon rage all over them or all the demons are behind security walls. I need some new skirts, blouses, and underthings. Maybe five of each."

"Anything special?"

"Well, for four of them, just work dresses. Use your judgment for fabrics. I trust your fashion sense much more than my own. But for the fifth, I was thinking of something quite special. Do you know those breeches working menfolk have been wearing, the indestructible ones?"

"That thick blue fabric?"

"Yeah, that's the stuff. How about a dress, designed to be durable, out of that? It has to be one piece with blouse and skirt in one because I'd need to get into it very quickly. Maybe like overalls with a dress at the bottom instead of legs."

"That would be ugly as sin, Stella."

"Yes, but it would take a beating, wouldn't it?"

Her thin face turns up, and her eyes close in thought. "I couldn't use any standard patterns. And to be really strong, I'd want to overlap the material and at least double-stitch everything. And to ensure no corner tearing, I can use metal rivets at strategic places."

"That sounds about right."

"I should warn you, Stella, that no fabric is going to stand up to the teeth, fire, or claws of any demon."

"I understand, Paula. Demons rarely get that close. Most of the time, it is something around the fighting that ruins my clothes, like dislodged bricks. The other day a bed fell out of a second-story tenement. One of the legs snagged the back of my dress and tore it nearly in half."

"That will definitely take a toll. Well, I'll have to double wash it so the material doesn't shrink when you launder it," she mutters to herself. I see her eyes roll back in deep thought. I'm giving her a professional challenge, and I can see that she likes it.

"Oh, another thing, Paula." Her attention snaps back to my face. "I'd like to get some underpinnings that are a little—" I trail off, not knowing how to broach the subject in polite company.

Paula gets me right away. "Oh, you want some see-through drawers? Maybe some lacey petticoats? How about a silky smooth brassiere that doesn't really hide anything underneath."

I feel the heat blazing from my cheeks. I must be seven shades of crimson.

"Don't worry about it, Stella. I do the underthings for many of the ladies of questionable virtue around town. I also sneak in a few for ladies who want to give their husband a treat."

"Err," I stammer with intelligence.

"I could also make up a dressing gown with a big slit up the middle so your paramour can see almost all of your legs."

I gulp, thinking about what Karie would make of that. Probably drop to her knees and make a meal of me. The whole thought process is making me slick down between my thighs. "Yes, to all of it, Paula."

"Do you have a choice in color? I know red is really raunchy, but I think your skin tone cries out for a bright iris-purple."

I swallow hard thinking about wearing those and nod.

"So, do you need them in any special hurry?"

"Well, if I could get that denim dress fast, and the, ummm..."

"Unmentionables?"

I nod again. "If I could get those quickly, I'd appreciate it. The rest of the dresses and underclothes, any time is fine."

Paula and I dicker over the price. She asks for an outrageous price for the unique dress. I counter that more working women would want them if they stand up to the roughness I can put it through. I wouldn't restrict the pattern to just me. We arrive at a price that barely lightens the coin pouch tucked down in my brassiere.

She glances at my figure for a moment. "If you were any other woman, I'd have to retake measurements, but we only measured you up a pair of months ago. I don't think we'll need to do so again. Come back Friday for the dress and your special underthings."

"Thanks, Paula. You are a godsend," I say, giving her a hug. "One more question, if I may."

"By all means."

"It's a little odd."

Paula laughs like little chimes. "I've known you five years now. When have you not been odd, Stella?"

"Guilty," I say, with a big smile back. "Who does all of the mechanics for your machine and other gizmos in the back?"

She pauses for a second with raised eyebrows. "You are right— definitely odd. Gearman Louis Archambeau."

"A frog?"

"Yes, he sometimes gets discriminated against because of it. His father emigrated right at the beginning of our monarchy. He's as American as any of us. But be that as it may, I think he is the greatest mechanic ever. He has a shop over on Mt. Vernon, right up against the seawall."

# # #

The chop on the surface of the Charles River sends up just a bit of spray. With the tide in, I smell the brackish water slapping against the seawall. A wooden gear, as big around as a large dog, hangs down from a wrought iron bar above a person-sized door, within a massive double carriage entrance.

I knock with one hand as I reach for the handle. To my surprise, the knob opens on a Saturday afternoon. I step over a six-inch weather sill carrying my bag full of metal bits. Beyond is an open space in which it looks large enough for the Boston Beacons to play soccer. The entire expanse is so tightly and randomly packed, I doubt I could walk to the other side of the room without getting my skirts greasy and torn. The area closest to me is a pin-neat office, sans walls. It sports a desk that has the patina of decades of use. Several comfortable-looking chairs, with the leather worn to suppleness, surround it. All of this is illuminated with electric lights dangling down from overhead. The remainder of the expanse is a random mishmash of hydraulic cylinders taller than I stand, great gears bigger than the poderabile, and bins with parts that defy description. The collection must be in some form of order, but I can't fathom its organization.

Somewhere back in the distance, I hear banging, the clatter of things falling to the floor, and even the sound of something like a mythical dragon's breath.

There is a sign on the desk next to a tiny bell, the kind you might see on a high-class hotel counter. The sign says, "If I'm not immediately at hand, please ring bell for service."

Dubiously, I step up and tap the bell. The sound is nothing more than I expect and can't possibly cover much distance. I wonder if I'm going to need to pound it with a hammer considering the size and scope of the chamber.

The racket in the distance ceases. "I'll be right there," calls out a pleasant voice from that general direction. A youngish man wearing patched overalls, stained with grease, dances between a crate, a massive gear, and a box containing large wrenches that I could have used to take the wheels off a locomotive. His face is smudged all the way up one side and into his blond hair—hair that stands out in no particular order, looking more like a haystack than something that belongs on the head of a businessman. He wipes his greasy hands on a rag of dubious cleanliness. "Yes, ma'am, how can I help you?"

"Mr. Archambeau, I have a puzzle that you may be able to help me with. I have pieces of a machine, and I'd like you to tell me what it is, and maybe who made it?" My voice rises on the end of my question, indicating my lack of belief in such a wizard-like capability.

"My time is valuable, ma'am."

"I'm sorry, I didn't mean to imply that I looked for you to use your time without compensation. I'm more than willing to pay. What are your rates?"

"Five dollars a day," he says, staring me down.

"Fair enough. Would you like a day in advance?"

The man bursts out in a guffaw that fills the entire space. When he settles down, he says, "You didn't even tick the top rail, ma'am. I apologize for being overbearing."

"Not at all, Mr. Archambeau. I am asking for your expertise, and for that, I will pay. By the by, my name is Stella Ochoa."

"Good enough. Let's see what you have in that bag, Mrs. Ochoa," he says, pushing a table on wheels toward me. Never have considered putting a table on wheels. It must make things so much easier to bring it to the source rather than carrying things to it. I dump the bits and pieces of metal that I'd gathered from the scene of the abattoir basement onto it.

"That's it," I offer.

Rubbing his hands together like a kid looking at the presents under a Christmas tree, the mechanic digs in. I smile at his eagerness.

He spreads the pieces out like a puzzle. "Good gracious, but this looks like what happens to a branch when it's put through one of those new wood chippers. What happened to it?"

"A demon probably stomped on it, at minimum."

The blond man looks up with his bushy eyebrows raised. "Surely, you jest."

"No, Mr. Archambeau, I am quite serious. I am a hellfighter." This gets me another furrowed brow. I sense more than a bit of disbelief. Fortunately, the mechanic's entire building is on a dirt floor. I simply will the ground to lift up a bit of ground no bigger around than a dime. I let it stretch out to form a narrow cylinder in front of me like a cane. The man takes a step back. With my fingers, I take the top inch off the thin structure. The rest of the earth oozes back to its quiescent state. I hold out the dirt clod.

It takes him several moments before he takes a step forward, with a tremor in his hand. "That is quite impressive. I'm sorry for my disbelief."

"You aren't the first. You won't be the last. I accept your apology." I avoid going into the implicit bias of men.

"So you found this in the hands of a demon?"

"Yes. I found this at the scene of a demon escape."

"Well, that gives me a place to start. Did you want me to reassemble it? That would take quite an effort and maybe impossible in the end."

"Heavens, no. I just want to know what it was and, God forbid, if it had anything to do with the demon's escape."

"That is fair." His attention turns entirely away from me. One by one, he picks up each piece and turns it over in his hand. He looks at it closely before setting it down and moving to the next one. His attention is so focused on the metal and rubber bits that I feel like I'm not even in the room. I sit down to stay out of the way. At one point, he flips a magnifying glass in front of one eye. The dollar-coin-sized lens is on an arm attached to a strap around his head buried under his mop of hair.

"Well, here is one piece of your puzzle, Mrs. Ochoa." He turns toward me, and his right eye looks four times the normal size through the lens.

"Oh? That was quick."

"I'm far from done, but I can give you some information right away." He brushes the glass up out of the way until it stands straight up. "See here." He comes over close, pointing to some indentations on a piece of pot metal.

I trace the tip of my finger across tiny symbols, not even the width of my wedding ring. "I see them, but what do they mean?"

"Well, that rounded-top T symbol means it was originally made by Umbrella Toys."

"A toy?"

"Were you expecting something else?"

"I'm not sure what I was expecting. Looks like I may have involved you in a wild goose chase."

"Don't jump to conclusions, Mrs. Ochoa. Where did I put that book?" He turns away and rummages through a bookshelf. "Here." He picks off a tome at least six inches thick, opening it up near the end. "Udaloy, Udder, Ulong. Here it is—Umbrella Toys. He traces down the page. "Em, Em, three. Those are the other symbols near the umbrella. That is a key-operated street sweeper toy."

"That's odd."

"Well, don't run away yet. This toy has been modified after manufacture."

"Modified?" I ask.

He picks up another piece and points at a joint. "Look here. There is silver solder in this joint here. No toy manufacturer would use silver solder. It's too expensive."

"So why does..."

"I'm sorry, Mrs. Ochoa, but that's all I can give you at the moment. Give me until tomorrow evening, and I'll be able to tell you more."

I open my purse and count out ten one-dollar coins onto the table.

Mr. Archambeau takes the top five dollars. "This is more than enough, Mrs. Ochoa. You've brought me a challenge. I don't get that very often."

"As you will," I say, dragging the remainder into my purse.

"Come back tomorrow and I'll have more for you."

"On the Sabbath?"

"Yes, ma'am. I work every day. Why not, when you love the work?"

"Why not indeed."

#

Climbing into my poderabile, I'm not looking forward to my next stop. Going another year without talking to my mother wouldn't distress me. Even before my first encounter with Gazzunreep, our relationship wasn't what anyone would call good. The closest word that comes to mind is adversarial. Sometimes I feel I should have a barrister at my side when I visit.

Now, I wasn't abused as a child. I had food to eat and a roof over my head. I was given good schooling. My mother's failing, in my opinion, is that she never shared love and affirmation with me. As she is the only parent I've ever known, I found that as hurtful and cruel as if she'd beaten me with a buggy whip. After often bringing home stellar grades from school, I received only acknowledgments. When I discovered my magical bent, I learned at twice the speed of any other apprentice. She never displayed pleasure at my skill. The servants tried to make up for her coldness, bless them, but they weren't of my flesh. As a result, I now find visits with her to be painful reminders of a childhood bereft of maternal care.

That being said, my thoughts go back to what I've been thinking all day—Professor Xavier's assertion of my lineage. *A demon! Fuck*, I remonstrate myself. Unfortunately, I know no other way to obtain more information about my ancestry than through my mother.

I put the coming confrontation out of my mind as maneuvering the poderabile takes a good deal of concentration. I wish I had someone back behind me to warn anyone coming that I am backing out. I do honk my goose horn several times. No horses or bicycles crash into me so I breathe easier as I set a course for *madre's*.

Fortunately, Senior Mistress Witch Josephine Romero lives on a wide street with plenty of buggy space for parking. Point in fact, there is a very fine rig out front as I pull up. A single black Irish Draught horse is between the service rails of an ebony coach with ivory inlay. The outfit would cost more than I make in a year, both from demon rewards and spelling coal dust out of the air. I don't recognize the coat of arms on the door. A driver sits atop, and two formal footmen mill around beside it, speaking in very low tones.

The three of them studiously ignore me as I go up and use the knocker to announce myself. Ozias stifles a smile as he opens the door. "Good evening, Mrs. Ochoa."

"Hello, Ozias. Are you and the others doing well?"

"Other than Iris complaining of a touch of rheumatism, we are all doing quite well."

"When didn't Iris complain about something?" I observe. "She isn't happy unless she is complaining."

"Oh, we are quite aware, miss. And how are you?"

"I'm confused at the moment, Ozias. My mother may be able to unconfuse me if that wouldn't be too much to ask."

"I'm sorry, miss, but she is entertaining."

Just as he trails off with his statement, I hear my mother talking to someone and walking in this direction. "Of course, Emil, I will have to check my social calendar. After all, the Royal Spring Ball is THE event of the season."

"But, *mi amor*, you promised you would accompany me," came the smooth Latin tones of a Spaniard.

"I will check and respond by Royal Post, Sir Serrano." That gave me the last piece of the puzzle. Sir Emiliano Serrano is a special envoy from the Spanish court to the court of our King Frederick II.

The pair of them come out into the foyer. The Spaniard's arm is around my mother's waist with his hand firmly on her bustle in a manner no gentleman would presume. My mother isn't much better, draped over his arm like a courtesan with her hand stroking absently up and down his thigh.

"Regardless, you will be my escort to court when His Royal Majesty Alfonso the Twelfth meets with your Frederick the Second?" It is less a question than a statement.

"Yes, I will definitely be at your side for that event, Emil."

"Very good."

"Do we have a better idea of when that excellent event might happen?"

"Alas, *señora*, I am not at liberty to discuss the plans of his highness."

"Of course, Don Serrano."

"Oh, my goodness, who is this charming young woman," the knight asks as they get closer to the door.

"This is my daughter, Mistress Witch Stella Ochoa."

"No, say it is not so. There is no way you could have a grown *hija*, much less one that is so accomplished and so radiant." He bends over my hand and places a kiss on the back. I've never seen a man butter up two women at the same time, but he is doing his best.

"You wolf," my mother says. She whacks him gently on the head with a collapsed fan. "She is not for the likes of you. Now get off with you before I write to your wife that you've been out carousing and engaging in drunken debauchery with lewd women."

"In that case, I will bid *buenos noches* to you, *Señora* Romero." I hear a whisper of *"querida,"* as he bends over, kissing her hand, much more thoroughly than the peck he gave mine. As he straightens, he addresses me directly. "Alas, *Señorita* Ochoa, I cannot linger for fear of my dalliances being revealed by your lovely mother. But I would be honored to entertain you at some future time." He bows and, without waiting for a response, turns to return to his expensive carriage, driver, and footmen.

"Madam Romero, Mrs. Ochoa desires to consult with you," Ozias says as if I'm not standing right next to the pair of them. "Will you see her?"

"Yes, Ozias. Daughter, will you be dining with us?"

"No, ma'am," I say, not wanting to give away that I've already got an engagement at the Helmses' home. It would lead to awkward questions I don't want to answer.

"Then, Ozias, service for coffee in my study."

"Very good, mistress."

Mother puts her arm around me and leads me. It isn't quick enough to hide the marks on her collar from the pearl-white face paint the knight was wearing, nor does it do anything to mask his musky cologne that wafts up from her dress. *Does the prim and proper Lady Romero play fast and loose with morality?* Come to think of it, I don't remember ever seeing my mother court anyone seriously, nor act in any way even potentially scandalous. The closest I can ever remember was her dancing the waltz with the Duke of Ontario at my seventh birthday party.

"So, daughter, why are you here? I know I'm not your favorite flavor.

You never show up unless you have something you want."

She isn't wrong so denying it is pointless. "After visiting with Professor Xavier, I have some questions about Grandmamma and Great Grandma," I inquire.

"So was she as quirky as they say?" Mother asks.

"You know I didn't know either of them."

She waves me to a chair. "I meant the professor, daughter. I heard a rumor that last summer she swam in the harbor just in her leopard skin corset and some Italian knickers that barely covered her *concha*."

"Oh, her. I'm sorry, Mother. I'm a little scatterbrained with all that's happened in the last couple of days."

"Please enlighten me. I get to hear so little about your life other than what is written in the papers."

I rummage around with what I can tell her. I figure the shooting probably won't make the papers so best not bring it up. "Well, this morning, I had it out with my landlady. We parted ways on not terribly amicable circumstances."

"Really? Where are you staying now? Your room is still available if you'd like."

"Ah, I have made other arrangements."

Mother waves it away as unimportant. "Probably for the best. Maybe now you can live somewhere worthy of your new status as Mistress Witch."

"I'm working on that," I say truthfully. "Also, I got a wonderful warming note from the NPP." Mother says nothing but directs Ozias to place the coffee service on the table between us. "And, I'd say my visit with *la professora* definitely has me shaken."

"How so?" she says, pouring a bit of cream in her coffee after placing a pale-blue, demitasse china cup of heavenly smelling coffee in front of me.

"Would you mind if I approach that somewhat obliquely, Mother?"

"As you will, daughter," she says, picking up her cup. I take a sip of mine, which makes a serious dent in the amount in the tiny cup. But the thick mixture lights up my brain and all but overloads my taste buds.

"Since when do you drink Cuban coffee?"

"A wonderful trader from the Consolidated Islands of Cuba introduced it to me. Quite refreshing, don't you think?"

I bat my eyes and arch my brows, thinking I'm not going to be able to sleep tonight. "I might have saved it for the morning."

"Nonsense. Anyway, you were talking about Professor Xavier."

"Yes. So what do you remember about your grandparents?" I ask as casually as possible.

"Interesting question in conjunction with Professor Xavier, but I'll answer. Not a good deal. I met Grandma Polly once before my father moved us from England. She had a Scottish brogue that you could use to bludgeon a sturgeon to death with. I seem to remember her telling me one time to be proud of being a McDonald. I never met my father's mother. Mixed marriages, a Spaniard and an Englishwoman, were taboo. Grandma Sally and Grandpa Jorge kept to themselves in the English midlands, living quietly and trying not to call attention to the different colors of their skin. My father told me it was so bad they never went out in public together."

"Anything more? How many kids did each of them have?"

"Well, Grandma Sally and Grandpa Jorge had only my father, Martin. But Grandmother Polly and Grandpa Ioan had eight, I think."

"And I'm assuming if you knew nothing about Grandma Sally and Grandpa Jorge, you knew nothing of their parents."

"Almost nothing. Somewhere around here, I have the Romero Bible that has names but nothing more. Why the sudden interest in family genealogy?" Mother leans back into her chair like a queen or goddess. She has that disconcerting ability to strike right to the heart of your soul with just a glance. She knows I am hiding something. I know she knows. And she knows that I know that she knows. I guess it is time to just grasp the nettle.

"Well, Xena Xavier provided me with an interesting explanation of why I wasn't cleft in twain by Gazzunreep's flame. She says one of our ancestresses copulated with an incubus. We have demon in our blood."

I don't know if there is such a thing as a ladylike chortle, but if there is, that is the sound that comes out of my mother's mouth. "Poppycock." This is the closest I recall my mother coming to uttering profanity.

"Excuse me?"

"You know the meaning of the word, daughter. The premise is ludicrous. I guess I should have suspected someone from Boston University would come up with such a fantasy."

"But you, yourself, said that she is an expert in demonology."

"That's what I'd been told. But I also have been told her husband used to be a circus performer, that she wears men's clothes, and that she would just as soon see our monarchy as a democracy like those foolish Germans."

I think briefly about sharing the proof that Xena gave me. Still, I decide that the fewer people who know about my special ability, the better, especially my mother. "So you sent me to a crackpot?"

"I gave you a pointer, daughter. How you choose to use it is your affair."

"OK, she did say that women who have this blood in them tend to have few to no children. What about you having me and no others, and Grandma Priscilla having only you and—"

"Daughter, I was lucky to live after giving birth to you as my womb detached. That is why you are an only child. There is nothing supernatural about it."

"But—" I try to get out.

"Seriously, my daughter. And just so you know, I wasn't an only child. My younger brother died in childbirth. My mother had three other miscarriages, not something you share in polite conversation."

Interesting, I think. I'm not sure it changes anything Xena told me, but I can see that pushing Mother isn't going to get me any more information. Someone in my mother's mother's lineage likely is the one who spread herself for a hellspawn, but it is never to be determined for certain. "As you say, Mother. I don't think it matters one way or the other. One could chalk it up to bad luck as easily as anything else."

"Well, that's better than that crazy old bat's idea of being some demon half-breed."

"Probably so."

#

I pull the poderabile up to the stable entrance of the Helms Estate. It's a little sluggish on the controls as I do so. That usually means I need to have the air bottles replaced soon.

Tommy comes running out to help. "I'll put it away, Miss Stella."

"Been itching to drive it, haven't you, Tommy?"

"Well, as a matter of fact, yes, ma'am. I been watching you every chance I get. I think I know how."

"Let's see. Climb in." I slide over and give him the operator's seat. Like me, his first attempt is a bit jerky, but it smooths out quickly. He eases my vehicle into the barn, sending the hay on the floor sailing into the air from the gas exhausted out of the gearing, like the steam puffs in the train station that sometimes blow up the skirts of unsuspecting ladies. I understand some men stand on the platforms just to watch for this. "Good job, Tommy. See this switch above your head? Always flip it off when you end using the poderabile. Flip it on just before you start using it."

"Yes, Stella."

"OK, question. How do the Helmses normally dine?"

"Whatcha mean?"

"When I was here convalescing, it was somewhat casual because I was an invalid. Do they normally dress up fancy or eat like the servants below stairs?"

"Oh, they usually change clothes just before they eat. Never knew that a person could own so many duds the day I got sent to Mr. Helms's closet for something. Musta had twenty suits and even more less fancy wearings."

"Bet you a penny that the viscountess has more."

"No way I'd bet on that. Laoise done told me that the lady has a room bigger than the bunkhouse just for her clothes."

"That doesn't surprise me, Tommy. OK, you told me what I needed. Off with you. Behave, and I might just let you bring Lady Justice out of the barn for me."

"Thanks, Stella," he says, scampering down with the agility of a monkey.

Well, dirty drawers, I mentally curse. If I'm supposed to dress up for dinner, I've only got one remaining good dress, the luscious green one that the Helmses bought for me. Fortunately, it is one of the things I brought with me from Chapman's. But, I can't wear the same clothes night after night. Monday, I'll stop by Paula Simpson's to add a couple of fancy dresses to my order as a rush, and maybe one formal gown. One never knows around the Helmses.

It won't matter too much as tomorrow night I'll be at Karie's for our weekly dinner and chat. Her seduction of me happens only infrequently, but my body has been crying out for relief. In the past, I'd not thought about it twice. Despite my mother's assurance, I now wonder if that lust is my human parts or my demon parts. In the end, does it matter? It is all me, as Xena pointed out.

I go into my room through its private door. Dressing for a formal dinner is a tedious affair. The gown is no problem as it is in my carpetbag; however, it's rumpled from me shoving it into my bags rather than being folded and treated with care. When I'd left the boardinghouse, I remembered to pack my second set of petticoats, but I forgot my bustle. I improvise by wrapping my two spare pairs of bloomers around themselves and tucking it betwixt the elastic of my bloomers and that of one of my petticoats. I find only one of my pearl earrings. I do find both my glass ones in the iconic shape of the Philadelphia Palace.

My makeup is a complete loss as it is spread across the bottom of my handbag. In fact, the purse itself is more likely to need a bonfire rather than a laundress.

The only *peineta* that has survived the journey, other than the one in my hair, is the beautiful jade one that the viscount and viscountess purchased for me. For that, I'm pleased. This move is becoming much more expensive than I'd anticipated.

In a panic, I can't find my wedding photograph. It is the only thing other than my memories that keeps my Aaron fresh in my thoughts. I must have left it at Chapman's. With a rush, my body aches to feel Aaron's arms around me just once more. Just let him tell me one final time that it will be alright. I know I will meet him again in God's kingdom, but that doesn't wipe away the tears I find on my cheeks. "I miss you, my brawny moor," I say, thinking of the stubble he always seemed to have on his chin. But he wouldn't grow a beard.

I shake my head and wipe the dampness from my eyes. It is funny how even five years later, I still can be swept up in grief for my husband—damned Ireland and England both.

I gather my thoughts and emotions back together. Dinner will be in a few moments, and I can't look like a grieving widow for my hosts. I salvage a bit of my skin powder and dust it over my cheeks to hide the puffiness there. After a spritz of rosewater, I start down the stairs to the dining room.

"Good evening, Stella. You are looking lovely tonight," the viscount says with a gentle bow. "Lady Helms will be down any moment."

"Like now, darling," Lady Helms says, sweeping into the room wearing a layered, shimmering silver gown that contrasts with her blond hair. The bodice stretches tightly enough across her chest that I can see the decorative Chantilly lace of her brassiere.

Oh, Karie, where are you?

5—Sunday, May 6, 1888

Waking up lately has been a mix of sensations. Thursday night, I'd been on my bed in Widow Chapman's Boarding House, lumpy as cold oatmeal and waking to the micturition of umpteen other women. Friday night, I'd been on a hard cot the size of a postage stamp. The hiss of a steam boiler shocked me awake in a basement lit by only a single candle and the orange flames of a coal furnace. This morning, I find myself enveloped by a marshmallow the size of a polar bear. I drift up to a sweet silence. No women getting up and ready in other rooms. No bang of a door by someone on the way to the outhouse. No coal-heated boiler.

I'm warm and snuggle down deep into my nightgown and fine cotton sheets, covered in down comforters. My breath doesn't fog the air. My green dinner dress and even my bloomers are pressed and hanging on the back of a nearby chair. A pair of diamond earrings and a heavy gold necklace, neither mine, lie on top of them. My hostess must have noticed my need last night, or the downstairs had been gossipy to the viscountess. This is better than the Parker House.

My morning ablutions in the warmth are like basking on the first day of summer. The only thing missing is the bright sun on my skin. I smile, thinking that my Aaron would have liked me in only my bloomers out in the sunlight. He'd cradle one breast in each of his enormous hands. He's the only person that has ever made them look small.

I sniff back a single tear with a big smile on my face. My husband was a good man.

All dressed up in my Sunday best and fit with the world, I come down to the dayroom. Coffee, croissant with butter, clotted cream, and two different preserves dominate a silver service. Next to them, a china cup and plate, silver, and an embroidered napkin. Perched atop the Sunday paper is an envelope. I slip out the pink paper scented with Adrianna's musky perfume. In a hand the envy of even the royal secretary, her neat cursive reads:

Stella,

The staff, Viscount, and I have all headed off to church services. We know you said you wanted to go off to your own church, but should you change your mind and visit our congregation, you will be welcome. We will be at the First Baptist Church at the corner of Magazine and River Streets.

If not, we will see you Monday evening for dinner.

Adrianna

Sometimes owning the poderabile is a blessing. It means I have some time for a leisurely breakfast before services.

I buttered a roll and dipped it into some cream as I read the paper. Seven hundred thousand German refugees have landed at Ellis Island in the last month. More than twice the number of people in Boston. And that didn't even count the continuing stream of Irish immigrants, Spanish fortune seekers, and even the odd boatload of Italians. The article wrote that over one and a half million people joined our monarchy this year alone. If it weren't for the northwest, our country would be bursting at the seams. The article went on to claim that more than a million settlers, mostly non-immigrants, moved west for the new homestead lands in the duchies of Oregon, Tahoma, and New Cadiz along the west coast. Even more adventurous ones talked about the fertile lands around Fairbanks, Aleut.

"My God," I whisper. "May you keep them, for I don't know what we will do with them all."

#

"Good morning to all of God's children this morning," Father Juan Dubois y Cantonio offers from the pulpit. His long, flowing hair cascades over the robes of his office. His high brows and black beard makes him look like a young disciple from the Bible itself. Like every Sunday, his preaching voice is deep and resonates, compared to his everyday pitchy tone. As a witch, the church doesn't know yet what to make of me. All of us with powers sit in the back pew of the nave, a practice that remains in the church since witches became generally known, yet I hear the pastor with clarity.

"God knows we are imperfect. We will all err. Be you a carpenter, factory worker, miner, farmer, or even a priest, you will at some time fall into sin. '...each person is tempted when he is lured and enticed by his own desire.'"

For just a moment, I believe he is talking to me. My repeated liaison with Karie is definitely not sanctioned by the church, not because she also sits to pee, but rather because we aren't bonded under God. Father Juan has more than once advised me to find a man and marry or, barring that, to wed the friend who sometimes shares my bed. If I ever marry again, it will only be for love, if even then. I value my independence too much. I do ask for penance for my sins, but my hot-blooded nature, human and demon, won't be denied.

Father Juan continues with "This morning's lesson comes from the book of James. It says, 'My Brothers, show no partiality as you hold the faith in our Lord Jesus Christ, the Lord of glory. For if a man wearing a gold ring and fine clothing comes into your assembly, and a poor man in shabby clothing also comes in, and if you pay attention to the one who wears fine clothing and say, "You sit here in a good place," while you say to the poor man, "You stand over there," or "Sit down at my feet," have you not then made distinctions among yourselves and become judges with evil thoughts?'

"So what is James trying to say? Is a prosperous man any better or worse than a poor one? No. God makes no distinction between them. And, even further, does God care about the color of your skin? Not at all. Is a Chinaman any better than a Spaniard? How about a Russian? An American? Or even an Irishman? None is different in the eyes of the Lord. What matters is that we live in the love that is Christ, not the hate and vileness that comes from the evil one."

Now, I know where this sermon is going. While it is to let us know we are all brothers, it is aimed directly at Archbishop Mendel Mrak, who recently declared Irish souls suspect. This is sending a straightforward message. Surely, someone in the congregation will deliver it, word for word, to the bishop.

"So, we are not perfect. We are but human. So what matters to God is not that we sinned but how we deal with our sin. Do we continue to sin and compound our sins further? Or do we fall to our knees and beg forgiveness from the lord of hosts for our misdeeds?

"And it matters not what position a man holds when sin comes to call. For the Bible says, 'Not many of you should become teachers, my brothers, for you know that we who teach will be judged with greater strictness.'

"It means we of the clergy must be held to even a higher standard—"

The tinny, two-tone bells of the Mission Church, some miles away, ring out loud enough to even cut through Father Juan's preaching voice. I check the pocket watch left to me by my husband, Aaron. It is not the hour or even quarter-hour. That means these bells are for my team and me. Another demon is loose.

Father Juan catches me by the eye, even at this distance. He holds his words.

The bells ring out a Morse code. Low tone, high tone, pause. High tone, low tone, pause. High, high, high, low. High, low. And more. It spells out the Naval Yard.

I stand up. "The members of the hellfighter team and any doctor will leave to pursue their own fight against evil. Go with God," he says as I stride out the door.

This is a new one—right in the *maldito* middle of service.

# # #

Having Lady Justice handy makes my trip to the Naval Yard in Charlestown a breeze, literally—straight up Prince Street, across the Charles River Bridge, and a right onto Chelsea. I can see, no more than the length of a football pitch away, a demon engaging in its carnage.

The hellspawn reminds me of the hydra of myth. Its body is thrice the size of the poderabile, standing on four pedestal-like legs and with no arms. It relies on its four necks, each ending in a skull-like face and each reaching the height of ship masts across the berm from it.

I slide to the edge of the road and park the poderabile. Jumping down, I bend over and run my finger along the clay road. Popping the digit in my mouth, I feel the willingness of the earth to move at my command.

It is pretty common that you see something new each and every time there is an escape as demons are destructive to anything around. Sometimes the greatest dangers are the surroundings. I remember battling a fiend amid a glass factory—the shards and crystalline dust alone could kill. But what is before me, I classify as an entirely newfangled experience.

The Royal Marines, maybe thirty strong, seem to be fighting the creature. I can hear their rifles popping off in precision groupings. Their bullets are ineffective, but they fight nonetheless. Groups of three or four take turns firing into the beast to keep its attentions cycling between them, either accidentally or purposefully copying our hellfighter technique. They are doing it well enough in that they seem to have the creature stationary, and it hasn't wiped the whole slew of them from this life. I give them full marks for surviving this long.

"YOUR TEETH WILL HANG ON A CHAIN AROUND MY NECKS AND I'LL FEED YOUR BRAINS TO MY DOGS!" the creature bellows in our minds.

I may have to save these well-meaning idiots from themselves if they fail in their timing. I move down the street with dispatch. As I do, I walk past a brownstone sporting a huge sign announcing "Science of the Miraculous." It bears the mark of a demon eruption hole from its basement. Sarcastically, I wonder how miraculous it can be if it released a demon.

As I get close, the hellspawn's heads fall into a new rhythm. Instead of attacking with all four heads simultaneously, the heads attack in sequence, one after the other. This causes a problem because even after its attention is diverted, the other heads will still attack the former target. I don't believe it is a conscious attempt to avoid the tactic the Royal Marines are employing, but that is why hellfighters make so much reward money. We must think on our feet and change when things get too dangerous.

The last head is coming in behind a group of soldiers. They don't seem to be aware of it. Like sliding a coffee service and everything on it across on a tablecloth, I pull the surface of the ground to one side. The gaping maw misses the men by several feet. As the danger passes, I let the earth move back to the status quo.

A dark-skinned man in the uniform of a major sees my activities. He orders me, "Save the vessels! They are the most important."

There is a tenet in demon fighting that is similar in most crises. When someone leads, you follow. It doesn't matter if they have the authority or not. The theory is that they have seen something you have not. It could mean life or death. If this marine feels confident ordering me about, I will comply, at least for now. I move between the beast and the docks, asking the earth to form a twenty-foot-high berm. I can go higher if necessary, but I must keep something in reserve to help the soldiers.

Upon seeing the wall, the creature turns on it, butting its faces into it in succession, inflicting fissures and rents in the earth. With my hands, at a distance of several dozen feet, I mentally knead the ground like a lump of clay and reform it again into the original hillock without damage. The body of the demon lurches forward and slams into it. I am glad I formed a berm rather than a wall. It might have breached that. Instead, it staggers back and again sends the heads after the soldiers stinging it with their popguns.

I feel the love of God being bundled nearby. Maxwell must be healing someone. At least one other member of my team is at hand. That is a good thing. It means the rest can't be too far away.

A roar, not of the demon but the report of a cannon, bellows out not too far from me. A steel ball, maybe eighty pounds, slams into my berm at almost the same instant. The scream that follows couldn't have been higher or more pure had a four-year-old girl made it. I peek around my hill to see a hole through the demon, like one left by a fire poker through a gelatin aspic. It must have pierced the creature before burying itself in my defensive wall. I've never seen a non-magical attack do any physical damage to one of hell's creations. It impresses me, not that it will make the slightest difference. There are no organs, muscles, or even blood in a demon. They don't follow any semblance of human or animal anatomy. They are more like slime with no weak points to target.

You can move it around. You can change its shape. But in the end, you can't kill it with a simple weapon. I see the reason the projectile had been effective at all. A naval chaplain is blessing the ammunition before it is loaded in an old cannon on the parade ground. The consecration gives it the extra damage against the foe, but it still doesn't matter. I've seen a demon in four pieces still reach out and deal death and destruction around it.

"I WILL USE YOUR BONES TO PICK THE LICE FROM MY PUBIC HAIR."

The hellspawn charges forward right at the cannon. The priest and the four men manning the piece dodge aside as the mass of the hydra-shaped creature rolls over the artillery piece, smashing its carriage into splinters and twisted bits of metal.

To keep the beast as far from the boats as possible, I move the berm up behind the unearthly pocket of chaos. A thorny bramble grows up out of the soil to the demon's right. Manaj has arrived with her mastery of all things natural.

"Cease fire!" yells the major. "Fall back by twos."

The white noise of a dust devil takes the place of the rifles to my left—Carlos. He must have taken over command of the situation. Maxwell's work, a flare of white light over the beast, distracts it for just a moment and tells me the team is assembled. It is time to really go to work. I set my earthen surge in motion westward back down Chelsea Street. With this escapee, I choose to nudge it along with the earth instead of just letting it move on its own. My actions keep the creature off balance and at least one head nipping at the soil to its rear. It causes me to dodge a bit more than I'd like, but it is one less head the people in the perilous positions have to deal with.

I urge the stone upward to form tines, like those of a fork, to parry the demon's head strike. A flock of pigeons, fifty thousand strong, arrow down out of the sky before splitting up and forming rings around its heads. They perform aerial acrobatics, mostly dodging the mouths. Occasionally a bird is snapped up in the beast's teeth, leading to an explosion of feathers and the clouds of birds dispersing for a moment before reforming.

I need to give Manaj a pat on the back for the brilliant idea. Each of our foe's heads is engrossed with the thousand or so birds swirling around, ignoring us witches entirely.

While it's distracted, I encourage my earthen mound to push for all its worth. I get help from vines and wind. I let some seawater creep up under my hill to make it slide easier. This is teamwork in its truest form. We don't even have to talk. We just naturally do what is needed to support one another.

On the plus side, the beast is too distracted to attack us. On the downside, it is exceedingly heavy. While walking two hundred feet may not seem like much, doing it pushing an unwilling load that weighs more than a wagon loaded with iron ore is quite another. Panting and wheezing, we force our burden to the building "Science of the Miraculous."

The whirlwind to my left clears enough for Carlos to catch my eye. "We got it, Stella," Carlos yells my way. Despite the earth's protestation that it does not belong in a wave-like tsunami, I leave my twelve-foot soil and clay berm in place.

White light, brighter than the cloud-filtered sunlight, pours out of the hole the demon broke free through. I frown. I crawl in, cursing at what it is doing to my best stockings and dress. The dirt I can spell out later, but the tears and runs I can't. I slip the rest of the way in, and my foot lands on something round. It skitters out from under me. The result ends with me on my fundamentals with my petticoats and skirt strewn up to expose my bloomers.

I expect to be covered in blood, but unlike every other demon escape of the last month, I don't find the shredded remains of a person. Instead, four men sift through the debris of a mad scientist's basement. They are examining papers and more robust metallic or rubber equipment and sorting it into piles. They are so intent they don't even notice me or my scandalous sight.

Putting my clothing back in place, I find the basement isn't a cold cellar like every other one I've seen. Instead of the dark abattoir that I've become recently inured to, limelights hang from the ceiling, giving the whitewashed brick walls a bright, almost cheery look—at least for something that has been hit by a hurricane, that is. Broken glass of all colors litters the tiled floor. Papers and remnants of books are strewn about. Wooden splinters of what may have once been bookcases lie smashed around the journals.

"Excuse me, gentlemen, but unless you want to be demon pâté, I suggest you leave the premises," I say, getting a bunch of blank expressions in return.

One, wearing a natty business suit and a neatly trimmed mustache, advances on me. His dark-brown hair, parted in the middle, is slicked out like a pair of osprey wings. If it weren't for the attire and the smirk at the corner of his mouth, I would peg him as a matador. "This is my place of business, miss. Why are you here?"

"I am here trying to put your demon back in place," I say, pointing at a broken pentagram in the far corner under additional wreckage.

"After this debacle, I want nothing more to do with it. Have it destroyed!"

"And who are you to make such a decision?" I ask.

"Nikola Tesla. Perhaps you've heard of me."

I just stand there and stare. I've seen his picture in the paper, and now I recognize him. I stand with my mouth open after uttering, "Ahhhhh." I might as well be an addled worm for all the intelligence I have, being struck so by someone famous.

"Miss, this is my property. You must be a hellfighter, or you wouldn't be talking about trapping the beast. I formally request that you rid us of the pestilence. I was experimenting and found—"

"Stella, are you ready for us?" Carlos calls from above.

"We got a problem, Carlos. Hold on a few more seconds," I bellow up. "You were saying, Mr. Tesla?"

"I was experimenting to determine how I could more efficiently harness the powers of a demon for the betterment of mankind, but the hellspawn interferes with well-known principles of physics. In fact, it was in the middle of what we thought was safe experimentation that it broke free. I hope no one was hurt."

Famous or not, genius or not, the man is an idiot studying to be an imbecile and failing. No one who doesn't want death and mayhem plays with a demon. "Some bruises, battered egos, and a good deal of property damage seem to be the extent of things. Luckily the alarm was sounded quickly. No deaths."

"I'm so glad. I sent a boy with the news as soon as it tore out of here."

"Good for you," I say with no little amount of sarcasm.

"I appreciate your services, Miss Hellfighter. Now, if you would be so kind as to destroy the beast. I'll pay whatever fee you deem appropriate. I will also make restitution for the damages it caused."

"I'll get on that right away. May I use your front door? Climbing out that hole would be indecorous, to say the least."

"By all means. Manuel? Please show the hellfighter out." Tesla turns and returns to his work as if I no longer exist. A striking young Spanish man, his dapper suit mussed by deep wrinkles and a smattering of dust, shows me the exit. While not the brawny type that was my late husband Aaron, this man's taut derriere, narrow waist, and smooth skin lend themselves to a second look.

"*Lo siento, señora. Señor* Tesla is very focused on a project for the monarchy. He means no...*como se dice—falta de respeto*...umm, disrespect."

"I understand focus, Manuel. What is your family name?"

"Gomez y Ruiz."

"Manuel Gomez y Ruiz, we will talk more after I've dealt with the immediate problem."

Manuel takes my hand in his and bends over, placing a soft, gentlemanly kiss on the backside. "*Gracias, señora.* I look forward to it." His moist lips give me a little shiver, reminding me that I've got a meeting with my best friend and sometimes lover, Karie Taylor, this evening. I've been a steam vessel without a relief valve for far too long. Business has been too brisk to provide the opportunity to release the pressure.

I run out to where the team is keeping the demon contained. With all the flailing of the multiple heads, now ignoring the flying rats, I think "contained" is maybe too strong a word. "Carlos, they don't want the demon back."

"What? Are you sure?"

"Yup. The demon was part of some experiment that went awry. They want it destroyed." I duck one of the flailing heads and dodge some green spittle that smokes and crackles when it hits the ground.

Carlos uses his air magic to amplify his voice. "Everyone. Change in plan. We are going to destroy this one. Everyone on their toes. Maxwell—you are up."

The monstrosity within our charge flails even harder, attempting to break free. "I WILL DEVOUR YOUR FLESH AND SCOURGE YOUR SOULS FOR ALL ETERNITY," it roars.

Maxwell bellows out, "Romans 6:23," his voice breaking in the middle of the numbers. Several globs of the ochre sputum arc out of our magic-made binding walls toward Maxwell. He dodges them with aplomb. The beast screams like a locomotive whistle carrying too much steam. "I WILL SNACK ON YOUR EYEBALLS AND MAKE MUSIC WITH YOUR ENTRAILS."

Undeterred, Max continues, "For the wages of sin is death, but the free gift of God is eternal life in Christ Jesus our Lord."

"HE IS A LIE. YOU CLING TO NOTHING BUT A LIE, MORTALS."

Max sets the chant timing and tone. "For the wages of sin is death, but the free gift of God is eternal life in Christ Jesus our Lord."

While dodging heads and maws, and working our magicks to control the monstrosity, six of us *Campanas* chant in time together. "For the wages of sin is death, but the free gift of God is eternal life in Christ Jesus our Lord." All hellfighters know their Bible, but you must agree on a specific version. Goodness knows they aren't all the same.

"YOUR HOLES WILL SERVICE MY HOUNDS!"

All of the goodness and love that we generate from God's love begins to saturate the area between us. I can start to see sunlight through the creature. It fades. Its strikes against the berm become less forceful. It's like watching ice melt in the summer sun. Even the heat he radiates cools. As we repeat the text from the book of Romans for the ninth time, there is nothing more to fight. It evaporates.

As one, our group whispers, "Amen."

After a reverent pause, Carlos barks out in my general direction, "What in the thunderation was that all about?"

I just look at him dumbstruck.

"I mean, why did we get balls deep in moving this cussed demon back if we were just going to destroy it? What zounderkite came up with this blazing shitstorm?" Carlos once again directs his fury in my direction. I don't mind the profanity. I've heard enough of it; hell, used enough of it for the lifetimes of seven hundred prim and proper ladies, but it is unlike him to shoot the messenger. Raquel's mouth hangs open. Maxwell's brows furrow together. Donny O'Sullivan's mouth is also catching flies. His body language shows he is ready to run away from this unusual confrontation after having successfully faced the fury of a demon from hell.

I cross my arms. "Carlos, I know you are stretched thin. We all are on edge from dealing with all of the demon escapes recently, but that doesn't give you the right to yell at me because I communicated.

"To the rest of you, I look forward to seeing you at the Bell in Hand, assuming some fopdoodle hasn't let out another hellspawn. Good evening."

I turn and pointedly don't pay attention to anything behind me. My team is family. Like siblings, we always stick together in a pinch, but we don't always get along. I make my way back to the "Science of the Miraculous" building.

Manuel leans on the balustrade, watching. "That was quite impressive, *señora*. Why don't you do it more often?"

"I'm sorry?"

"Destroy demons. Aren't they a pestilence?" he asks. The muscular neck under his firm jawline definitely could use some kisses. I shake my head. I'm not that much of a *puta*. I'm choosey about my sexual companions, and since my husband's death, they are not male. In fact, there has been only one. If I'm lusting over this stranger already, I'm glad that Karie is serving me dinner this evening. I have a feeling she is going to get a very friendly thank-you. I take a deep breath before answering.

"They are quite expensive, *Señor* Gomez *y* Ruiz. They have their place. Being a hellfighter is like being a firefighter. Firemen protect lives and property...and demons are property. But even a firefighter wouldn't eliminate all fire. It is a tool."

Manuel advances on me like a predator stalking its prey. I stop moving toward him and even take a tentative step backward as my insides become somewhat moist. But he stops a comfortable six feet away. "Even when, like a runaway locomotive, it will harm others?"

"Then my team works to stop it. Are you trying to be offensive, Mr. Gomez?"

"I'm just trying to understand better. My boss, Mr. Tesla, wants to eliminate further demon testing. I just want him to have all the data he needs to make a viable decision."

"Would you care to accompany me to the theatre tomorrow night? I have tickets to *Dr. Jekyll and Mr. Hyde* at the Globe Theatre," he throws out in a radical change of direction.

"Excuse me? I hardly know you." I'm glad I swore off men; otherwise, I might have to accept this offer. My husband, Aaron, is the only man I'll ever love, much less obey. Dating leads to sex, which leads to love, which leads to marriage, which is nothing better than being property. If you are extremely lucky, you are a pampered and well-kept slave. I won't have it.

"I'm a professional man who finds you fascinating after only a few moments of talking to you. No other obligation, *Señora* Ochoa."

"Technically, I am *Vdo* Ochoa. My husband died in the war."

"My condolences," he says, bowing low.

"Thank you, but it was many years ago."

"That doesn't alter my invitation, *señora*. Would you care to accompany me on an evening of fun?"

He has looks, manners, and he smells yummy—clean with only a hint of male. I'm going to regret this. "Do you know Viscount Helms?"

"I am so acquainted, m'lady. I attended a party at his home just last week."

"Excellent. Then please pick me up there. I'm temporarily staying as a house guest of the Helmses."

"Marvelous. I'll pick you up at seven, *señora*. I look forward to investigating your marvelous brain."

"Adios, *Señor* Gomez. Until tomorrow night," I say, turning toward my assignation. It seems odd to me that I'm going to my lovers after just making a date. Am I fickle? A cockchafer? *Puta*?

#

"LEAVE NOW, ABOMINATION," claims a badly painted sign nailed to the side of the poderabile. I grit my teeth as my jaw works back and forth. *Why now?* I wonder. I've spent years practicing witchcraft. *Why now?* The only thing that makes any sense is Quarrels's upcoming trial. But if they are trying to get me to leave, why try and kill me? Why both attempts?

The red lettering covers a set of broad fir planks made from the side of a milk or produce crate. I touch one of the galvanized nails holding it in place. I feel the zinc and iron beneath my fingertip. I convince the five nails to reform into disks. The vandalism clatters to the ground with one end in a partially frozen puddle. With the mercy of God, it lands with the vile message face down. On the back is stenciled "Knapp Dairy."

I pick up the offending placard and toss it onto the poderabile's bench. As I have a date for some canoodling, I'm not going to let this ruin my evening.

#

Karie has a carriage house. I pull the poderabile right inside, knowing I won't be blocking her from leaving. Instead of knocking at the nearby back door, I go the long way around to the front.

Once, not so long ago, I feared Karie meant to make me her wife, or maybe it was the other way 'round. She thankfully disabused me of the thought. I am but one of many that share her charms. Nevertheless, I'm still as nervous as the proverbial long-tailed cat in a room full of rocking chairs about anything that might indicate overt familiarity.

That may sound odd coming from someone who fully intends to tear the woman's bloomers from her body and place kisses in places that would make a doxy blush. I want (and, frankly, at the moment need) the sex. I have always desired her friendship both in and out of bed. At the same time, I don't want to be owned.

"Good evening, Miss Ochoa." Karie's butler says, opening the door. His face wouldn't have the same lived-in character without the oft-broken nose that seems to dominate it. The ex-boxer's broad shoulders and narrow waist are actually well displayed within the tailored traps of his office. Karie wants none of her, ahem, customers to take liberties beyond what they pay for, of course. Alejandro's employment ensures that they at least understand the rules. My belief is that he's only twice been called into acts of his former profession rather than his exceptional brain. One man was fool enough to pull a knife. I emphasize the past tense. The police gladly removed the body and gave Karie and her staff a rousing, "Thank you."

"Alejandro. It's nice to see you again."

"And you, miss."

"Still haven't gotten over-thinking me a lady? Despite all of the proof I've given to the contrary?"

"No, Miss Stella."

"Very well. On your head be it."

"Yes, miss. The mistress is waiting for you in the parlor."

I twist my mouth to one side. The parlor? Usually, we start in the dining room and end up in the blue room after some quiet seduction and not a little bit of her cook's excellent fare. If she is particularly randy, we skip the dining room entirely.

"Thank you, Alejandro. I'll see myself in."

"Very good, miss."

Walking into the parlor, I realize right away what is up. Karie, without a trace of makeup, reclines on her deep green divan. Her simple cotton nightdress might as well be a chastity belt. For Karie, this is one step away from being dowdy. She clutches one of the new rubber hot-water bottles to her stomach. I know why immediately—she is *descongelando el bistec*. If that doesn't make it clear, it is also known as the red balloon, strawberry week, or in more polite society, perhaps just her courses.

Usually, when either of us has our time, we focus on the other, or if really needy, we ignore the mess so I've earned my red pollen pin. But this is obviously different.

At one time or another, every woman has been wracked in cramps during this time of the month. Karie is no exception. For the first time in recent memory, my lover seems frail. She is always so vibrant and full of life. Now her face bears worn lines, and she sinks in on herself. I rush to her side, asking, "Is there anything I can do to help?"

Even through a grimace, Karie jokes, "Get Frankenstein to give me a new body?"

I smile and massage her middle around the warming bottle. "So tonight is going to be about food and sleep, *querida*."

Karie manages a weak smile. "And plenty of your tummy rubs."

# # #

Over an intimate dinner, between gentle touches, I sneak into the conversation, "I was shot."

"*¿QUÉ?*" Her eyes go wide. She tries to leap from her chair but instead grabs her aching middle.

"I'm sorry, *querida*. I don't think there is an easy way to break that news. I'm fine." I reserve the fact that I still ache and might be dead if it weren't for a twist of fate.

I'm obviously here and not in some surgeon's clutches so Karie's practical side comes to the fore. "Tell me everything."

I give Karie chapter and verse of the attack. I add the messages about the NPP. Her frown grows to a complete scowl.

"That gunman is no joke, *novia*. Be careful and do everything you can to kill him before he kills you."

Her vehemence makes me wonder if the police can possibly catch him before he sends me to Saint Peter. I need to think about what my response will be next time. I've got a plan, but it is defensive rather than offensive. While the constabulary is sincere in their desire to bring the blackguard to justice, can they?

"I'm not sure I'm up to killing a man without warning, Karie. I also fear the rule of three. Whatever energy anyone puts out into the world comes back threefold."

"Threefold law be damned," she hisses through a spasm in her middle. "There really is no other outcome, Stella. At this point, it is self-defense. Think it through. He's already killed one. It is only luck that kept you among us mortal souls. Remember the papergirl."

I do. I have. "The Witchcraft Rule doesn't have a self-defense clause in it, Karie." She opens her mouth to speak, but I just put my hand up to stop her. "I will at least think about it."

"Do, because I want *mi amiga* around for many years to come."

"Absolutely, Your Highness," I tease to lighten the mood.

"It is about time you have learned my superiority," she slings back as good as she gets. "Oh, and when, not if...When you catch one of those NPP maggots, make sure no one finds his body." Tonight Karie seems bloodthirsty instead of her typical lecherousness.

This makes me think about something I'd never considered. What will I do if I find one of them scribbling their slogans of hatred? I have some intense fantasies about what I might do, but running counter to them is the fear of witches' prison. Part of me can see such a violent act with regard to the gunman. To kill just because someone scribbles some vile words seems out of place.

"To move off of that morbid subject, did I tell you that I'm homeless?"

Her eyes search my face like I may be playing a joke on her. "What did that bitch of a landlady do now?"

"I've been thinking of finding a new situation for some time. Her intransigence just sealed the deal."

"Did Alejandro move your traps up into the blue room?"

Sometimes I'm an idiot when I'm dealing with people. "Ah, no. I'm not staying here except when invited to share your bed."

"You are invited," she says deadpan.

"We've been over that, Karie. I'll not be your pet."

She purses her lips. "As you will. You aren't staying at any fleabag motel, are you? I don't want you to have to deal with that at least."

"No, I'm not." In desperation not to reveal my circumstances, I change the subject again. "Did you know that I found out that I'm a demon?"

"You are full of interesting news today. I think I need to stop taking the paper and just have you visit every morning."

"Pshaw." I relate my visit with the professor in great detail.

"A demoness, eh? I always wondered what it would be like to have a succubus in my bed. Looks like I already know, you insatiable wench."

The heat in my face stains my cheeks red.

She continues, "Too bad I'm in no condition to sample it, but I will be, demon girl. Looks like you will just have to warm my bed tonight."

6—Monday, May 7, 1888

"Miss."

I feel something tapping so gently at my wrist.

"Miss. Please wake up," says a voice that sounds like a harpsichord playing about a league away.

The tapping continues. It must be a dream. I'm warm. I'm cuddled from behind like the small spoon. I'm in a soft bed. I snuggle back against my partner.

"Miss, it is time to get up."

A tiny drop of something as cold as the night is long lands on the back of my hand. I feel the wetness drip down to my wrist.

"Good gracious!" My eyes snap open as I wipe the offending droplet of water onto the bed linens. Standing next to me is Karie's lady's maid cum housekeeper, Edwina, or just Winnie below stairs. She is about six pounds heavier than a sack of feathers but with a face that I sometimes think of as Medusa's visage. It's hard to describe why it isn't an attractive appearance, but take my word for it that God didn't favor her. I'm sure her mother doesn't flinch at it, nor I'm sure does Alejandro. The cook has shared with me more than once that the pair of them have spent more than just a little amount of time playing the game of see-saw.

Winnie is a wonderful girl with as sweet a disposition as you've ever met. Alejandro must be one of the few men that can look to a woman's inner beauty.

"Thank you, Miss Ochoa. I've been trying to wake you for a good five minutes now. I don't want to wake the mistress."

"All too right," I whisper back.

"Do you require a bath, miss?"

"No, Winnie. I just need my clothes."

Getting from the bed is every bit as tricky as getting awakened. Karie has spooned me. It works best for us that way when we actually sleep. If I try to be the big spoon, my breasts are in the way. I either find myself aching by squishing them like one might oranges for juice or so far away that I can't wrap my arms around her. Besides, she says she likes the warmth my fundamentals give her middle. With gentleness, I unwrap her arm from around my chest and ease out from underneath.

I do some minor ablutions, including a much-needed pee behind a dressing screen. With the long practice of dressing Karie, Edwina is busy on the other side. I come out in only my bloomers. I find my freshly laundered clothes laid out in the order that I'd put them on, except perhaps the brassiere that for me must go on first.

"Breakfast?" Winnie murmurs as she hands me my boots and a buttonhook. "Cook has already got scrambled eggs and chorizo cooking. She also has *porras* warm on the back of the stove."

"That sounds wonderful. After cook's *sopa de picadillo* and apple *flan* last night, I'm thinking I might have to start wearing a damned corset."

"Not likely, miss. Begging your pardon, miss, but I am very jealous of your figure as you have what all the menfolk want. Me, I need all the help I can get."

"Seems like Alejandro likes what you have." Tact has never been my strong suit.

Through a blush that might light up the greater portion of Boston, she says, "Yes, miss."

"Are you two going to make it official, or just riding the hobbyhorse for fun?"

"Miss? I am thinking that is quite a personal question."

"Well," I say. "I'm a nosy bitch. And I like my friends to be happy, no matter what choices they make."

"Yes, miss," is the only answer I get as she changes the subject. "By King Frederick, I had no idea what that is or what to do with it," she says, pointing at the coil of metal stripping that I'd just left on the floor last evening. I'd really like to leave it off, but someone still has a bullet with my name written on it.

"That, my good woman, is my temporary corset," I say with a wry smile.

"You are having me on, miss."

"Not at all, Winnie. Are you afraid of magic?"

"No, miss."

I witch the metal coil into a long band that climbs my legs like a snake might a tree. Winnie watches with astonishment, not fear. The iron flattens out into thick ribbons that overlap one another to encircle my torso from the bulge of my hips over the line of my brassiere.

"Miss, that must weigh thirty pounds. How can you carry it?"

I chortle. "That's all you can say? I put on a show for you, and you ask about the weight? How anticlimactic."

"Should I have clapped, miss?"

I stick my tongue out at her, but it is spoiled when Edwina slips petticoats over my head.

"I can dress myself, Winnie," I say, struggling through the crinolines.

"As you say, miss. I'll get Cook to put you a plate together down in the dining room." She slips out quietly as I pull my overdress on.

Dressed, I look down at Karie, still giving off tiny little snores, as I fasten a leather belt around the middle of my work dress. Her countenance is beatific. I'd love to stay and even just rub her tummy longer, but in reality, my lust is more than simmering under my umpteen layers of clothing. It demands for something a bit more prurient than a gentle petting. I lean over and place a chaste kiss on her cheek before heading down for the ambrosia Karie's cook usually dishes up.

# # #

Well tucked in, I slowly weave the poderabile through the crowds and traffic that are the morning usual in downtown Boston. A raucous goose-horn honks as a dapper man on a bicycle trundles past. A country gentleman directs his plodding horse to one side, his eyes are wide, and his jaw clenched as I chuff by him. Six men carry pony casks over their shoulders across the road to a waiting wagon proclaiming "Winston's Whiskeys." Another wagon loaded with barrels heaped with fish and ice lumbers past.

This isn't the first time I've learned that it doesn't pay to drive the poderabile to work. However, as Karie's home is so far from the Coal Syndicate, I'd still be walking next Christmas if I chose to ambulate. At least the first part of the journey goes quickly. Tremont Street is closed for most of its length as they install the new clay pipes to carry sewage from town and all of the outlying villages as well.

Instead of my stable, I steer my horseless wagon to Forever Power. I make the back lot well before the workers clock in. I park in the poderabile's assigned spot before shutting down its air source. I know that when I return, Henry Helms's people will have replaced all the played-out air cylinders with freshly charged high-pressure ones giving the poderabile motive power for weeks more. Slipping down from the driver's bench, I head out the back gate, closing it behind me.

Now time to get to work, the rest of the four blocks or so via Shank's mare.

"France continues pogroms!" calls out the newsvendor outside the gates of the Coal Syndicate. "Towns burned!"

Jesus, Mary, and Joseph! The French really aren't paying any attention to the fact that the Germanic lands are a Spanish protectorate. If England supports France by helping to blockade the English Channel, all of those poor folk will have nowhere to go but toward Russia. Not an inviting thought for Russia or the Germans.

I hadn't gotten to read the paper at Karie's because I needed to hurry off. I offered the newspaperman my penny and got the paper. The headline, which fills up the entirety above the fold, asks, "European War Looms?" I tuck it into my bag for later reading.

Walking up to the gates, with minutes to spare, I find Mark Carlton standing there with two of the company's security guards. They confront the air witches of my coal remediation group. In the background, I feel a tingle of someone doing earth magic creeping up and down my spine like an itch.

"I'm sorry, but you are all fired," I hear in Carlton's most supercilious voice. He has a smile on his face the size of the Ozarks, emphasizing his nearly chinless face. The women all bombard him with questions that I can't hear.

"Excuse me, Mr. Carlton," I say as I get closer, my voice cutting through the more mousey voices of the other ladies. "Did I hear you correctly?"

"You heard right, *Widow* Ochoa. You, and all these ladies, are out on your arse." I manage to peek back at the bins where we would be working. I get a glimpse of a group of robust German women, still wearing their peasant attire, spelling down soot. An entire coven of earth witches must have become available among the German refugees. "Cost-cutting measure. We've contracted the work out for a fraction of your salaries. Now, here are your final pay packets. These gentlemen will escort you to pick up anything in your company lockers." He looks me deep in the eye as he says, "Then if you will quickly disperse as you are trespassing on private property."

I can tell that this is his petty vengeance over my forcing him to humble himself in front of everyone after firing me the last time. I knew he'd find a way to retaliate; I just hadn't realized it would happen so soon.

The air witches collect their packets. Some even go collect personal items. I'd never left anything in my locker overnight. Carlton steps up and hands me my envelope with a sneer. "Vengeance is mine," he says quietly.

"Romans 12:19—Beloved, never avenge yourselves, but leave it to the wrath of God, for it is written, 'Vengeance is mine, I will repay, says the Lord.' You are not the Lord our God, Mr. Carlton. But, I prefer Matthew 6:14—For if you forgive other people when they sin against you, your heavenly Father will also forgive you. But if you do not forgive others their sins, your Father will not forgive your sins.

"Goodbye, Mr. Carlton. I forgive you, but I fear for your soul."

I turn and walk away. I can feel the daggers he is drilling into my back, but he has become part of the anonymity of the city to me. I care no more for him than I would the peddler on the corner or the horse that walks across my path. I do worry about my status now that I've lost both my home and my job. Maybe I shouldn't have been so quick to discount Karie's offer of being her kept woman.

For now, I need the comfort of a kindred spirit.

# # #

The receiving dock of Forever Power is as busy as the backlot had been still and quiet first thing in the morning. A dozen wagons proclaiming themselves of the Richmond Iron Works bear stacks of sheet-steel so high their springs have flattened down to the axle. A half dozen more unmarked wagons carry stout wooden beams, likely from the duchy of Maine. An ungainly monstrosity of gears, belching steam and smoke, strides out of a massive building. It stands twenty-five-feet high and twelve across on six legs. The loader straddles the wagon like a woman climbing atop her man. With gigantic crab-like pinchers between its six legs, it reaches down and lifts the contents of each wagon as easily as one might a pint at the pub. The teamster drives the wagon away. A flat conveyance only a foot or so off the ground slides in under the massive metal insect. I can feel an earth spring inside powering the low truck. The spider-like machine slowly lowers its load onto its new transport.

The flatbed is driven away like a trolley but with a driver.

"You, missy! Get out!" yells a familiar voice. "G'damned women got the brains of a baby chick."

"*Señor* Delgadillo, its Stella Ochoa."

"Well, get the hell out of the way, you stupid bitch. Now! B'fore you get kilt!"

Ignoring the narrow view the dockmaster has against my sex, I duck around a slow-moving cart to the cavernous opening of Forever Power. I catch the swirl of petticoats and red hair in the distance and make that my destination. Only one woman has Delgadillo's grudging approval to be there. She writes in a tremendous ledger with her back to me.

Patty Smith is a brilliant woman. She acts as the stock mistress of the firm, ensuring everything is checked in and everything is checked out. By concatenation, she knows exactly what material is within the four walls that is Forever Power. Mrs. Smith is fierce at protecting her charge, but I've learned soft as a marshmallow in other ways over the last few weeks.

The noise of the industry outside and the regular pounding beat of the shaping hammers inside the room would mask anyone's approach. Not wanting to intrude, I wait patiently.

Patty turns, pulling back from me in surprise if her face has any bearing on the matter. "STELLA!" she yells out, leaping into my arms. As a hug is what I really need, I encourage it by leaning into it as long as possible.

"What's wrong?" she whispers into my ear as I hold her close.

"Nothing," I blubber, trying to keep the tears from leaking. It isn't until this time that I realize just how much emotion I'm holding in.

"Let's go talk."

"What about your job?"

"I've got everything here accounted for. And even Delgadillo knows to contact me if there are new deliveries. Last time he didn't, I tore a strip off his hide big enough to cover a prairie schooner." Her dimples light up her face. She leads me to an office where two chairs fight for space with not only the bookcases bursting with papers, references, and ledgers but also samples of materials—here a chunk of tar soaked beam, there a sliver of steel, and yonder a canning jar of clear fluid.

"Sit," she orders, flipping the door closed. I do so, digging out a handkerchief to daub my eyes with. "Now, tell me what's wrong. We haven't known each other long, but I can tell when someone is hurting." She may at that. Patty has empathy enough for a dozen women.

I know I should be sharing with Karie, my best friend, but dumping even more of my troubles at her feet would likely just renew her demands that I move in with her.

"I don't even know where to start—demons, assassins, homeless, fired—"

"Hold on. Slow down. One piece at a time." She rolls her chair as close to me as two women in petticoats can manage. She takes one of my hands and holds it between hers.

I again spill the story of fighting massive numbers of demons, of being shot, of leaving my boardinghouse in a snit, and even the vile NPP. I leave off being a part demon. I don't know how our nascent relationship would fare under that bit of news.

Patty doesn't say anything but occasionally squeezes my hand. Her face looks like a thunderstorm on an otherwise clear summer day. Throughout it all, I daub at my eyes with a handkerchief to keep them clear.

"If that isn't enough, my bloody boss fired me this morning. Seems as if he got a coven of refugees to do his bidding and not put up with my attitude. I guess I knew he would as soon as he could find a replacement. This, on top of everything else, has me about ready to explode."

"You poor woman." She leans over and wraps her arms around me. I lose control and just start crying. A part of my mind is appalled at my weakness or even depending on such a new friend. On the plus side, I don't devolve into bawling. As I get some semblance of control back, we break. She hands me her handkerchief as mine has turned into a soggy mess. The logical part of my brain reminds me to launder it and return it to her as I blow my nose.

"Let's deal with one problem at a time, shall we?" she says, less a question than leading me by the nose. I manage to nod as I wipe my nose. "You can come and stay with Brian and me. We have a couch in his office that is quite comfortable." Patty is too practical for her own good sometimes.

I shake my head. "I'm staying with the Helmses. They are being very good to me."

"Good. They should be. Now, do you have money for expenses? Brian and I could help a little if needed—"

"Oh, no, Patty. I wouldn't take your money."

"Don't be proud, woman. You are a friend. Ecclesiastes 4:10—If either of them falls down, one can help the other up. But pity anyone who falls and has no one to help them up."

"I didn't mean it that way. If I were in real need, I would, Patty...or at least I think I would. I have more than enough money for my needs for any foreseeable future. Hellfighting pays well, if sporadically."

She smiles. "Good, then we have two of your immediate problems dealt with. I know naught about demon escapes other than to tell you Lord Helms is in full attack there. With all of the raw materials coming in and going out, you'd think we were a bloody regiment of the King's own. He even has a chart in the breakroom that shows that we are eighty-three percent retrofitted with the new sheet-steel enclosures."

"That's good," I manage.

"Better than good," Patty replies. "We are working three shifts, and we'd be doing more if it were possible. This isn't just Lord Helms's fight. It belongs to all of us.

"But that is neither here nor there. Let me get to the most important item you listed. That you were shot! Are you hurting? You don't appear to need medical attention."

"Max patched me up good as new," I dissemble just a tad. I still ache in places and don't have my full wind.

"That's good. I wouldn't like losing a friend that I just found." She smiles at me. "Have you told the police?"

"Yes."

"And what did they say?"

"They want me to hide away until after I testify before the bench."

"And?" she asks like a disappointed mother.

"And what? I told them no."

"Knowing you even as little as I do, I'd wager you said more than just no."

That gets a grin to break through my self-pity just a little. "Well, I refrained from taking the name of our Lord in vain."

"Such restraint." I just shrug my shoulders as she continues. "Well, be that as it may, there is one more thing I might suggest. As far as a new job, I'm sure Lord Helms would hire you in an instant."

Patty's door opened just as she finished the last sentence. "You have that right," Viscount Henry Helms says, peeking into the room.

We both stand. "My lord."

"Oh, pshaw. Just Henry. You both know that by now. Ladies, I'm sorry for intruding, but I just heard the news that Stella was here and without gainful employment."

"How could you possibly know that?" I ask in confusion.

"It comes in two parts, Stella. First, not much happens here within these walls that doesn't come to my attention. You know that this company is my baby," he says, stroking the door with his white-gloved hand. Part of me wonders if it is more like a mistress than an offspring.

"Point taken, M'lord Henry," I reply. "But that only speaks to my being here. Unless you have very long ears or spies, you couldn't possibly know that I am without a situation at the moment."

"That is a little less tricky. Just minutes ago, I received a telegram. I understand it has been distributed to just about every company in the Boston area. It reads...Well, read it for yourself."

Lord Helms hands over a yellow telegram form. Patty takes it in over my shoulders.

Western Union

To all company owners:
    Stella Ochoa fired for insubordination and neglect. Considered ill-suited for any form of employment. Contact Mark Carlton for details.

The Coal Syndicate

"That scumbag!" Patty exclaims over my shoulder.

"This looks about right," I mutter. "This level of vindictiveness is just Carlton's sort of low work."

Henry steps in with, "I did a quick calculation, and this mass delivery probably cost in the neighborhood of two thousand dollars."

"Excuse me?"

"That's about right. I may be off by a few hundred dollars one way or the other, but that about sums it up."

"Carlton couldn't afford that just to be petty. Maybe as much as a hundred dollars but not twenty times that," I say with my brows crinkled together. I'm so stunned at the costs involved that I don't realize what it could mean for my prospects for employment.

"That's why I brought it up, Stella. This wasn't the spite of one man but rather something larger. I smell the handiwork of Bruce Jasperson, the president of the Coal Syndicate. This smells like something he'd cast out there."

"But why?" I ask.

"Well, if your initial reaction about him being behind the demon-release plot in the first place, it would make some sense. He can humiliate you and discredit your testimony at the same time."

"But I'm not testifying against him."

"That would assume that Quarrels only knows as much as he's offered thus far."

"*¡Madre Dios!*" Patty exclaims.

"I think this is worth a trip to the constabulary," I say, my jaw tightening. If that pig wants a fight, he will get one. And I won't be limited by the Marquess of Queensberry.

"Unnecessary, Stella. I've already sent the information by courier to Inspector First Guizzetti."

"Thank you, Viscount." My teeth clench and grind against one another.

"Now that piece of unpleasantness is dealt with..."

Not by a longshot! I mentally scream.

"...I was wondering if I could borrow Miss Ochoa. We have some other business to deal with."

Henry's soul should hang on a plaque in heaven with every other good person that has ever been born; however, he loves to shock and keep people off balance. He's done it again. "Other business?"

"Yes, quite."

"I guess so," I hedge, wary of his sense of humor.

Patty gives me another hug and whispers into my ear, "If you need anything, anything at all, come, and Brian and I will see what we can do."

"Thank you, Patty."

As we break our hug, she asks aloud, "Dinner tonight?"

"Sorry, but, on top of all things, I have a date."

"Oh? Tell me more," she says.

Henry stands there looking bored. He is at least smart enough to recognize that his right as president of the company and viscount doesn't warrant him any special consideration when two women are talking.

Patty spies her boss's impatience. "How about Tuesday night then?"

"I'd be glad to."

"Seven?"

"I'll be there."

I toss back a wink for my female friend. Henry is obviously taking me to his office. "I hope you aren't going to offer me a job," I say with just a little exasperation.

"I wouldn't dream of it, Stella. Our relationship, dare I say friendship, is still in its infancy. I've learned enough about you to avoid that pitfall. You are a strong woman who loathes letting people help, even those in your debt. Taking something that might seem charity would make you dig your heels in." As we are walking side by side, he can't possibly see my open mouth. "Please don't get me wrong. I'd hire you in a minute for any number of positions I have here, not the least of which would be vice president of installations, but you won't take it. So, I won't deign to offer it to you. I have my pride."

"It's not that, Henry..." I sputter. "OK, it is a little bit of that. I won't give up my spot on the *Dos Campanas*. Any job I took from you would have a conflict of interest."

"True enough. That's another reason offering you something that would require your sacrifice is just wrong. Just know that if you ever decide to move beyond fighting demons, there is a place for you here—a good place."

We walk along in silence for a few moments. "So if offering me a job isn't the reason for our business, then what is?" I ask as we enter his office. Four chalkboards stretch out along one wall. A bookkeeper, by the looks of him, sits at a table facing the boards, diligently scribing something.

"This," Henry says, waving at the calculations, charts, and even graphs in white on black. The title on the first board says it all. "How Stella Can Buy a Home."

"*Cacafuego*," I mutter to myself. Then out loud, "Henry, I no longer have a job. How in God's green earth can I afford a house? This is out of my reach."

"Poppycock!" Henry refutes. "Barton here is my head bookkeeper. He knows money better than anyone I know, myself included. Tell her, Barton."

The unassuming (as all good men of numbers must be), mid-twenties man clears his throat before continuing with a voice so precise as to be found only in a watchmaker's toolkit. "Miss, I don't know you other than by reputation. Viscount Helms has assured me that you have at least five thousand dollars in funds and a property worth in excess of ten thousand dollars. He has told me that you prefer the company of others in your home. With only that and no other money from you, I can assure you that you can not only buy a home but make a profit on it." He waves the papers he is writing at me. "This will give you all the generalities and many of the specifics you will need. Let me assure you that this is, in the vulgar slang of our time, a done deal.

"If you like, I can go over the specifics with you now or at another time of your choosing."

"Thank you, Barton," the viscount says in a way that means a dismissal.

As he gets up to leave, the accountant hands me his introduction card. I smile sweetly and tuck the card in my bag.

After the door shuts, Henry says, "There it is in black and white. You've had three people tell you that this is not only possible but likely. Stella, you can make money doing this. And a lot more than your pittance at the Coal Syndicate."

"But the risk? And how am I going to save for my old age if—"

"Damn it, Stella, but this is the beginnings of how rich people got rich."

"I don't want to be rich, Henry."

"Then take the comfort it will provide and be content."

I shake my head slightly as I look over the chalkboard. The crisp lettering and order of logic make it easy to follow the train of thought. There is a wide range of property costs, graphs that show how much rent to charge. Startup costs are included. The staggering numbers open my eyes and make the once tiny doubt in my belly now feel like a hog rooting around for more slops.

"I just don't know, Henry. This looks good, but…I just am not sure."

"OK. I have one more ace up my sleeve, Stella." He hands me yet another yellow form of a telegram.

Western Union

Henry Helms,

Regarding the late Snowdonia lands. I would gladly pay $1000 per year for the right to crop and use the land. Pls advise.

Reginald Cornwall

"I took the liberty of asking a friend who has property bordering the Cardiff Estate if he saw any value in leasing the land. There is his first response."

"A thousand dollars?" I ask, my mouth dropping open and my eyes wide.

"Yeah, he's trying to get a bargain."

"Wait, did you say a bargain?"

"Yeah. I'd hold out for at least three thousand."

"Three thousand dollars?" I repeat, the incredulity of it in my pitchy voice.

"Why are you so surprised?"

I stagger back and sit hard into the chair the bookkeeper left. "Henry, I'll be honest in never thinking that the land was worth a wooden nickel."

"That is the advantage of having friends in different places. We can help educate you."

"But why is it worth anything at all?"

"Jesus H. Christ, Stella. Sometimes you astound me with your lack of education. Let's make it simple. The Snowdonia land is just over six hundred acres. Modern corn cropping gives about twenty bushels per planted acre. Corn is running eight to ten dollars a bushel. I'll leave the total as an exercise for the student."

I ran the numbers in my head. "Over a hundred thousand dollars! My God!"

"Oh, that isn't all profit. There is seed, farm labor, equipment, and whatnot. Likely, even if Reggie pays you three thousand a year, he will still make a tidy thirty thousand or so."

I've never been a fainter, one of those women that are so overwhelmed by her circumstances, and likely an overtight corset, that she just gives up on consciousness. What Henry describes so casually has me wishing for some smelling salts. Oddly, I'm beginning to understand the term "landed gentry."

"Oh, you could sell the land for considerably more if you don't want to hold it."

"Sell it?"

"Yes, it would bring probably forty or fifty thousand dollars. You might get more, but it is a ways out of any town. But I wouldn't sell. I'd crop it out so it continues to pay. You can always sell it later."

I just sit there in silence. Henry goes over and sits behind his desk with a smug look on his face. He signs a few papers and consults a book as I try to rearrange every thought of working and wealth that I've ever had. I struggle with the idea of having my entire future secured by something I had mentally tossed in the rubbish bin. I started the day happy with a mere job. My emotions dropped like a stone when I found myself without a regular paycheck. Now I'm some kind of lady of leisure with funds coming in without doing anything. The bucking waves of feelings today have me not knowing what to do or where to turn. Frankly, I feel like I've been kicked in the head by a mule.

Five or maybe even ten minutes pass as my mind sorts itself enough that I can open my mouth coherently. "Lord Helms," I begin. He looks up from his concentration on his work. "I thank you more than I can possibly express."

"Balderdash. My part in this has been something simple, showing you what you own and can do with it. You earned it. You saved me and my business."

"Be that as it may, m'lord, you have taken me under your wing, and I will do right by it. In the meantime, if I can impose on your time and knowledge further, how do I negotiate with your friend, and how do I buy a house?"

# # #

"I'm not sure why I kept this property on the list," Henry says with some distaste as we climb out of the freshly recharged poderabile. "It was a concrete block factory."

I had tried to convince my benefactor that taking the whole of his valuable day to show me available properties around town is overmuch, even if he feels gratitude. He threw off my objections like a duck might shed a spring shower.

Henry had shown me six different houses throughout the morning, from an immaculate three-bedroom brownstone, not two blocks from my mother's home, to a twelve-room flophouse. None of them feels right. I can't describe it any better than that. I test the earth at each place and feel only the sadness of something abused and without hope. Blocky and drab, this building looks so much like a factory it's hard to imagine living in it.

"I almost agree with you, Henry," I say, looking dubiously at the derelict cinderblock workshop that takes up the entire block. It once produced the cement bricks, but it is also made from them as well. Its lack of visual appeal adds to its location on the industrial side of Beacon Hill, among other equally glamorous buildings. Saws, steam engines, and other loud implements of production add to a low din around us.

Lord Helms produces a key and opens the door for me. I bat at cobwebs across the doorway as I enter. Like many of the properties we've seen today, the place is little more than walls and rubbish on the floors. A battered display rack leans against one wall, pegging this as likely a showroom of some sort. In silence, we wend through offices on two levels, a production floor, and a storage room. I wrinkle my nose when I open the door to a basement and a smell of molded papers and rusted metal issues forth. I decide to move on and leave that for another time. In the center back is a large courtyard open to the sky with a well in one corner and a plank privy that had seen better days in the other. The locals had chosen to use the enclosure to discard their trash, adding to its slum-like appearance.

Kneeling down, I pick up a pinch of the earth and touch it to my tongue. Expecting the same sad, tired emotions of the other places I've visited, the vibrancy and energy locked in the bitter taste drags my eyes wide. "Wow!"

"Wow, what, Stella?"

"This ground is fresh and alive." I can feel the urgency of the bits to embrace my care and commands.

"Come again?"

"I don't have the words, Henry. It is a witch thing. This ground is young and energetic. Let me guess. A single owner?"

"Yes, a single family all the way back to the founding of Boston. The Brick Baron, and yes, he really is a baron, owns this. Having manufacturing and corporate offices in town just didn't pay. He built a newer factory up at Haverhill where many of their raw materials are found, and ships finished product by rail."

"Well, despite the dilapidated state of this place, this is the one."

"Really?" Henry asks, eying the refuse and rusting tin roof.

My mind is already making mental changes to the inside and cleaning the place to within an inch of its life. "Yes, sir. Can I afford it?"

"Well, Baron Jordan is asking the exorbitant sum of twenty-two thousand—"

"Twenty-two thousand?! ¡Dios Mío! We should just—"

"Hold on a moment. Let me finish, Stella. *Señor* Jordan has been trying to sell for some time. And frankly, it isn't worth that much. If we can get him down to twelve, then it is more realistic." He looks up into the sky, and I see his mouth moving in mental calculations. "You'd have to have at least six boarders to make the place pay."

"Only six?"

"As a rough guess. But this place could hold maybe forty comfortable bedrooms with the correct modifications."

"I think I should start more modestly. How about eight rooms where the offices are and carve a room for me out of the production floor?"

"It can be done easily, Stella. It leaves you lots of room for expansion if you find you like being a lady of business."

"First, let's see if I can buy it."

The viscount chuckles. "Stella, Conner Jordan owes me more than one favor. He'll sell, and I'll get you a good price."

#

The Mission Chapel sounds the four o'clock hour as I drop Viscount Henry at Forever Power, just five blocks away, but only two as the crow flies.

"I know the first time is scary, Stella, but trust me that you will not regret it."

"My mind and heart are all twisted up in knots. Part of me regrets it already, Henry. You see, I've never been in debt to anyone. You seem to think that by taking on more obligation than anyone can rightfully earn in a lifetime that I'll somehow make more money." His mouth is open to speak, but I continue before he can reply. "But in this case, I will trust in your friendship and expertise."

"There is a certain risk in any business, Stella, but in this venture, the worst I see is no profit."

"Then I leave you with my trust, Henry. Thank you again."

The viscount bows and turns back toward Forever Power. With its customary chuffing, I ease the poderabile out into traffic. I squeeze between a horse-drawn trap and a hansom cab. The afternoon traffic keeps my attention away from the sinking feeling in my stomach at even owing so much money.

I swerve around a mechanical street sweeper before being stifled by the mass of traffic coming off the Canal Bridge. The American Royal Navy has used the fishing docks to offload cargo much more of late. I remember a similar uptick just before our men sailed for the liberation of Ireland. The blockage is so severe that after sitting for fifteen minutes without moving so much as a buggy whip length, I pull out directly behind an automated trolley into an opening in the traffic made for it. It earns me a few goose horns honking for my impertinence. It is a quarter of the hour before I finally make it to my former home, a walk that would have taken me considerably less time.

To my great surprise and delight, three youths with a dogcart are sitting in front of the boardinghouse. Between Chapman's and the laundry next to it is a narrow alley used by the garbage collectors and other service men. I ease Lady Justice in there, leaving me just enough room to dismount on the left side without soiling my dress against the filthy walls.

"You must be Mikey," I say to a young girl wearing grubby boy clothes. If it weren't for the ponytail of flame-red hair down from under the damaged woolen hat, I wouldn't have even picked her out as a girl. She has two boys, both at a brawny stage just between youth and manhood.

"Mum," she says, giving something akin to a curtsey. It looks strange in breeches.

"I'm pleased you are early. It will make my evening plans easier to meet. Now, who do you have with you?"

"Bob and Tom. They ain't got much smarts, but they got good backs."

"Watch it there, Mikey."

"Shush, now!" she barks back even though he would have made three of her, maybe four. "You be behaving yourself, or I ain't gonna pay you nothing." Bob backs down.

I admire her spunk and didn't contradict her in that I would be paying. "First off, my name is Stella—not ma'am, mum, or lady. Just call me Stella.

"Yes, Stella," they all three say at the same time.

"I'm glad to see the initiative in bringing the cart. I didn't think of it."

Mikey smacks Tom with her hat, exposing even more of her brilliant hair. "See. I told you."

I inwardly chuckle at the exchange. "I'll reimburse you for its use. Now we are going into Chapman's Boarding House and retrieving my things. There is a bed, a chifforobe, two night tables, a dresser, a coal bin, and poker. I'll try to collect other things together."

"Mu—Stella, I brought a few crates," Mikey says, pointing to the back of the dogcart.

"You are a girl with a head on your shoulders, and I seem to have lost mine. Thank you. I'll go in first and then call you in."

They nod in agreement. The front hall of the boardinghouse is pleasingly empty. If I can get my things without meeting either Mrs. Chapman or any of the other boarders, I'll be happy.

I march up the stairs, and I open my door. The scene before me takes my blood from cool to boiling in the space of a glance. There are crates around the room filled with my clothes and incidentals from the drawers and other places.

"CHAPMAN!" I bellow, not caring if the whole of Massachusetts hears me. Ladylike is not in my current emotional vocabulary. I dig around in the crates for the prized possession of my wedding picture. I find it, but the frame is twisted and bent. The picture itself has a scratch in one corner. "CHAPMAN!"

I hear pelting up the stairs. The dowager runs into my room panting and out of breath. I lapse into Spanish so vile that I can't believe it myself. The most polite thing I say is to call her a fish fucker. I'm shaking, and my voice is at least three levels louder than it should be.

"Mrs. Ochoa. I don't understand what you are talking about, and I'd appreciate it if you stopped waving that in my face."

"Appreciate? You want any appreciation after you violated my room. Touched my things and damaged my possessions? How dare you ask for ANY rights or privileges? If I had any self-respect, I'd smother you in sand."

My ire is up, and I force down the earth below me that rattles the building like an earthquake. She takes half a step backward. "MRS. OCHOA! Calm yourself!"

"Oh, no, you worthless *puta*, not this time. I've put up with your snooping, your interference in my affairs, and your invasion of my privacy, but this..." I wave the damaged picture at her again. "...will not go unpunished."

"Mrs. Ochoa, I had no reason to believe you would ever return for your traps so I crated them up for disposal in the case you didn't return."

"You lying *coño*," I hiss. "I was clear I would return for my possessions. I paid you for this room until this coming Sunday. I did both in front of witnesses!"

"You said no such thing." She looks me square in the eye as if daring me to brand her a liar again.

"Then let me be perfectly clear. If anything else is damaged or missing, I will send for the police. And if they don't give me satisfaction, I will take this house off its foundations and put it over the privy. I'll stoke the earth to such a fervor that no one would dare purchase it, ever. And you know that I can do it, too."

Her eyes go wide. "You wouldn't dare."

"I would gladly spend my time in witch's prison gloating over the fact that you have been ruined."

"It is moot as I've damaged nothing."

"What do you call this?" I say, pointing at the bent frame and scratched photograph.

"It was like that when I came in the room. I merely put it in a box."

I feel a spike of earth reaching up, begging for the right to come all the way up through the floors to impale her. I do consider it as my whole body shakes and flushes. The *puta* isn't worth the cost. I close my eyes and take three deep breaths. The rage I feel remains but is held in check at the moment. I urge the earth to resume its quiescent state. With more than a skosh of reluctance, it complies.

"Mrs. Chapman, I will bring in three young people to move my things from these premises. You will not interfere with them or me in any way. Once I am out, I will ensorcell this room so that anyone entering it will be...I'll just leave it up to your imagination as to what will happen. And before you object, the enchantment will be removed on Monday morning at twelve-oh-one in the morning." It is a bluff. There is no such capability in the witch's arsenal. But *la puta* Chapman doesn't know that.

She opens her mouth to object. Nothing comes out other than an indignant squeak. She turns and marches partway down the stairs before she shouts out up to me, "You better not damage any of my property, or I'll have you arrested. And I want my crates back."

I sit down on the bed. Closing my eyes and clutching my husband's picture to my chest, I just take repeated deep breaths, thinking about the joy I had in my life with him. His deep-throated chuckle. The way the sweat glistened across his chest after a long day of work. Running my fingers through his thick hair as he kissed my neck. The resentment within melts away. There is still a frown on my face, and my hands still shake, but the anger is put into perspective against love.

I have too many people who care about me to ruin it for the merely momentary pleasure of quashing the old hag. With a much lighter soul, I go down and open the door to my waiting moving team.

# # #

The trio works exceptionally well with the two muscular boys handling the heavy furniture. Mikey helps me transfer my belongings from Chapman's crates to the ones the short redhead brought. We are all loaded in less than forty minutes.

"As you can see, Mrs. Chapman, the room is in good order, better in fact than when I moved in."

"I'll be the judge of that!" I stand there with the patience of Job as the obnoxious woman rummages around. "I guess it will do." It had better. I did multiple repairs on that room after I'd moved in.

"Then I'd ask you to write a receipt to that effect, Mrs. Chapman."

When she scowls at me, I knew I'd just scuttled her plan for doing me in after the fact. She scrawls out a release and hands it to me.

"Thank you. And as you have been so kind, I will not magick this room." I hand her the front door key and the key to my room. "I will trouble you no longer and not even ask for prorated rent. You may do as you will with the room."

Outside, my three helpers are huddled down next to the cart to be out of the cutting wind.

"That weren't friendly, Stella," Mikey says.

"No, Mikey, it wasn't. I'd just as soon talk to her back as she walks away."

"My momma once been telling me that bad apples can ruin a bunch. Bad people can be doing that, too."

"Ever so true. Let's take this where it is going to be stored. I've got a stable somewhat near here. I'll drive the horseless carriage, and you three follow on behind. I'll go slow."

Through the thick of evening traffic, we weave over to where I've been stabling the poderabile. I unlock the shed, and together we load everything except my precious photo inside. It takes up just a tiny corner of the small area. Sad that my entire life fits there.

"I think you deserve a bonus, not only for working so fast but also for having the foresight to hire the cart and bring crates." Not to downplay her self-defined role, I give Mikey six quarters and six bits instead of paying the boys.

She hands Tom one of the bits. "Take the cart back to the fishmongers and pay him. And here is the rest of your pay. Good job. Now don't go spending it on liquor," she admonishes as she hands each of her workers two quarters each.

"Thank you, miss," they say as they pull the two-wheeled wagon away.

I don't say anything as I don't know if they are talking to her or me.

"Thank you, Miss Stella," Mikey says, tipping her hat at me. She turns to leave.

"Mikey, can you wait a minute?"

"Absolutely, Stella."

I don't know what is wrong with me. I don't have a job. Until (if, I mentally reserve) my business opportunity starts to pay for itself, I have no income. Despite all of this, my mouth speaks by itself. "How would you like Tommy's job?"

"I'm not fond of horses, miss. They don't be liking me much."

"Sorry, Mikey, I should have been more clear. I was paying Tommy a dollar a week to run errands for me. Would that interest you?"

"What do I have to do?"

"Show up where I'm staying each morning round about seven. If I'm there, I may have you go do something for me. If I'm not, you leave at quarter past and have no duties for that day."

Her eyes get steely and narrow. "I'd say that would be costing you a dollar and a quarter a week."

"Dollar and a bit."

"You be cheating me, but done," she says so fast she's already decided in her head. I hand her a dollar and a bit. "Climb on to the poderabile then, and I'll show you where you need to be every morning."

"What is being the pod her bile?"

"The horseless carriage," I reply.

"Oh, the magic machine. Is it being safe?"

"Yes. I've been driving it around for months with no danger."

"Then it beats horse-drawn anything. Thems horses'ud rather be biting me than much else."

"I can't say I'm fond of them either, Mikey. I took the trolley most times."

My young employee takes to the poderabile like I had. She leans into the wind and seems to love the stares of people as she leans forward of the dash. "It be just like flying, Stella, but it is being cold."

"I think that often myself."

The six o'clock bell rings as I cross the Charles River Bridge. I'm going to have to hurry if I'm going to make my date with *Señor* Gomez y Ruiz. I need to get a sponge bath and dress in my best for a night at the theatre. I've heard such wonderful things about *Dr. Jekyll and Mr. Hyde*. And I daresay that the thought of being on the arm of Manuel Gomez y Ruiz tickles me as well. He might have given the ghost of my husband a bit of a nudge to make room for himself. Once off the bridge, I push the drive levers forward. I ignore the honks of protest as I barrel by all the traps and hansom cabs as if they are standing still.

"This is a long way out, miss," Mikey says.

"Not to worry, Mikey. I will be moving in-town soon enough. In the meantime, I'll give you an extra bit a week to make it worth your while to come out this long way."

"Aye, Stella," she says, unable to keep out the tone of victory. Mikey is quite the rascal. I smile as I drive. I like rascals.

"Here we are."

"Great Mother Mary! Stella, you live here?" The Helms Estate is quite impressive, even to me after being a regular guest off and on for several months.

"Temporarily, Mikey. Very temporarily. Now, I don't mean to be rude, but I have just forty-five minutes to pretty for a date. You will have to make your way back."

"Yes, Miss Stella."

# # #

"We missed you at dinner, Stella," Viscountess Adrianna says as I enter the foyer, freshly pressed and perfumed. She is wearing a stunning three-tier dress in periwinkle blue, dripping with silver glints like icicles. The diamonds clinging to her earlobes probably would have purchased her entire mansion.

"I'm sorry, Adrianna. My errand to clear out my previous home took longer than expected."

"Would you join me in the parlor? I have some teacakes being sent in. I can just as well have a late supper brought for you."

"Thank you, no. I have a theatre date with a gentleman tonight."

The cheerful expression slipped from her face for only a moment. In that brief tick of time, I read disgust, jealousy, and anger all in one before her façade of a smile returns. "Of course, I can't hope to monopolize such a lovely woman's time. You and your gentleman friend have a good evening." She turns in an abrupt swish of fabric and strides away like a storm cloud on a windy day.

I am still processing her demeanor when Charles, the Helmses' butler, walks up to me. "Miss Stella, you have a caller."

I check the clock in the hall to see that it still lacks five minutes of the hour. I know social convention is to make a man wait. I understand the practice in the abstract that making him wait makes him desire even more, and it sets the tone that she is calling the shots. I've never subscribed to such a coldly manipulative view. If I don't appeal by myself, then no level of gameswomanship will change things. Or, worse, if it were to make the difference, how solid could that relationship be?

"Tell him...Never mind, I'll go and see him now."

"Very good, Miss Stella."

I lower my voice. "Remind me to tell you the one about the daughter in the oaken cask."

"A bunghole is a bunghole?"

"Damn. Thought I would get you on that one," I say.

"That one has been around at least since my grandfather was a boy, Miss Stella," he replies with a smile.

Charles wins that round. "OK. I'll try to find something more original."

"As you will, m'lady."

I find Manuel waiting just inside the door. He is resplendent in a freshly-pressed, tailored suit. His hair, just one shade browner than auburn, is much longer than other men care to keep it. It curls up in a wave in the front and hangs down his back like the fall of a wedding dress's train. The cleft of his chin is clean-shaven enough to be shiny, and his eyes give me an appraising look.

"Mrs. Ochoa, you are a delight in every sense of the word," he offers with the lilt that a born Spaniard can't help but lace throughout his speech.

I catch just the hint of lavender wafting from my date. "Why thank you, *Señor* Gomez y Ruiz."

"*Señora*, just Manuel, if you please. I am not of noble birth and don't need the, ah, *hinchado*...inflated title or my complete lineage. I'm a common man."

"As you will, Manuel."

"Shall we be off? We don't want to miss the show."

"By all means."

He offers me his arm in such a gentlemanly fashion that I can't recall ever having received. I like it enough that when my hand feels the deceptive strength beneath his coat, I get a bolt of lightning striking in an all-too-familiar place. It reminds me that my visit to my paramour's hadn't provided the opportunity to slake my lust. I'm holding onto just a little too much passion at the moment.

The evening's darkness is well lit by four gas lamps, two flanking the door and another two on poles on the other side of a magnificent carriage. *Señor* Gomez has spared no expense. It makes me wonder what he is expecting out of our evening. I mentally chuckle, wondering what he might think if he were granted the privilege of undressing me and finding my wrought iron corset. It is wound tightly enough not to show under my best dress.

Our footsteps crunch the paving shells beneath them, but the sound doesn't cover the bark of a weapon's fire. It also does nothing to hide or lessen the shock of a bullet slamming into my wrought iron underthings immediately below my right arm. I let the impact tumble me into my date.

I've always been both proud and dismayed at my prodigious *trasera*. This time it bites me as the second slug ricochets off the bottom of my impromptu armor and imbeds itself in my *gluteus maximus*.

I let out a yelp, but I'm too busy to give the pain any further heed. I cut my fingers on the sharp shells digging down beneath them until I reach earth. My senses magnify as if each bit of soil, rock, and sand is a separate individual sending me information. I always imagined it similar to the way a fly might see. But the earth doesn't see. It feels the vibrations of the third shot very near the Charles River's edge.

My companion cries out and grabs for his calf. Ignoring this irrelevancy, I realize that it is too far to entangle our attacker in stone. I reach out with a slightly different sense, feeling for metals in the area of the vibration. There are several, but the range is extreme. I settle for letting each of the chunks of metal deform in a way that suits it best. A fourth shot doesn't come.

I jump up with a hiss at the pain. I start in the direction of the river but stop after only two steps. With a slug still in my buttocks, I can't hope to keep up with a man running away, a fact that the earth assures me of.

Charles, Henry, the stableman, whose name I've forgotten, Tommy, and basically every other living soul of the house bursts out onto the front drive. Every man is carrying a firearm, including, to my surprise, Tommy.

"Tommy, hitch up the buggy to go tell the constable," Lord Helms barks.

"Yes, Mr. Helms!"

Jimmy Marsden, coachman and head groundskeeper, says. "Fan out. If you see something, cry out, don't get involved. Back in five minutes whether you see anything or not."

"Check toward the river. About five hundred yards that way," I point. I check on Manuel, but his wound is superficial. He is up and moving, with a limp, almost before the spectators arrive. I look down at my own injury. Blood stains my dress and continues to leak down my stockings. I'd be more worried about the rust color ruining my outfit if it weren't for the two large holes having made the point moot.

"Excuse me," I say, putting my hand up under my dress. Mentally, I commune with the metal shot still in my ass and convince it to narrow and return the way it came. I grit my teeth as it squeezes out the wound. I take my arm out to find the slug in my palm, both coated in red.

"Stella, are you alright!" Adrianna screams, coming over to my side. "Fetch a doctor!"

"No need, Viscountess," I say, offering her the narrowed bullet.

"Still, you need to get patched up."

"Adrianna, I've had worse, much worse, herding demons. I'll be fine."

"Maggie! Fetch my sewing kit and hot water. Bring garlic and honey. To the library."

"Yes, m'lady."

"Stella, come inside. There may be more of them."

"There aren't. Even he got away," I pronounce. "But I'm not sure I want to be on this leg too long."

Adrianna gets her shoulder under my right arm. I wince at the bruise underneath. "You're not hit somewhere else?"

"Yes and no. It hit me, but I'm just sore, not penetrated."

Ignoring Manuel entirely, she helps me into the library. I realize at once why—leather furniture. They can be wiped clean of blood. Manuel follows but is rebuffed.

"Sir, if you would please wait in the foyer, I'm sure Charles will help you. To dress Stella's wound will require some privacy."

"Quite right, *doña*."

After his retreat, Adrianna continues. "Stella, let's get that dress off of you."

"You seem to get my clothes off of me quite a good deal since you met me, Adrianna," I add, teasing just a bit. I slip off the damaged green frock that the Helmses had given me. At this moment, I feel as hurt about its loss as by the pain in my injured bottom.

"If you wouldn't get hurt so much, maybe I wouldn't have to. Jesus H. Christ, what is that?" I don't understand what she is talking about until I see her point and the other hand over her mouth for her blasphemy.

"This is my armor. Like it? I thought it might start a fashion." I reach around to pluck off the bullet that is smashed up against my metal girdle. A metal disk, maybe two inches across, probably started as a slug half-an-inch wide. The area is tender enough that I might have broken a rib. With the shot in my hand, I mentally talk to the structure of the iron around my middle. It loosens its coils like taffy in the hot summer sun before slumping over my bottom, held only by my petticoats. I untie the frilly layers, and the metal and crinoline both drop to the ground, my armor singing out a muffled ring like a leather sack of gold coins.

"Ah, isn't that heavy?"

"A bit, but it saved my life. Besides, I've been getting used to it," I say, stepping out of the ring of cotton and metal. The underskirts are more stained in my blood than the dress. Fortunately, unless I'm with a lover, no one is going to see them. My bloomers reveal even more burgundy. "Good grief," I say, wondering just how much blood I lost.

"That's more than a scratch, Stella. Get on your knees on the sofa," Adrianna orders, setting aside the oddity of my underwear construction.

The door opens, and we both look. I mean, I'm just in my bloomers and chemise. I feel the next thing next to naked to anyone that might intrude. Maggie enters, carrying an enamel tray laden with any number of items.

"Here you are, ma'am," Maggie says, setting it down next to me. "I also brought the alcohol. I sent Nayeli for some of Stella's clothes."

"Good thinking, Mags. Now go guard the door so that no one else comes in."

"Yes, ma'am."

The door closes. "OK, let's see it," Adrianna says.

I slip my fingers inside the waist cord of my bloomers for the second time of the night. I slide the drawers down, just enough to bare my wound. As big as my arse is, I can't see it, and no one has been thoughtful enough to offer me a mirror. I feel my hostess's fingers touch firmly to hold me in place. It feels like a brand and makes me suck in a breath. Not in pain but as my sex responds to her ministrations.

"I'm sorry, did I hurt you?" she says, pulling her hand away.

"No. It just surprised me. Go ahead."

"It is barely oozing now. I'm going to clean it and sew it up. I'm afraid you are going to have a tender bottom for some time."

Her touch returns. This time I feel a washcloth carefully clean the area. It stings a bit. I'm not kidding when I say that pain is something I deal with most every demon hunt. After I've been hurt so many times, it becomes a secondary thought, not something that breaks my concentration or even troubles me up to a point. I find it about the same as a splinter.

"I doubt it will even—yeow!" I cry. Then, through clenched teeth, "You might warn a body before pouring alcohol on a wound."

"Would it make it any better?"

I think about it. "Probably not, but it would be polite." I decide to shut up and let her do what I can't. Her work is gentle even when she sews the hole closed. She is almost done when there is a timid knock at the door. It opens.

"Ma'am, Witchdoctor Bartholomew is here."

"Excellent. Stella, do you want to cover before he comes in?"

"He has to see it sometime. Let him in, Maggie."

Witchdoctor Bartholomew looks more like an aged undertaker than a doctor. His severe black suit fits him like a glove. The pallor of his skin would make me think of a vampire if I didn't know such things are only myths. Even his voice is deep and creepy. I feel a blush come to my cheeks, the ones on my face, as I kneel on the sofa with my buttocks hanging out for the witchdoctor to see.

"Good evening, ladies. I take it one of you has taken an injury?"

"Two injuries, Doctor," Adrianna says for me like I'm some kind of invalid who can't talk.

As he moves closer, the chill that ran down my spine from his appearance and voice is smoothed over with the love of the Lord, our God, which he exudes. His hands, rough and callused, cool any ardor that my hostess may have coaxed from my too willing innards. They manipulate my arse like a cook might a ham she is preparing for dinner.

"This is excellent stitching. Did you do this, ma'am?"

"I can't very well stitch my own ass," I say.

"No, ma'am, I was talking to Madam Helms."

"Thank you, Witchdoctor Bartholomew. I just sewed it up like I might a rent in fabric."

"Just doctor is fine, Madam Helms. More healing is done without witchcraft than with it. From the looks of things, you would have made a fine doctor yourself. Did you remove the item that caused the wound?"

I hold up the narrowed of the two bullets.

"A bullet wound?" he asks, taking the narrowed lead from my hand. "I will have to report this to the constabulary."

"They are on their way now," Adrianna says.

"Excellent. It looks as if the bullet is intact. Did you clean the wound, madam?"

"Yes, with both water and alcohol."

"Good. You really would have made a fine physician. If you ever have the desire to proctor for the art, please let me know."

I can hear the embarrassment in Lady Helms's voice as she thanks him.

"Well, let me heal this one from the inside." His fingers physic my ass cheek like I used to knead a roll of dough to make bread. I can feel the warmth I associate with Sunday mornings at church. It is softer and smoother than what Maxwell does. Perhaps with experience and learning, one can do more miraculous things than just a crude patch? I hear him muttering under his breath, "'But I will restore your health and heal your wounds,' declares the Lord."

"Jeremiah 30:17," I say, unbidden.

"Very good. Most don't bother to learn the Bible anymore, Miss—"

"Widow, actually, Witchdoctor Bartholomew. Widow Stella Ochoa. I carry the title of Mistress Earth Witch and hunt demons."

"Ah, a hellfighter. That explains many of the other marks I see upon your flesh. I'm sorry our first meeting is so...intimate," he offers.

"Second meeting, Witchdoctor. We met briefly at a fete given for me by Viscount and Viscountess Helms."

"Yes. You wore this same magnificent green dress."

"Good memory, Doctor, but I'm afraid this frock took both of the bullets and probably is bound for the rubbish bin."

"That is a shame. But you say two wounds. I see no other injury. Is it hidden beneath your chemise or bloomers?"

I lift up my arm again with a wince. With it, I slide up the chemise. "Right there, under my brassiere strap."

"Ah, yes, that is bruising quite nastily. I see no entry wounds. Were you struck by a blow?"

"It is a long story. For the sake of simplicity, just say that I was shot, but it hit a corset stay." I hold up the flattened bullet for him to examine.

"Exceptionally lucky. That might have torn up your lungs or other vital organs had it entered."

"Agreed, Doctor."

"Well," he says, stopping with only the word. I feel the searching gaze of the Lord deep inside my flesh. "I'd say you have a greenstick fracture of the rib. 'The man said, "This is now bone of my bones and flesh of my flesh; she shall be called woman, for she was taken out of man."'" He eyes me as if searching for an answer to a question he hasn't asked.

"Really? I'd guess even Adrianna would know that one. Viscountess?"

"Genesis, I believe."

"Genesis 2:23," I clarify. Doctor Bartholomew nods.

"Mrs. Ochoa, I can feel the power of God's love in you. Why did you not heal yourself?"

Jesus, I mentally curse. *I've already claimed to be an earth witch. How can I now claim white witch powers?* A witch with more than one focus is as rare as scales on a buffalo. But, fortunately, most men will fall for the dumb woman act. "I do?"

"At least I so feel. I'm not a teaching witch, but I think you have a second gift. You should have that checked."

"Checked" like I have some curable rash, I think. The fewer people know about my unique nature, the better. Besides, at wielding white magic, I am a rank amateur, like a tyro violin player. While the novice instrumentalist can be painful on the ears, an untrained witch of any type can be dangerous. This is why I use it so infrequently and almost always in a situation of desperation.

"I'll do that, Doctor." I am not sure he bought into my dissembling, but if nothing else, I put doubt in his mind.

"Whilst these two injuries are minor, and I've healed them, they will remain tender for the next week or so. I suggest rest and minimal movement."

Adrianna couldn't let that pass. "Good luck with that, Doctor. I nursed her through her last injury. I just about had to tie her down."

"Viscountess, it is her body. One thing I've learned in thirty years of practice is that people know their own limitations, usually, even better than a doctor."

"See?" I taunt Adrianna, sticking my tongue out at her like a child. She acts as if she doesn't see it.

"Thank you for coming on such short notice, Doctor. How would you like your fee?"

"Hey, it's my body. I'll pay my own bills."

Adrianna ignores me. "Will banknotes be acceptable, or would you prefer coin?"

"Either works for me, madam." They both move out of the room, and I start to follow, intent on putting a kibosh on this whole Helmses' charity business. "Mrs. Ochoa, you can resume your clothing now," the witchdoctor says.

I stop in my tracks with the realization that I am in just my boots, chemise, and a crimson-stained set of bloomers. Worse, there is nothing but my petticoats to put on. *Damn that woman.*

Nayeli, a young native girl, comes into the room as they leave with an armful of my clothes. In a high-pitched voice that would have done a bird credit, Nayeli asks, "Would you like help getting into your clothes, Stella?"

Nay is a great young woman. I met her when I was invalided here a few months back. Reticent in speaking, I did manage to worm out of her that she works as a servant for the Helmses so she can save up money for college. She plans on becoming a telegrapher.

"No, thank you, Nayeli. I'll manage."

"Very good, ma'am," she says, dipping a knee and leaving.

#

Unfortunately, the cut of my second-best dress, a severe black frock that I primarily wear to church, shows in the mirror as if I am an additional thirty pounds heavier. Thirty pounds is correct, not in flesh but in iron. My dignity, if not my beauty, repaired, I emerge from the Helmses' library.

The foyer is a hive of activity. A number of constables are roaming around doing goodness knows what. A handful of men I don't know are also moving in and out the front door. Lord Helms is talking to Inspector First Antonio Guizzetti. Manuel Gomez y Ruiz sits in one of the dining room chairs brought out for him and his injury. The Spaniard is attended by the witchdoctor who tends his wounds and a constable who picks his brain. Adrianna fusses over most everything and everyone. Within the hubbub, Bastogne takes refreshments around the room with the dignity and serenity that only he can manage convincingly.

"Ah, Stella," Antonio says as he spies me exiting my cocoon. "Might I have a word?"

"Absolutely, Lieutenant. Here or in private?"

"Privacy would be preferred if your dignity and chastity wouldn't be endangered by being alone with me."

"Not at all, sir." I lead him back into the library. He closes the door behind me.

"You stupid little bitch!" he barks as silence falls around us. "I should have locked you up to protect you. I warned—"

"Lieutenant, I don't think that cursing me is appropriate when you are on duty. That is also, as I recall, the second time you've referred to me as a dog. I think even as a remonstration, it falls out of bounds of propriety." I do soften my retort with a wink.

I wonder if the look in his eyes might shoot flames out like those of Gazzunreep, the demon I'd fought. He swallows hard. "Yes, Mrs. Ochoa." He mutters a low curse in Italian under his breath. I only recognize it as such because of its similarity to Spanish. He bites his lip before continuing. "Would you please give me your account of the event?"

"Much better, Inspector." I give my version of the evening's festivities: chapter and book, with a table of contents and index for good measure.

"Armor? Can you please show me?"

"Why, Inspector, are you trying to get me out of my clothes? I thought my chastity was safe with you," I tease. It must hit home as his cheeks each take the appearance of halves of a Tahoma apple.

"Uh, no...I mean..."

"Relax, Antonio." I pull down the skirt-half of my dress away from the bodice, just a few inches, enough to show my flat metal spiral. He eyes it professionally.

"You know that won't protect you from being hit in the head?"

"I do know that, but I felt at least the first time the assassin would go for my heart. I wasn't wrong."

He pauses for a moment. "Do you have any idea who might want you dead? I mean, after reflection on the *second* attempt on your life?" His emphasis is his new way of chastising me while maintaining his professional demeanor.

"Still have the same list of suspects. Although I did receive another threat from the NPP."

"Do tell?" he says, scribbling furiously.

"I have the offending *thing* in my poderabile. I'll have someone fetch it for you. It was another attempt to get me to leave Boston."

"Interesting. Maybe I can get prints from whatever this thing is."

"It's the side of a milk crate from one of the dairies out west of town."

"It might show fingerprints. We'll have to see. Speaking of which..." He walks over to the door and says, "Robles, bring that over here."

I don't hear a response, but Mr. Guizzetti of the sweet buns is handed a revolver long-rifle, or what may have been that at one time. It now sports needle-thin spines all over it like a porcupine defending itself against a polecat.

"Recognize this, Stella?"

"Can't say that I've ever *seen* it. I felt it, sure enough, earlier this evening, in more ways than one."

"Well, one of these points jammed the action. The assassin has the luck of the devil himself. If one of these had hit a primer, it would have blown up in his face. As it is, even with the, uh, distortions, we should still have a better than average chance of getting prints off of the wooden stock, if nothing else. Know anyone that owns one?"

"Antonio, I don't even know what it is, other than a rifle. I don't have much need for such a thing in my day-to-day life."

"It's an Irish liberation sniper revolver. They were much prized by the men in the field. Six shots without reloading and accurate to five hundred yards. More than a few redcoats went to the devil because of our boys in blue and this little toy. But they weren't in wide service."

"Interesting, but rather useless information for me. Do you have any other questions, Lieutenant?"

"Yes, Mrs. Ochoa. We can sit down," he says, waving to the nearby chair. I curse my memory for that befitting of nothing better than belongs in a mouse. Sitting on my freshly healed ass stings. Antonio takes a chair at a comfortable distance for talking.

"Are you ready to be put into protective custody now, Mrs. Ochoa?"

"Only two more days," I temporize. "I doubt that goon will try anything now. He doesn't even have a gun."

"Stella, sometimes your hard head matches the stone you can manipulate."

"Mayhaps," I offer without commitment.

He continues, "With the trial of Quarrels only two days off, you are in more danger than ever. If this killer doesn't come back, someone else will."

"Then he'd better watch his back," I say with not a little malice.

Antonio sighs in surrender. "If you remember nothing else, you know where to find me."

"I thank you, Inspector. Now, if you will excuse me, I have to cancel a date." This time he frowns at me. Why are so many people making unspoken commentary on my personal life?

I make my way back out into the entryway. I don't even have to find Manuel as he comes limping up to me. He performs a theatrical bow. "I'm sorry for what occurred this evening. I should have prevented it."

"Nonsense. If there is anyone that should apologize, it is I. This is the second time I've been shot in less than a week. I inadvertently put you at risk."

"It would be my honor to put my life at your disposal any time you should need it. I am only sad that my injury prevented me from chasing down the culprit or protecting you from harm. Please accept my word that I shall devote my honor to discovering the identity of the cretin." The chivalrous man actually thinks it is his fault.

"Thank you, *señor*, but I assure you that it is not needed. This should all be over and forgotten within a pair of days."

"Be that as it may, my honor has been damaged, and I will have it restored. It will be my great pleasure to serve you in this way."

"As you will, Manuel, but that leaves us with the tatters of our evening."

"Yes. The play is well into its second act, and it is too late, with propriety, to take you out. I beg forgiveness for ruining your evening."

"Oh, Jesus, Mary, and Joseph. Manuel, you weren't the cause. Trust me that I would round on you proper if you did mess up, but this isn't your failing."

Manuel stands up a little straighter and puffs his chest out as if remembering his manhood. He lifts his cleft chin. "Then may I be permitted to call on you some other time?"

I think about the trouble I'm getting myself into before answering, "Yes, you may. You can contact me here for the nonce or the viscount or viscountess will know where I have relocated to."

"Thank you, gracious lady." He bows low over my hand and gives it a thorough kiss that melts my middle.

"Until our next meeting, I will be adrift of heart without your startling company."

His words make me want to drag him, with little concern to social convention, to my room and...Well, let's just say we wouldn't be playing Tiddlywinks. Instead, he bows again and hobbles out the door favoring his game leg.

I'm left with damp bloomers and the sole option of auditioning the finger puppets—rubbing myself—when the opportunity presents itself.

7—Tuesday, May 8, 1888

The tinny chimes of the Helmses' hall clock edge into my consciousness. Without waking, I count the bells. I twitch a bit when I've counted eight and then nine. My mind tries to prod me that I've forgotten something, but it won't tell me what it might be. I snuggle down into the bedding. Then, as if being splashed with water, I go from pleasant almost-slumber to full wakefulness. *I'm late for work*. With only the time it might take a rattlesnake to strike, I realize *but I've been fired. But nine o'clock? I've missed Mikey*.

I silence my thoughts by pulling the covers up over my head.

#

One of the mid-hour chimes stirs me from sleep once again. Which one, I have no idea. *No matter,* I decide. Staying flat aback, I stretch, feeling just the slightest of twinges up under my armpit and my bottom. *I'd better not sleep the whole day away,* I think. But there is a niggling little thought of, *Why not?*

"'Cause you have to find a job, you silly witch," I say out loud.

I pick up my husband's pocketwatch from the nightstand to see that I have slept most of the day away. It is ten-thirty. Slipping out of bed, I wrap a dressing gown around me and put my feet into the luxurious plush slippers that Adrianna bought me last time I was here. They are so decadent that when I left, I couldn't bring myself to take them.

I shuffle out of my room. This proves that the hole in my arse isn't nearly as healed as I'd like. I manage something of a limp down the hall, thankful that I don't have to go to a frozen outhouse. As my muscles limber up, my gait improves but not to anything resembling normal as my right ham twinges with every step.

The water closet here at the Helmses' is to die for. The extravagance of not having to hover above a privy hole so cold you'd stick to it is priceless. There is even a water basin to wash in before I leave. If it costs me my last penny, I'll make sure my new house has a room like this.

"There you are, Miss Stella," Nayeli says as I exit the indoor outhouse. "Be you feel'n alright?"

"Moderately well, Nayeli. I don't think I quite need a cane yet," I joke.

"Well, if you would, the mistress has ordered me to make sure you rest. I know you be'n a strong woman with her own mind about things, but to save me a tongue lash'n, could you please go back to your bed?"

I consider a few choice curses, but Nay doesn't deserve any of them. "I will," *for now,* I don't add with my fingers crossed behind my back.

"Thank you much, ma'am."

My stomach grumbles at me as I make to hobble off. "Nay, any chance an invalid can impose on Cook to rustle up a pair of scrambled eggs and some toast?"

"Cook has food keep'n warm for you on the back of the stove—Mistress Adrianna's orders. I can fetch it right up if you like."

"That would be wonderful, and the morning paper if there is one."

"Absolutely, ma'am."

It reminds me that I should do something sweet for Nay, Laoise, and Maggie. They have been so attentive. Although, how I'm going to get out of the house with a pair of guards in service uniforms and an assassin intent on closing out my accounts, I don't know.

I keep going back to the "Why?" and the "Who?" of my attempted murder. The pair are obviously interlinked, but I decide to examine "Why."

I review recent significant events in my life. Mainly it involves lots of demon internments. In fact, that reminds me that it has been several nights since the last escape. It looks like Henry's new locking enclosures are making a positive impact in that area. Is there any reason someone might be cross at me about that? Obviously, whoever is letting them out, if anyone is left alive, may be upset but not at me specifically. None of the other hellfighters have been killed, or it would have made the newspapers. That seems to be a dead end.

I returned Gazzunreep to hell, where he belongs. He might be angry, but unless he's found some new agent on earth. I mentally scoff at the thought that anyone would treat with a demon, but Baron Snowdonia had. At the same time, I participated in the event that killed Franklin Cardiff, the same said noble. In doing so, I got a large portion of his estate. Perhaps there is a relative that expected some of that? Something I should kick over to Inspector Guizzetti to see what he thinks.

Without much trouble, my mind turns to the most likely issue, that I thwarted the plans of someone trying to discredit the demon power industry, and I will testify about it. That can point at either Quarrels or the CEO of the Coal Syndicate, Bruce Jasperson. But as Quarrels is well and truly behind bars, I don't see how he could have done anything. Jasperson, on the other hand, is a loathsome rat. I'm confident that he was behind the scheme to send demon power into disrepute by releasing them to cause death and destruction. Unfortunately, I have no proof. As wealthy and powerful as the man is, he is all but above the law. So why would such a man care if I lived or died?

The whole mess is a puzzle that I don't have an answer for. And for the nonce, it will have to remain that way. If Antonio's fears have any basis, I'll give the assassin little opportunity to hone in on me before my appearance in court. Barring dinner with my friend Patty tonight, I'll remain comfortably ensconced and safe within these opulent if temporary lodgings.

I select a book on modern mythology before setting down into the wingback chair in my room. Reading is an excellent way to while away an afternoon, but I so rarely have had the opportunity. I don't even get into the foreword when, good as her word, Nayeli is up with a breakfast tray. She sets up the day table in my room with a mound of scrambled eggs, four rashers of bacon, and tea cakes on a china service. The heavenly but bitter aroma of Columbian coffee issues forth from a matching carafe. The morning paper is folded neatly next to my place, as is a yellow Night Letter envelope.

"Thank you, Nay. This looks yummy." Nay giggles. "Did I say something funny?"

"Kinda, ma'am. The way you growl 'yummy' tickles me. Sorry for be'n unprofessional," she says, ducking her head.

"Oh, fiddlesticks on that, Nay. You know me well enough now that I don't stand on ceremony. I'm a working girl, too."

"That may be true, but the mistress orders I am to be treating you like a lady."

"Does she, now? I knew I should have gotten my own damned breakfast. I can still cook a damned egg or two."

"No, no, ma'am. I didn't mean it that way. You treat us right, not like some of them snobbies that the lord and lady have over. We think of you more as downstairs rather than a guest. I'da done this for any of us servants that been ill, mistress's orders or not."

I take the opportunity to chuckle myself. "If I had been some highfalutin woman, I'd box your ears for calling me downstairs. But as I am not stuffy, come here and let me give you a hug. Thank you for claiming me as one of your own."

"You be mighty welcome, ma'am. And thank you for reminding Charles of the barrel joke. I near peed myself laughing so hard."

"Let's just keep that downstairs where it belongs, Nayeli. I have no wish to have Lady Adrianna round on me for corrupting you. Off with you now before my eggs get cold."

"Yes, Stella."

I've never received a Night Letter. It demands my attention even more than the food. I open the envelope with the butter knife. No, I have no shame—or very little.

Western Union Night Letter

Mrs. Ochoa,

I received your counteroffer on using the Snowdonia Estate and accept your offer of $1,800.00 for the year. I've sent down a contract by post and authorized the Bank of Boston to remit to you the total amount upon delivery of signed same.

Reginald Cornwall

My Lord above. Eighteen hundred dollars. That's like getting more than thirty-five dollars a week! And now I get it for doing nothing much at all. I need to ask if I can get this every year. I'm hoping. Maybe Mr. Cornwall would be willing to negotiate a slightly lower rate for a longer-term. Thirty-five dollars a week! I imagine all kinds of luxuries from being a patron of the arts, my own private library, new wallpaper every year, or maybe even owning my own train car.

Then practical Stella comes in and throws hurricane-driven storm surge onto my crepe paper beach. My memory throws up the image of my one and only visit to my old schoolteacher, Mrs. Hogarth, in that squalid poorhouse. Bedridden with crippling arthritis, her body lay wasted and bearing a mass of sores. Her shift looked as if it hadn't been washed in a month. Bugs crawled over her skin with near impunity. A chilling moan issued from her mouth, which was bordered by the crusted slop she might have had for a meal two days prior.

To my shame, I'd run away without saying a single word to her. I'd been fourteen when I called in response to her letter. It shames me still. The vision still makes me wake up from time to time with chills when nightmares put my face over her pathetic body.

Gritting my teeth, I hiss, "I'll never be in that position." I still have to save for my dotage. That land won't give me an income forever. I'll take what I can get, indeed, and stuff every spare penny into the bank. I won't be destitute. It seems like such an overreaction considering my plush surroundings, but I will never be so...so...pathetic and helpless as she had been.

I focus on my breakfast to erase the all-too-vivid remembrance. While excellent and filling, I decide that the viscount's cook has nothing on Karie's kitchen staff. Daubing my mouth with a napkin, I push the empty plates away and grab the newspaper.

The headline above the fold offers, "Peary's Third Expedition." I read this article through because Robert Peary's explorations, in this case, to reach the North Pole, always interest me. This time instead of sled dogs to make his final leg of the journey, they'd packaged three specially manufactured dirigibles into his ship. Peary's team includes three air, three fire, and three ice witches. The picture in the article is of the entire team in New Murcia Harbor in front of the ice breaker *New Worlds*. I don't give him one chance in twenty of being successful, but I hope he is. I like the idea of knowing more about our world.

There is another article about people finding the wreck of the airship, *The Princess*, in the frozen wilds of Siberia. *Princess*, flown by the famous and rather dashing Edward Simson, had been attempting to circumnavigate the globe. It had left Basildon, England, on February twenty-eighth at seven AM. Its last known position was when it dropped a message down onto Salsnes, Norway. For seven years, people have speculated where it had gone. The reporter went to great lengths to hype the grisly condition of the scene and hide the cause of the wreck. Rest in peace, Mr. Simson. We are all a bit sadder without you.

The help-wanted section of the paper is depressing. With hundreds of thousands of German refugees, jobs that I qualify for are few and far between. I'll have to keep looking and maybe even head down through the manufacturing ward to see if anyone can use my talents.

Before I can even work up a good funk about my joblessness, Nay comes up to collect my tray. "All done, ma'am?"

"Yes, Nay. Could you please let Tommy know that I want to speak to him? There is no rush. When his duties permit."

Nayeli blushes. "Yes, ma'am."

There is only one reason I can imagine why Nayeli might be embarrassed about my request. I wonder who seduced whom. Now, I have another reason to talk to Tommy.

I pick up my book and lose myself in gorgons, medusae, and ghosts. After an hour, I feel stiff and need to get up and move around. Not for the first time, I lament that being lazy can be more exhausting than working.

There is a knock on the doorframe to my room. "Stella, you wanted to see me?" His silhouette there makes me reevaluate the young cutpurse I'd taken pity on just a few months ago. Tommy has grown. He's put on at least an inch in height and twenty pounds of muscle. His shirt is damp and wafting his musk all over. From a purely prurient standpoint, I understand any woman's interest in him. I still consider him more like a young brother.

"Close the door, please."

"Did I do something wrong, ma'am?"

My left brow comes up in confusion. "No. Why would you ask that?"

He closes the door. "Oh, it's just that Lady Helms rounds on me in private if I done something wrong."

I chuckle. "Nothing like that at all, Tommy. Come here and sit down." He does but perches on the edge of a chair.

"First, let's do the easy one. Can you have the poderabile outside the garden's back gate for me at four o'clock?"

"I thought you was supposed to stay in until you go to court tomorrow."

I lay down an exaggerated sigh. I won't have anyone defining my parameters. "Tommy, who decides when and where I go?"

He gives me a smile that I'm sure would get any number of girls to lift their skirts and show him their ankles. "Only you, Stella. I done learned that the first time we met."

"Good boy. So…"

"I'll be having the poderabile behind the north gate ready for your use by four o'clock."

"Much better! Now to the delicate part of my conversation. Do you know how babies are made?" I really do mean I feel like a big sister.

Tommy's tanned face erupts in purple. "STELLA!"

"Hmmm. That isn't an answer, Tommy. I know it's a sensitive topic."

"Yeah, and not one a lady be talking about, ma'am."

"So you learned it out behind the woodshed looking at French postcards? Or maybe with the other menfolk talking about dirty things while drinking liquor?"

"Ahh—"

"That's what I thought. First off, I'm no lady. So let me give you a crash course because I don't want you getting none of your lady friends with child."

Tommy looks like he wants to crawl under a rock. "Ahh—"

Why are men so timid about something so natural and easy to define? I never understand their timidity. "When you pull on the thing between your legs—"

"Stella! Please, stop. I done watched animals doing it. I know hows mens and women are supposed to make babies. I don't need you learning me."

"So, have you being doing it with any women?"

"No, ma'am. I mean, I wants to, but I ain't got no right to make a gal in a motherly way."

A mental weight is lifted off my mind. "That is a very responsible attitude. Keep that thought until you do have the right, Tommy." There is a pause before he speaks again.

"That don't mean I ain't been sparking, Stella."

"So if you know how animals, and girls, get babies, that means you know what to do…or maybe what NOT to do if you don't want to get a girl with child?"

"Yes, ma'am. Only one girl I am courting. We both done agreed we could do most anything 'cept that."

I'm pleased but decide to tease him a bit. "Yes, things with hand and mouth can be quite pleasurable."

"STELLA!" he barks and, if possible, he's getting even more colorful in the face.

"I have been married, Tommy. But if you want to keep your partner happy, you will do it back for her, too."

Tommy is looking for somewhere to go to avoid any more of this conversation. I smile and say, "That's all I wanted, Tommy. Just wanted to make sure the poderabile will be ready."

"Absolutely, ma'am," he says, sprinting out of the room. I hope I may have just bolstered both of their enjoyment, for which I must ask for absolution from Father Juan this coming Sunday.

# # #

"STELLA!" comes Adrianna's command from downstairs. I make my way to the banister to see her there with Tommy and four other grooms, as well as Charles, all laden with bright boxes so high I can barely make out their faces. "Up there, Charles," she says, pointing toward me. The group troupes past me into the guest room.

"Umm, what is—"

"I have some surprises," her ladyship says with a wicked grin that makes me sorry I teased Tommy. They do say it comes back threefold.

I follow the procession into my temporary quarters to find boxes and bags all over the bed, which Nayeli somehow had managed to make in my absence of thirty seconds or so. Multiple chairs and even the writing table are likewise adorned.

Adrianna collapses into one of the two empty chairs where she sets up court. She pats at the other one. "Sit down here, Stella.

"And would you gentlemen be so kind as to fetch the rest of them?"

This reminds me of nothing but a stage comedy. "What is this?"

"Well, Nayeli mentioned that you only had four dresses, and two of those were in the worst state of disrepair. One of those, the one we gave you, mind, was damaged beyond repair last night. Your undergarments are even poorer quantities and in worse reputations. So it was time." Alarms start ringing in my head like I am standing right in the church steeple, listening to the painfully loud sound of them striking the hour. My mouth twists into a grimace as I sit down. The viscountess continues, "I actually started this a couple of months ago. But, you have been such a stick in the mud about what we offered as a reward to you, we held off on this and only gave you the one dress—"

"And the poderabile. And the nursing. And paid my rent. And—"

"Yes, yes. All trifles."

"Trifles? Madam, are you insane? While your praise embarrassed me, I did endure it. Having a mother as cold as a whaler's feet, your approval did warm my own heart. But the gifts are outrageous in nature already."

"*Merde*," she says using a French curse word that has come into fashion of late, at least down near the dockside. "I daresay you saved us literally hundreds of thousands of dollars, if not perhaps more than a million. Henry could tell you much more accurately, but he didn't even raise an eyebrow when I suggested we outfit you in more appropriate attire. Honestly, woman, he was willing to buy you a home. That should show you just how high we hold you in esteem."

"I didn't do it directly for you—"

"I know. You've told me more than once. 'I wanted to save lives and prevent damage.'" She scoffs.

"Well, that is nothing but the truth."

"Even if we were just to give you a five percent reward based on the amount you saved us, it would amount to ten thousand dollars, at least."

"I'd rather just have you as friends rather than patrons."

"You have our friendship and more, darling. We'd never try to be anything else, but demon hang us if we wouldn't be unchristian if we didn't show at least our gratitude. I know it feels like we are showering you with gifts, but it is no more than your due, please."

I sit, locking eyes with her. Her green eyes take on the solidity of jade. Maybe I can wiggle out of all this with some of my dignity and self-respect intact. "I will acquiesce under one circumstance: that this ends it, once and for all. I will no longer be in your debt. I will be only your friend."

"Agreed, Stella. Now let's dig into these boxes. I'm eager to see you in what they contain."

As we while away the afternoon with me playing dress-up dolly, not a small part of my mind wonders if seeing me in various outfits isn't the ultimate reason for her largess. There is more clothing in these piles of boxes than I've ever owned in my entire life: dresses, blouses, and skirts, all from the most prestigious Spanish *modista*. I try one on. Adrianna has me spin around, comments before I take it off and move to the next. Nayeli is kept busy putting them away neatly. Petticoats, bloomers, chemises, a few brassieres, and even two corsets explode from the packages so that I have foundations for the expensive dresses.

It takes me a good half hour to get into the spirit of things, but soon I'm joking and laughing and have forgotten about someone trying to murder me. I've forgotten about the possibility of being dragged out to reinter an escaped demon. It is only my friends and the feel and swish of new fabric, all in bright colors and patterns. For this brief moment, I feel like the girl I was just before Aaron and I married—carefree and excited at what is to come.

#

At four bells, I feel resplendent in a brilliant blue dress with three layers in the skirt. The fabric is a vertical stripe pattern in a subtly darker blue color. The neckline and hems all carry gold lace. When topped with a matching blue hat sporting a white ostrich feather, the only time I've felt more attractive is when I climbed in bed, nude, with my husband for the very first time.

I've never had the wherewithal to go in for such frippery. But as someone else is footing the bill, I get the luxury of proving to myself, at least, that I'm a pretty woman. It's a morale boost. As an added bonus, I have foregone my iron underwear this evening as no one can possibly know where I am off to.

I guide the poderabile to the police station, hoping to find Antonio there. Inside the door, I find the duty sergeant booking in a middle-aged woman in her jugs. She isn't helping by sporting an excess of ardor.

"C'mon, Sarge. I'll make ye feelin' like a real man. I's gott'n the best t'warm yer baton. Lookie here." She lifts her skirts above her waist, exposing her legs all the way up to a bare bush that could use a scythe. Her clothes scream middle-class. If she remembers any of this in the morning, she will be scandalized with behavior shunned even by a two-bit streetwalker.

Using his nightstick across the desk, the sergeant brushes the skirts from her hands, allowing them to fall decently. "Wa's t'matter. I jus' wan' yer lovin', no' like tha' hussssban' o'mine."

"Ma'am," he says directly to me with a blush, "what can I do for you?"

"Sergeant, I don't mean to interrupt but is Inspector Guizzetti available?"

"Please come back. I'll have someone take you there immediately."

"Hey! Youse le' tha' floozy back 'ere. I's more purdy." She begins unbuttoning her dress as proof.

"Patrolman," the sergeant says to a passing constable, "please take this lady back to Inspector Guizzetti while I try to deal with this other one."

The woman's actions don't completely shock me. I've done the same or even worse for Karie, but not in public. But then again, that incident in the Commons where she diddled me under my dress probably qualifies. I had to bite my tongue each of the three times I crested the mountain to keep everyone around me from knowing what was happening. She'd made me lock eyes with a young gentleman sitting on the bench across the path from us. I'm sure he knew exactly what was taking place.

"Stella! I can handle it from here, Constable." The look in Antonio's eyes matches that of a demon fighting gamely not to be interred. It wars with the appraising look he gives me. After the policeman leaves, he closes the door and barks, "What are you doing here! You should be safely inside the Helmses' home."

Any show of contrition would give him the advantage. I will have nothing to do with that. Instead, I dive into why I'm here. "I got to thinking about who might be shooting at me."

"The very reason you should be somewhere safe!"

"Is not the constabulary a safe location?" He glares—one point for me.

"It is the trip between that matters, as you well know it."

I once again ignore his irritation. "As I was saying, I wondered if there were any relatives of the late, unlamented Baron Snowdonia that might be aggrieved at my having taken their inheritance."

The inspector purses his lips at me and says, "I don't think so, but I can check quickly enough." Antonio pulls out a folder with the baron's name emblazoned on it. Opening it, he flips through three pages before scanning down with a finger. "There is an umpteeumpth nephew three times removed that still lives in England who doesn't seem to know anything about his distant uncle. And Snowdonia has some remote relationship to the royal Hanover family lineage, but as far as I can tell neither knows or cares about the baron. Remember, his family was exiled from England some years ago. And the money is a pittance to the queen or her family."

"I wouldn't discount them so quickly. Royalty often has *amour propre* about anything they believe is in their purview, especially Victoria. That English *puta* would crawl into a sewer for a penny."

Antonio laughs. "I won't disagree with you. We'll look into it, but with all of the political tension, there aren't many channels toward England or back this way. I don't know of any way they could even get a message over here, and if they could, would they waste it on you? Oh, sorry. I didn't mean t—" His face falls as he realizes his gaff.

It is my turn to laugh. "That is alright, Inspector First," I say, emphasizing his title rather than his name. "I realize that I'm a small fish. I don't have a big target painted upon me like someone like, say, the prime minister does."

"Harrumph," he grunts and then changes the subject. "We did find usable fingerprints on the gun that shot you last night."

"Excellent. Whose were they?"

"That's the bad news. We haven't matched them to anyone yet. I had our fingerprint section up all night comparing them. We've tried all of Quarrels's known associates with no success. None of them were military snipers in any case."

"Have you tried the NPP?"

"Our file on them isn't nearly as complete as we'd like, but we will try it against those parasites next. Also, Lord Helms has allowed us to fingerprint all of his employees."

"All? Did they agree?"

"My reports thus far are that two of them quit rather than be printed. We are watching them closely. But this is going to take several days to make full comparisons."

"Well, it was worth a try."

"Don't give up yet, Stella. Our plodding methods often get results. If you will just stay home!"

"As I don't have a home to stay in, that would be rather difficult, Inspector."

He grins back in a way that a cat who is about to pounce on a mouse might. "Then I shall have to arrest you as a tramp or maybe even a trollop." One point for him. "That would keep you safe until court tomorrow."

"Dear Inspector, I have but one stop this evening before I return snug to the bed being provided graciously by the Lord and Lady Helms. I am to dine with one of Lord Helms's employees, Patty Smith, and her husband, Brian Smith. Mr. Smith works for the Ministry of Defense. Surely I can be safe in their hands?"

"Hmmm. Straight there?" I nod. "Straight back to the Helms Estate?"

"Antonio, I assure you that I value my own life. I will risk myself as little as possible. I wish nothing more than to survive to give testimony against John Quarrels."

"Then I will detain you no further, Stella. Please do be careful."

# # #

The Smith residence is a three-story brownstone home, modest for a civil servant and just opposite the Naval Yard in Chelsea. It bears the overly lived-in look that characterizes the barracks and housing of most military posts. It sits just a block away from the building labeled "Science of the Miraculous." The Smith's door proudly displays the acorn and stripes flag of the monarchy. Beneath it hangs a carved wooden sign, "Make Merry. Patty and Brian Smith."

I hear the chuffing of steam pumps, sounding vaguely the same as the poderabile, only with a slower, more forceful beat. Three of the noisy devices shoot water out of the drydock of a ship into the bay beyond.

I twist the doorbell, hearing the tinkle inside.

The door opens, and Patty all but launches into my arms, more a greeting for a lover than a friend she has seen recently. "Stella! Welcome." The bun of her flaming red hair and her lavender scent each tickle my nose.

"Nice to see you again."

She disengages with a kiss on my cheek. "Come in. Brian is just bursting at the seams."

"Why would your husband be so excited by my presence?"

"He wants to give you a tour of the Naval Yard. He is very proud of the work that he is doing and wants to show it off to someone new. And I'm sure he is going to like you, Stella. You are a very likable person."

Inside, the Smith home is as warm and inviting as any good home should be. It is clean and presentable but cluttered and lived in. This is in direct opposition to the museum that my mother lives in with every item in place, all the time, and where dust is turned away at the door like a beggar. There are no children's toys or pasteboard books lying about. The Smiths have not yet been so blessed. Patty once told me that, God willing, she wanted five or six.

Brian is as short and round as Patty is statuesque. They look like a meatball and a fork. His face is kind and gentle, and he has that quiet, unflappable presence of a librarian. Countering this are his mischievous gray eyes like those of a schoolboy dreaming up six different ways to glue your skirts to the chair. He takes his wife's hand and kisses the back.

"Not now, Brian. We have company," she whispers, turning to me with a smile. He desists his oral assault but keeps her hand in his, interlocking her fingers with his.

"Welcome, Mrs. Ochoa. Welcome again to our home."

"Thank you, Mr. Smith, but I'm just Stella. You do have a lovely home."

"You are so gracious, Stella. I'm so sorry I was unable to be available last time you visited us."

"You are quite the busy man, Mr. Smith. I totally understand. I'm glad I have the opportunity to meet with you this time."

"Oh, and if I have to call you Stella, then you must call me Brian. No formality is required here." He pats his wife's hand and smiles up at her. She smiles back but says nothing—an almost impossibility. Patty's daily form is that of a chatterbox.

"Thank you, Brian. I understand you are anxious to show me your work."

"Patricia told me of your inquiry about my job at the Ministry of Defense on your last visit. I thought it only polite to give you a quick tour."

"By all means, Brian. I'd love to see your boats."

"Ships, Stella. Boats are for day sailing, fishing, and travel along the coast. Ships are ocean-going vessels. Sorry, but it is a distinction that I feel is extremely important."

"My apologies, sir."

"None needed. I'm just trying to keep the lexigraphy correct. Dear, did you wish to accompany us?"

Patty speaks for the first time since we are all in the same room. "No, dearest. I have to make certain supper will be ready when you return."

"And will you, Stella, feel safe without any chaperonage?"

I giggle. "The last time I worried about that, I was knee-high to a grasshopper. And as a widow, I have no need to protect my reputation. I assure you it is quite sullied and worn."

Brian laughs deeply. "Then, in that case, Patricia, we will return in just a few minutes. After you, Stella," he says, motioning toward the front door.

He leads me across the road to railroad tracks. On them sits an ingenious vehicle looking like an oversized handcart. Two benches are fastened to the bed next to a mechanical drive box containing an earth spring. As an occupational hazard, I feel the unmistakable tension in it. The drive connects directly to the wheels via a gearing system that I don't completely follow.

Brian motions me up to the forward of the two benches, offering his hand as support. "It is quite safe," he says. I scamper up without his assistance or even concern.

"Looks a good deal safer than the poderabile," I say.

"Yes, Patricia has mentioned your marvelous car. But this device has an added feature," he says cryptically as he sits next to me. The benches look like they could easily hold three men across or two women in our bulky skirts.

Unlike the dual levers of my conveyance, Brian pushes a single lever, and we set off at a moderate clip that slowly increases speed until we outrace the nearby road traffic. "This vehicle comes close to perpetual motion. We expend energy to get moving, and then when we slow, it collects the energy. We call it motion vampirism, or MV for short. There are still losses, but it makes this an efficient mode of transport around the Naval Yard. We only have to wind it up about once a week."

"That is quite smart. So what do you do here? Patricia was very unclear with her remarks."

"All new ship designs are done in New Murcia with its more extensive harbor. It has more space for the massive construction programs the Royal Navy is about now. Boston Naval Yard, by contrast, is a refit station. I am the head of all naval ship conversions.

"As you know, most of our vessels are still wooden ships powered by sail. With the tensions with the damned-all British, we need to modernize our fleet. It is my job to quickly give new life to these older, sometimes tired ships."

"That sounds like an incredible responsibility."

"It is. No, please don't think I'm blowing my own horn. Unofficially, I believe war between the monarchy and the British, and therefore the French is a foregone conclusion. The striped pants brigade in the Foreign

Office still thinks they can make diplomacy work. By contrast, the Admiralty isn't going to wager the future of our monarchy upon the soft soap of wishful thinking. So, if war does come, we must have the naval strength to project force and aid our ally, Spain.

"The new vessels are nothing short of miraculous, but they will likely be few in number before the outbreak of war. These vessels," he says, waving his free hand at more warships than I've ever seen in one place, "and the ones waiting at anchorage, will be our primary force."

"What kinds of conversions are you making?"

"Well, there are the simple ones, like changing the cannons for rifled artillery and adding bunkerage for coal. And then there are the much more onerous ones, like adding a steam plant and installing a drive system. The latter one is the most tricky. We've tried paddlewheels as they don't impact the hull and are the fastest to make and install, but they are too bloody slow. With a decent wind, sailing ships run circles around them. So we've gone to a propeller-based drive system. It is non-trivial to build, modify the hull, and install."

"How so?"

"I'll show you. Here is the *Independence*. Just at the right stage for you to see what I'm talking about."

Brian gently slows down our speeding car. I feel the tension in the spring increasing as he does so. *Quite a good invention,* I think. Once stopped, Mr. Smith dismounts and walks us over to the edge of a tremendous oblong pit where I can see the bottoms of the boat, I mean ship. Two great holes have been opened at the back end of it below the normal level of where the water might reach up to. Metal plating and other doodads are being fastened into place.

"The holes the driveshafts are going to be placed through are quite obvious. We must shore up the damage we have done to the structure. Down in the bottom of the slip, you should see the two driveshafts that will be installed."

I see two long, metal toothpicks with each end mangled in some way. It isn't until I see the men walking beside them that I get the scope of their size. The toothpicks are nearly as thick as a man is tall. The flies crawling around the holes are men, not insects.

"Not only do we have to get them in place, but they have to spin without wobbling and not let seawater in. It is an enormous task, made more difficult in that each ship is different."

"This is quite an effort, Brian."

"We should head back now. Patricia won't want her dinner spoiled by it being overcooked."

"Definitely don't want her upset," I say with a smile.

Brian chatters about redesign time, how they employ three shifts of workers to modify as fast as possible, and more. As we head back to their home, he talks about the length of time it takes to bring in each vessel and empty the dry dock. He points to the ship directly across from their home. "That is the *Ice Maiden*. You see those three large pumps? They are emptying the water from the slip, a process that takes three to four days. We do have one dock that we can empty in a day, but most of these older slips take pumping for days, and we only have a small number of pumps."

"Why don't you—" I clamp my mouth shut. I don't know what I'm talking about. It is his job, not mine.

"Why don't I what, Stella?"

"Well, why not use witchcraft? If this is a major problem, I think I can speed it up for you...maybe. All you want is the water out, right?"

"Yes." He looks at me with his head tilted in confusion and skepticism. "How?"

"Why don't I try it and see what happens?"

He nods and leads me to the edge of the pit. It is like a bathtub about one-fifth full. "It's not like I can hurt a big old boat like this." Brian nods again. I can't tell if the set of his mouth is anger, consternation, or just stubbornness.

With a mental sigh, I admit to myself that this will take just about everything I have. I bend down and root around the brick to get to the earth beneath it. I manage to pinch just a tad. I bring it up to my tongue. I undo the laces on my boots and remove them along with my socks. Brian blushes and looks away.

"I'm sorry, Mr. Smith. I don't mean to embarrass you. This is large enough that I'm going to need a firm contact with the earth."

"Quite alright, Mrs. Ochoa. If you aren't feeling shame, then I should not be so squeamish. I just hope my wife is as forgiving."

I stand and twist my feet around for a good purchase on the earth. Standing still, I take a deep breath and let it out slowly. Like a concert conductor, I urge the ground in the pit to swell up. The mass resists in its weight and bulk. The sluggish seabed finally agrees and pushes upward.

I wrap the earth around the ship like the shell of a taco around the filling of the hull. Time has little meaning as I take on the countenance of the earth itself who, in a fast year, might move a quarter inch. We are instead moving with blazing speed. As the pit vanishes, my communion with the earth slips away.

I open my eyes and see that the *Ice Maiden* is no longer in water but in a cradle of stone. Mr. and Mrs. Smith both are looking on in wide-eyed wonder.

"Patty, when did you get here?"

"About two minutes ago. I was worried about you both and that infernal contraption of my husband's."

"Mrs. Ochoa, that was the most impressive thing I've ever seen!" Brian says, ignoring his wife's slur on his invention. "That ship is entombed! I don't know how we will ever get it back out."

I ease the rock and mud back down a few feet at a time. "Easy. But what I don't know is what will keep it upright if I put the pit back beneath it. Should I let the water back in?"

"No! Wait. Let me think," Brian says. "I'll call workers over, and we can shore it up as you lower the ground. You can do it slowly, right?"

"As slow as you want."

"Bugger me all to hell," he says in a fit of profanity. "Wait, if you can move earth, can you shape stone?"

"Yes."

"How about three, two-foot-wide stone cradles under the hull. It has to be stone, and it has to be a single piece, or it might fall over."

"No problem," I say, urging some of the granite beneath the seabed up to form the shapes he asked for. I continue to lower the ground. "Like that?"

"Stella. I understand you are without a job right now. Patricia told me." She nods.

"Yes."

"How would you like a job as...well, I don't know what we'll call you, but you will be essential to our efforts. Say yes. Be a patriot."

I can't think of any reason to say no. Work is work. "Yes, if we can come to terms."

"You just tell me what you want, and I'll make sure you get it."

The rest of the evening is a bust. After I manage to get my feet covered, with as much dignity as possible, I find the convivial air has been punctured by Brian's enthusiasm and energy. Patty's carefully planned meal had been left on the stove too long. We try to eat the roast beef, but it is like chewing on a horse's bit. The broccoli is gray and has no form to speak of. Something has gone wrong in each dish. Patty fusses and apologies, but it isn't her fault but rather mine, for opening my big mouth. Brian alternates between nonstop talking about the possibilities and staring off into space dreaming up the next idea. I don't think he eats a single bite and ignores the both of us when he is not talking.

Neither of my hosts seems interested in a quiet evening reading aloud by the fire so I make my excuses. I'm not sure whether to consider this a success or a failure.

8—Wednesday, May 9, 1888

"Repeat after me," says the bailiff. "By God and King Frederick the Second..."

Standing under the skylight in the darkly-paneled courtroom, I mimic him. "By God and King Frederick the Second..."

"I do solemnly, sincerely, and truly declare and affirm..."

Beads of sweat drip down my chest to be absorbed by my brand new brassiere. Standing here under the gaze of eleven good-and-true jurors, the judge, the attorneys, and a crowd of spectators has me nervous as a mouse trying to sneak across a cat show. The defendant, John Quarrels, didn't matter to me in the slightest other than as a reason to be here.

"I do solemnly, sincerely, and truly declare and affirm..."

"That the evidence I give shall be the truth, the whole truth, and nothing but the truth."

I've faced down reigning lords of hell, but none of them made me sweat as much as being about to testify in a courtroom. I've never had as much as a citation, even for drunken walking. "That the evidence I shall give shall be the truth, the whole truth, and nothing but the truth," I vow, giving John Quarrels the only look I have since his arrest.

"State your name and occupation for the court," the prosecuting attorney says, not as a question but rather a demand.

"Stella Edwina Ochoa. I..." I stammer as I remember I am actually not gainfully employed at the moment. "I am a member of the *Dos Campanas* hellfighter team."

The crown's prosecutor, Juan Ortega, stands up. I never understand how those silly perukes manage to stay on their heads as they move around. It looks more like a poodle perched on a loaf of bread than a wig.

"Mrs. Ochoa, do you carry a title under the Coven of Massachusetts?"

"Yes, sir. I have been awarded the title Mistress Witch by that organization," I say. I didn't share that I hadn't sought the title. I'd been warned to answer the questions and provide little else.

"And how long have you practiced witchcraft?"

"I've held a practicing witches certificate for seven years." Standing in one place without fidgeting is not easy. Thankfully, I wore my comfortable boots, not one of the new pairs so at least my feet aren't completely unhappy with me.

"And how many of those years have you been a hellfighter?"

"Almost all of them, *Señor* Ortega."

"Please try to be more precise, Mrs. Ochoa."

"I joined the *Dos Campanas* approximately two months after completing the practical witch test and being issued my license." That had been a wild buggy ride of a summer. Between my early failure at keeping Gazzunreep ensnared, to healing from the burns he inflicted upon me, to retesting for my license, to following Carlos around like a puppy, I racked up some serious karma debt.

"Excellent. So after seven years in trapping escaped demons, would you consider yourself to be an expert on demons?"

"Objection, Your Honor," says Grismire Pollux, the defense lawyer of John Quarrels. His voice is high and just this side of being screechy. It makes me flinch. "No foundation laid for Mrs. Ochoa being a credible judge of demon expertise, especially that of her own."

"Sustained," the judge rules from his seat eight feet off the floor.

"Very well, would the Coven of Massachusetts consider you an expert on demons?"

"Objection. The witness can't testify as to the beliefs of other persons or organizations."

"Sustained."

Mr. Ortega didn't miss a beat. "Mrs. Ochoa, can you tell me how many demon reinternments you have done?"

"I've never kept an accurate count. Approximately seven a year, maybe eight until this last year. In this last year, at least twenty, maybe thirty."

"So, at the low end, you are saying at least sixty, maybe as many as a hundred."

"Yes, sir."

"Do you know all of the hellfighters within the monarchy?"

"No, sir, but I do know many of them and have knowledge of most of the rest, on the east coast at least," I offer.

"How many witches have interred more demons?"

"Objection. No foundation," Quarrels's attorney interjects.

"Overruled," the judge says.

"Can I answer now?" I ask.

"Yes, Mrs. Ochoa," the judge reassures me.

"Maybe fifteen other hellfighters have interred more demons than I have."

"Out of how many?" the prosecutor asks.

"I know personally of fifty or more hellfighter teams on the east coast."

"At six members per team? Or about three hundred hellfighters?"

"Yes, sir."

"So only fifteen other hellfighters have more internments than you have?"

"Correct."

"So only five percent. Wouldn't that make you an expert?"

"Objection. Your Honor—"

"I'll withdraw the question. Mrs. Ochoa, in your own words, can you tell the court how you came to suspect a human agency in the release of demons in the early part of this year?"

"Yes, sir. Earlier this year, I received information that several escaping demons were installed by the same witch."

"Some, not all?" the prosecutor probes.

"That is correct, sir. As my resources were limited, I chose to investigate only the installations of witches who'd had multiple failures."

"And were those of the defendant, John Quarrels, within that list?"

"Yes, sir."

"How many demons had escaped his protections?"

"Thirteen." It is hard not to look at the jury as they and the gallery above us murmur and shift in their seats.

"Thirteen?"

"Objection. Asked and answered."

The judge is quick to reply. "Sustained. Be careful, Mr. Ortega."

"My apologies to the court, Your Honor. What did you do next, Mrs. Ochoa?"

"I obtained permission from home and business owners to examine all of the other demon entrapments by the defendant."

"And what did you find?"

"Three installations contained salt contamination."

"And what is salt contamination?"

"If salt is placed into the binding circle chalk, over time, the salt crystals will suck the moisture out of the air. This muddies the chalk and eventually breaks the ring and the spell, allowing the demon to escape."

"Was there anything special about the installations of the three that were contaminated?"

"Objection. How can the defendant define special? Pink chalk might have been used, or even done in block letters rather than cursive," the defense attorney argues.

"A witch of Mrs. Ochoa's experience, in the top five percent of her peers, would know the difference between normal and special or different," the prosecutor argues back.

"Gentlemen!" the judge barks. "I will allow the question only if the counselor lays a foundation for the term special."

I'm beginning to feel like a badminton birdie.

"Thank you, Your Honor. Mrs. Ochoa, can you describe what was different between the installations that were contaminated and those that weren't?"

"The contaminated sites all were in high profile locations."

"What do you mean by high profile?"

"Most demon escapes happen where very few people outside of the block or so where the hellspawn escapes would notice or care. The places that were contaminated couldn't help but be noticed by the entire city."

"Since there were only three, can you list them?"

"Young's Hotel, the Boston Opera House, and Boston General Hospital." The mumble that races through the people in the court is palpable enough it doesn't even need to be heard to be understood. The image of the carnage of these three great institutions being torn to shreds by a demon is enough to cause the ruckus.

"The court will come to order," the judge says, banging his gavel. The crowd does quiet as the sensational nature of my claim settles in their minds.

The prosecuting attorney picks back up again: "And what did you do with that information?"

I swallow hard. "I informed the constabulary, who set a trap for the defendant. We created an opportunity for him to contaminate a high-profile site while we watched the installation."

"And what happened?"

"The defendant summoned a demon and then polluted the protective circle with salt."

"Objection. Calls for speculation."

"I'll rephrase. What happened after the defendant summoned the demon at this location?"

"I saw the defendant sprinkle salt on the chalk of the binding pentagram."

"Objection. The witness is offering speculation on the substance," Pollux says.

"Sustained."

"Mrs. Ochoa, do you recognize this plaster cast formerly marked as Crown Exhibit One?"

"Yes, Mr. Ortega. It is the cast we made of the salt contamination of the chalk."

"And did you check the chalk before it was delivered to the defendant and just before the summoning?"

"Yes, I did."

Mr. Ortega looks over at the defense table. "And was there any salt in those supplies?"

"No, sir."

"And there is *salt* contamination in this cast."

"Yes, sir," I offer, emphasizing my affirmative.

"So what happened after you saw the defendant sprinkle the white crystals over the spell ring?"

"The constables took the defendant under arrest."

"Thank you, Mrs. Ochoa. No further questions."

"Mr. Pollux, your witness," the judge confirms.

"Mrs. Ochoa, you say you have held a practicing witchcraft license for over seven years. How many demon installations have you performed?"

"Two."

"Only two?"

"Yes, sir. I am not an installer."

"Were both of your installations successful?"

"No, sir. The fir—"

"No is sufficient, Mrs. Ochoa. Did either of your installations escape?"

"Yes, sir. As I tried—"

"And so you are a poor installer, then."

"Objection. My learned colleague is being argumentative."

"Sustained," the judge intoned.

"I'll rephrase, Your Honor. You don't have an exceptional record as an installer, then?"

"No, sir." I bite my tongue because I know anything I say in my defense will just get cut off.

"Your elevation to the rank of Mistress Witch. Did you put forth an application to make this happen?"

His question confuses me. So far, everything at trial has been obvious and straightforward, as a thief cutting a purse for the coin. This seems off-topic. "No, I didn't."

"Then who put your name forth?"

"I don't know, sir."

"Oh, come now. Didn't your own mother pin you to your new rank?"

"Yes, she did."

"So, isn't she the one that put forth your name?"

"Objection. Asked and answered," Ortega says.

"Your Honor, I'm asking the witness to answer on further reflection."

"I'll allow it," the judge says. "But be on your guard, Mr. Pollux. This is His Majesty's court, not a debate club where you can define to your own rules."

"Yes, Your Grace."

"The witness may answer the question," the judge orders me.

"Sir, Judge, I have no idea who put forth my name for my rank."

"Your Honor," Mr. Pollux says, "I would like to introduce Defense Exhibit One, the sworn testimony of Senior Mistress Witch Anya Lopez. It states that the witness's mother put forth her application."

Pollux hands the sheaf of papers to the prosecutor. He gives it a cursory glance. "No objection, Your Honor." The defense attorney hands the documents to the bailiff.

"It is so entered into evidence."

"Now, Mrs. Ochoa, doesn't the Coven of Massachusetts handbook on witchcraft standards require testing to obtain the status of Mistress or Master Witch?" the defense attorney asks.

"I believe it does."

"Did you test for that grade?"

"No, sir, I did not." I steal a look at Ortega, but he is quietly writing notes on a pad in front of him as if he has no care in the world. Well, he isn't up here getting abused by this pompous arse. To my surprise, Pollux doesn't take it any further. He instead changes the subject.

"Let's now go to your statement about receiving information that several escaping demons were installed by the same witch. Who gave you that information?"

"Viscount Henry Helms."

"The owner of one of the largest demon power companies in the world?"

"Yes, sir."

"And was Lord Helms under considerable pressure in the news because of the demon escapes?"

"Yes, sir."

"So he could have given you false information."

I glower at the man. "Yes, sir, but—"

"So it is possible you could have been looking at the wrong man."

"I did not have the origins of the information Lord Helms shared with me. I was operating as if that was the gospel. So, if I was given bad data, yes, I could have been looking at the wrong man."

"Is Lord Helms your friend?"

I actually start at the question. What in God's creation does this have to do with anything? "I'm sorry, sir?"

"It is a perfectly simple question," Mr. Pollux continues. "Is Lord Helms your friend?"

"I think you would have to ask him that question. I am friendly with him."

"Are you not living with him and his wife at this time?"

"Yes, I am, but that is—"

"So, he is a friend enough to beg a bed from."

"Yes, sir," I say through gritted teeth.

"So, shall we turn our attention to the actual event my client is charged with?"

"As you will, sir," I say.

"You say a trap was laid for the defendant?"

"Yes, sir."

"Where?"

"Miss Taylor's residence."

"Miss Karie Taylor?"

"Yes," I say, trying to follow the advice to keep my answer short.

"Is Miss Taylor a friend?"

"Yes, sir."

"Is she not Daring Karie, Boston's most infamous prostitute?"

"Objection," Ortega interjects through the buzz in the court. "This is direct examination and has no basis."

"Mr. Pollux?" the magistrate asks.

"It goes directly to credibility, my lord. If the witness will consort with whores—"

"My lord! At best, this is argumentative, and at worst, it is slanderous."

The judge leans over the edge of his high bench before answering. "I have to agree with the prosecution. Please drop this line, counselor."

"Yes, lord," Pollux says calmly as he knows he's already made the point he wanted. In the minds of the jury, he's paired my name with streetwalking.

"Who chose the place of Miss Taylor as the trap location?"

"I believe it was my suggestion, sir."

"And why did you suggest Miss Taylor's residence?" he says, turning his back to me to get something from the desk.

"As I mentioned earlier, she is a friend, and I felt certain she would oblige."

Pollux spins and snaps off his next question. "So why would anyone risk releasing a demon in an ordinary residence?"

"Well, Miss Taylor is anything but normal, sir. As you've already pointed out, she is a famous courtesan." I do my best to elevate my friend's status in the eyes of the court. Courtesan is a so-much-nicer word than whore.

"Ahem," he says, looking away in fake embarrassment. A buzz of moral disapproval runs through the crowd.

"So you obtained permission and lay in wait like a spider."

"We watched, sir," I offer, trying to remove the connotation of the man's meaning out of it.

"And while you watched, you say that you saw the defendant in some way damage the spell circle?"

"Yes, Mr. Pollux. He sprinkled salt on it."

"So you say. How far away were you?"

"I was hiding thirty feet away."

"In a cellar?"

"Yes, sir."

"In the dim lighting, you can tell salt from sugar or chalk?"

"No, sir," I reply with a tight jaw.

"Then how do you know my client put the salt across the chalk?"

"No other possibility exists."

"So let me see if this is correct, Mrs. Ochoa. You, someone who can't accurately summon a demon who can remain bound, whose mother got her promoted, who is a friend of the person most likely to gain from a guilty conviction of my client, and who is best friends with a trollop, want the jury to believe that you, and you alone, can speak to the fact that my client tampered with the demon imprisonment?"

"Objection, my lord. The defense attorney is making closing statements. It is argumentative and insulting to the witness."

"I'm only posing a hypothetical as allowed for within the rules of examination, Your Honor."

The judge is silent for a moment as he takes a sip from a glass. "I sustain the objection. Mr. Pollux, that supposed hypothetical is argumentative, and I'll caution you for your behavior."

"I beg the court's apologies," the defense attorney says with a bow. His tone doesn't sound as if it carries any genuine contrition. "Your Honor, at this time, we are done with this witness."

"Does the crown have any more questions?"

"Yes, my lord, we do."

"Your witness then," the judge says.

"Mrs. Ochoa, did you seek the rank Mistress Witch?"

"No, Mr. Ortega, I did not."

"And what caused the Coven of Massachusetts to award you this title?"

"I am not privy to their decision process so, I don't know," I offer. "I have my own surmise, but from the point of view of the law, I can't say."

Ortega says, "Your Honor, I'd like to introduce Crown Exhibit Ten. It is the sworn statement of Elijah Beckworth, Senior Master Witch of the Coven of Massachusetts. It states that the witness's elevation was granted for the singlehanded return of a ranking demon prince to hell."

"No objection," Pollux says as if it has no meaning.

"It is so entered."

Ortega turns back and asks me, "So, you accomplished something much more difficult than the tests for senior witches to obtain your position?"

I prevent myself from giggling. "It was difficult, sir, but I have never taken the test so I cannot say for certain."

"Did you ask your mother to put forward your name for your new rank?"

"No, sir. I never sought rank of any kind."

The crown's prosecutor changes his stance as he looks over his notes. "Can you describe your two attempts at summoning a demon?"

"Yes, sir. Both times I was still under instruction. The first was my solo attempt to gain my practicing license. I wasn't ready, but my proctor allowed me to call it and fail." I do not show them the scars. "She had to send the demon back lest it escape."

"And the second?"

"It was my reexamination for my certification. It went quite well. I summoned a low-ranked demon who is still under imprisonment as a power source in the Boston Public Library."

"Why have you never done further demon summoning?"

How to answer a question that even I haven't decided in my mind. "I just don't like to do so."

"So it is not lack of skill?"

"No, sir."

"I'd turn your attention to your friendship with Lord Helms. Were you friends with him before you saw the defendant contaminate the chalk in Crown Exhibit One?"

"No, sir."

"But you now have the friendship of a viscount as well as that of a lady of negotiable virtue?" The stir in the crowd is minimal.

"Yes."

"And does either affect your ability to determine salt contamination?"

"No, sir."

"The crown is completed with this witness, Your Honor."

"Anything more, Mr. Pollux?"

"Only one more point, Your Honor, if I may. Mrs. Ochoa, did you receive a reward from Lord Helms for your actions?"

"Yes, sir."

"A substantial one?"

"It wasn't monetary. It was a vehicle. I would say it was substantial."

"Did you know about the reward before you aided him?"

I think about this for a moment. "The viscount did mention that if we were successful he would be grateful, but he didn't mention a vehicle or even coin."

"Thank you. We are done."

"Last chance, Mr. Ortega?" the judge asks.

"No, Your Grace. I suggest the witness be excused."

"It is so ordered. Thank you for your testimony, Mrs. Ochoa," the judge says. "Court recesses for a fifteen-minute necessary break."

# # #

"Read all about the trial of the Demon Killer!" calls out a huckster on the steps of the courthouse as I rush outside for a deep breath of fresh city air after my ordeal. For as clean and truthful as the crown court is supposed to be, I feel like I need a bath after escaping the building. The defense attorney should be boiled in used pig fat and seasoned with molten tar. Infuriating. Perhaps it is a necessary evil, but I feel as if I were on trial for my own freedom.

"Good job, Mrs. Ochoa," says Juan Ortega as he walks up behind me.

"Good God almighty. You do this for a living? This is more stressful than fighting a demon."

"In some ways, it is exactly like fighting a demon. But in this, as in your skill with fighting hellspawn, you were exceptional."

"I certainly didn't feel exceptional. That bloody nonsense about my mother getting me my rank and Karie being a whore," I say, spitting on the ground. In the past, such behavior would have gotten me slapped by my mother for being unladylike.

Juan chuckles. "Yes, the defense sometimes goes after irrelevancies. But you were convincing and honest. The jury heard the sincerity of your words."

"Doesn't everyone give honest testimony to the crown?"

"No, Mrs. Ochoa, they don't. They lie. They cheat. They contradict themselves. On the whole, those brave and true citizens the crown has asked to make a verdict will usually perceive the truth of any given matter."

"So how much longer before the trial is over?"

"Actually, and primarily because of your testimony, I've been given overtures from the defendant that he may wish to change his plea to guilty. For that and giving up some damning information that may get us to those who ordered the demon escapes, he would get a lighter sentence."

Part of me wonders if that would include the president of the Coal Syndicate, Bruce Jasperson. "So what punishment would Quarrels receive?"

"That is open to negotiation, but based on my experience, I'd say ten years hard labor. Maybe as many as thirty, but that will depend on who he gives up to the crown."

I think of all of the deaths and the mass of destruction caused by the demons Quarrels released. "It isn't enough."

"I've been doing this job for thirty years, Mrs. Ochoa. It is never enough. But this isn't about revenge or even an eye for an eye; it is about restitution to society. Sometimes it works, and sometimes it doesn't."

"It still isn't enough."

"You are preaching to the converted, Mrs. Ochoa."

# # #

My room in the Helms Estate is a peaceful place to read a novel. I'm safe from marauding assassins, defense attorneys, and over-zealous policemen. I need something to clear my head after the morning's abuse. Stevenson's *Kidnapped* is washing the foul taste from my thoughts.

There is a knock on my doorframe. "Ma'am?" Nayeli's voice comes from the same direction.

I put the book into my lap. "Yes, Nay. What is it?"

"There is a gentleman caller for you."

"A gentleman?"

"Yes, ma'am. Your caller from the other night."

"The one taking me to the theatre or the one that put a bullet in my buttocks?" I say with a smile.

"Ma'am?" Nayeli giggles. Manuel has returned. Not completely a surprise.

"I'm just teasing you and making fun of myself, Nay. Tell the gentleman I will be down presently."

# # #

"Mr. Gomez y Ruiz," I say, offering my hand.

"Mrs. Ochoa, it is a delight to see you again," he says, bowing over my hand and kissing the knuckles. A shiver runs up my arm and lodges itself in my bosom. He makes me wish I'd not foresworn relationships. Maybe just a dalliance? But then there is always that chance of becoming with child.

"And what can I do for you on this beautiful afternoon, sir?"

"I have just learned that a carnival has come to town." He hands me a gaudy orange flyer for Otto Schmitt's Spectacular Amusement and Freak Show. "Our theatre trip was rudely interrupted. I wondered if you would do me the honor of accompanying me to this show tomorrow night?"

Traveling entertainment shows are a new fad, and I've yet to see one. "Yes, I would enjoy that, sir."

"Shall I pick you up at six then, Mrs. Ochoa?"

"I'll be delighted to receive you then."

"Very well, then. Until the morrow."

# # #

"I hear your testimony today went very well," Henry says as he spears some pot roast. The beef is so tender I have difficulty picking up a piece without it falling apart. I swallow the rest of the honey-glazed carrot I'd popped in my mouth before answering. The delicious fare my hosts provide makes me eat enough that I worry about buttoning my dress in the mornings.

"I've never been so uncomfortable in my life," I say before doing a double-take. "My lord, how did you know that?"

Lady Helms smiles at me over her wine glass but looks to her husband for an answer.

"Assuming that I didn't read it in the afternoon papers, I did happen to testify some short time after you did."

I guess my mind has been numb with the events of the day. I offer an intelligent, "Oh. That would make sense."

"But neither is how I came about it. The judge recessed early so I had afternoon tea with the prosecutor. He mentioned that there is a deal in the works for Quarrels to change his plea to guilty for a reduced sentence. That and provide evidence against other people. According to Mr. Ortega, the scum threw a couple of names around just as a teaser but says he has two names that will rock the entirety of the monarchy." Lord Helms looks as calm as I've ever seen him. Given that when I first met him, his business was being sabotaged and falling apart around him, I'd say he deserves to relax just a bit.

I twist my mouth into a frown. I hate that as a murderer, Quarrels has any leverage at all. "I will await his pronouncements and more arrests with all the eagerness of a willing bride."

Nayeli is refilling her mistress's glass as she snorts, trying to cover up a laugh. Adrianna gives her a stern look that shoos the young woman from the room.

"Sarcasm doesn't become you, Stella," Adrianna offers.

"Oh, yes it does," I counter. "That is about all I am—witchcraft and sarcasm."

"Hooey," she retorts. It's the closest I've heard her come to profanity. It gives me pause. Henry jumps into the awkward pause.

"I have one other bit of news." He holds up a telegram sheet. "I have a sale price agreement for the brick factory. I got him down to twelve thousand, five hundred. He wouldn't budge lower."

I can feel tension forming in my shoulders as they creep upward. "That's a lot of money."

Adrianna jumps in. "Dear, do we have to go over this again?"

I put up my hands in defense. "Please, no. I understand it intellectually, but emotionally I am still trying to cope."

"Tell your emotions on this to go to sleep, Stella."

"I agree," Henry adds. "I've done many a business deal. This one is rock solid. I wouldn't hesitate to put my own money down. In fact, why don't you borrow from us instead of going to a bank?"

My hesitancy evaporates, and I bark, "No! I'll do it myself, thank you." *Bloody meddling people.*

I slide into something of a sulk as I mull over how in *el infierno* I would convince tightfisted bankers to loan me over twelve thousand dollars. I don't taste the rest of my meal. I don't actually read the evening paper that says the pope will be arriving on the eighteenth.

After saying my "good nights" to my hosts, I walk in a daze up the stairs. As I change into my nightclothes, I think about the insanity of the day. After finally drifting off, I even dream of demonic financiers waving banknotes under my nose and yanking them away before I can grab ahold.

9—Thursday, May 10, 1888

My head throbs as I wake up. I feel like a vise has decided that my temples are its new home. Sand crusts the corners of my eyes like someone tried to cement them shut. I manage to sit up. Cupping my chin with my palms prevents movements that my skull interprets only as an attempt to rip it off my shoulders. I remember drinking past my limit by more than two glasses of burgundy.

The pale light coming through the curtains proclaims it is morning, but I can't guess within four hours what time it actually is. My dreams hadn't allowed a restful night's sleep. I even remember at one point signing away my soul for the money to buy that brick factory.

The pressure in my bladder is driving me to feats of superhuman performance. With a grimace, I stand and slip on a dressing gown and slippers. Making my way to the water closet, the house is mercifully silent until the hall clock chimes. I have never come so close to smashing a timepiece as in that very moment. Only the fact that it would make more sound than suffering through the rings it emits saves its physical being. I instead opt to put my fingers into my ears to muffle the infernal racket.

"Jesus, Mary, and Joseph," I mutter until after the seventh chime it desists.

After watering the dragon, I stand before the washbasin and look into the mirror. Bloodshot eyes, hair that would make Medusa proud, and crusty bits around my mouth greet me. "*¡Dios mío!*" Probably a good thing I'm not in a relationship. Anyone I was sleeping with would have run for the hills upon one look at me.

Inside the cabinet the washbasin sits on, I find a bottle labeled "Mr. Trawley's Tincture of Willow Bark." I uncork it and take a long draw. As bitter as it is, I know it will begin to ease my head and other aches.

With reluctance, I sponge myself off and trundle back to my room to get dressed. The latter isn't as easy as it used to be. Not long ago, when I had only three or four outfits, the choice of wearing the least threadbare one is easy. Now, with a chifforobe full of dresses, skirts, and blouses gifted to me by my hosts, it isn't half as easy.

"What should I wear to beg for a loan?" I mutter to myself, my fingers dancing over the fine fabrics. I decide on a conservative blue skirt with a cream-colored blouse bearing a bluebird print. My hair needs to be up so I braid it and make a coil, pinning it in place at the back of my head with a whalebone *peineta*.

I hustle down to the front door to find Mikey standing out in the cold wind. I'm pleased to see her in the stout overalls, a heavy coat, and mittens I'd yesterday sent her to buy. "Come inside, Mikey."

"Thank you, miss, and thank you for the new duds. I feel like royalty." As little as I know about her background, she just might. I decide not to press the point.

"I don't have much for you today—"

"Miss Stella, did you hear the news 'bout that there damned Demon Killer?"

"The one in the paper?"

"Yes, ma'am. The one you told the magistrate about in court. He be killed last night."

"How did you learn that?"

"Every huckster be yelling 'bout it."

Out of the corner of my eye, I catch Bastogne moving across the hall. "Bastogne?"

"Yes, Miss Stella," he says, changing direction.

"Has the morning paper arrived?"

"Yes, ma'am. I have it right here. I was going to put it on the breakfast table."

"May I see it for a moment?"

He hands it over with his white gloves as if the rag is the jeweled Scepter of India. "Will there be anything more?"

"No, Bastogne. I'll put the paper on the table when I'm through."

"As you wish, miss." I barely hear him as I am drinking in the headline.

"Demon Killer Murdered!" screams the headline that takes up the majority of the paper above the fold. Ignoring my charge, I dive into the article. "John Quarrels, awaiting the second day of his trial for the release of multiple demons, was found dead in his jail cell at four thirty this morning. A rolled-up prison bed sheet was found around the victim's neck. A detective inspector at the scene says they have reason to believe that this was not a suicide." I read on, but it is more about the trial yesterday than more information about his death.

"Widow Stella Ochoa, Mistress Witch, testified clearly and strongly in court today against the defendant. She withstood several determined attempts by the defense to impugn her integrity and bring into question her renowned reputation as a witch. Her evidence alone would have put John Quarrels behind bars for many decades had he not been slain." A few paragraphs later, I read, "Viscount Henry Helms testified for the crown. His acerbic tone toward the accused was quite noticeable. His Lordship proves his noble birth by providing his evidence with a crisp sense of its veracity. Upon cross-examination, Lord Helms's responses often caused the court to dissolve into mirth. Still, to this reporter, it denigrates the solemnity of the crown's system of justice." I chuckle to imagine Henry's vitriol for the defense attorney's impertinent questions.

But now, I direct my thoughts toward my own predicament and how this might play into it. Who killed Quarrels? What does that mean about the assassin who is targeting me? Why did Quarrels have to die? These questions and many more race through my head. Whatever the answers are, unlike the assurances I have from Inspector Guzzetti, I no longer feel confident that I'm protected now that I've testified.

"Alright, Mikey, my plans have just changed a bit. I want you to go to Paula Simpson's. She is a seamstress on Portland Street. Do you know her?"

"No, Stella."

"She is catawampus from the American Hotel. Her sign is a needle, bobbin, and thimble. I want you to tell her to let out all of the outer clothes I'm having her make by half an inch at the bust, waist, and hips. Make her understand that I want the underclothing to remain at the original size."

"Yes, Stella. Is that all?"

"I think that will do for today, Mikey. Thank you."

Making my way to the dining room, I smell bacon and pancakes. My stomach rumbles. *How prosaic. Food.*

I slide into a chair in the big dining room, thinking how absurd its opulence and service considering that I still have no job and no home.

"Is that the newspaper, Stella?"

"Yes, Henry. Here you are."

"And what are your plans today, Stella?" Lady Helms asks.

"They have changed radically upon reading the headline."

"Oh?" Adrianna says. Henry slides the morning news to his wife. "This is good, isn't it? The trial can stop. The guilty have been punished." My mouth hangs open as I stare at Adrianna in disbelief.

"Dear, you've oversimplified the problem. I don't disagree that the scum deserved to die, but think of what his murder means."

"Conspiracy," she says after just a few moments.

"Exactly. And a brazen one at that," Henry says. "To kill a prisoner in the middle of the constabulary takes balls of iron."

"Henry! We don't need to use that sort of language."

"My apology, Adrianna. It is true, but I should have chosen a better phrase. Be that as it may, Quarrels must have known something and was about to talk."

"I agree," I add. "And that means I probably should continue to be on my guard."

"I would think so!" Adrianna snaps.

"And it probably warrants another visit to Inspector Guzzetti." The statement elicits a silence from my hosts. Henry looks pensive. His wife is trying hard not to purse her lips and failing.

The hush continues for several moments before Henry breaks it with, "I should get to work. Dearest, have a pleasant day." Adrianna smiles at Henry. "And Stella, be safe."

"Of that, you can be assured, m'lord."

"I should be getting to the greenhouse. Would you like to come in and help me, Stella?"

Now I'm torn. I love tending plants. It is almost the exact opposite of the violence of demon fighting. The green calm is an anodyne to my soul. And I do enjoy the vicountess's company. But, on the other hand, I very much need to find out what hasn't been reported in the paper about Quarrels. My brain dredges up a decision. It can wait.

"I'd love to, Adrianna, if you would let me finish breaking my fast."

"But of course. I'll go make certain I have a second apron for you. We wouldn't want to get your pretty things mussed."

My temporization is to give me time to read the paper. I need more than just a quick skim of the pertinent facts. I delve into it only to find there is no additional information in the Quarrels's article that I find worthy of reading. I let my questions lapse at the next headline, which the local news surprisingly trumps. "Ten Days to Pope's Arrival—Boston First."

I've been looking forward to attending mass delivered by his holiness. That he is stopping in Boston before his meeting with the King bodes ill for Archbishop Mrak. That worthy's proclamation that Irish souls are not to be the same as others is in direct contravention of Pope Leo's orders. I am expecting the pope to deliver an ecumenical tongue-lashing. Following that will surely be a public apology by a penitent archbishop.

Nayeli doesn't interrupt me but fills the toast rack and departs. Setting aside the paper, I take a piece of bread and absently butter it. After some strawberry preserves, I nibble on toast as my mind does the same to the death of the prisoner. There are no new revelations. I daub the crumbs from the corner of my mouth with a napkin and set out for the conservatory.

#

The morning passes agreeably in the summer-like warmth of the glasshouse, with Adrianna and me transplanting basil and cucumber seedlings into larger pots. We chat about nothing of consequence, assiduously avoiding dead prisoners, assassins, or even the viscountess's attraction to me (and vice versa).

Yes, I can be dense when it comes to romance, but I'm not oblivious to multiple signs wagged in my face. Her vexatious countenance every time I even mentioned a man, much less go to see one, is more than a hint. She also dotes on every word I utter, and she glances at my skirt hem in the hope that I might flash an ankle. The flush on her pale skin as I tried on all of those clothes, or even more when I was taking them off the other morning, gave me the final clue. I guess I only have to be slapped about the face with a wet fish two or three times before I catch on to the obvious.

But her attentions are at best an infatuation. It must be. What of her husband? They are a couple consecrated together before God. I can think of much better ways to rack up sin against my soul. At the same time, I can't deny the way my heart beats faster when she is near me. I'm not sure what draws me more, her ability to boss her household without losing her femininity, her font of compassion, her quick intelligence, or maybe I'm so shallow that I can only fantasize about kissing her flawless skin and stroking her blond hair.

Get thee to a nunnery, I think. For now, I'll escape by performing another task. We are just finishing the cucumbers. "Adrianna, I've enjoyed this," I say, taking off my gloves, "but I really need to be getting on to my errands for the day, not the least of which is finding gainful employment."

She sketches a pout on her face cute enough that I just want to kiss it off. "I understand, Stella. Have a good day. Will we see you for dinner?"

"God willing, and the creek don't rise," I say with a smile. "Oh, may I borrow Tommy for a couple of hours?"

"Certainly, Stella. It will give me some peace and quiet to have that noisy rapscallion out of here," she jests.

"Thank you, m'lady. With your permission, I'll take my leave."

"I'm not the queen, Stella. Just do be careful."

"Yes, mum," I say with a curtsey before scampering out of the hothouse before she can throw something at me.

In my room, a twisted pile of iron bar sits in the wardrobe where I've left it out of the way. I rub my fingers over the dark surface, feeling the rough of the metal. Its eagerness to bend into some new form jumps up in my mind. I slip off my blouse and my skirt and lay them neatly on the bed. I pick up the ferrous metal and wrap the mass around my waist. It twists and squirms, forming and reforming until it creates the coil of bands that is my first line of defense. I urge the strips to cinch firmly about my middle.

If I have to wear a corset, I might as well get its benefits. This time I don't stop at my bosoms but rather bring it all the way up to my neck. I make sure that the neck of the armor is left loose around my throat to make it easier to breathe, even if inflating my chest isn't much of an option underneath my breastplate. Redressing over the top of it, I check myself in the mirror. The only difference I can see from before is that my natural endowments don't budge, not even like they would if captured under my stiffest brassiere.

"That will have to do," I mutter to myself before heading out to the stable.

I find Tommy grooming the Helmses' horses.

"Tommy, pull out the poderabile. We are taking a trip."

"We, ma'am?"

"I have the Lady Helms's leave to take you with me. So, yes, we."

# # #

"So what do you know, Antonio?" I ask after being shown to his office. I don't even make a pretext of pleasantries. Tommy stands respectfully behind me.

"I assume you are asking about Quarrels?"

"No, I'm talking about the pope's visit—of course I'm talking about Quarrels."

Behind his desk, Antonio shakes his head and leans back in his seat. His rumpled suit and the dark circles under his half-lidded eyes say more than anything about his mental state. "Honestly, Stella, I haven't the barest clue."

"But it wasn't suicide?"

"Not a chance. First, the ligature wasn't fastened to anything. His fingernails are broken off with blood on the sheet where he tried to claw it off. If that isn't enough, there is a nasty bump on Quarrels's head. The coroner says he's rarely seen such a savage blow. As for the murder itself, I have a motive, but that's about it."

"Motive?"

"Yes, he was about to turn crown's evidence on someone—"

I interject with, "Jasperson. He was going to give evidence on Jasperson."

"Possible," Detective Guzzetti continues, "but unless we can catch the killer, there is no way we will know for sure. Quarrels never said the name of the ringleaders."

"Do you have any suspects for the murder?"

"Nary a one. He was alone in his cell. He had no visitors. I don't have the foggiest of who or even how it was done."

"How about a policeman?"

Antonio vaults up from his semi-reclining position, his eyes wide. "What?! We are Royal Constables, not thugs for hire."

"And all of your officers are paragons of virtue? I can't even say that about the clergy."

"True enough, but you don't just go waving that accusation around, especially in the middle of a constabulary. Do you have anything to back that up?"

"Maybe," I offer. "Remember when we were hunting Baron Snowdonia a couple months back? I told you that Tommy," I say, gesturing toward my friend, "saw a policeman warn that scum?"

"*Si.* Now that you mention it, I do. We've been so busy with

Quarrels and his other installer compatriots that it has dropped off my mental list."

"Well, let's put it back on, shall we? Let me just run this by you. The same cop that was feeding information to the Baron also is working for..." I don't want to repeat Jasperson for fear of looking like a one-note band, "...the big boss. Then they find out Quarrels is getting ready to spill his guts like a butchered hog. The policeman goes in and removes Quarrels from any future computations."

Antonio rattles it around in his mental attic. "Quite a bit of conjecture there, Stella."

"Hellfire, it is all conjecture except the constable that Tommy saw talking to Quarrels just hours before he took it on the lam."

This seems to make up the detective inspector's mind. "Son, did you get a good look at the policeman?"

There isn't a response right away. I turn to see Tommy fidgeting. "Tell him, Tommy."

The youth twists his face up and turns red. "Yes, sir, I seed him." His speech drops to more of the street talk he grew up with than the more polished accent and words he's come to use in the Helms household.

"Can you describe him?" Antonio says, picking up a pencil.

"He looked like one of them jungle monkeys," Tommy says.

"An ape?"

"Yes, sir."

"Why do you think he looked like an ape, Tommy?" I ask, beating the policeman to the question.

"His shoulders're wide, and he be short. Oh, and he be mostly bald."

"Bald? How would you know that?" Antonio asks. "Constables wear hats."

"He took his cap off when he were talkin' to the baron like he were bein' respectful-like. That copper's got some gray hair around his shiny head like a halo."

"I wish I had cabinet cards of each of our policemen. We take them of the mugs, but not the constables. However, Tommy, your description is rather clear. I'll ask the wardroom to see if we have anyone that matches your description."

"Ya believe me?"

"Why wouldn't I?"

"I's been in the hack more'd'n onest, sir. Most of them constables

e

never trusted me to tell 'em the God-fearin' truth."

"Tommy, that was different in a number of ways. First, you don't have any dog in this fight. And second, I am not asking you as evidence. I'm just trying to narrow down suspects. Honestly, if it went to court, with your checkered past, I don't think the prosecutor would rely on your testimony."

"That's right honest of ya, sir. Many of them Bobbies 'uld just a lied their arse off ta me."

"Would you like to know which of your constables we believe it is?" I say.

"*Madre Dios!* You know who it is?"

"We think we do."

"Why didn't you say that before?" Antonio snaps.

"I wanted to make sure you were at least on board with the thought of a bad policeman," I say.

"I doubt that is your motive, Stella. You are too much of a drama queen. You probably wanted to draw this out."

If DaVinci himself had been accused of copying someone else's paintings, I don't think he could have been more affronted than I am. I avoid drama like the plague. But, this is too important to get myself into a snit. I trace out the outline of what we know and let Tommy provide details.

"Officer Heinrick Meier? I don't know him," Antonio says. He stands up and goes to the door, flagging down a junior officer. "Bring me Constable Heinrick Meier's personnel jacket."

"Yes, sir."

"So, now that you have at least something to look at, Detective Inspector, I have to ask about me. What should I be doing? Should I hide or go about my business?"

Antonio closes his eyes and shakes his head. "By the crucifix, Stella, I haven't the foggiest idea. Part of me screams that you aren't safe and should stay holed up somewhere. You are important to—" Antonio stops short and continues along a different line of thought. "Another part of me thinks that's silly over-reaction."

"So, no words of wisdom?"

"Keep a sharp eye out," he says, his cheeks red. I don't understand why he might be blushing.

But all of this means my metal girdle is going to remain a regular feature. "I always do."

"Here's your file, Detective," a downy-fresh policeman says, offering a thick folder.

Antonio mumbles thanks as he opens it and starts reading it. Tommy and I wait patiently through several curses of our host, not directed at us but rather the documentation in front of him. Finally, he slams his fist down on the stack. "*Cacafuego.*"

"What's in there?" I am literally on the edge of my seat, ignoring the ache in my derriere.

"Meier resigned this morning. His background includes a tour in Ireland as the battalion sharpshooter. Three guesses what weapon and the first two don't count."

"Revolver long rifle."

"Got it in one," he says. "He won his regiment's marksman competition in 1885."

"So, I've been lucky so far."

"Something like that, Stella. And this particular individual is mean. There are numerous cautions and warnings in this file for having used a little too much of the truncheon on suspects. Many of them had to visit the surgeon before being booked."

"Sounds like quite a champion of justice," I add with more sarcasm than all the water over Niagara Falls.

Antonio either doesn't hear or ignores my jibe. "Hell, there is even a note by a former sergeant that says he suspects Meier of taking a bribe. No sergeant would pen such a note if it weren't true. If there were any doubt, any at all, it wouldn't have been mentioned. Unfortunately, removing a police officer without a smoking gun is nearly impossible." The corners of the detective's mouth pull down and together in a scowl. Antonio goes quiet for several heartbeats. "This is the one. I can't prove it yet, but it looks you hit a bullseye again, Stella."

"I can't take the credit. It was Tommy's sharp eyes."

"Let me dig around some, Stella. In the meantime, you and Tommy both be very careful. This is one dangerous bastard."

# # #

I walk out of the police station with Tommy at my side. My emotions fly in all directions. With some trepidation, I check the windows of some of the buildings across the street for a rifle barrel poking out. I don't see one.

"You OK, Stella?" Tommy asks.

"I've been better, Tommy, but I'll live—I think."

"You should get Mikey to rustle up some bodyguards for you. That'd make anyone think twice about messing with you."

Tommy means well, but he thinks in terms of what he knows—street fighting. If it were only that, I'd be fine. But, a bullet doesn't care about how big and brave a bodyguard is. And while I can protect my body, some of those damned snipers can hit a head. I can't go around in an iron mask for the rest of my life.

As a bicyclist rides right up to me, I step backward, forgetting my own mental assurance that a street encounter isn't an issue. Tommy steps between us. My fear drops when I realize the man is wearing a navy uniform, not a Royal Constabulary one. I put my hand on Tommy's shoulder, restraining him from doing something unnecessary.

"Ma'am, are you Stella Ochoa?"

"Yes."

"Ma'am, I have a message for you." Without dismounting, the young naval officer hands me a yellow telegram form. With no more than a perfunctory nod, he pedals off in the direction of the naval station.

I unfold the night letter and read,

Royal American Navy Official Dispatch

To: Senior Mistress Witch Stella Ochoa
From: Dockmaster, Royal Naval Yard, Boston

Mrs. Ochoa, I have it on the good authority of Brian Smith that you have a skill that would aid our work here. It would be my pleasure if you would attend me at the dock office at your earliest convenience to discuss a paid position in our shipwright efforts. We remain open from seven AM through seven PM.

Your servant,

Collin Murphy

I read the note twice. I have nothing demanding my attention, and frankly, being somewhere I might not usually go will make me a more difficult target. Part of my mind tells me that the task itself is a waste of time. Because I'm a woman, I'll probably be ignored by this Murphy person or, at best, given a cursory look because of Mr. Smith's introduction. Then later, they'll hire a warlock to do their bidding.

"Phaa!"

"Excuse me, ma'am?" Tommy asks at my outburst.

"Tommy, could you make your own way back home?"

"Sure, Stella. I'd be happy to." The wide grin on his face makes me wonder what he's planning.

"No stopping at any pubs, young master."

A scowl rewards my guess. "Yes, ma'am."

"Normally, I wouldn't care, but I promised Lady Helms I wouldn't keep you long. Off with you then, and no dawdling."

#

By day, the Naval Yard resembles nothing like what it did when Patricia's husband Brian took me around. A mass of workmen and women weave in and out of one another, all somehow failing to collide. Even those carrying significant burdens keep from bludgeoning their fellows. The chugging of steam pumps delivers a deep base to the growl of conversations, shouted orders, high piercing whistles, and even the buzz of an electric arc welder.

I grab ahold of an unburdened laborer in coveralls. Beneath the face, three-quarters covered in smeared soot and grease is the body of a stout young woman. This makes me revise my previous rash evaluation of the message the dockmaster sent me. Maybe this isn't a snipe hunt after all. "Miss, where is the dockmaster's office?"

"Over yonder. See the big, yaller building?"

"Yes. Can't miss it."

"Well, it is the boxy gray building just seaward of it."

"Thank you very much," I offer with a great big smile.

She looks me up and down and gives me an appraising wink. "My pleasure, miss. Very much, my pleasure."

The young lady is attractive in an androgynous way. In other circumstances, I might have given her my card, but I've got too many people panting after my petticoats as it is, if it isn't too vain for me to even think such a thing. I'll have to ask my confessor about that.

Instead, I give her another smile and something approaching a coquettish tuck of my chin into my shoulder before walking off toward the canary-colored warehouse. I hear a wolf whistle behind me. I opt not to offer the woman any further encouragement by turning. I walk on.

I've strolled through Saturday markets that aren't as crowded as this is. It takes me nearly thirty minutes to cross a lot that is not two football pitches long. I confess as to be confused by some of the activity. Two men stand over a circular metal doughnut sized for one of the mythical Jack and the Beanstalk giants. They keep using words I've never heard before, like "toroid." It sounded like some horrible affliction that one wouldn't want to sit down because of. Two workers squabble over the use of some tool that looks like a round-topped waste can with two tubes running out of it. And what in God's green earth are two men doing carrying boxes labeled "Parts, dirigible, furnace, 1 each?" I don't think I'll ever live long enough to find out.

"Make a hole," says a man as I finally reach the dock office. I must be standing still blocking the entrance.

"Excuse me," I say to the naval officer.

He pays me no-nevermind after I scoot aside. I follow in behind him through the door. The interior room is open and more raucous in its own way than the outside. In the center of the room is a red-haired man who bellows with enough bellicosity for six noblemen being forced to sit in third class on a train. In a thick Irish accent, he snarls, "No. No. No! Look at the plans! You have to drill inside the third stern timber, or you risk weakening the entire stern by damaging the cant frames." He doesn't wear a jacket but instead has the sleeves of his grease and soot-stained shirt rolled up, exposing arms that would do a gorilla proud, both in the amount of hair and musculature.

"But if you do that, the screw won't have enough action lever. It will take six years to turn the beast," a naval captain bellows back right in the face of the ginger.

The redheaded man takes off his wire-rimmed spectacles. Calmly he cleans the captain's spittle off the lenses before speaking. "Captain Tolgard, you are telling me what you want. I'm telling you what you can have. If the *Ice Maiden* had been built for steam screws from the keel out, you probably would have a wider stern and a shorter turning radius.

Unfortunately, it wasn't. This is a refit to take that outdated wooden beauty from sail to steam. We use the bones we have, and she just won't take the screws farther apart without having a glass jaw...on the stern, of course."

"I'll take this to the Admiralty, Mr. Murphy."

The redheaded man shakes his head. "By all means, Captain. However, I suggest you hurry. The *Ice Maiden's* slip has emptied faster than expected. We will be refitting it tonight. I have my orders as well."

I had to dodge out of the way of the storm-faced captain as he stomps out.

"You! What is your business here?" barks the ginger man who dominates the spotlight despite fifty-odd other people occupying the room.

It takes me a moment to realize he is talking to me. "Yes, you! I know everyone else here, and you don't belong."

I can't remember ever being so cowed. "Ah...You sent for me."

"I did?" His tone drops to something more conversational. "Then you must be Stella Ochoa."

"Yes, sir."

"Come over here, woman. I don't bite—"

"Much," someone else adds.

"Margery, I'll have your hair cut off and used to calk boat seams," he snaps back in a good-natured, if aggressive, way.

"You and what platoon of marines," teases a young woman with a remarkable ponytail that stretches down below her derriere.

"I'll make the Admiralty send out the entire corps as a matter of national security."

"Pah!" the woman scoffs, turning back to her work.

"So, Mrs. Ochoa, am I going to have to call out those marines to get you over here?"

"I'm sorry, no, Mr. Murphy." I walk over to a massive draftsman's desk, which holds seventy or a thousand-odd drawings in folders each four foot long on a size and several inches thick.

Dockmaster Murphy gives me an appraising look up and down, not in a way a woman is so used to receiving but rather like a man sizing up a new horse or tool. "So I have you to thank for mucking my schedule all to hell and gone."

"I'm sorry?"

"I bloody hadn't planned on working on the *Ice Maiden* for another three days, mainly because I couldn't empty its slip faster. You did it overnight?"

"Oh, that. Well, yes, that was me. And it wasn't overnight but over less than an hour."

He plops down on a tall stool. He isn't a particularly tall or physically impressive man. Only his presence attracts attention. His hands are heavily calloused and covered in a panoply of scars. His clothes look as if he started the day out as a well-turned-out businessman—spotless and creased. Now they have stains of any variety of colors on them. The knee of one breeches legs is ripped. There is a smear of mud across his shoulders. His tie has been stuffed into the shirt in a vain attempt to protect it. He seems oblivious to his own appearance. "Brian Smith told me as much. Mrs. Ochoa, would you be willing to demonstrate this to me?"

"And slaughter your schedule even further?"

He laughs. "*Scoth*, Mrs. Ochoa! Yes, if you would. I can always hire more laborers."

"So, what do I get out of this demonstration?"

"Mrs. Ochoa, if you can empty a slip as fast as you say, I'd be willing to pay you thirty dollars per slip."

I try not to show any emotion. Thirty dollars is twice what I made in a week of spelling coal soot from the air, and that was after I extorted a colossal raise from my then-boss Mark Carlton. "Well then, where do you want me to perform for you?"

"The *Queen's Gift* has just been moored at the slip outside. If you would follow me..." I tag along as the rest of the office turn from our interaction to suddenly find something to work on. "The *Queen's Gift* is in one of our older slips. It's rather small. If we pumped it with our three steam pumps, it would take about forty hours, give or take."

I look at what had been a graceful frigate, a fierce lady of the sea. All that remains is a wooden anachronism that needs help to even be a participant in the current global discourse of naval affairs. Even her moorings look tired and sagging. For her small comparative size, the *Gift* barely fits in the dock with a scant eighteen inches on any side.

I sit down and untie my boots. The Irishman looks at me quizzically. "If you will excuse me, Mr. Murphy. I don't mean this in any way intended to be forward, but I must have physical contact with the terrain." I slip my footwear off, tucking the stockings inside the shoes to keep them from being soiled.

Mr. Murphy pulls out a stopwatch to time me. "At your leisure, Madam Ochoa."

This afternoon the earth seems even more eager than before, like it knows that it will get to stretch after decades of slumber. I urge its action, and it responds by surging forth, relatively speaking, to cradle the warship as one might a babe.

I get lost in the sensuous slide of mud, sand, and rock over one another and lose track of time. As I open my eyes, water pours over the caissons, and some even laps up onto the stone dock itself. To finish, I decide to do it exactly as I had with Brian, with three stone bands holding the vessel in place. I recall what I had drawn forth from the ground to leave a gaping hole in the ground with only a damp trace of water remaining.

"¡Madre Dios!" cry out several of the dockworkers witnessing the event.

"Saint Nicholas preserve us," the dockmaster mutters. Belatedly, he looks down at his stopwatch and shuts it off. "Seven minutes, fourteen seconds." He just stares at the empty slip for several moments. "Mrs. Ochoa, as a man of God, I'm awed. And while I don't know that I approve of such power under the control of one person, I am not stupid enough to fail to take advantage of it when it presents itself. You're hired."

"Hold on just a moment, Mr. Murphy. How often would you need me?"

"I don't know if you are aware of this, Mrs. Ochoa, but the monarchy is gearing up for a probable war with England and France."

"Unfortunately, I am not blind to that," I say.

"Do you think we should appease them?"

"No, Mr. Murphy, I don't. I am a widow myself of a man doing his duty for king and country. I only say it is unfortunate for all of the men who will die in battle and all the women who will mourn their loss."

"On that, we can agree. But to answer your question, our current rate is about one to two ships a week. If you can empty dry docks as fast as you have shown, I think I can double or likely even triple that output for the foreseeable future."

Sixty dollars a week is a lot of money. It gives me a good deal more faith in spending a huge sum on my own home. "And what about time that I'm not emptying your berths?"

"I don't understand."

"Would you expect me to stand around waiting for you to have a need?"

"Oh, bollocks no, Mrs. Ochoa. Your time is much too valuable for that. We could provide you with schedules, just as we do to every worker. They would tell you when and where you need to be. What you do with the rest of your time, I couldn't give one g'damned lamb's hoof."

"In that case, you have hired a witch, Mr. Murphy."

# # #

Over the last few days, I'd had more items on my mind than getting back to gearman Louis Archambeau. As I'm on my way back to what I hope will be a quiet evening, "Knock, knock," I say, walking through the open door of his shop.

Mr. Archambeau is sitting at his desk working on a watch with a loupe in his left eye. He pops the magnifier out into his hand as he turns. "Ah, Mrs. Ochoa. I'm glad to see you. I worried I'd lost you when you didn't show up earlier this week."

"I'm sorry, Mr. Archambeau. I got wrapped up with other activities." I am not about to share with any more people than necessary that I'm the target of an assassin. I do have my pride.

"Well, I do have something for you." He reaches into a box next to his desk and hands me a fully intact metal model of an automated street sweeper.

"This is mine?"

I didn't know a person could chuckle with a French accent, but the gearman manages. "Yes, it is. I bought that one new to have a model to more accurately reproduce this," he says, lifting a board with a similar but ragged metal shape glued to it. Metal bits are soldered together, making up this figure. Patches stretch around missing pieces to give it some structure. "Having the second makes it more clear where the original was modified."

I see immediately what he's talking about. There is a rectangle carved out of the back of the toy. In its place, I see a horizontal wheel with gearing back down to the spring. The wheel looks like the end of a chimney sweep's brush. It sits just right to scrape the ground.

My hair on the back of my neck stands up. I understand immediately what the modified toy is for. If you aimed it for a demon's capture pentagram, it would spray the chalk away as it traveled, releasing the prisoner. Used correctly, or incorrectly as the case may be, it would act something like a gunpowder fuse. The perpetrator wouldn't even have to be in presence when the beast is released. Jesus, Mary, and Joseph!

"I'll admit that I'm not sure why the modification was made. I'm thinking a new sweeping gadget for a housewife?" He makes it a question as it really is a guess on his part. "I'm just not sure—"

"I do know what it is for, Master Archambeau," I say rather coldly, more out of fear than anything at all against this incredible man.

"I also have to tell you that these were very intricate changes and required a good deal of skill."

"Oh? How many in New England could have done it?"

"Maybe a hundred or so. Any good gearman or watch smith could have done it. But here in Boston, there are only three, two if you eliminate me, and only one if you consider the material used."

"You are keeping me in suspense for a reason, Mr. Archambeau?"

"Ustov Wilsdorf. He has a watch sales and repair shop at Columbus and West Chester."

"Expensive neighborhood."

"He imports only the finest Swiss watches. He makes a good living."

I mull this over and decide this is good information but nothing I need immediately. "Could you load both your reconstruction and the unmodified toy into my carriage outside?"

He nods. As he loads them into the passenger seats, he looks over the poderabile with interest. "I'd heard of a horseless wagon about town, but I'd not seen it before now."

I scribble a quick note onto the back of one of my cards. "Mr. Archambeau, if you are interested in this remarkable vehicle, take this to Forever Power. It will get you an audience with Viscount Henry Helms, the inventor. I am certain the two of you will hit it off.

"In addition," I say, handing him ten more dollars from my purse, "here is an additional payment. I will also say that your work may have just saved many lives."

The gearman stood looking puzzled as I drove off.

#

"Good afternoon, Karen. Is he in and available?" I ask the receptionist at the front desk of Forever Power, plunking down my mounted, metal reincarnation of a toy on her desk. Since I stopped thinking of Karen Vasquez as just a decoration who got her job by repeatedly flashing her ankles, we've become friendly. I've had her as a guest to the Bell in Hand more than once. I have no ulterior motives on her, nor is she inclined to the Sapphic bent. It is just nice to have another friend. And boy, can she get rowdy with the rest of the patrons at my normal watering hole.

"Hi, Stella." Her face lights up. "He doesn't have an appointment. I'll send a runner up to make sure he can see you. Is it just a social call?"

"No, if it were, I'd wait until dinner. I'm staying with the Helmses at the moment."

"Oh?" Karen packs a great deal into that one-word question. I've shared my beliefs about the infatuation of a certain viscountess on my personage.

"Nothing like that. They offered me the guest room when I lost my room at the old bat's boardinghouse. And yes, it is important. It has to do with the recent rash of demon escapes."

"Edwina!" Karen snaps. A young tomboy with more freckles than stars in the night sky races up to the desk in less than three breaths. "Take Stella up to the boss's office. Interrupt if you have to.

"Bell in Hand tomorrow night?" she asks me.

"Sorry, but I have a date."

"Oh? What's her name?"

"HIS name is Manuel Gomez y Ruiz."

"Color me surprised," Karen teases.

"Better be careful, or I'll color you black and blue," I tease back. I give her a smile. "I'll talk to you later about when we can carouse together."

"You ready, ma'am?" the young runner asks.

"Lay on Macduff and damned be him that first cries hold, enough."

"Huh?" the tomboy asks. Karen twitters, recognizing my quote.

"Sorry, Edwina. It is a quote from the playwright William Shakespeare. It means let's go and whoever stops first is a chicken."

The young girl twists her head to the side and wrinkles her mouth for a second. "If you say so, ma'am." In silence, she leads me up to Viscount Helms's office door. When we get there, she reaches for the handle but pauses. "Ma'am. Where could I learn more about that Shaking Spear fellow?"

"Shakespeare. Can you read?"

"Yes, ma'am."

"Here then," I say, taking out one of my cards. With a pencil, I write down the bard's name and *The Tragedy of Macbeth*. I hand her the stiff paper and say, "The public library is certain to have all of his plays."

"Thank you, Mrs. Ochoa," she says, cribbing my last name off of the card.

"You're welcome."

She opens the door. "Mrs. Ochoa to see Lord Helms," she announces in a crisp, piercing voice.

"Thanks, Edwina," I say, handing her a pair of bits.

"Thank you, ma'am."

"Stella!" Lord Helms greets me happily from the other side of the room. "Come in. I'll be with you in just a second." He isn't alone.

"Sir, there isn't any more sheet steel to be had in all of New England," offers an older man with a neat salt-and-pepper beard. His white hair is in a neat braid down his back.

"How about aluminum?"

"That is still readily available, but our current plans for the demon enclosures won't take aluminum."

"Get Joshua Candor to redesign our enclosures using aluminum. I want rough plans by the end of the day and the final design by tomorrow's close of business. As soon as he has his specifications, I want you to lay hands on enough aluminum to finish every installation we have twice over."

"Yes, sir," the white-haired man says and turns to perform his duty. The older man whispers to me as he passes, "Good luck. He's in a bit of a pet."

Walking across the room, I say, "Sorry for barging in, Henry."

He sorts through several stacks on his desk. "Nonsense. What brings you here this afternoon?"

"I brought the reason all the demons have been escaping."

Putting down a sheaf of papers, he replies, "Really? If you didn't have my full attention before, you certainly do now."

I plunk the reconstruction down on his overcrowded desk, finding it leaning precariously on top of the uneven supporting surfaces. "I found all of these pieces at one of the demon escape sites. I hired someone to figure out what they were." I show him the unmodified wind-up toy. "Someone is starting these some distance from the pentagrams and then leaving."

As an example, I wind up the unmodified device. Setting it on the floor, I point it toward a rug in the middle of his room. Henry watches with fascination. It growls as the spring drives it at a crawl toward the carpet. As it reaches the fringe, I say, "And now there is another demon loose. The toy itself isn't enough. While it is a model of a street sweeper, it doesn't actually brush the ground. That is why this additional wheel is needed," I say, pointing at the pieced-together version on his desk.

"Judas Priest! That's just like a fuse!" The dark frown on his face doesn't match the strain when I first met him, but it isn't a far second.

"My thoughts exactly. I'm going to go show this to the constabulary next."

"Please do. Also, share with them that my demon enclosures will stop this sort of device."

"How close are you to retrofitting all your installations?"

"Eighty-six percent complete. The lack of available sheet steel has us flummoxed."

"I overheard. I'm sorry, I wasn't trying to eavesdrop."

"Not a problem, Stella. Heck, if you want to invest, I'd buy stock in steel or aluminum companies."

"Not my thing, Henry. Besides, knowing that Forever Power is going to buy that much from them would be cheating, wouldn't it?"

Henry chuckles. "Yes, it would. But that wouldn't stop many people."

"One thing that witchcraft teaches us above all things is that your actions come back to you threefold. Why would I want that level of negative karma on my soul?"

Henry shrugs. "Not everyone has your morals, Stella. I've known men who would not only cut your head off but drink wine from your skull while cavorting with your widow."

"If you are trying to shock me, you can't, Lord Helms. I know that just as well as most and better than some. Well, I've done my duty to you, my lord. I'll be off now to share with the constabulary."

"Looks like I owe you another one, Stella."

"*Madre Dios*," I curse. Well, I guess it is better to have friends in high places than be bereft of society.

"See you at dinner?"

"Barring being held by Inspector Guizzetti, I will be there."

# # #

"Did you hear that Tesla was hired by the Royal Defense Ministry?" Charles says, more as a statement than a question.

"No!" Nay denies.

"Yes. There are rumors he is going to create an earthquake machine to lower the whole of England into the sea."

"Now, wouldn't that be a grand sight? I'd pay real money to see that," Maggie says.

I wasn't trying to snoop, but the servants weren't exactly quiet about it. "Good evening, all."

Charles looks up from his work setting the table. "Good evening, Lady Ochoa."

"Balls to that. It's just us chickens here, Charles."

"Yes, Stella, but you never know when the mistress or master might show up."

"I'd lay twenty to one that you can tell exactly when and where the lord and lady of the manor are at any time." Charles just lifts an eyebrow. "That's what I thought."

"I've been led to believe by the below stairs gossip that you've saved Lord Helms again," he states.

"Good God, no. I found some information and passed it to him and the constables. Nothing more. I didn't save anyone."

"I'll make sure that the correction is noted," he says with a voice that seems all too flat.

"But?" I ask.

"But what, Mrs. Ochoa."

"Oh, not that again. You said that the correction will be noted, but you weren't telling me the whole truth."

"Really, ma'am?"

I growl at him.

"You should have a witchdoctor look at that throat, ma'am."

"I'll doctor you. What aren't you telling me?" I notice that Charles is now the only other person with me in the dining room.

"Stella, you have developed quite a reputation."

"What reputation is that?"

"There is a good deal of heroine worship below stairs directed at you. You battle demons. You are good to us servants. You don't think you are better than anyone else. You genuinely care. Because of all of this, no matter what I say, everyone is going to think you performed another miracle."

"Jesus, Mary, and Joseph. I'm not Artemis reincarnated. I'm just Stella. I fornicate out of wedlock. I can't control my temper. I save my own skin at the expense of others. I..." I trail off before I reveal my ignoble ancestry.

"Be that as it may, ma'am."

"Well, you can tell them this from me. Don't put me on too high a pedestal as I don't want to break any bones when I fall off."

# # #

Dinner at the Helmses' paroles my tastebuds from the prison of years of swill from Chapman's Boarding House. The table sports long-cooked navy beans thick with chunks of ham, cornbread so light that angels must have baked it, freshly harvested peas, hot and crisp, and a dish of strawberries with a dollop of cream. Nothing on the table is extraordinary fare, but it all has been prepared with joy and grace rather than grudgingly. I eat much more than my metal corset will allow with comfort.

As Lord and Lady Helms and I reach the napkin and toothpick stage, Laoise enters the room. This is odd enough as her duties don't lie in the dining room. Her normally jovial face is red and blotchy. Tear stains trace down her cheeks.

"Lady Helms?"

Adrianna does a doubletake at her lady's maid as well. "What is it, Laoise?"

"Ma'am, I've come to give you my notice."

"I'm confused, Laoise. Are you unhappy here?" Adrianna says more gruffly than I might have.

"No, Lady Helms. 'Cause you've been so good to me, I figured it would be better 'fore I start to show. I am caught."

Pregnant. I am beginning to realize what the tears have been for.

"Does the baby have a father?" the viscountess asks, a bit crassly.

"Oh, yes, ma'am." She smiles for the first time since entering the room. "Albert Glass, he is head groomsman for the Garretts down the road. We are to be married next week."

"Then I fail to see the problem, Laoise."

"Ma'am, I was gonna go live with him, but the Garretts won't let me move in. They say they don't have the room for a family. But Al already has his own room, and we didn't ask for nothing he doesn't already have.

An' I can't have him move in with me and Maggie. So we need to find a new place and probably new situations."

Adrianna twists up her face before harrumphing. "Well damn that all to hell. I won't be losing a perfectly good lady's maid just because of some silly domestic issue."

"Henry." Lord Helms's eyes are at the ceiling, and his mouth working numbers in his own world. Even his fingers absently trace on the table, likely drawing plans only his mind can see. "Henry! Join us here." Adrianna repeats.

"Sorry, dear. What can I do for you?"

"Did you hear anything that Laoise said?"

At least he doesn't dissemble. "No, my lady, I did not."

"She is with child."

"That's wonderful!" Henry says, jumping up, arms wide to give Laoise a congratulatory hug. He stops as suddenly as he started when he realizes the serious air. "What's wrong."

Adrianna purses her lips, not saying the curse about clueless men I feel she has on the tip of her tongue. She calmly says, "Henry, there is a problem in that her fiancé, Albert Glass...you know, the groomsman for the Garretts...can't have her with him."

"Well, move him in here. I'd hire him in a minute. He is mechanically minded, and I am going to need more than one additional pair of hands when my new workshop is finished behind the house."

"I will not have a squalling infant in my nice, quiet home," Adrianna says. "But, I wondered if we could repurpose your workshop as a dormitory for the servants. I could use the extra space inside to expand my conservatory."

I bite my tongue hard. Adrianna has confided in me more than once that she barely has the time to deal with the plants she has. She isn't doing this to get more space but rather as an excuse to give Laoise what she needs.

"Possible, but as the workshop has specialty points within its construction, it would make more sense to build a separate building, maybe off the carriage house."

"That might be acceptable."

"Dear, may I note that you told me my workshop couldn't be off of the carriage house because it would mean losing a chunk of your formal garden."

Adrianna doesn't accept her hypocrisy. "Well, if it means keeping a perfectly well-trained lady's maid, it may be worth it. Please get Mr. Krieg to draw up plans for our review."

"Yes, my dear."

"Laoise, you can tell your young man that he can have a home and situation here if he so chooses."

"Oh, ma'am, this is wonderful news!"

"But don't think I'm going to let you shirk your duties! You will keep doing everything until you are big as a house," Adrianna says in what I take to be bluster. Something makes me think that a particular babe will get some expensive baby shower gifts from Auntie Adrianna.

"Yes, ma'am. Yes. I won't let anything go by the wayside."

10—Friday, May 11, 1888

"No! I won't have it!" I snap. What had started as a pleasant breakfast with me sharing my good fortune of finding new employment has devolved.

Lord Helms gives me a look that one might give a precocious but favored daughter who is throwing a temper tantrum. That I am in a pet makes it all the worse. "Stella, it isn't like I'm trying to buy the building for you. It would only be a loan, no different than you got from any bank."

"Henry, you have already done more for me than I have had any right to expect, and I'm grateful, but you can't just keep giving me things. Your wife has already agreed that your obligation is done."

"That's true, Henry," Lady Helms says, smoothing her dress over her lap. "I did agree that the dresses were the last thing—from me. That doesn't bind you, husband."

"What?" I squawk again. "You devious..." I trail off my words so I wouldn't have to do even more penance on Sunday.

"Yes, Stella, I am somewhat cunning," she says over the top of a cup of tea. She takes a ladylike sip before returning the china cup to its saucer.

"Be that as it may," Henry picks up where he left off, "I'm just offering you the payment price and the renovation price as a loan."

"No." I can feel the muscles in my jaw cramping as I grind my lower teeth on the uppers. I decrease the pursed draw on my mouth as I take a deep breath, trying to relax. "If I can't get a loan from a bank, then it is an ill-conceived notion in any case."

Henry looks pensive for a moment. "Fine, then how about I have Barton go with you and pitch the merits to a loan officer?"

"Barton?"

"You remember, my bookkeeper."

"Oh, yes, Mr. Barton Olds. I'm sorry, but this still is you influencing the outcome. If I can't articulate the plan, then how can I implement it? And if it can't stand on its merits alone without your captain of industry backing, how can it be mine?"

Henry looks vexed with me. Adrianna steps in. "How about a compromise, Stella? Let Mr. Olds go with you—" I start to object, but Adrianna holds up her hand to stave off my comment. "Let Mr. Olds go with you and only step in if there are fine points you can't remember. Think of it as a second, like they have in duels."

I remember one other time I failed to avail myself of a backup. My mother, bless her heart, allowed the demon Gazzunreep to burn me for my missteps. It grates against my sensitivities, but I nod.

"Is that a yes?" Lord Helms asks.

"Yes. I'll agree to that, but Mr. Olds is to warrant nothing. And for that matter, say nothing unless I specifically require it."

"Agreed. When?"

"I plan on doing it first thing this morning."

"Then I'll hustle off to work and send Barton back in my coach."

#

"Welcome, Mr. Olds," the manager of the Royal Bank of Boston says. "We always welcome the business of Forever Power."

I bite my tongue as I stand next to Barton. Before I can even open my mouth to speak, I am interrupted.

"I'm sorry, Mr. Farmington, I'm not here representing Forever Power."

"You aren't?"

"No, sir."

"I am the one here to discuss business," I say, working my entire willpower to keep the sarcasm out of my voice.

"I'm sorry, miss." He doesn't make it seem condescending. I'll take that as a good start. "What is your name and business," he says, waving me to a chair opposite his.

"My name is Stella Ochoa. I have been doing business with your bank for nearly seven years. I'm looking for a loan to purchase a home with which to start a boardinghouse." Barton stands behind me without saying a word.

"Interesting, Miss Ochoa."

"Widow, actually, Mr. Farmington."

"Ah, Widow Ochoa. I apologize again."

"No reason you should have known."

"Wait a moment. You wouldn't happen to be a hellfighter, would you?" I nod. "Then I've read of you in the papers. You broke those vile men who were releasing demons."

"I was part of a larger team, but my part seemed to be overblown by the newspapers."

"So back to business, Mrs. Ochoa. You want to buy a home. I do know you are a hellfighter, but that is infrequent work at best. How do you plan on paying back a loan from us?"

In my own words, I break down what Barton and the Helmses have indoctrinated me with: purchase price, rents, tax credits, depreciation, owner improvements, and more. I recite for twenty minutes. Fortunately, the bank manager doesn't interrupt as I'd lose my place in my mental spiel.

A couple of times, the manager looks at Barton but true to Henry's word, the accountant says nothing and just points back to me.

When I finish, he says, "Mrs. Ochoa, I've been bank manager here for six years and in the loan department for ten years before that. With the exception of some very highly skilled businessmen and businesswomen, that was the most articulate business plan I've ever been presented with.

"However, what if you end up with no tenants and your hellfighter income drops precipitously? The bank must understand how it will be repaid under adverse conditions."

I say nothing. Instead, I hand over my current passbook, my deed to the once-Snowdonia Estate, along with the telegram from Reginald Cornwall about his paying to crop my land. "If that isn't enough, I can bring even more cash into this account from others I have in the city. Also, I have been recently employed by the Naval Yard to the tune of sixty dollars per week minimum."

"No, Mrs. Ochoa, this is quite adequate. We are willing to loan you your requested fifteen thousand dollars at four percent interest."

I look back to Barton. He smiles and nods.

"We will ask for a lien on your property in the Duchy of Connecticut as well as the property you are purchasing. Do you have a sales contract?"

With breakneck speed, I find myself signing seventeen thousand and three papers. Barton previews each one before handing them to me. Only one does he balk at—something to do with a prepayment penalty. The manager passes it to one of his staff and moments later gets a modified sheet that Mr. Olds approves.

"That does it, Mrs. Ochoa," the manager says, offering me a folder containing more paper than an encyclopedia. "The moneys amounting to twelve thousand, five hundred royal dollars will be wired to Mr. Cornwall. The remaining two thousand, five hundred will be placed into your building and loan account, for which you have a passbook. Any amount not used by the close of business one year from today will be paid directly against the principle. Do you have any questions?"

"Only about six million, but nothing I can articulate at the moment, Mr. Farmington. I assume I can return with anything that comes to mind later?"

"Absolutely, Mrs. Ochoa. Or, with such a good friend, you might just ask Mr. Olds. He has a good deal of expertise in these matters."

I don't know how I get my feet to carry me outside the bank. I feel faint. "Merciful Lord, what have I done?"

#

Barton spends the trip to Forever Power trying to console me. I'm quiet after my one outburst. He talks about buyer's remorse and how things will all work out. My brain just wallows in the enormous debt I've just undertaken. My silence is as rude to him as possible without telling him to have sex with farm animals.

After dropping Barton at Forever Power, I speed back to my lodgings. The sounds of the poderabile mock me. The chuffing speaks to me. "You shouldn't have bought. You shouldn't have bought. You shouldn't have bought." A chill creeps up under my hairline. There is the sour taste of vomit in my mouth even though I've not regurgitated.

I pull up to my room's back entrance and jump out. Tommy smiles at me from the stables. I just turn and dash into the house, fumbling with the key as my hands shake.

Locking the outer door, I race to the portal to the rest of the house. I slam it with a bang, sliding the deadbolt into its slot. I lean my body against the wood, trying to keep my anxiety at bay. Peace from my folly comes to me only for a moment. *Too bright!* I rush to the windows and yank the drapes closed until only muted slivers of light sneak in. My tears start falling of their own accord. I don't discourage them. Through my blurry vision, I make my way to the bed, tossing myself on it, pulling covers up into a ball under me as I sob.

# # #

"Miss Stella, there is supper for you," comes Nayeli's muted voice through the door. It drifts into my conscious thought, breaking up yet another dream where I'm shackled and forced to work for pennies to pay the debt, which only gets bigger.

"Go away!" I try to bark the command, but it cracks in the middle.

I spend the rest of the day holed up in my room, drifting from one nightmare to the next. A giant ball of money tries to crush me as I run away from it. It rolls after me, getting bigger and bigger.

"Stella?" comes Tommy's tentative voice through the locked entrance. "Is you hurt?"

"Leave me be!" I snap at my friend. This spawns a new round of bawling at my insensitivity. I'm being selfish and I know it, but I need to purge myself.

Three or four hundred years later of evil dreams, tears, and snot, there is another knock at the door. "Miss Stella," calls Charles softly. "The Helmses are sitting for dinner."

"Charles, if you don't have a bag of fifteen thousand dollars to hand me, you had better make yourself scarce before I open the earth beneath the servants' quarters." Footsteps pad away from my doorframe.

This is the most coherent I've been since I indentured my life by signing all of those papers. Cold rationality comes over me—what's done is done. I can only live with the actions I'd already taken. Sleep and a good crying jag seem to have stolen my self-recriminations.

I pull myself up from the nest I'd made of the bed linens. From the dampness and snot covering the outer layer, I'd sobbed through the entire day. Maybe I can make something of the evening that isn't—

My mind slams the memory of my promise to Manuel Gomez y Ruiz into the spotlight. I am to attend the circus with him tonight, and I have no idea what time it is. I tear around, looking for my purse. I find it on the floor just inside the back entrance. Inside, I pull out my husband's pocket watch. Seven minutes to six. Oh, sweet Mary. I'll never get ready in time. I am certainly not in the mood to spend a gay evening with a man. I'm sure the Helmses and their staff would cover for me if I chose to claim woman problems or just downright sickness.

But that wouldn't be fair. I decide to make the evening work, no matter what. It means speed. I light a couple of candles to give me illumination to work with.

I barely want to look at my face, but it has to be first. My dressing table mirror shows me what I already know. My normal olive complexion is swollen and mottled with pink and red around my eyes, nose, and cheeks. My upper lip and nose are crusted in a way I'd rather not remember. I douse my face with water several times. A good scrub with a washcloth and soap takes out the worst of the damage. This and a smile will have to do.

Next, clothes. I'm rumpled and in a more conservative attire than would be appropriate for a rendezvous. A woman's clothes should shout out flirty and fun, not to mention sans wrinkles. I open the closet, and my eyes immediately fall upon a white dress with large yellow sunflowers printed all over it. That goes onto the bed as I struggle out of my current outerwear.

In the mirror, my buttery and white, empire-waist frock gives off a sprightly image. I opt to keep my jade *peineta* and accent it with jade earrings, compliments of my hostess's largess, and a green cameo broach.

A timid knock on the door interrupts my makeup, sparse as it is. "Miss Stella?"

"Come in, Nay."

The door rattles. "It's locked, miss."

I forgot that I'd dead-bolted it. I open the door. Nay looks like I'm going to beat her. "What is it?" I realize my tone is just a touch frosty as she stepped back. "It's alright, Nay. What can I do for you?"

"You have a gentleman caller."

"Please tell Manuel that I will be down in a moment." Nayeli didn't leave immediately to deliver the message. "Is there something else?"

"Are you alright, miss? We are all worried for you."

"I'm quite fine, Nay. I was just feeling sorry for myself. Tell everyone that everything is good."

I get a wan smile. "Very good, miss," she says dubiously before returning to Mr. Gomez y Ruiz.

Without closing the door, I sit back down at the makeup table and put a daub here and there before mentally proclaiming my look at least worthy of not pulling a gunny sack over. Grabbing my one white, lace *mantilla*, I make my way down to the foyer, where Manuel sits wearing a smart day-suit.

Standing, he offers, "Good evening, Miss Stella. You look quite lovely."

"Why, thank you, Manuel."

"Are you ready to go?"

"At your pleasure, Mr. Gomez."

He offers me his arm. I slip my arm through his as he escorts me out to a waiting landau. He opens the door and hands me up into the carriage. "The fair, driver."

"So, what do you and Mr. Tesla work on?" I ask to start a conversation.

"Oh, Mr. Tesla is interested in all manner of things. Primarily his attention is given to electric fields and how they propagate. I've been a student of Michael Faraday's work through college. Nikola read my thesis and hired me before the ink on my diploma from the University of Barcelona was even dry."

"I missed out on higher education," I offer, "but I've always been interested. What was your thesis on?"

"It might be too complex for someone not in the field." He turns to me with an ashen look. "I mean no disrespect, *señora*. It is just quite esoteric. It was titled '*Corrientes de Foucault Complejas Dentro de los Núcleos de Hierro en Relación con las Densidades de Campo.*'"

I consider my Spanish quite good, but he has me baffled. My face must show it.

"*Me disculpe, señora.* My paper talks about the electric fields generated by...*cómo se dice*...unusual electric flows inside a metal core."

I chuckle. "Yes, Manuel, you were right. I know the words, but I don't have an earthly idea what that means even in English."

"Not to worry, Miss Stella. My paper even baffled the men judging it. I had to explain every nuance to them. It is well that they have open minds, for they gave me my papers of graduation."

"Do you like working for *Señor* Tesla?"

"Si. Si! He stretches my mind sometimes to the breaking point. He is a most brilliant man. I cannot speak on what we are now working upon as your government has declared it *Secreto del la Corona.*"

"*Si*, I understand, Manuel. With the war with England and France looming, I'm surprised more things aren't Crown Secrets. So what about some things you were working on before you got pressed by the King?"

"Oh so many things. Sometimes Nikola would come up with six different ideas before he got us working on the first. You must know we built a functional electric motor more efficient and cleaner than any steam engine of its type."

"That is impressive."

"As you know, we experimented on electric fields against demons." Fortunately, the darkness of the evening swallows my frown. "We'd hoped to create amplified power signature. Well, you know the result of that one."

"I can't say I was pleased, but I understand the need for all sorts of research."

"So tell me more about yourself, *señora*. I know so little about you other than you are a hellfighter and have powerful friends at court."

"Friends at court?"

"The viscount and his lady have allowed you to live with them."

"Oh, no. Lord and Lady Helms are just friends. I've just bought a new home and will be moving out."

"But, as you say, they are *amigos,* and they have a title."

"True enough," I concede. "Well, I was born of an earth witch. When I reached womanhood, I learned I also have earth witch powers. My mother taught me. When I passed my practical witchcraft tests, I joined *Dos Campanas.*"

"So you mentioned you were *viuda*—widowed."

"Yes, I married Aaron, my husband, not weeks before he was sent to Ireland."

"*Si.* Bad business that. You have my condolences."

"It is something I try both to remember and keep close and at the same time push to arm's length."

"Understandable, *señora*. So he was a good man?"

"He treated me well. He loved me and I him." I tried to imagine Aaron in the coupe with me rather than the pretty Spaniard. I just ached to wrap my arms around his brown arms one more time—to smell his sweaty shirt covered in horsehair after a day of work. I longed for Aaron more than life itself.

"I'm sorry I bring up a topic most troubling."

"Not at all, Manuel. The feeling is bittersweet."

"Excuse me. What means bittersweet?"

I dredge up my Spanish vocabulary before answering, "*Agridulce.*"

"Ah, thank you. My English is still not perfect."

I laugh. "Mr. Gomez, most Americans' English isn't perfect, and many of them aren't even good."

"*Gracias, señora.* I try. I've been living here in your country for three years now, but I still sometimes miss what is being meant."

"As do I, and I've lived here all my life."

Manuel chuckles. There is a dead space in our conversation. I'm loath to let awkward silence reign.

"Is your leg all well after our excitement of the other night?"

"It still pains me lightly when I walk on it, but it will heal with barely a *cicatriz*—scar. Thank you for asking. Did *la policía* capture the bad man?"

"No, but they have a good idea who did it. Worse it appears it was a constable. It is sad when the shepherds turn on their flock."

There is a pause before Manuel responds. "*Lo siento*, but is it not good that such filth is removed and the rest can be assured of safety?"

"On that, we agree one hundred percent."

We manage to fill the rest of the time on the way to Boston Commons with trivial chitchat about people we know in Boston. With his work, he has been all over the Northeast as far north as the Duchy of New Foundland. While he hasn't been in this area long, he has met some of our city's more famous and infamous denizens. At parties where Tesla is invited, he has met journalist Henry Adams, poet Hattie Griswold, photographer Helen Murdoch, lawyer Austin Abbott, and murderess Sarah Robinson.

The lights spilling all over the commons create a gay bit of day in the middle of the surrounding darkness. The sounds of a calliope trip off into the night at counterpoint to a brass band. Lights and motion are all over like an Independence Day celebration. People weave in, out, and around in festive enjoyment.

"Driver, let us off in front," Manuel orders in a very authoritative voice. It is more than I expect from a mere assistant. It makes me wonder if he would be so commanding playing at mother and father. Goosebumps form up and down my arms. My Venus triangle also threatens to dampen my bloomers with such thoughts.

All of this reminds me that it's been too long since I've had a thorough loving. I need to find out if Karie has finished her courses. I will make a point of an inquiry tomorrow.

Manuel hands me down as a good gentleman should. He again offers his arm. We stroll up toward the excitement. I'm bubbling inside with joy. The first thing we come upon is a brightly colored booth where if you toss a ring onto an upward slanted peg, you can win a prize.

"C'mon, friend, win your girl a ceramic dolly, or maybe a pocket knife for yourself. Step right up. Two tries for a nickel," came the smooth patter of the man. I watch as a man tries four times. With the first three, he doesn't even touch a peg. The fourth ring circles the second pin from the right only to bounce off.

The barker doesn't stop his talk. "Aww, just missed, young gentleman. You have the knack of it now. Try again?"

The mark fishes out another nickel from his coin pouch.

"Watch, Stella," Manuel whispers. "Winning at that game would be the grossest of luck. The kinetic energy of any of those small rings will bounce off those very bendable pegs. I'd guess they are made of bamboo and hollowed out."

True to his comments, the game player this time put each of his throws right on the stick only to have them spring off like an untied corset off a chubby woman, one of the reasons I gave up on the devices.

We continue to walk up a fairway with games of chance on either side of us. Manuel provided a running commentary in my ear as we watched each one in turn. His knowledge of science is impressive as he debunks the games one by one. Some might find it boring, but all of the colors, music, and movement have me captivated. My date's explanations also add to, not detract from, the joy.

"Oh, here is one," he says, pointing to a football game. "Now, see the angled net on either side of the minuscule goal? Most people would think if they kick it anywhere in there, they will score. That net would just cause the ball to ricochet away. But this one at least has a measure of skill." Manuel gently leads me up to the game owner.

"Show your woman just what a good footballer you are. Win her affection by proving your manhood. Win her a dolly or a stuffed animal. Three tries for a dime. Two goals win a big prize. How about you, sir?"

Mr. Gomez fishes into his pocket.

"Don't do it, Manuel," I insist. "You don't need to prove anything. And, as you mentioned, the game isn't fair."

"Oh, I didn't say it isn't fair. I just say everyone will think they can kick it anywhere in that wide maw. If you kick it straight into the goal, there isn't a problem."

"That can't be more than twice the diameter of the ball."

Manuel hands the man a dime and steps up to a row of three footballs. He looks odd wearing a suit about to kick a soccer ball. His windup is minimal, but the ball sails about six inches off the ground and curves to the right, missing the goal by six inches.

"Really close, mister. You got two more tries."

Manuel cocks his head to one side. Before kicking another, he reaches down for the ball.

"Whatcha doing, mister. You can't touch a soccer ball with your hands."

"Very well," Manuel says. With the tip of his shoe, he rolls the ball to one side before letting go. On the flat surface, the sphere rolls back. "Weighted to make it wobble. *Que estafa.*"

The Spaniard kicks the second ball right through the goalposts. There must be a bell behind the hole as it clangs loudly. This is followed almost immediately by a second ring as his third ball drills directly through the winning zone.

"Congratulations, mister. You win one of the prizes on the upper shelf."

"Miss Stella?" Manuel says, indicating I should choose.

"If I may have the stuffed purple bear, please."

The carnie uses a stick to pull down the prize my date had just won for me. I hadn't realized just how big the stuffed critter is. It almost takes both arms to reach around it.

"Thank you, Manuel. How did you do that?"

"I lettered in football at university as a left striker. One year, our rival college started the game with a skewed ball, very similar to those. It took us two periods to convince the referee that it had been tampered with. Personally, it didn't matter to me. I scored two goals with that wobbly football. We beat them five to three."

"You are brilliant. Thank you, Mr. Gomez."

"You are quite welcome, Miss Ochoa. Oh, goodness, what is this?"

We walk arm in arm down the rest of the causeway. At the end is a contraption going round and round that makes me quiver inside.

"Come ride a fierce unicorn, mount a wild bear, or float in a dirigible on the merry-go-round."

"That sounds fun," I offer.

"I agree, Stella. Let's get in line." He is correct. There is a queue of at least seventy people long. I haven't seen anything of this length on this side of the yearly column to vote. As we wait, we look about the rest of the fair. A massive tent boasts a show including a bearded woman, a three-armed boy, the lion-man, and a demonic beast, and the women who charm it. The last makes me wonder if the viscountess has already gotten our idea of having public demons in motion or if this is just a coincidence.

"The big tent looks interesting," I offer. A gaudily dressed man in front of the big top breathes fire around a torch like a dragon. Three or four more times, he repeats the blazing event. If that isn't impressive enough, he takes the end of the torch and puts the flaming end down his throat. Moments later, he removes the extinguished brand and belches a smoke ring. "Oh, my!" He may be nothing more than a fire witch, but it is still impressive. It reminds me of the professor's husband.

Manuel gives a smile. "We'll go there after the merry-go-around."

"Thank you, sir."

"How about you thank me with more tales of your hunting of the demonic?"

While the good girl of the church that I...well, sorta am, I'd almost rather him to allow me to kiss his trouser serpent. I've told my hellfighting stories so often it isn't a burden, only dull. People with no or little power are fascinated by the descriptions of our fights.

I regale him with the time we fought a snake-like demon that could burrow faster than I could order the earth to close around him. We reach the front of the line just as I'd gotten to the point of my tale where the beast swallowed Menagerie.

Manuel hands the operator a dime for our fares. "Please step onto the platform and find an open seat," the operator says in a voice only slightly more excited than someone asleep.

"What would you like to ride, Miss Ochoa?"

"They all look so fun. Let's ride the dirigible. I've always wanted to fly in one. Sometimes I wish I'd been an air witch."

"I've been a passenger in one several times."

"Really? Tell me?" I ask like a schoolgirl with a crush.

"They are quite heavenly. You feel as if you are a god so high above the ground. They float so smoothly it feels as if you aren't moving at all, but in fact, you can sometimes outrace a locomotive."

"That is something on my wish list. Until then, this will have to do," I say as we find the dirigible with two comfortable seats beneath the fake gas bag made of pastel-painted wood.

We no more get seated in place when the calliope restarts its gay tune, and the ride begins to circle. Our dirigible slowly takes us up into the air eight feet or so. It is a giddy feeling similar to riding in the poderabile. Driving my horseless carriage requires too much concentration to enjoy it this much. The bear takes up a good deal of my lap, but I'm feeling more than a little friendly. I reach down and take Manuel's hand in mine. He toys with my palm with his fingers. As denied as I've been lately, I wonder just how far I might take this.

As we spin at great speed, I catch sight of what I think might be Carlos. When we round back, I don't see him. At one point, I think I catch sight of my teammate Menaj and her mass of hair askew in all directions. All this spinning in circles must be messing with my vision.

The merry-go-round stops a few seconds later, and we depart, hand in hand. Manuel points to a half-moon of cages illuminated in limelight. We meander that way and find a menagerie of animals.

A giraffe sticks its neck up to nibble off the newly budding leaves from the elm next to its cage. A lion paces behind the bars of his cage. His restless energy makes him look capable of taking on a demon. A hunch-backed dog, a hyena I recognize belatedly, cackles as it tracks from one end to the other of its eighteen-foot pen. A rhinoceros lies in an enclosure snorting into the hay. An elephant drinks water from a trough and then picks up a peanut from a small pile. I never knew how dexterous its trunk is. It operates at least as well as my hand. The monkeys are a bit scary in their similarity to humans, with the bigger one beating on a smaller one for some slight that I didn't notice.

I've never actually seen all of these magical creatures, only read of them in books or seen in poor illustrations. It makes me wish that Duchess Massachusetts, Maria Kincaid, would commission a zoo for Boston.

"Should we investigate the big top?" I ask as the unique aroma of so many different animals wrinkles my nose.

"This way, m'lady," he says, leading me onward.

"Step right up. Only one dime to witness the wonders of the ages, and the abominations of nature, and the depths of hell itself. You there, missy. You are an attractive woman, but what if you woke up in the morning covered in every square inch of your body with tattoos? Would you feel so beautiful then? Our inked lady is so afflicted. If anyone can find even a single inch of her skin uncovered below the neck, we will pay him or her the handsome sum of one hundred dollars.

"Or you, sir, if you suddenly found yourself with another leg? Could you cope? Well, Mansfield does have three fully formed and functioning limbs.

"Come one, come all to visit these, and other attractions only brought to you by Otto Schmitt's Spectacular Amusement and Freak Show. One thin dime of the realm grants you access to our continuous showing." The man seemed to be able to talk until the cows come home and then a few hours for good measure.

Manuel walks up and pays our twenty cents. He is given a pair of orange paper tickets with "Admit One" printed on them in fancy calligraphy. As we approach the tent, a young boy in gaudy attire takes the coupons and tears them in half, and we are ushered in through a flap.

The oblong tent is enormous and is held up with three large poles. Bleachers cover three sides of the canvas walls with three stages or rings in the center. Acts are taking place in either end, but in the middle, ominously, is another smaller tent, this one white and coarse. I recognize it at once as an asbestos-embedded cloth. That must mean that the demon is beneath it if they truly have such a thing.

Manuel leads me up to some seats in the middle section, seven rows back from the edge. The seats are high enough that we are afforded an unobstructed view. There, in the middle of the center ring, is a master of ceremonies in a great red and gold coat wielding a megaphone. "And to your right, this small wagon can't carry many people to the westward duchies, or can it?" The Conestoga-style wagon couldn't be more than four feet high and six long. Maybe one adult could lie down inside. But, a clown climbs out of the back, big floppy feet and all. He begins to perform antics as if he is grooming the pony. Another clown climbs out as a satire of a dowdy old woman who begins berating the first. Before she can even get fully started, more clowns climb out. Then more. I count ten adults and twenty children-sized little-people clowns. The antics are hilarious as, at one point, they all try to pull the pony to get it moving. I nearly bust a gut laughing. Manuel also smiles and chortles.

"If you will turn your attention to your left, the Inked Lady performs the snake dance. As this is a family show, she retains enough clothing to keep her decent, but any man that wants to inspect her more closely after the show may come to the far tent." I watch as the woman squirms around in loose silk and veils showing more skin, or in her case, tattoos, than any woman has any right to do in public. I'm not a prude, but I'm sure at one time or other I see all of her skin as she undulates. There are catcalls aplenty. I think I hear three or four shouted proposals, none of them of the honorable variety.

By this time, the clowns have cleared off. "Back to your right, up in the top of the tent, you will see the flying Ponterbo family." A family of five, the youngest couldn't have been more than seven, are in woven clothing in bright red that fit them like a glove, all over their person. The father and two children are on one platform, and seemingly halfway across the rooftop, the mother and the youngest wait on a second. Below them, a net is stretched out by a group of large men.

The father takes a trapeze bar held by ropes and swings across the upper reaches. Back and forth he goes until he flips over and wraps his knees around the bar. He lets go and is waiting with his arms outstretched.

The orchestra plays a dramatic beat. The mother pats the youngest, a girl from the length of her hair. The little one swings out and back on a second bar. Out again she goes, before releasing her grip at the far end. Flipping around, her father catches her by the forearms. The orchestra plays a triumphant measure. Together the pair swing back, and her father deposits her on his platform.

The music gets dramatic again. The mother swings from the second platform and, like her husband, turns over to hold onto the bar with her knees. Now the eldest son jumps out over empty air. You would think that he would just plummet, but his father snatches him from death by the forearms, just as he had his younger daughter. They swing back and forth a couple of times. Just when you think the father might drop him, the son releases his father's arms, and flips twice before soaring right into the hands of his mother. She gives him a little help until they are both standing on the bar swinging back and forth with their arms stretched up and a hearty ta-da from the band.

"Now, Crystal Ponterbo will perform something never before attempted on any stage anywhere. A quadruple somersault onto a bare bar. She must have absolute silence."

Next to me, Manuel whispers, "If you would excuse me, señora." He stands up and starts moving through our row of onlookers. He is too polite to even mention he is off to the necessary.

My eyes are glued on the trapeze family setting up for their incredible stunt. "Hurry back, or you'll miss it." I absently notice that he repeatedly apologizes as he passes across the view of people as he probably heads for the necessary.

The music builds in eerie intensity. The girl, who couldn't even have had her first period, leaps out across the open area and links arms with her father, who is still swinging by his knees. The pair move back and forth three times. The mother, now on the other platform, flings the second empty bar toward the center. At the bottom of their arc, Crystal is flipped by her father. She rotates about her middle almost faster than I can follow through one, two, three, four somersaults before grabbing at the empty bar. Her fingers don't hold their purchase. There is a gasp as she loses her grip. With more aplomb than I might have had, the girl continues her rotation. With her back to the ground, she flattens out and is caught in the net. She uses the net almost as a spring-loaded bed and bounces up to her feet with her arms held high as if she had just won the derby.

"Unfortunately, it remains an unperformed feat," the ringleader says. "Maybe next time, Crystal." I wonder what an act with an air witch might look like. They don't have to be afraid of falling. I don't wonder long as a drumroll begins. "But if you will now turn your attention to the center ring." Lime lights spring onto the gray/white tent. "What is inside is likely to be upsetting to women and children. We recommend those individuals leave the tent."

There is a loud argument of a child, no more than seven, demanding to stay as his mother takes him forcibly by the arm out of the big top. No one else leaves. The audience leans forward. I have to admit to a certain amount of curiosity myself.

"Beneath this canvas is the most vicious, cruel, murderous spawn of the devil himself. It would eat you as soon as look at you. I present, the demon!"

The canvas is lifted off of what looks like a gigantic birdcage. Inside is a demon that looks very much like a king-sized hyena but with four tentacles out of its back. It doesn't cackle like the one back in the menagerie but instead roars.

"YOU WILL ALL BAKE IN HELL AS I EAT THE FLESH FROM YOUR BONES."

I know that the cage is superfluous. The demon could destroy that with three tentacles tied behind its back. My professional interest draws me to the chalk circle on the ground. As best as I can tell at this distance, it looks solid and well-constructed.

"See the evil, yet we are unscathed! The ladies will dance just outside its cage to prove how safe we are."

A troupe of attractive women traipses in, showing enough of their stockings that I wonder where the sheriff is. The band strikes up a saucy tune. They create a live band around the cage, bouncing around in a circle and occasionally kicking up a leg to give the men at least the chance of more than just their stockings to look at.

"YOU WILL DANCE AT YOUR OWN WAKE AS I DRAG YOU INTO MY MASTER'S DEN, WHERE YOUR EYEBALLS WILL BE BOILED IN YOUR OWN BLOOD."

"Windbag," I mutter under my breath. I look around, but Manuel isn't to be seen. *Watering the nag must have turned into something else,* I muse.

The cage in the center begins to raise. I notice that it is on a chain that goes up through a pully and off to a pair of highly groomed and decorated horses that are slowly pulling it up at the urging of a trainer. People start pointing and calling out in terror as it lifts, uncovering the beast within. The crowd begins to stand and move. I stay seated, urging the people nearest me to do the same.

The dancers seem oblivious. They swirl and kick to the stirring music.

Finally, the ringleader bellows through his megaphone, "Fear not, people. The cage isn't what holds the abomination of nature in place." The cage lifts rapidly, now giving everyone an unfettered view of the ochre-colored demon. The dog-thing smashed against its invisible prison before bouncing back. "As you can see, it cannot escape the love of the Lord, our God!"

The girls just dance closer now that the cage is gone. I notice that they stay a good two feet away from the chalk ring and only kick outward. They are taking no chances that something might release the hellspawn. A slight irregularity in the dancers' pattern catches my eye. The break comes from where a metal object, maybe twelve inches long, crawls along the ground toward the pentagram. It bears a spinning wheel covered in bristles.

"No," I say softly at first. Then I stand up and yell, "NO!" I'm too far away from the earth to make it move, or I'd throw the damned thing away or put up a wall. "Stop that thing!" I bellow.

The ringmaster looks around in confusion. The dancers continue to dance as I watch the disaster unfolding. I try to push my way through to an aisle so that I might get to the earth but know already I'm too late.

"Run! Run now!" I command as people look at me as if I'd turned blue and poured a bucket of molasses over my head.

"Really, there is no danger," the red-tuxedoed man urges.

Everything slows down. A man puts his arms out to keep me from passing, saying something I don't hear. My attention is almost entirely on that brushed wheel. The demon also eyes it like a lion might a wounded doe that hobbles toward its hiding place in the grass. The first grains of white chalk spray out from under the metal toy like a rooster tail. The dancers have lost rhythm and are just gadding about now. I bat the man's arms away with difficulty as he is strong. "Run!" I repeat. "The demon is about to be loosed."

The pentagram is severed with one last cloud of white dust from the modified toy.

Roaring, the demon lunges forth, growing to the size of the elephant as it crosses the line of its former prison. Its rush wraps up two dancers. Tentacles miss two others who have finally realized their danger and dodge away. As the demon squeezes the two women it has in its clutches, literally in half, blood and less savory internal bits spray out like bursting a pig's bladder.

The horses, which had been holding up the massive cage, bolt, snapping the ropes. The weighty enclosure bounces off the monster, drawing its attention for a moment. As the metal shakes the ground, a massive maw snaps through the iron as if it were no more than strings of taffy.

Guilt wells up in my chest. Now is a time for action, not wallowing in what-ifs. I have to get to the ground to provide at least some protection. The crowd, belatedly realizing its danger, stampedes for the exits. I find myself caught up in the flow, taking me farther away from the demon and any possibility of slowing its advance.

"Please! Let me through!" I plead above the shrieks and screams of the people, and the white bass noise coming from the demon. I watch a little girl get pushed over. Her mother tries to help her up. They both go down and don't emerge from the chaotic mob.

With some thought, I realize there is one part of the earth that I can reach. It is the iron wrapped around my waist. I coax it into two points that rip from beneath my dress about my middle. I form them into a single cow catcher, pointing in the direction I want to travel. The mass of people finally split to stream around me. My speed is slow, but finally

I've parted the Red Sea and reach the earthen floor of the tent.

The demon is licking its tentacles from the bloody mess on them. It eyes me as its next meal.

"I won't be so easily taken, you bitch," I taunt.

"I WILL TAKE YOU TO FEED THE WORMS THAT FEED THE SINNERS I SUP UPON. FOR ALL ETERNITY, YOU WILL FLOW THROUGH MY INNARDS."

As I bend over to get contact with the dirt of the ring, the most wondrous and delightful sight appears—a hedgerow. My teammate Menagerie is here! A whirling dervish forms to another side.

"We don't know if this demon can fly," I hear Carlos's gruff voice call out. "Bea, lay down some sleet above it."

Before I can say Rumpelstiltskin, the beast is surrounded by barriers on each side, including a wall of mud and a sheet of pure goodness.

"Stella!"

"Yes, Carlos." I can now see the group in the far bleachers, moving to take up more strategic locations.

"As we are right over the portal it was summoned through, I want you to send this one back to Hell."

"Got it." My mind falls into that simple reverie of doing, almost by reflex. As much as I hate to have to do it, I am happy to be in that space. It is one thing I am made for.

I reach with my soul for the planes of existence, like multiple slices of swiss cheese. I need to line up the holes in the exact location that is occupied by the demon. It is a spiritual exercise that leaves my mind open to other input.

"Everyone, it's tearing down the tent pole," I warn, too late.

The fabric roof collapses on us, blocking our view. This wouldn't have been such a problem, but the demon's heat sets the canvas on fire. Donny changes his wall of mud to a spray of protective water that falls over everyone like heavy rain. I'm assuming Menagerie's wall of vines is burned to a crisp. With some walls gone, I don't want our quarry to escape. I lower the ground in the area where I'd last seen the demon to put it into a deep bowl. I hear a scream before the heavy fabric is lifted free of me.

"YOUR SOUL WILL FUEL MY EXCREMENT."

Carlos's vortex spins the fabric and flames up and away. "Bea, freeze that so it doesn't set anything else on fire."

"Got it, Carlos," she replies.

The demon is in a pit with broken bits of wood and burning remains of the canvas. I see it start to climb a tree-trunk-sized remnant of a tent support. The pole burns readily under its touch, creating a new inferno. Donny expertly changes his water's focus to douse the timber.

Within moments the original witched walls of my team reassert themselves.

I return to moving the plates of existence, feeling the thought-twisting and nausea that it prompts. Fortunately, I've been working on inuring myself to this effect. Once burned, twice shy. Nevermore would someone like the unlamented Baron Snowdonia mess with my mind. I'd practiced the mind-twisting movement of the planes regularly over the last months and have become somewhat resistant.

"I MUST DESTROY. RELEASE ME, PUNY HUMANS!"

The best action to a demon's demands and blustering is not to respond unless you are trying to provoke it. I concentrate on my work until I manage a sliver of a portal. Like a wet rag being run through a wringer, the demon thins and becomes partially insubstantial. It screams in defiance as I endure the headache to wrench the tiny opening wider. "I WILL BURN YOUR WORLD. I WILL...AAAaaaa." Like the pop of a cork, the demon squirts through.

There is a heavy sigh. Police whistles toot in the distance. Screams of panicked people continue. "Wasn't expecting that," Carlos says, breaking the relative silence. We slowly mingle together into the center of the destruction.

Now, free of the need to act, my brain starts up again. "Why are you all here?"

There is a pregnant pause. All my comrades look at Carlos, who says as he puffs up his chest, "Can't we enjoy the circus, too?"

"No. I don't buy that much of a coincidence."

Donny nods his head to Carlos while saying, "Just tell her."

"Tell me what?"

Menaj speaks up when Carlos fails to. "I'll do it. Because of the attempts on your life, your boyfriend sent us to keep an eye on you."

"Manuel?" Thinking of Manuel, where did that worthy get to, I wonder.

"No, not that Spanish fop." Inspector Guizzetti and sixteen constables come rushing forward. Menaj points at Antonio. "That one."

I bark, "What?" The incredulous look I lay on Guizzetti must have spoken volumes.

"What did I do?" Antonio asks.

"Boyfriend? Since when are you my boyfriend?"

"I'm confused. I came here because of a loosed demon."

My friends...FRIENDS...try to sneak away. "Don't you dare leave," I hiss.

"This is between you two lovebirds," Donny offers.

"Wrong answer," I say, getting the earth to engulf his legs.

"Hey, I was just teasing," Donny says, looking down at the stone that now encases him from the waist down.

"Now back to you, Inspector First. Boyfriend?"

"I said nothing of the kind, nor did I intimate anything like it."

I steal a glance at Carlos and Menaj. "Well?"

"Maybe we misinterpreted something he said?"

My ire is up. Too many things all happening at once. I direct my next attack at Antonio. "And what did you say?"

"I just said I wanted to keep you safe as you are important to us."

"You said 'me' not 'us,'" Maxwell offers.

"Both mean the same thing," Antonio directs toward Max.

"*Pendejos!*" I snort as I stomp off, still sporting my metal crowd breaker. I almost mow down one policeman who doesn't move out of my path fast enough.

I make it as far as the causeway before I hear, "Stella? Are you alright?" Manuel is standing there looking a bit more disheveled than is his normal countenance.

"Stay away from me, Manuel. I just bring death and chaos." The prissy man takes a step away from my glare.

# # #

My consciousness spins, not because of the planes, but rather with everything that I've dealt with. I don't even know how I end up back at the Helmses' home or how my metal corset disappeared. I storm through the door and find Adrianna alone in the parlor. I must make quite a sight. Her eyes show the concern of a good friend.

I flop down on the settee next to her. All the things that have happened over the last fortnight come to a head—assassination attempts, demon escapes, everyone trying to spark me, houses, jobs, and murderous toys. I gush everything to her. It comes out of my mouth like some vomitus mass. As tears start leaking down my cheeks, she wraps her arms around me.

"I don't know what to do. Too much. All too much. I can't—"

Adrianna kisses me.

Not with a friendly peck on the cheek but an open-mouthed buss on the lips that offers much more. I'm startled speechless. She backs off and studies my face. I sit there with my jaw hanging somewhere around the floor level.

The moment stretches on as my thoughts completely freeze up as my body churns and burns. I stop thinking and throw myself into her arms, crushing my mouth to hers. She welcomes me in. Our tongues dance and swirl in sweet abandon.

Without a by-your-leave, I reach up under her dress and petticoats and start grabbing her limbs and arse, where I find slippery silk lingerie. I run my hand inside the waistband of her bloomers and yank down. It catches on her garters. I won't be denied. I take both undergarments and strip them off her legs in one brutal motion.

She isn't idle, unbuttoning my dress in a fashion only an urgent lover would employ. More than one of my clothes' whalebone clasps is torn from the garment. As she takes too long, I just clasp the seams and yank. The rest of the buttons skitter across the floor. I slip my arms out and shove as much of my dress to the floor as possible. It leaves me in only my brassiere and shift.

She reaches for my breasts, but I push her back, diving beneath her skirts. I want nothing more than to drown my sorrows in the orgasmic cries and nectar of this goddess. It really is like a little woman in a boat. Even through multiple layers of fabric, I get the former. My face is generously anointed with the latter multiple times.

11—Saturday, May 12, 1888

Tangled in a lover's arms, I wake. There is no hurry. There is a calm in my soul that overwhelms even the need to empty my bladder. The musky perfume of sex tickles my nose in the most pleasant way. My vulva throbs between a desire, not a need, for more and the stings of the thorough loving it has already received. I can still taste her in my mouth, along with a strand of her long, blond hair. Her head is nestled in the crook of my arm, using one of my breasts as a pillow.

Half of our nakedness is covered with a blanket, which I find odd as we are on the parlor floor. A sun spot from one of the upper windows lands on us. As I look at the beautiful, disheveled mess of my hostess and friend, guilt reaches up from within me to snatch away my calm.

Did I take advantage of her? What will she think of me? Have I've defiled her marriage? My brain begins a running monologue of fear and doubt. In the middle of my self-flagellation, I notice her eyes are open, and she is looking up at me with a dreamy smile on her face.

"Good morning, beautiful," Adrianna purrs, nestling in closer to me. About half of my guilt drains away. I order the other half to go peddle its wares elsewhere for the nonce.

"Good morning." I comb my hand through her hair.

"Mmmmm. I'll give you a fortnight to stop that." Her voice is soft and not at all the authoritative voice of her public self.

"We probably should get up before someone finds us like this," I say with little enthusiasm.

Her head snaps up to look into my face. Little worried lines form around her brows, and her mouth is pursed. She looks like a puppy that has been caught ripping up a bed pillow.

Adrianna searches my face for several moments. She snuggles down against me, wrapping her arms around my chest before offering a muffled, "I don't want you to stop cuddling me."

"Oh. I was afraid you might think I forced myself on you."

"Really? If you recall, I kissed you. If anything, I took advantage of you." She hugs me tight, like I might try to get away.

"Come to that, why did you kiss me? I've been trying hard to be just a friend and keep this part of me buried away." I continue to play with her hair and stroke her shoulders.

"I've been trying the same. You didn't need the complications," Adrianna says, her voice rumbling against my chest.

"Me?"

"Yes, you. Demons, assassins, rogue witches, hate groups, work, and even sans a place to live. Most of all, I didn't want to mess up our friendship."

"So why, then?"

"I couldn't think of any other way to calm you down," she says, loosening up the hug just a bit and stroking the underside of one of my breasts. I offer her a sigh for her efforts. Thinking about it for a moment, she isn't wrong.

"I am definitely calm," I say.

Adrianna does something that is so out of character for her that I have to look to make sure she is the woman in my arms—she giggles like a schoolgirl maybe a third her age. "Then you are pleased?"

"Adrianna, if I were any more pleased, I'd just be a pile of goo that you'd have trouble getting out of your rug." I receive another giggle for my comment.

"I'm glad. Stella, I've had hot bloomers for you almost from the first minute I met you. When you brought that silly letter from Daring Karie here for my husband, half of me was furious that you might have been a trollop, and the other half soaked my gusset all the way through. Last night you were so discombobulated that I took advantage of you. I'm only a little sorry," she says, punctuating it by using the tip of her tongue to flick over my stiffening nipple. Her confession is adding to my ardor.

"And here I was going to apologize to you for my untoward behavior."

Adrianna smiles. "Stella, when you told me about Manuel, Antonio, and everything you had been through, I was ready to tie you down to have my way with you. You were losing your virtue last night regardless."

"Virtue? I left that behind long ago. My confessor already thinks the worst of me." My remorse roars back to life. "But what about Henry? Your husband?"

Her face becomes more serious as she holds me. "I love my husband, but not in the traditional way. He and I have engaged in marital relations exactly once, to formally consummate our union. He knows I don't desire his carnal attentions. So we both pretend. I ignore his dalliances with, as I gather, Daring Karie, and he looks the other way when my female guests are wearing the same clothes the next day as they wore the previous night." She pauses for a moment. "Oh, neither of us flaunts it or rubs each other's face in our unspoken arrangement, but we both know it is there. We are both realists in the art of love."

"But what about the servants. Surely—"

"Stella, they already know."

"What?!"

"After you fell asleep—" I'm horrified that I may have left Adrianna without good loving. The look on my face must tell enough of a story because she soothes me with, "Oh, I have no regrets. None at all. You gave me pleasure many times. But as I was saying, after you fell asleep and well after my normal bedtime, Nayeli came in to check on me. She was the one that brought us the blanket. I actually asked her to wake us after Henry leaves for the office."

"What are they going to think?"

"Who? The servants? Darling, I don't know if you've noticed, but they think you walk on water. I don't think you'd lose their love if you stabbed one of them to death in a church.

"Now, I think we might just have some more time." She cups my breasts and nuzzles down between them.

I'm still stunned. "But—" I manage to get out before her hand spider-walks up my thigh. Her fingers start teasing my pubic hair with the lightest of touch. "Mmmm." I moan. "You convinced me to—"

A knock at the door startles both of us into immobility. We look at each other and laugh.

"Come in," Adrianna says, her voice returning to one of command. We both pull the blanket up to cover ourselves.

Nayeli steps through the door, obviously not looking our way. "Ma'am, you asked me to—"

"Yes, thank you, Nayeli."

"Here are your dressing gowns. I'll leave them here on the chair."

"Very good."

"Ma'am, there is a message for Miss Stella from the constabulary," she says, holding out the letter at random. She is doing anything she can to keep from looking at us.

"Leave it there on the coffee table. Serve breakfast in the dining room in fifteen minutes, please."

"Yes, ma'am. Also, the master left a note for Miss Ochoa on the dining table."

I don't know what to say in my less than adequate dress so I just blush and grin when Nay breaks down and steals a quick glance. The maid pulls the door closed after her.

"Oh, dirty drawers," Adrianna exclaims. Her tone shifts down, and her aggressive vulgarity changes to something more like a little girl pleading for some more gruel. "I wanted more loving."

I tilt her face up to meet mine to deliver a soft kiss on her lips. "Thank you."

Her open mouth invites something more, but I don't take her bait. I still don't know where I stand. She pouts, "Well, I guess that's it. Let's get the day started. What do you have planned?"

She gets up, and I get the first look at her fully naked. Her heavy curves start to overheat my boiler. And her bottom is something that poets try to write about but can never hope to convey even in one part in a thousand of its splendor. Standing with her back to me, she slips into bloomers and dressing gown while I watch, wishing I were that lace covering her.

Turning, she says, "What, are you staying there, slugabed?"

"Nope, just enjoying the sights."

In that soft voice I'm becoming partial to, she says, "Thank you for your pleasant fibs." She bends down and kisses my forehead. Unfortunately for my middle, that just gives me a front-row seat to gawk at her breasts. "See you at breakfast?"

"Wild horses couldn't keep me away."

She gives me a smile and leaves the room, closing the door. I decide I need to get decent, but not without thinking about what all this means for us. Was this one night of passion? Am I to be her muffin? Or maybe just her fancy girl? What does it all mean? The answers are important because I've fallen for my hostess in more ways than just having her in the biblical sense. She warms my heart and always seems to put me first. I would be more than happy to be her wife. I also need to know where I stand because I have dinner with Karie tonight.

The letter on the coffee table thankfully attracts my attention. I tear open the envelope and pull out three pages in the inspector's horrible script. Why is it that men can't write?

Stella,

Let me start with professional items.

1) We discovered another of your sweeper toys in the wreckage last night.
2) Ex-constable Heinrick Meier is now the head of security at the Coal Syndicate.
3) We have found fingerprints on the long gun but no match.
4) We have discovered in an interview that Meier's fingertips and thus fingerprints have been obliterated with acid.
5) Meier and CEO Jasperson both have an alibi for last night.

I do not know what all of these pieces together mean except that I believe you are still in danger. Please take the appropriate precautions. My concerns for your safety are why I enlisted your team to follow and protect you.

With those things in mind, I want to delve into the personal.

I've never expressed feelings for you as you have held everyone at arm's length except Miss Taylor. I never have been given any indication that you desire anything more from me than friendship. I care for you deeply as a friend and colleague. If, and I stress that small word, it ever progressed beyond that, I would be proud to be considered a suitor for your hand. However, I will not pine over you like a lovesick puppy. Until the day comes when you would accept something more from me, if it ever comes to pass, I will remain your friend and confidant and ask nothing more than that in return.

Your friendly neighborhood inspector,

(s) Antonio Guizzetti

Goosebumps raise on my skin, partially for the lack of clothing but also because of the contents. I'd dodged one of cupid's arrows and added an assassin's bullet with my name on it. It's not an even trade.

A knock at the door precedes Nayeli coming in. "Oh, I'm sorry, miss. I thought you were being done in here. I came in to straighten up. I'll leave you be."

Before she can leave, I ask, "Nay, is what the viscountess and I did OK below stairs?"

"Why yes, miss. We all been rooting you on."

"You have?"

"We wondered if you were blind, Miss Stella. The mistress has been sending googly eyes at you since you first came over to see the master."

"But what about that? Am I getting in the way of their marriage?"

"I ain't no nun. I can't tell you the right nor wrong of it, but we all say why not? You ain't taking nothing away from the master. They don't sleep nor do any bundling, but they still love one another in all them other ways."

"So all of the downstairs are OK with this, then?"

"Heck, ma'am, we've been betting how long it would take before you would know each other biblically if that ain't being blasphemous."

"I'm not a nun, either, Nayeli. You take that up with your confessor, not me. By the way, who won?"

"Tommy won twelve dollars fifty."

"That little rat."

#

A small ring of keys drops out of the envelope onto the dining table when I open it.

Stella,

Welcome to the wonderful world of homeowners. Enclosed you will find the deed to the Brick Factory, as well as the keys. I had Mr. Jordan send them ahead, knowing that the sale would close, one way or another.

I've also arranged for a bricklayer/carpenter I know and trust to meet you at the factory at noon. His name is Otto Krieg. Tell him what you want. Listen to him and his suggestions. He isn't one of those bunco men that will charge you and then not do half the work.

Unfortunately, I can't be there as I have an important business meeting with a competitor.

(s) Viscount Helms

I have so many different feelings right now. First and foremost, shame burdens my soul. Henry trusts me, and I have made him a cuckold by enjoying the charms of the woman that sits across from me.

Adrianna calmly reads the newspaper, fully and properly dressed. I try to interest myself in the muffin on my plate or the coffee in my cup, but all I can do is try to understand what our relationship is. On the one hand, I'd like to drag her back to the guest room and make her as disgracefully noisy as I'd managed last night. But, still, she sits nibbling on buttered toast, all but ignoring me while reading her own periodical as if I haven't wallowed in her charms the night before.

Then the keys remind me of the Rockies-sized debt I've racked up for a decrepit old building that must somehow be fixed up. I still have someone trying to kill me. Demons are still being released.

As much of an emotional mess as I had been last night, I believe it might be worse this morning, even if I'm calmer in other ways. It all makes me want to bury my head in the sand until it is all over.

Get a grip, idiota, I remonstrate myself. I bite the muffin, and the sweet blueberries explode in my mouth, warm and gooey. Good as it is, it isn't enough to derail my self-destructive mental processes.

"Demon Powered Train Breaks Speed Record," says the newspaper in front of me. It distracts me, at least momentarily. I try not to look at Adrianna and instead focus on the paper. The headline interests me. All attempts to put a demon on a moving surface have failed. When I dig into the details, it says that the demons powered engines that controlled some sort of pulley and cable system. I think that is sort of cheating. Also, the test rails were an unused siding only three miles long. Probably not feasible over long distances. Keeping all that cabling lubricated and unbroken would be a nightmare.

"Stella, what do you have planned for the day?" my hostess says, interrupting my reading and dredging up passions that had begun to fade from my consciousness.

"Goodness, but I have many things I should do, but would rather find time to play," I say, trying to score some more information.

"Oh? What do you do for hobbies, Stella?" Shot rejected by the goalie.

"Nothing important," I dissemble. "I really need to get to the constabulary again." I wave Henry's missive. "I've got to meet with the builder about the Brick Factory. Then, there is the watchmaker I should interview. My seamstress should have some of my clothes ready. That doesn't include apologizing to my date last night for running out on him." That one gets Adrianna's face to form a small frown. "Oh, and I have my regular dinner date with my good friend Karie Taylor." My hostess's face is now all but stony. I kick that one into the upper corner of the net for a score for the visiting team. "I really wish I had been able to catch Mikey this morning, but I was more pleasantly occupied." Adrianna's face changes in a flash to a coy smile and a blush over her pale cheeks. "She could do some of these errands for me."

Nayeli must have heard this as she entered the room to refresh coffee. "You might check to see if Mikey is with Tommy. She often stays some of the mornings with him."

"What?" I ask, my own issues dissolving before me. "Mikey and Tommy are sparking?"

"No, nothing like that, miss. Cook usually gives her something to eat, and they just talk. Tommy is too much of a rake to settle for one girl."

"Rake? Tommy? The young man I hired as an errand boy?"

"Yes'm. If the mistress will forgive me, he's gotten into the petticoats of half of the downstairs girls within a mile of here. There even be rumors he might be pitching woo with the Clarks' youngest."

"Adrianna, I apologize for saddling you with a monster. I just hope he doesn't get anyone, especially your neighbor's daughter, pregnant."

"T'isn't like that, miss. He don't use his..." Nayeli trails off, realizing what she is talking about over the breakfast table. I try to erase the mental image I have of Tommy playing patty-cake with a young woman, but it's hard. I can't unsee it.

"That will be all, Nayeli," Adrianna says in her stern public voice.

"Nay?" I interrupt. "Could you check to see if Mikey is here for me? If she is, tell her I'll meet her out front in fifteen minutes."

"Yes, miss."

"Well, that left a sour taste in my mouth," Adrianna says.

"Hopefully, it didn't counter the sweetness of last night."

She clears her throat and turns back to her newspaper. I do detect a darker rose color creeping up from her neck. *What is with her?* I'm more confused than ever. I need a clue, and I'm not getting anything.

I tear through three muffins, each with more ferocity than the last. It slakes my physical hunger but not my other needs. With no feedback from Adrianna, I excuse myself from the table, my mind and body in chaos.

# # #

"Mikey, I'm glad I caught you this morning." The smell of horse is all but overpowering. Nayeli had informed me that Mikey would be waiting for me in the stables. I use a kerchief and reach over to wipe some egg from the corner of her mouth.

She smiles at me and says, "Shore, Miss Stella. You are payin' me so I'm totally ready to do anything you be needin'."

"The list is long today. The first thing is I want you to go back to Paula Simpson's and collect any clothes she has ready for me. Bring them back here and give them to Nayeli, Maggie, or Laoise to put away in my room."

"Yes'm."

"Then I have a pair of jobs that I need doing. I'd really like your smarts on both of them, but you can't be in two places at once."

Mikey nods, her freckles flashing somewhat hypnotic.

"I have something a bit dangerous. I want you to pick one of the bigger boys you know to follow an ex-policeman named Heinrich Meier. He's short and broad about the shoulders, making him look like an ape. He is working for the coal syndicate now. Talk to Tommy, and he can tell you where he lives with his mother. I just want to know what he is doing and who he talks to.

"I can't stress enough that this is dangerous. This *pendejo* is meaner than a mother bear before her first spring breakfast."

"Yes, Stella. I know just who to use. Prolly cost you two bits a day."

"Give him this," I say, handing her two dollar coins, each bearing the face of His Royal Majesty Frederick II. "He gets another one every second day until I call him off. It really is dangerous, Mikey. Warn him and don't stint on the coin."

"Yes, ma'am."

"The second is much less dangerous, but I need your ability to boss around the kids."

She chuckles. "That I do good, Stella."

"Don't I know it. Do you know the old brick factory on Irving?"

"The haunted one?"

"It's haunted?"

"Yes'm. Some of us kids used to bed down there until spooky noises and things magically moving around made us stop staying."

"Great buy," I mutter to myself. Then aloud, I say, "Well, be that as it may, I need the thing cleaned from top to bottom. Is that a problem?"

"Naw, Stella. It be only scary at night."

"In that case, anyone that wants to work, I'll pay two bits for a day's work to scrub and clean it from the basement to the chimney. I'll give you another half dollar to supervise them all. And here is a dollar to get some buckets, brushes, and rags."

"I'll get it done, Stella. You can count on me."

"I know I can, Mikey. Here are the keys." I mentally add a trip to a locksmith to rekey the entire place. Who knows how many ex-workers have keys.

# # #

"So is your gut telling you the same thing mine is?" I ask Antonio in his microscopic office. He hasn't mentioned his gaffe or the personal portion of the letter. I vow to myself not to bring it up either.

"If you mean that Heinrick Meier is the assassin, the shooter, and the releaser of demons, then it isn't telling me anything, but rather screaming it to the rooftops."

"That's what I expected."

"I would go even further in saying that I'm certain he is at least the assassin who shot at you. When we interviewed him, he was bandaged all over in random locations. One gets you fifty that if I put that gun you porcupined in his hand, the spikes would match his wounds."

"And that isn't proof enough?"

"No. He'll have some excuse, backed up by any number of witnesses, that explains his injuries. No proof," Antonio says. "Further, he has a solid alibi for last night. Meier and Jasperson were at a party being held by the mayor. I have at least thirty solid citizens that confirm it."

"Maybe an accomplice?" I opine.

"Possible, but that is clutching at straws. Only go where the evidence leads."

"That's your job, Mr. Inspector. I can theorize wherever I want."

"Oh, we do plenty of that here as well, Mrs. Ochoa, but we just can't act on it. And a good thing, too, else we would be jailing everyone who looked sideways."

"Too true. So you have nothing more that is helpful to me personally."

"No, *señora,* I'm sorry. But please protect yourself."

I'd replaced the iron underwear that had gone missing with some old scrap that Tommy found in the stables. I now wore banded armor from my knees to my neckline. "I will. I'm even considering bodyguards."

"Not your worst idea."

"No. I think that involved a large jug of absinthe and two longshoremen."

Antonio laughs. "From any other woman, I'd consider that flummery. From you, I'll take it at face value."

"You will excuse me if I don't go into details?"

"As you will."

"Well, I have a million and a half things to do today. I should get moving. I'll let you know about what I learn at the watchmaker's business."

Antonio cocks his head at me like a dog trying to make sense of what his master just said. "Pardon?"

"Didn't I tell you about the watchmaker?"

"If you did, I don't have any recollection of it."

"The toys used to release the demons could only have been modified by one or two people in the city. Based on the silver solder, it is likely only to be Ustov Wilsdorf. He has a watch sales and repair shop at Columbus and West Chester."

"Yes, I know the place. I purchased one of his creations not six months ago. Watch hasn't lost a minute in all that time. And no, you never told me this." He picks up the toy that released the demon from the circus. "I've been ripping my hair out trying to find where these were made. God, but you are infuriating, woman."

"Thank you," I say. A woman should balance sarcasm with modesty.

"This is constabulary business, Stella. We will talk to the watchmaker. Don't worry yourself about it. Go and stay safe instead."

It feels like I've been patted on the head and told to go play with my dollies. If I didn't have so much to do today, I'd tell the inspector where he could put his suggestion. "Alright, I'll be good." *For now,* I think.

# # #

The Bell in Hand has been my *cantina* long enough to know the patrons, day or night. Bill Mattingsly's boat, *The Jumping Nelly,* must be in dry dock, for he isn't usually here during the days. Jason Rumsley, a night watchman down at the dock, nurses the one ale per day that he allows himself. Horace Appleton plucks at a guitar, whiling away the day before his night-fishing trips. Brenda Marcusdotter prefers drinking here to the bawdy house she works in. Gentleman George Lee, a solicitor with an office around the corner, upends his breakfast, also known as his fifth whisky of the morning. And, of course, Michaeleen O'Flynn, owner, and barman. To my surprise, the entire *Dos Campanas* team is sitting in the booth playing cards.

"Stella!" Michaeleen says in an over-exuberant welcome. It alerts my comrades who turn and wave at me—at least all but Carlos.

He holds up his hands in front of his pockmarked face like a shield. "Antonio made us do it."

"Did he now," I reply. I just want to make him sweat for good measure.

"We figure you are competent enough to protect yourself. You don't need us hanging around, but he insisted."

"Oh, well, as long as it was insisting. I wouldn't want you to feel like someone had twisted your arm," I growl. I can be a cruel bitch when I want to be.

"Don't be like that, Stella," Menaj interjects. "We really did have your best interests at heart. And look how it turned out."

I bark back, "Yeah! And that is why..." I soften my voice to finish, "I want to thank you all very much for protecting my skin."

"What! All of that, and you thank us. I figured we'd be skinned and sautéed by now," Maxwell says, his voice cracking at the worst possible moment.

"Amen!" several of the others say.

"Yes, I'm thanking you. I can't say I like being followed around, but I won't look a gift horse in the mouth. Thank you all," I say, throwing my arms around the three of them I can reach. The group hug lasts for more than a few seconds before dissolving on its own.

"Michaeleen, how quick can you whip up about thirty of your trenchers?"

"Excuse me, did you say thirty?" he says from behind the bar.

"Yes. I have a cleaning crew to feed."

"I don't have enough for anything like that. If I run down to the baker's, I could put together that many salami and cheese hoagies. Maybe scrounge up enough pickles to go with them. Say half an hour?"

"Do that."

"Watch the bar for a second?"

"Sure," I say. Michaeleen never even mentions a price. I know he won't cheat me. He knows I'd not ask if I couldn't pay.

"That's a lot of food, Stella. Did you hire the entire Boston Beacons to clear your new place?"

"No, but close."

"Which reminds me," Carlos says. He hands me a pouch of coin. "The circus was so happy that we stopped the creature dead in its tracks, with so little damage. They paid up before we could even put out the last of the fires. And they weren't stingy."

"Hurrah for circuses," I say.

"I'm not complaining," Donny says. "I might even propose." The entire table groans. Donny's girl is, at best, a gold digger. All of us know it, except Donny. "What?" he asks as if it is news.

"Don't," Carlos orders, ex-officio. Our leader might argue with decisions in his own person, but when he uses that commanding tone, we follow it. We may ask why, but we don't buck it without serious talk with the whole team. "We'll talk more later," Carlos says directly to Donny.

"On another note," I say to change the subject and fill the silence that has formed from Carlos's proclamation, "We have identified the assassin—an ex-cop named Heinrick Meier."

"So, when is the constabulary going to arrest him?"

I shake my head. "No evidence that would convince a jury."

Bea gives a heavy sigh, and Maxwell massages his forehead as if he is in pain. "So we know who to go after if he succeeds," Menaj offers with cynicism dripping from every syllable.

# # #

I walk out of the Bell in Hand with a big smile on my face. Michaeleen and I carry some heavenly-smelling sandwiches and jugs of cider. It should assuage the hunger of my cleaning crew.

When I reach the poderabile, a frown replaces my grin. I begin to boil as I grit my teeth. Someone has used blood to write "*Non Patiatur Phythonissam*" in twenty-inch high letters across the side. I walk around to find it on the other side as well.

"Do people have no respect?" Michaeleen says.

"Michaeleen, most people are good and decent as the day is long, but there are some who believe in only hatred and fear. The vermin that wrote this shouldn't even be considered human."

"You won't hear me disagree. If I ever catch them in my pub, they will get the working end of a billy club until they can't move."

"I won't say nay. Nothing I can do about it now, and better yet, I have a group of workers at my house that should clean that in short order. Let's get this loaded. I'm meeting someone at noon."

"You going to be alright, Stella?"

"You're asking the witch that takes down demons?"

"True, but I don't like my friends hurt."

"I appreciate the sentiment, Michaeleen. I'll be fine," I say, climbing up around all the victuals. On the driver's bench is a handwritten letter saying, "Get out while you still can."

One day I'll catch those worms. While they might not suffer a witch to live, I would have to spare them, not because of the law of the land but rather the witch's three-fold rule. I wouldn't suffer for scum like that. But there isn't anything that says I can't imprison them in a stone jail until the constables arrived.

The sweet daydream lasts me until I get to the brick factory, some five minutes past noon. The place is a hive of activity. There must be fifty kids cleaning the walls, doorframes, gutters, and many more places than I even know the building has. Mikey comes bouncing out like a girl half her age with a new dolly before I can even climb down. Halfway to me, she slows down, and her brow wrinkles, looking at the malicious messaging on the side of the poderabile.

"Hello there, Miss Stella. Did you do that to your magic cart?"

"No, I didn't."

"I thought I could read but don't have an earthly what that is."

"It is in Latin. It is a vile saying that says that witches don't have the same rights as everyone else."

"That's one of the stupidest things I ever heard. Ain't you just like the rest of us? Ain't being a witch nothing different than how tall you are or what color skin or hair you got?"

"Pretty much, Mikey, but those scum, also known as the NPP, don't care. Witches are different so we have to be bad."

"NPP, huh? Well, I can get some of the boys to scrub that right off your coach if'n you want, Stella."

"Yes. And I have to say they have been doing a bang-up job on the building. Goodness, but the place looks like a shiny new penny."

"They are working well, but we aren't done yet, miss."

"Well, call them all in for food," I say, pointing at the butcher-papered sandwiches and jugs of cider. "Share it among everyone."

"You didn't need to do that, Stella."

"I know, but they'll work better with a full stomach. Not only that, they'll be much more likely to want to help out in the future."

"Miss Stella, you do more for us than all the charity ladies put together. You don't give us nothing. You make us work, but it is all we want. We want to show everyone we are worth something."

"Each and every one of them that is working in there has proved something to me. Now a practical question. Do you want me to give you the money to distribute or pay them when they take lunch?"

Mikey pulls her ponytail around and chews at the end. "I ain't comfortable with that much money, Stella. I think we can trust them to stay after you paid 'em. Most of 'em are too proud to leave, miss."

"OK, we'll risk it, but sometime soon, I'm going to be busy with a builder—" a horse-drawn dogcart pulls into the lane, "—and that is him now, I assume. Tell the workers I'll pay them after lunch."

"Yes, ma'am.

"LUNCH CALL," she bellows so loud I wonder where she could have gotten that much breath from her small frame. Kids aged nine to fifteen scramble down from their perches and pour out of the doors.

A sweet little bay pony pulls up a well-used dogcart filled with more tools than I'd seen most anywhere I can remember. "Vould you be being Fraulein Ochoa?"

"And you would be Mr. Krieg," I say to a muscular man with a mostly bald head and a babyface. What little salt-and-pepper hair he has remaining is trimmed down to nothing much more than stubble.

"Please, fraulein, just call me Otto."

"Then just call me Stella."

"Goot, Stella. The Vizegraf Helms tells me that you are needing verk on your building."

"Yes, Otto."

"Tell me vat you vant, and I'll tell you how long it vill take and how much it costs."

"Come on in, and we can go over it."

When he climbs down, I realize he is a good eight inches shorter than I am. He wears shorts, exposing legs that might have looked small on a gorilla but large anywhere else. His feet would have made two of mine, and, as my cobbler has mentioned more than once, I'm not exactly dainty of foot. "Is all these children yours?"

I give a hearty belly laugh. "I thank you for the compliment, Otto, but I'm not sure anyone can be that fertile. I hired them to clean for me. In fact, I'm partial to them and would like you to use them as unskilled laborers. They might learn something."

"Ve have a saying that if you vatch, ve charge you double, and if you help ve charge you triple," he says with a belly laugh that startles many of the people in line for food.

I laugh with him. "I understand, but that will be part of the deal."

"I understand, Stella. Now let's go over your needs."

We walk in through the front door. The workers have done me proud. Light pours through clear windows. Garbage and broken furniture no longer clutter up the spaces. What had been a dingy, dirty mess is now bright and smells only of soap and bleach.

"Well, first of all, I'd like to take this wall down and open this up for a sitting room," I say, going through the first doorway. He grabs the doorframe and thumps it with a hammer.

"It holds no veight. Easy." Krieg scribbles something in a notebook.

"Then through here, I want to take down all of these small walls and split this large room into a kitchen and a dining room."

"Ja. How many people dining room?"

"Twelve?"

"So about here," he says, marking the floor with chalk dividing a third off for the kitchen.

"I think closer to half for more room," I say. He frowns and writes more. "With a swinging door from the kitchen into the dining room."

"Ja."

"And out here, I want a hallway all the way from the front down to here. That way, people don't have to go through the dining room to get to the rooms." He nods and waves me to continue as he notes my requests. "This big double-level area I want to convert to bedrooms. I'm thinking six."

"Stella, I vould think zat six bed chambers vould be enormous. Eight

vould fit vith much space bigger than all rooms I been seeing anywhere."
With chalk, he marks off how big a room would be if he fit in eight. I
stretch my arms out in it and envision a bed, chifforobe, and dressing
table. They would be swallowed up in each space.

"Yes, eight sounds much better." I lead him out onto the production
floor. "Up here, I want another room twice that size above here."

"*Entschuldigen sie, fraulein*—sorry, excusing me. How are you to get
to upstairs rooms?"

I feel like an idiot forgetting the need for stairs and a landing.
"Where would you suggest?"

"If vee put it up the middle between zee rooms, it vill use up less
space."

"That sounds perfect. And let's keep the stairs there already off the
biggest bedroom."

"And each room has its own fireplace?"

"No, I'm going to install a demon."

"I don't be doing that vork," he says, making more notes.

"No need to worry, Otto. Lord Helms will do that. I'll have him
coordinate the ductwork with you."

"*Danke*, Stella. And outhouses?"

"Oh, do you do water closets?"

"*Ja.*"

"Can I get one for each floor and another one only accessible to the
big bedroom? Each one should have a big porcelain tub."

"Expensive, but I can do."

"And windows. This place doesn't have much in the way of light.
Two per room?"

"Cinder blocks make vindows harder because must support veight,
but I can do. No electric lights?"

"No, thank you, Otto. The electricity gives me shivers."

"Goot, I vould haf to hire it out. Any more?"

"One more thing, I want a stable out back," I say, taking him out
back into the courtyard. "I don't need anything more than an enclosed,
weather-tight structure to park my...my wagon in."

"*Ja.* Access through that door? Double doors for the vagon? No
horse stalls?"

"Yes. Yes. And no," I say. "I think that is all of it."

He looks down at his book. "Vat about all this other space?"

"Nope. Keeping it just the way it is."

"*Ja.* You vant stove, ice chest, and finished valls?"

"Yes, please. Do I have to pick out colors now?"

"*Nein.* Ven vee get close, I get Mrs. Krieg to take you to pick that out. I don't see color gut."

I smile. I've heard of those who can't see specific colors but have never met one. "OK, so what's the damage?"

"Paint or wallpaper?"

"Wallpaper, of course."

He wrinkles his mouth and mouths some things under his breath.

"Two hundred for carpenters and plasterers. Another one hundred for your unskilled young'uns. Two hundred to buy materials. Two-fifty for the best appliances. Another hundred for finish vorkers, and add another one-fifty for my time and overhead. Nine hundred dollars. Three veeks."

I mull it over. "If I up it to an even thousand, can you get the master bedroom done in three days and have it all done in two weeks?"

"Master bedroom in four days 'cause I must build it up. Longest part."

"Start Monday?" I say, reaching out my hand. He takes it and shakes. I don't do much, as his massive paw completely encompasses mine. I hand him a pouch I'd specially prepared for this case. It contains banknotes equaling seven hundred dollars.

"*Ja.*"

"I'll need a receipt so I can get reimbursed. The rest when you are done."

# # #

As the afternoon at the Bell in Hand goes on, my beer tastes off, and sparrows are loose in my innards. The closer it gets to dinnertime, the more the conversations slip past me. I can't concentrate on anything going on around me as a creeping dread swallows me.

No, I am not worried about being murdered in the middle of my friends. Instead, it is much more sinister, something I'd managed to not think about all day with pressing issues. To wit, what do I do about my dinner with Karie? Or maybe a better question might be, what is my relationship, if any, with the viscountess?

"Stella? Stella? Hello, Stella!"

"I'm sorry. What was it, Carlos?"

"I was asking if you were alright. You seem to be sweating and preoccupied." My teammates are more siblings than friends. No couth man would tell a woman she is sweating.

"And the horse you rode in on," I reply. "I'm fine, but I do have to leave soon."

"Dinner with Karie?" Donny asks.

"As always on Saturday. I have to give my *real* friends some time," I say as I swat at him playfully.

"Save some for us," Maxwell interjects.

"What, dinner or Karie?" I tease. "If you want her, you have to put up your doubloons just like any other bloke."

That gets a raucous round of laughter but doesn't get me any closer to solving my dilemma.

#

"Are you alright, miss?" a man in a suit asks. I pull a few strands of my hair back to keep them out of my vomit. I don't think I can speak so I just nod. He shrugs his shoulders and walks on. He really has to think I'm in my cups. I do have the smell of bitter on my breath.

No one else pays any attention to me bent over. I had managed to stop the poderabile before emptying everything I'd put in my mouth since before lunch. The chunky mess is much better in the drain than in the floorboards of my vehicle. Shivers go up my back as I try to swallow down further nausea. My stomach rebels once again, depositing another semi-gelatinous mass at my feet. I've worshipped the gutter before, but always when I've had too much to drink. I had one and only one pint.

I'm sailing into a minefield. I look up at the sky and ask, "What do I do?" I guess the lord of hosts isn't listening to one Stella Ochoa today because there is no answer.

I use my kerchief to mop my brow, cheeks, and lastly, the remaining traces of my spew from around my mouth.

"Should I just cancel?" It would give me time to understand the new dynamic in my life. "Buck up," I say to myself as I straighten up. "It's just dinner."

For the remaining drive to Karie's, I clamp down on my nervous tummy. I almost change my mind after I knock on the door. Alejandro, of the broken nose, opens the door. His broad shoulders effectively block the doorway. Even with his graying hair, he intimidates most people he meets. I happen to know he is a pussycat studying to be a kitty cat, at least as long as you are good to his employer. "Good evening, Miss Stella."

"Is it really?" I reply as soon as I swallow some vile tasting near-vomit.

"Are you alright, Miss Stella?"

"Not even kinda."

"I'm sorry to hear that."

"Where is Karie?"

"In the parlor, waiting for you, miss."

I steel myself for the reaction my body is threatening. "Could you bring some bicarbonate, please?"

"Right away, Stella."

Karie is in the parlor alright. She lounges on the divan, wearing a lace gown over nothing but her delectable skin. Instead of going over to nuzzle her neck, I think about how I might mess up Winnie's floors if I lose more of my lunch. My self-control allows me to swallow the saliva that forms in my mouth and bite back the reaction my stomach urges. I'm standing there shaking like I've got the chills.

"Stella! Are you alright? You're white as milk." She jumps up, bare feet and all. She wraps her arm around my shoulder and eases me over to the couch. As soon as I'm sitting, she bellows, "Tea! Now!"

I just sit there as she cuddles around me. It reminds me of a discussion after my ninth birthday. I'd convinced myself that the cake had been for my birthday so I ate the remaining three pieces in the root cellar. As part of my punishment, my mother had sent me to talk it over with my confessor, Father Juan. He had put his arm around me, making me feel safe as he explained. "Stella, God has given us the best gauge of right and wrong. Have you ever had the feeling you were about to do something wrong? That's God's voice speaking to you. When you ignore his words inside you, you will almost always be wrong. When in doubt, listen to that feeling."

I never heard God's words, but I certainly knew the feeling he spoke of. Right now, my belly overflows with that feeling.

"I can't. I just can't," I mumble to myself.

"What can't you? Here is some tea," Karie says as the cook brings it in. "It will make you feel better."

I snap out of my funk. "I can't do this tonight, Karie."

"I'm confused, *querida*. Take some tea."

"No tea!" I snap.

"I have your bicarbonate, Miss Karie."

I snatch the cup off the silver tray and down the entire thing in four swallows. At least all of it that doesn't dribble out of the corners of my mouth. It soothes but doesn't wholly quench the fire in my middle. Even though I don't see them leave, Cook and Alejandro make themselves scarce.

"I've gone and done something dumb," I start my confession. Karie's empathy oozes off of her as she strokes my back. For twenty years we've been friends; she knows not to interrupt. "I had a tryst with someone else. Now I don't know what to do. I mean, I do know what to do, but I'm confused." I lean into her cuddle, wanting to get more, but my middle fills with more acid at the thought.

"So the viscountess finally fed your pussycat," Karie says.

"Karie!" I snap as I pull back.

"Your reaction is all the confirmation I needed. You, dear, are smitten."

"But I don't know. What do I do?" Tears start dripping down my cheeks. "I don't want to hurt you, but she hasn't...I mean, she didn't... Oh, I don't know what I mean."

"Stella, you can't hurt me. I thought we went over that before. I have no hold over you but friendship. That you have let me share your charms is a bonus, not a defining characteristic. Now tell me everything, *querida*. I've got a good deal of experience in this area."

So I spend the next hour talking. My tears dry up as I unburden my soul. I give her every detail except the intimate ones. Winnie serves dinner in the parlor without even being called. As I run out of things to talk about, we polish off the fish tacos with refried beans and flan for dessert. Winnie clears the low table and brings in coffee before leaving us alone again.

"My dearest friend, you are a knothead."

"Excuse me?"

"You've told me all the things you wanted to hear from Adrianna, but YOU didn't listen. She told you everything you needed to know with one simple question. 'What do you have planned for the day?'"

"Huh?" I feel like I've just walked into Alice's looking glass.

"You are a wonderful person, Stella, but your one marriage didn't prepare you for courting and all of the nuances. If I translate Adrianna's question, it comes out, 'I want to spend much more time with you doing anything you want.' You told her that you were going off to spend time with your weekender. If that isn't bad enough, it is with her husband's fancy girl." I gasp. How could I have been so stupid?

Karie looks earnestly at me. "Stella, let me ask you a question. Are you serious about this?"

I bite my lip. "Yes. No. Maybe."

"Not very definitive, *amiga*."

"I do want it, but I'm worried about how it will affect her relationship with Henry, and for that matter, my immortal soul by coming between husband and wife."

"I am not a priest or your confessor. That last piece you have to take up with them. But as far as Henry, he probably would urge you two on, as long as you were discrete."

"Really?"

"Yes, but I can't speak for him. But I'd probably bet my house on it."

"In that case, I'm serious. Even before we kissed, I found myself looking forward to being with Adrianna. I wanted to make her life better. I want to grow old with her. Now that has only magnified. Can I fix my idiocy of this morning?"

"Yes. If you do it right now. You have to let the viscountess know that you didn't canoodle with me and how much you care for her."

#

There is just enough light that I don't need to break out the lanterns. I push the poderabile like I've never done before. After I clear the busy Charles River Bridge, I mash both throttle levers all the way forward. I wind my way around carting traffic as if they are standing still. More than one goose horn blows as I charge home at a speed that might very well break my neck as I careen around corners and dogcarts. One part of my mind is ashamed that I've only one thing on my mind.

I'm comforted by the sound of the poderabile's wheels on the crushed shells of the Helms Estate. I pull back on the throttles so hard I'm pushed forward into the seat straps. I jump down and storm into the house. Laoise is the first servant I run into.

"Where is the viscountess?"

"In her bedchamber, miss. She asked for dinner to be served there." I don't even say thank you to her but rather storm off in the direction I'd been pointed. I found the door closed. I finally stop, considering my next move. For a good ten seconds, I consider knocking. I instead barge through the portal.

Adrianna is on a pile of bed linens. Her cheeks are puffy, and her eyes red. "Stella?" she says, looking up. The kerchief that she holds in one hand is streaked with mascara and lip color. "But I thought you were sta—"

I march on her in the bed before kneeling down. I take her face in both of my hands. "I'm sorry. There was never a choice for me. It is you and only you." I kiss her softly on the lips and then again on her eye and down her cheek. They are not in the need of the body but the passion of my heart. Her tears renew, and she blubbers, reaching out to pull me closer. I climb up onto the bed and wrap around her as best as possible, stroking her hair.

"I thought you just wanted me once," she blubbers. "Like I was a trollop or streetwalker or something." She clutches me tight enough to feel my iron girdle. She gives my middle a look. I urge the metal to flow out the bottom of my petticoats like quicksilver. When she can only feel me, she squeezes my middle hard. I may have bruises in the morning, but I don't care.

"I wondered the same thing about you until I realized just what I'd done." Karie had made it emphatically clear that I shouldn't mention her part in my education at all. She clings to me like a drowning woman, weeping.

"Please tell me that last night wasn't a one-off mistake, Stella."

I stroke her shoulder and wish I could let her feel my soul like I can that of the earth. "No chance, *mi amante*. I want you here...today, tomorrow, and as long as you can stand me."

# # #

I wake up in darkness that is only pierced by a single guttering candle in a wall sconce. Adrianna and I are fully clothed and yet intertwined on the top of her bed. Her soft, regular breathing against my neck is reassuring. Based on the state of the candles, the lack of a glow through the curtains, and the silence, I assume it is somewhere around midnight.

The arm that is under my sweetheart tingles with numbness. As I slip it out from underneath her, Adrianna moans and tries to wrap around me like a python. I trade a pillow under her head for my limb. I then flail my hand around to restore circulation.

"¿Querdida?" I say, nudging her. "¿Amante? Annie, please wake up." I need to go back to my own room before someone notices, but I don't just want to disappear.

"That's sweet. Say it again," my lover mumbles around my neck.

"What? Annie?"

She giggles in a higher register than her normal voice. "No one ever gave me a nickname before."

"Not even in school? I assumed Anna. It seems so obvious."

"I didn't attend school," she says, releasing me for the first time that evening. "I was tutored in different subjects from arithmetic, business, chemistry, all the way to womanhood."

"I'm sorry."

"Why? I learned what I needed and then some."

"But you never had the chance to make friends in school."

"Close relationships were discouraged with anyone outside my family. Too much risk."

"That must have been lonely."

She brushes loose hair away from my face. "I never thought about it until Henry and I married."

"And lovers?"

In the pale light, I just see her cheeks go pink. "Her name was Maria, the scullery maid. Sounds like a cliché doesn't it." I smile back. "We remained lovers for nearly two years until I married Henry and my husband moved us to Boston."

"Ever see her again?"

"Once. She married a sweet girl, and they live in the capital. I had dinner with them, but her wife politely made it clear I wasn't welcome. I've left them alone to their happiness. What about you?"

"Well, I played kissing games with both boys and girls when I was in school," another place I need to avoid Karie's name. "Nothing really stuck. My mother tried to bring me out in society. That was a disaster of biblical proportions. The only time I got kissed there was by a stupid little *pendejo* who thought he could take advantage of me."

Adrianna giggles again. "I'm sure you educated him to the error of his ways."

"I had barely started my witchcraft training, else I might have done something more serious. I had to rely on the tried and true. I kneed the *pendejo* in the family jewels. It doubled him up while I left."

"Good girl. Sometimes those brutes need to be taught a lesson. But what about your husband?"

"Met him when my mother went to complain to a wainwright about her carriage. Aaron was there getting a replacement wheel. He just happened to be shirtless. The sweat shining on his chocolate brown skin just gave me shivers."

"Moor, African, or Cuban?"

"A moor. I got the first thing I might define as excitement watching those muscles straining. Later as I got to know him better, the accent to his Spanish alone would get me wet."

My lover lies quietly for a moment. "Is that going to be a problem between us?"

"Aaron has been dead for more than a few years now."

"No, I mean that you won't have...Do you need a man to have..."

"*Cariño*, I have only ever had one man inside me. I've only ever had one woman until you touch me." She flinches. It's barely noticeable, but with my entire attention on her, she couldn't have hidden it. *Damn*, I cursed myself. "As nice as sex is, it can't hold a candle to love. It is probably premature to call what is between us love, but I feel you in my heart like only my husband managed." I am unprepared for her response. She pounces on me like a lioness on a crippled gazelle. She shoves her tongue down my throat. And as quickly as she attacked, she pulls back.

"Thank you," she whispers. "It's been a long time since I've cared for someone this way."

"I won't ask, but I'm jealous of her. Now shut up and get your clothes off. I intend to get something from you for being blubbered on."

"How about this," she says, starting to undulate and unfastening her dress, one slow button at a time. "I saw a woman in Cotton Candy's Lady Parade doing this, driving every man in the place crazy." She leans over and whispers, "It did the same to me."

She lifts up her skirts and underthings so I can see her bare ankles all the way up her calf. Then to tease me some more, Annie pulls her bloomer bottoms up above her knees. "If the goal is to get me to attack you, just keep doing that," I threaten.

She slips her upper blouse off her shoulders along with her chemise, giving me a glimpse of her bare shoulders and the beginnings of her full bosoms. Like a cockchafer, she draws the chemise back up. As I try to sit up, she pushes me back, waggling a finger at me. Still weaving back and forth to imaginary music, she undoes the buttons to her teal skirt. It slides down to the floor in a puddle leaving her in blue-green petticoats and flashing her ankles. I take a deep breath to keep from exploding. My sex has gone beyond just mere slickness. I'm worried I'm going to soak the entire bed.

Sitting on the wingback chair, she reaches up under the colorful swirls of fabric only to toss her cotton bloomers my way. Her smell is already overpowering me, but her underthings reek in the best possible way. She dances around, lifting her crinolines to give me peeks of more. She stops moving with her legs spread wide. She lifts her undershirt over her head, spilling her glorious breasts out. The nipples are hard and sticking out like acorns. Her gyrations start back up again, making my attentions focus right at her hips. She slides down her petticoats with her bloomers in one motion, leaving her bare all over except for a gold chain around her neck and a pair of black pearl earrings.

She stops moving and stands in front of me, legs spread and her hands on her hips as if defying me to do anything. I climb off the bed and walk around behind her. She tries to watch me, but I just put a hand on her cheek and point her vision back to the front.

Out of her sight and with the lightest touch I can manage, I run my fingers down her back and over her derriere. She draws in a long breath but remains statue-still, only her heavy breathing allowing her body any movement. With both sets of fingernails, I draw them gently up the inside of her thighs. I see her ass and legs quiver. Continuing my line, I rake up her back until I reach her neck. Her whole body is shaking.

"Now, please," she says, not moving. "Please. I need your love. Please." I bend over and run my fingers up under her hairline, baring her neck, where I place a gentle kiss before flicking my tongue across the fine hairs I find there. "Stella, please."

I push her over onto the bed, bending down behind her. I place my lips on her sweetness. "Thank you. Thank you. Thank you," she repeats until a crisis overcomes her ability to talk.

12—Sunday, May 13, 1888

I drift up into that glorious feeling of being married. The warmth of skin on skin cradles my back all the way down to my feet. An arm cups one of my breasts from behind. I hear just the faintest little snores behind me. My well-being quotient is very high. If it weren't the Sabbath, I could easily spend the entire day in bed just snuggling and talking to my girl.

That she is my girl gives me a certain level of satisfaction all by itself. I don't know where, if anywhere, this can go, but I will happily go there with Adrianna. I am not sure how I fell so hard and so quickly for her, but I feel like the missing piece of my soul has just fitted into place. It isn't the sex. To be honest with myself, sex is a part of it. Still, I have an overwhelming urge to protect her and do everything I can to make her happy. It is an emotional attachment that I've only had one other time in my life, with my husband, Aaron.

"Mmmmm," she offers as she squirms, if at all possible, closer to me. Her fingers start massaging my breast and are casting about for my nipple. With my size, that can be a challenge for someone who can see them. But Adrianna snags that proud little bit of flesh. This elicits a moan from me as well.

"Stop it. We have to get ready for church, the one day that your husband doesn't go to work."

"Don't worry, sweetie. Laoise always wakes me up two hours before we need to leave. Henry won't even stir until about thirty minutes prior to services. That men can get ready so quickly should be a crime."

"I guess life isn't fair. But you were last night, my Annie." I roll over to face her. "Thank you for a wonderful night. I can't recall ever being so pleased." I pull the hand that is tracing my curves up and kiss it. I take my time, pressing my lips to the back, the palm, and eventually popping her index finger into my mouth, licking and sucking on it.

"You weren't and aren't a slouch in that area, either. Of course, I had been emotional all day. That may have had something to do with it," she says with a mischievous wink.

"So, is your mind at ease on that point?" I ask, taking her finger from my mouth.

"I'm sorry, Stella. I'm normally not so needy or clingy with my lovers, but I've never felt this way about anyone, even Henry. As long as I have you in my life and my bed, I'm quite content."

I lean forward and plant my lips against her but say, "I feel the same about you, *querdida*. I have no intention of letting you—"

I'm interrupted by knocking on the viscountess's door. Oddly I don't remember closing it last night. Of course, there were too many emotions flying about.

"—go."

Muffled comes Laoise's voice, "Mistress, it is time to wake and get ready for church."

"I'll be dressing myself this morning, Laoise."

"Yes, ma'am."

We giggle together after we hear her walking back down the hall.

"I'm going to keep you to that promise," Adrianna says.

"I hope so. Now, dear, as pleasant as this is, I need to get back to my room before your husband, or too many of the staff get moving."

She pulls me close into something akin to a bear hug. "Thank you for giving me something I never thought I'd have." I hear her sniffle. I pull back to see a pair of tears leaking down her cheek. "Tears of joy, Stella," she says in a way that answers my unasked question.

I respond only by kissing them under her eyes.

"Now get your sweet fundament dressed and back to your room." She playfully swats me as I climb out of bed. "Will you be joining us for church this morning?"

"I think maybe in the future, but for now, I have to see my confessor. Too much has happened. I need a padre I understand and who understands my past."

"I'm not surprised, but it would be nice to have you sitting next to me," she says as I sponge off the worst of our rutting smell.

"Agreed."

"When do I get to have you in my arms again?"

"We will have to work something out that will keep us together without rubbing your husband's face in our canoodling," I say, strapping my bosoms into the Torquemadan vice that is my brassiere.

She wrinkles her nose as if she just walked downwind from an overripe privy. "You make this sound so dirty. I think it is beautiful."

I pause, in only my undershirt and petticoats, and lean over and kiss her thoroughly. "'Beloved, let us love one another, for love is from God, and whoever loves has been born of God and knows God.'"

"John 4:7. A nearly perfect passage."

"But lest we forget, there is someone who can be hurt by our love. That makes it dangerous and potentially vile. I will NOT hurt your husband and my friend."

I slip my dress over my head, noticing that I'm missing most of my buttons again. I collect my stockings, boots, and bloomers and plant one last kiss. I open the door and cast about each way. Seeing no one, I dart out.

I don't look around because I feel guilty. I do it only to keep Henry from being hurt.

# # #

Father Juan's sermons usually keep my attention. This morning, however, I find my mind wandering. There is the overarching warmth in my chest for Adrianna. My mind wonders briefly if I may have confused love with lust. I know I overthink things, but it is how I am.

I sit in church, and here I will confess my sins. Have I fallen for the classic tool of the devil to pull me away from my Lord God? Even as I think it, my mind flashes not to our time in bed but rather the hours we've spent pouring over newspapers to head off issues with the demon power industry. Images flash in my mind about her nursing me back to health after the Snowdonia affair. And then, I imagine time together as we age, with me helping her from my sickbed into her rocking chair and reminding her of the medications she is to be taking. I imagine us caring for a young baby and the mutual sleepless nights that entails.

No. Lust isn't what drives my emotions. We would face any issue together as a partnership.

As wonderful as this daydream is, it just reminds me that I have other issues in my life at the moment. Not the least of these concerns is that I've had someone try to buy me a pine box, which is causing me to wear metal underwear. Also, I've somehow drawn the attentions of the unrighteous scum, the NPP. Add all of these to the uncertainty of my new house. All of this adds up to enough to take my mind away from the beauty that is love.

So focused on my musings that the concluding rite is upon us before realizing just how deep my thoughts had led me astray. I give my responses automatically. I even remain seated as people get in the queue for the confessional. Father Juan Dubois y Cantonio, resplendent in his black cassock, steps into the priest's side to do his part in forgiving the sins of his congregation.

I wait. I want more than just the formality of "...it has been one week since my last confession..." What I have to say I want to be face to face.

Father Juan has more than once kept me on the right path with his counsel. I won't say I always liked what he said or even how he said it, but in the end, I believe it led me down the righteous path. No one says faith is easy. Just look at Job. With that worthy man forefront of my thoughts, I compose myself to wait. I spend the time muttering biblical passages to myself from Second Corinthians as I look at the image of Mary. I have no reason for picking that scripture. As a hellfighter, I have to keep my biblical knowledge fresh.

".. momentary troubles are achieving for us an eternal glory that far outweighs them all. So we fix our eyes not on what is seen but on what is unseen since what is seen is temporary, but what is unseen is eternal."

"Stella, what are you still doing here?" Father Juan asks. His question makes me realize I'd lost track of time again. The nave is empty except for the pair of us.

"I need your guidance, Father."

"I can slip back into the confessional if you are in need."

"Can we just sit and talk? You've helped me many times in my life, and I want your thoughts."

"Sounds serious," he says, sweeping his cossack underneath him. Sitting, we are at much more the same height. Standing, I have to look down, something I'm not used to doing, at least to a man.

"It is, Father. I'm in love."

"Blessed be all the saints," he says like an Irishman. "The Lord has decided to act on my prayer. What's his name?"

"Her, Father."

"OK, what is her name?"

I hesitate for a moment. "Can we keep our conversation under the seal?"

"Daughter, anytime you ask for guidance, I keep it in the strictest of confidence. Barring a direct papal order, your secrets are safe."

"Her name is Adrianna."

He cocks his head at me. I can also tell that he purses his lips because the pink gap between his thick beard and mustache disappears. "The Viscountess Adrianna Helms?"

"Yes."

Father Juan's face goes blank and unreadable. "Tell me."

For the next fifteen minutes, I explain. He concentrates on my story. I share how my love for Adrianna grew from less than nothing, how she is without physical love in her relationship, how I want to keep her safe and grow old with her, and even how we will do everything not to hurt her husband and my friend.

There is silence when I run down. There are frown lines around the priest's eyes. In a calm and soothing manner, he says, "My daughter, this is the first time in my life that I've been ashamed of you."

Not the reaction I'd expected. "What? I'm confused, Father. I thought you would be overjoyed that I'd found love."

"I would be, but what you found was adultery, not love."

"But I'm taking nothing away from Henry. Theirs is a marriage of—"

"It is a marriage, Stella, not a corporate merger. They can't just take the parts of it they like. She, as his wife, is his to take as he deems fit. That he chooses not to take those rights isn't her choice or yours." He looks into my face that must mirror my own inner confusion.

He takes my hand. "Stella, you are too close to it. Don't you realize that coming and asking for my guidance is your own conscience speaking out?" My befuddlement deepens. "How many people come to their Father confessor before continuing a relationship? In the twenty-some-odd years I've been doing this, the answer is two. The first was a girl who wanted my advice before getting involved with a Jewish boy. The second is you.

"You know this is wrong, but want me to bless your union to salve your spirit. I can't and won't do it."

"But..."

"There are no buts, Stella," he dictates. "Think it through. You said that you needed to keep from hurting Henry. You've turned him into a cuckold, and you want the Lord's blessing for this? No, daughter. Nor can I turn my back and give you absolution like with your semi-regular indiscretions with a certain other young woman. At least she is single and available. There you always have a hope of a union between you. What you would be doing with Adrianna is a mortal sin that can't be washed away with a few Hail Marys or Our Fathers. I can see no way you can form a union with Adrianna. You must end it."

I've never been spoken to quite so firmly by the father. Worse, he wants me to tear my heart out and walk away while it pumps my love all over the dust. Around the tears leaking down my face, I respond with a little girl whisper, "I don't know if I can."

"This is your immortal soul you are talking about, Stella. Find a nice available man or even woman to give your love to, and I'll not only give my blessing but gladly officiate. But, your relationship with the viscountess is doomed before it even starts. It doesn't mean you can't have a close friendship, but nothing more." He wraps his arms around me as I weep. It may not be professional, but he is a compassionate human. "Now, daughter, you have to go out and face this reality. You can't hide here in the nave. Come back to me when you have ended your affair, and we will talk about penance."

"Yes, Father," I manage to choke out. I stand and walk away without looking back. I left not with what I came for but with much less than I had come in with. I can feel Father Juan walking me to the church doors, but he stops as I walk through the portal.

I stumble down the steps, blackness filling me with the emptiness that awaits me at the Helmses'. Oblivious to what is around me, I stumble forward like a trolley with a broken guiding cam. That is until I feel the impact and sharp steel penetrating my back. The blade must have slipped between the bands of my armor. I can feel the edged dagger inside my torso. I let out a wail.

From hundreds of miles away, I hear Father Juan shout, "Stella!"

An arm grabs me from behind. The knife withdraws. Blood spurts.

My armor merges, becoming a solid sheath. There is another impact on my back. My armor holds. And another. And another.

"Beat the blighter," comes an unknown voice from the bottom of a well.

"Get the knife," responds a similarly distant and unknown person.

My legs won't hold me. The arm around me is yanked away. The world spins. I collapse to the ground. Five muscular kids grapple with a bum holding a bloody knife. One of the boys stomps the fist holding the weapon into the ground.

More screams, mine and others, as the boys wrestle the man away from me and my vision.

"Kick him."

"Don't let him up."

Blood pools under me. Whistles. Running footsteps. Kicking. Dull thuds. Ebbing. Pain. Cold. Blurring vision. Darkness. Whistles. Boots hitting cobblestones.

"Stella!" I peel open my eyes enough to the unfocused image weaving in front of me. I hear Father Juan's voice speaking in its deep, sonorous preaching tone. "So do not fear, for I am with you; do not be dismayed for I am your God. I will strengthen you and help you; I will uphold you with my righteous right hand." The familiar warmth of God's love burns through the chill that has taken hold of my body. The magic is rough, like having a deep cut abraded to be fully cleaned out. Sandpaper of God's love is pulled across my wounds. I scream.

Father Juan continues, "Heal me, Lord, and I will be healed; save me, and I will be saved, for you are the one I praise."

My eyes open fully, no longer clouded in agony or the fuzz the brain uses to protect against traumatic injury. Father Juan kneels over me with God's magic swirling around him like a hurricane of biblical proportions. I still feel the harshness of the power forcing my body to knit itself together.

My life has been broken apart. My love has been shattered. My body has been torn and pierced. All I can think is that all of this blood and knife work has cost me another dress.

"Sleep, Stella."

"What a bossy *pendejo*."

13—Monday, May 14, 1888

The faint sounds of a choir make me wonder if I've gone to Saint Peter. But then the smell of frying potatoes makes my nose twitch. My stomach growls. Food draws a craving from me like blood might for a vampire if such a thing exists. I try to sit up, but my middle doesn't bend. If that isn't enough, a stab of pain rewards my effort. I pull back the covers and find myself flat on my back, missing my outer dress. Black iron covers me from thigh to throat over my underpinnings. It spurs my memory. I'd solidified the bands around my middle into a tube to protect myself. My saviors couldn't do anything to take it off.

I, on the other hand, with little effort, get the edges of the metal to spin off into little coils. It takes counting seven chimpanzees until the entirety of my armor is nothing more than long, weak springs lying beside me.

Wary of the ache in my back, I roll over the spongy metal to sit on the edge of a bed. I reach around my right side and probe at my back. I can feel the wound. It is mildly feverish, and the ragged edges make it clear I'll bear yet another warrior's mark. At the rate things are going, I'll be nothing but one big piece of scar tissue before I'm a crone.

"*La mujer esta despierta. Aqui rapido, padre.*" I hear outside the half-open door. Father Juan comes through the door.

"Stella, I love you, but it would be very nice if you could keep your blood on the inside and your outsides intact."

"Yes, Father. I'll remember to ask for my next attack to be a clubbing," I say with as much sarcasm as my aching body will allow me to muster.

Juan chuckles. "I'm glad to see that you could get that iron lung off of you. We tried any number of things without success. In the end, it probably saved your life, for my skill is not well-honed. Had you been more badly damaged, I don't think I could have saved you. I just threw a quick patch over the hole to keep your insides in."

"Come to that, how come you didn't tell me you were a witch? You have power that matches just about any other white witch I've ever met.

You could have been a doctor or a hellfighter, either one. Why not help people that way?"

He gives a sigh. "I'll start with the first question. I didn't tell you as it is between God and me. Do you tell me all your secrets?" I just open my eyes wide at him in incredulity. "Well, then maybe you do, but it matters not to my profession. Second, I've been offered both of those paths many times before. I chose to go where my vocation is. Could saving someone's life, as a hellfighter might, be any more worthy than saving that person's soul? Is curing the corruption of the body more valuable than erasing the taint of their spirit?"

I stammer for a reply but instead swallow and shake my head.

"My powers are inconsequential compared to the good I can do as shepherd of the people in my congregation. I almost never use these skills, even to those dying, even to those I could save."

"Why?"

"Who am I to thwart God's will? Why should I put my wishes above those of the almighty?"

My brain, sharpening up from sleep, alerts me to his hypocrisy. "Then why save me? Wasn't it God's will that I should die in a pool of my own blood at the foot of the church stairs?"

I can see several lies go across his face before he offers a non-lie. "That's complicated and something I'm not willing to discuss with an invalid. Now, let's get you fed. I know how draining spiritual healing can be." I may not be at the top of my game, but I catch the change of subject. However banal, my body is demanding something to replenish itself so I let it drop. "You should be able to walk. The witchdoctor touched up my healing and pronounced you fit for light efforts. Apparently, it punctured your liver and gallbladder, but it has been repaired.

"He recommends that you not get attacked again for a fortnight or two," Father Juan jokes.

"I'll take it under advisement. Now can we go get some of that food? I'm about to waste away here."

"*Señora* Caledon left you a housecoat to cover your underthings. From what I understand, the viscountess is still outside. My guess is that she brought clothes for you." I am surprised and not surprised both that the padre didn't bring up our talk of yesterday.

"Food first."

"A wise choice, ma'am."

I slip on the keeper's frock and follow Father Juan to the kitchen. There are plates heaped with fried potatoes, scrambled eggs, and a towering stack of pancakes covered in syrup and melting butter. A big pitcher of buttermilk sits beside jam, butter, and a vase of tulips and branches of cherry blossom.

I lift up one of the tulips. "You've outdone yourself this morning, Maria."

"*Gracias, señora.* The padre doesn't seem to care about a well-set table."

"Hot and in large quantities. I need to keep up my spirit for bridging the gap between God and his people."

"See? I feed better food to the pigs in my hometown of Badajoz."

"I doubt that, Mrs. Caledon."

"Shall we have grace?" the padre asks as he sits. We all bow our heads. "Lord, please bless this, thy meal to bring us strength in your service. We give thanks that you have seen fit to allow Stella to remain in the mortal realm and continue your good works. Amen."

"Amen."

The padre loads his own platter from a serving dish before passing it on. Before long, I'm tucking in those golden pancakes and the lightest, fluffiest eggs that I've ever tasted. The food is restoring at least the perception of mental well-being.

Around a mouthful of fried potatoes, I ask Father Juan, "You said that the viscountess is outside?"

"Well, she was two hours ago. Along with a pack of street children and a pair of constables waiting to either take you to the constabulary or send word to bring Inspector Guizzetti here."

"The padre won't let them in. He told them they have to wait. I thinks the lady was gonna attack him. If it weren't for the *policía,* she might have done it. She looked very worried for you, *señora.*"

"I was worried, too. And, I've failed to thank my healer. Thank you, Father Juan."

"Anyone would have done it."

"You did it. I thank you." There is a silence as we all eat as if one of the others might pounce on our plate. "So I don't remember much of what happened. Father, can you fill me in?"

Juan lets out a belch that I swear rocks the windows in their panes. "Excuse me.

"The attack, right. I was distracted during the attack as a group of big street kids were running in your direction. With my attention diverted, a man without a situation came up to you on the steps and shoved a boning knife into you."

"Yes, and it hurt like the devil himself had branded me."

"With the repeated stabs, I thought you surely were dead. The kids tackled and, ahem, detained your attacker until the police, not a few hundred yards away, showed up to take custody of the man. I ignored the scuffle and played my small part." I snort mentally at the self-deprecation of his role.

"By the time you were stable, your attacker was in shackles and sporting more bruises than an entire gym of boxers.

"Inspector First Guizzetti showed up, took statements from everyone but you. He wanted to stay by your bedside, but I'd already enlisted the entire church staff to haul you into the rectory. I then claimed sanctuary for you and ordered him away. He opted to post guards at the front steps.

"Forty minutes later, the viscountess arrived in her carriage along with seven of her staff. She insisted on taking you back to the Helms Estate to nurse you to health. I told her that I'd release you as soon as you were well enough and send word of your condition if it changed. She commanded me to release you to her, and I demurred."

"The Lady Helms screamed and yelled at padre," Mrs. Caledon says.

That is my love, I think. I'm proud of her. And it tears a new strip out of my soul to need to break her heart.

"You should have heared him, *señora*. He told her to *jodete*. I never knew the padre to curse. He protect you good."

"Yes, Mrs. Helms started organizing things amongst the people she brought with her." There is a slight emphasis on her title, probably to remind me of what I've not forgotten. "I don't know what she was doing, but I'm assuming that everything will be like an army ready for battle when you finally emerge."

"Thank you both for your support. You've been wonderful. I probably should be on my way."

"That wasn't a request for you to leave, Stella."

"*Si*. Please stay. You must rest."

"I don't want to inconvenience you."

"*No es un inconveniente*—it isn't. Please stay."

"It really isn't a burden," Father Juan added. "Wouldn't that help you with certain other issues?" There is a pregnant pause as my mouth opens just a little, looking at him. "I mean, I doubt an assassin could get into the rectory. They seem to be getting to you everywhere else."

"True, but I have some business to attend to, Padre—personal business."

"God's work is never done, is it, Stella." I scowl at him. For the first time in my life, I really would like to tell him to go to hell. But then that wouldn't be appreciative of him saving my life. The way I feel right now, I wonder if his act had been a kindness to Adrianna or to me.

"Mrs. Caledon, would you go out to the Lady Helms and see if she brought me a change of clothes? I would be grateful."

"*Sí.*"

# # #

Mrs. Caledon brings me a complete change of my own clothes. It hurts my heart knowing where they came from and what I still needed to do.

"Do you need help getting dressed, *señora*?"

"No, thank you, Maria."

"If you change your mind, please just call out."

"I will. *Gracias.*"

I'm alone with my thoughts. My mind, body, and spirit all feel like I've been pegged out on the intersection of Charleston and Causeway to let all the traffic trample and roll over me. I've always been able to ignore physical discomfort by pulling in on my intellect. I find no respite there with people trying to kill me at every turn. Now, even my proud spirituality has been wounded. The padre has shined a light on a darkness within me I can no longer ignore.

I wince, lifting up my arms to pull on my slip. I've felt worse but never with the rest of my life in such turmoil. I don't even have a private retreat where I can hide until I've sorted it because I'm living in the home of one of my problems.

I don't hesitate to urge the metal springs I'd left on the bed to form armor around my waist, chest, and hips. I have become accustomed to the weight. And, I recently received a rather pointed reminder that someone wishes to plant me under the earth.

Moving slowly, I reach down and pull up my petticoats. It hurts more bending over. I'm glad they left my boots on last night because

I don't think I can endure the pain of being bent over long enough to button them up. I may be healed, but I'm definitely not well yet. I tie my crinolines in place, lift my gray cotton dress with red paisleys over my head, and let it fall. I do wonder when, or if, I'll ever feel good again.

#

The moment I hobble out the front door of Saint Leonard's church, Adrianna marches toward me with Tommy and Laoise at her side. Mikey and five of her bigger kids rush the steps. A reporter from each of the three Boston dailies bolts in as well. Off to one side, I see a pair of constables. One points to me, and the other says something to him, and they focus their attention outward. I bless them in my thoughts for not joining the surge.

The reporters arrive first and barrage me with questions.

"Mrs. Ochoa, how do you feel after your attack by an immigrant?"

"Is it difficult living with a price on your head?"

One stands out. "Susan Queensbury, *Boston Globe*. Do you feel up to answering questions for our readers this morning, Mrs. Ochoa?" This question came from the only woman reporter.

"Actually, Susan, I don't. But as you were so kind as to ask about me, I will consent to an interview with you tomorrow at your office."

"Thank you, ma'am," she says, beaming at the other two reporters.

"Now, if you will excuse me, I need to be with my family." The remaining two don't want to give ground or stop with their questions.

"You hacks hear the lady," Mikey says. Her brawny friends step forward. Just with their presence, they give more of an obvious threat than I could, even when at full capability. The reporters take a step back, grumbling, and compare notes.

"Thank you, Mikey. I appreciate that."

"We do what we can, Stella."

"Well, this went above and beyond. Give each of those who saved me five dollars," I say, giving her a wad of banknotes.

"No!" Mikey doesn't take the cash. Instead, she crosses her arms over her chest. "We didn't do it for no reward. You wanna give them who saved you a kiss on the cheek and your thanks, that's one thing. But don't be paying them for doing something they are proud to have done."

Contrary to popular belief, I am often at a loss for something to say.

I'll have to think about this one before I commit myself to any course of action. "Well, I'm sure I'll have plenty to talk to you about later, but for now, I really need to speak with Viscountess Helms."

"I know. I just wanna tell you that you'll have a visible bodyguard from now on. Enough patterfooting around."

"And if I say no?"

"Then we will do it anyway. You don't know how much you mean to us, Stella."

What witch needs a bodyguard? I think. *I do, apparently,* is the obvious answer. "For now, I'll allow it, but first, I need to talk to the viscountess alone.

"Yes, mum." Mikey and her friends depart to a discrete, out-of-earshot distance. I'm sure their presence is still quite obvious to anyone looking upon the scene. Not that anyone would try something with two constables at hand. Of course, until yesterday, I probably would have said that about anyone attacking someone else on the steps of a church.

Adrianna, on the other hand, has not been out of hearing range. She steps forward, waving her retainers back. Her eyes are red and puffy. Her pale complexion is blotchy crimson. Her smile is forced. "Are you alright, *querida*?" I notice that she doesn't come quite close enough to hug me or be hugged by me.

"For someone who's had six feet of steel poked through her gut, I'm in fine fettle," I joke, trying to lighten the somber mood.

"That's not funny. I've been worried. Are you ready to come home for some pampering until you are well?"

"Ahhhh." My heart jumps into my throat. "I don't think I can come back to your home, Adrianna." I may have put too much emphasis on the determiner.

She purses her lips. Her chin quivers. She closes her eyes and turns her head away. "Your priest told you, too?" she asks.

I would nod, but she isn't looking at me. "The least vile thing Father Juan called me was an adulteress," I whisper.

"Mine was positively lurid with visions of hell and damnation. Why does love have to be so hard?" she whispers back.

"I don't know, but I think we need to be away from each other and the temptation that we pose to one another."

"In some ways, I agree. In others, I just want to wrap my arms around you and make you all better."

"That wouldn't end well," I say with nothing jovial in my tone at all.

"We won't throw you out on the street."

"I'm sorry, Adrianna, but I can't be under your roof. The attraction would be too great, for me at least. I don't want to seem ungrateful or angry. I just can't stay with you any longer." I can't even trust myself to reach out and give her the hug we both need.

"I don't think you thankless, Stella. But where will you go?"

I think about it for a moment. I only lack three days before having my own room in my own home. "Until my house is ready, probably the Parker House."

Adrianna nods before hanging her head. Then, two steps away, she turns back. "We'll send your things. Henry and I will miss you, Stella." Tommy and Laoise each give me a pained look before following their mistress.

Mikey waits a respectful few moments before coming back to me. "Are you in pain, miss?"

"A bit, why?"

She points at my cheek, which is wet with tears. "I sometimes cries when I get hurt bad."

"Yes, you could definitely say I hurt bad."

"Mum?" The constables, who have been very respectful to this point, interrupt.

"Yes. I recognize you both, Constables Fredrick and Running-Bird. What can I do for you on this day that *se folla un pez*."

"I'm sorry to hear that, mum," the Native American, the senior of the two, says. "Inspector Guizzetti wonders if you would spare him a moment down at the stationhouse."

"*Mierda.* I seem to be spending more time at the constabulary than most criminals." The pair of them chuckles. "I'm glad someone thinks it's funny."

"No, mum," Running-Bird says but doesn't lose the smile on his face.

"Mikey, I need you to do some things for me."

"Of course, Stella."

I fish out some cash from my purse. "Go down to the Parker House. Give them my card. Tell them I want a room for three nights. Then go to the Helmses'. Tell them to what room to deliver my things.

"I'll be along as soon as the inspector is done with me. Meet me at the Parker House as I have about eight hundred more errands for you."

"Yes, ma'am!" Mikey says with more enthusiasm than I expected. She streaks off, leaving me with the five teens that each would have made two of most adults.

"I don't think I need five of you," I object to such a crowd.

"Tommy would skin us if'n he found out we left you."

I must not be up to speed as I miss the connection. "Can we compromise? Two of you at any one time. The other three can go off and get breakfast or, heavens, sleep." The five huddle together. I won't dignify the conversation they have with the word logical, but they do eventually agree. "So I don't have to think of you as numbers, can I at least have your names?"

"Well, I's Roger, this is Kid, Milton, Aria, and Aston."

"Aria?"

"Yup, she is a girl. She just don't act like it much." The tall, broad Aria hauls off and slugs him one. "And 'fore you ask, Kid never had no name. Him mum and dad dies 'for he knew a name. Kid stuck." The one identified as Kid nods.

"Thank you all. So the three of you not on bodyguard duty scat. You can find me at the Parker House later. I've got things to do, not to mention recovering." Roger and Aston stick with me, and the other three head out into the street traffic.

"Alright, officers. I'll head over to the constabulary now. I'd offer you a lift, but I'm afraid my cart is going to be full," I say. Looking at my escort, it seems silly that a grown woman should need four wolves to protect her.

"Could we beg you to swap one of your bodyguards for one of us?" Before my friends can object, "He can come with my partner in a police trap. You see, the inspector would have our badges if at least one of us isn't with you."

"That seems reasonable. Roger, go with the other constable. Aston, you and Running-Bird come with me." I shuffle off toward where Lady Justice is parked.

"Ma'am, would you like a shoulder or arm to lean on?" Running-Bird asks. "I didn't know you were so hurt."

"No, thank you, Officer. I've fought a demon for three hours feeling worse than this." I say with my own version of machismo, or would that be machisma? "I just need to take it slow and get some good rest after your inspector is done with me."

We move around the corner to find the poderabile, right where I parked it, and once again, it is covered in the bloody letters, "NPP."

"*Mierda*," I exclaim without much energy. "Aston, remind me to get Mikey to have some of the kids scrub this off...again."

"Yes, Stella."

Driving Lady Justice through traffic is a handful. Every push or pull of the steering levers twinges my back. I'll need to have someone look to make sure I've not torn the new skin apart.

We arrive at the same time as the police trap with the other pair of my protectors. I'm escorted inside in the center of a box. I would feel more ridiculous if it weren't for the three or four attempts on my life in just the last week. The police whisk me right to the inspector's office.

"Stella, are you OK?" Antonio asks as I limp into the office. My lower right back is starting to cramp.

"I'd be better if people stopped having to ask me that question," I offer. I lower myself with great care into the chair across the desk from him. There isn't much room in his boxy office, but Roger and Aston manage to squeeze in behind me like I'm in danger in the center of a constabulary. I wonder if Quarrels felt that way in his cell. After the thought, I don't feel quite so silly any longer.

"So, I see you've taken at least a little advice," he says, nodding toward my escorts.

"I didn't get a say in things."

"Boys, make sure you keep her safe."

"Yes, Inspector. And if there's another one, we'll leave the—"

I interrupt. "I have to ask. Will any of my kids be charged for attacking the man who attacked me?"

Antonio's face goes blank. "Excuse me? What kids? You were very lucky that there were several constables close by to save you from further harm from that man." I can read between the lines as well as anyone else. I look up at Roger and give a slight shake of my head, hoping he will get my meaning.

"So, what did you want to talk to me about, Inspector?"

"First of all, we talked to the watchmaker. He remembers the project quite vividly and identified the samples."

"Why do I think you are giving me the good news?"

"I am. He made twelve of those nasty devices for Heinrick Meier."

"¡Madre Dios! We've only positively identified two of them. That leaves ten still out there."

"Yes. Now on to more pressing matters. What can you tell me about the attack?" Antonio breaks out a notepad and pencil.

"Practically nothing. I don't even remember seeing the face of who stabbed me. I couldn't tell if it was a man or a woman. He did stink of stale beer."

"Well, take me through it step by step. Where were you coming from, and where were you going to?"

"This morning, I traveled in from the Helms Estate in my wagon. I participated in the service at Saint Leonard's and then took confession and visited with Father Dubois y Cantonio." He doesn't need to know the why. "Shortly afterward, I walked down the steps of the church. Next thing I know, a knife is shoved into my back."

"How did it get through the metal sheath your body was encased in?"

"To move, I have to make the metal in bands around me. The knife must have slid between a pair of them. As soon as the knife was out of my body, I instinctively spelled the metal into a solid barrier for protection."

"Ah, that fills in a hole I had."

"Pun intended?"

He smiles. "No, sorry. So what happened next?"

"My attacker stabbed me three more times, I think. None of them penetrated. I think I may have felt his knife break on the third strike."

"It was snapped. It wasn't a very good quality knife."

"Well, next I know, he's on the ground, and so am I. Then your, ahem, constables apprehended him. I passed out shortly after that." The inspector makes some notes.

"So, does the name Adolphus Rubio mean anything to you?"

"No, should it?"

"It's the name of the man who attacked you. He is a recent refugee from Germany through Italy." I shrug my shoulders. "So, no idea why he would want to attack you?"

"Everyone else seems to want me dead, what's one more?" I add with enough sarcasm to sink HRM *Independence*. With the look Antonio gives me, I add, "No. I have no idea."

"I know why, copper," Roger says behind me. Both the inspector and I give him an incredulous look. "We done saw him talking with one of them Coal Syndicate bigwigs. We overheard him say something about killin'. We didn't know who or when until that boche rushed Stella."

My mouth is in my lap, but I'm wondering if this might be the edge to finally put Jasperson behind bars or maybe even dangling from a rope. Antonio takes over, and I get to just listen in.

"Could you identify him if you saw him again?"

"Shore. We wasn't but a few dozen feet away trying to cage some breakfast from the food vendors."

"We?"

"Me, Little Bill, Jason, and Carson." Antonio is scribbling fiercely.

"And who is me? I mean, who are you?"

"Roger."

"Surname?" I just shake my head at Antonio. Few of these kids have a family name. "Did you hear the event that Roger just told us about?" he asks, directing his question to Aston.

"Nawsur. Tommy done paid us to watch over Miss Stella and keep her safe. I were watchin' her."

"Wait a minute," I say. "Who paid you?"

"Tommy done it, Stella, only I weren't supposed to let you see us."

I seethe inside. Tommy and I will have a talk on this subject sometime in the near future.

"Stella, can I get back to my questioning?"

"By all means, Inspector."

Antonio gives me a funny look but continues with Roger, "So, how did you know he was a manager from the Coal Syndicate?"

"I done seed him come out the gates wearing a suit. And it twern't the business doors but the gates all them workers go in and make all the smell and dust. The German bloke called him Mr. Carlton."

My own eyes go wide. Antonio looks up from his notes with a start. "The manager that asked the German to kill was Carlton?"

"Well, that were what he sayed is his name. I don't know for shore."

"Can you describe him? Any marks or scars?"

"The man got a big head over his brows and not much of a chin. Dark, wavy hair. Kinda thin and tallish. That's all I 'member." I nod to the inspector, who nods back. He's met Mark Carlton on more than one occasion.

"You've done quite well remembering so much, Roger. If you ever want to try and become a constable, come ask for Sergeant Anderson at the front desk. I'll leave a good word for you." Roger beams. "Gentlemen, would you mind if I have a word alone with Miss Stella? You could wait in the outer lobby. I promise that I'll deliver her to you in good health in just a few minutes." My two protectors look at one another and shrug. They leave the room, and we hear their heavy footsteps down the hall.

"You know that their testimony won't hold up in front of a magistrate?" Antonio says. "Not even with the four of them."

After what I've seen of court, I understand. "I believe that."

"But, what it will do is let me bring in Carlton and sweat him. I'll make sure he sees the German, but they won't get to talk. Not that I doubt your friends, but that look will be enough to tell me, not a judge, that he is guilty or not. Maybe we can get him to incriminate himself by telling him a little fib that he's been identified, but I won't tell him by whom."

"I'm sure that if he does crack open, he'll tell tales on everyone. He is quite brittle," I offer. "You might even insult him. Angry, he is more likely to spill something, and he is too dumb to understand he is being manipulated."

Antonio shakes his head. "You really should have been a detective."

"Nope. I already have more troubles than someone who has a wasps' nest tossed into her open window."

# # #

"Welcome to the Parker House, ma'am."

"My name is—"

"Stella Ochoa," the man behind the desk says. "I recognize you from your picture in the paper a few months back."

"That's sweet but old news. I'm sorry, but I'm quite tired. Could I have a key to my room, please?"

"Yes, ma'am. Here is your key—suite 1412."

"There must be some mistake. I just ordered a standard room."

"Yes, Mrs. Ochoa. You were charged for a standard room, but as a courtesy, we improved your room to a suite for the services you have performed for this city."

"That is quite unnecessary," I object.

"Probably, Mrs. Ochoa, but if we fail to recognize those who do good, then fewer people will do it. Now, do you have some luggage?"

My back hurts, and I'm too tired to argue. "No, that is coming later."

"Excellent. If we can do anything to make your stay here more pleasant, please let us know." He hits the service bell, and a bellhop pops out of a cubby near the desk. "Take Mrs. Ochoa to suite 1412."

I'd like to say I am sparkling company, but my eyes are barely open even though it isn't lunchtime yet. The damage to my back must be taking more out of me than I think.

My protectors station themselves outside in the hallway.

I give the young bellman a tip. I don't even know how much before falling into a bed soft enough to be made by ten thousand geese.

I seem to remember sounds now and again throughout my nap, but nothing breaks through my wall of fatigue.

#

The room, bright as it had been when I'd crawled into my eyelids, is now dark. A single gas lamp is on in the separate living area. I hear some minor movement in there. Stiffness in my back urges me to stay in bed but not as much as before I'd slept.

"Miss Stella?" Mikey's quiet voice asks from the other room.

"I think so," I reply. My head is throbbing.

Mikey comes in tiptoeing. I think a little man with a sledgehammer sounds a brass bell with every single step she makes. *Why do I feel like I've been drinking absinthe all night?* I ask myself as I hold my head still.

"You said you needed me for errands."

"Jesus, Mary, and Joseph, but what time is it?"

"'Bout seven thirty."

"I've been out over eight hours?"

"Looks like it, miss." Mikey sits with exaggerated care onto the edge of the bed.

"You should have gone home, Mikey."

"I didn't mind staying, miss. It's quiet, and I don't have to worry about nobody bothering me."

"Bothering you? Is that a problem?"

"Not so much anymore, Stella. My boys keep a close watch on me. Before, if some of thems found out I was a girl, I could have a problem." I didn't have to think hard about what she means by the problem.

"Do many of the girls have that kind of problem?"

"Every day, miss. Most of 'em eventually give in and in the end become cat house girls for protection."

At what cost? I ask myself. There is a lot of difference between a woman making a conscious choice to become a horizontal worker, like Karie, and someone forced into it because if they don't, they will be abused.

I know I can't save the whole world, but maybe I can make a small dent in the evils. "What if I said all the girls could come and stay with me?"

"What do you mean, miss?"

"I'm going to have lots of extra room in the Brick Factory. What if I bought bunches of cots and let the girls stay there. It won't be much but a bed. But it will be warm and safe from boys at least at night."

"Ma'am, that would be nice, but what's in it for you?"

"Turn it around; look at it the other way 'round. What am I losing? Some space I'm not using?"

"Still seems like charity."

"OK, do you kids make at least some cash?"

"Yes, Stella, by begging if nothin' else."

"What if I charge any girl a penny a day?"

"Most of the girls would jump at that, miss."

"And, we can also spread the word that I'll intervene if any boy won't leave a girl alone at any time."

"That might get you in trouble, Miss Stella. Them boys ain't gonna believe that any woman is going to be a problem to them."

"Even after I prove it by putting one in a stone cage for a few hours? Remember what I did to Tommy?"

Mikey smiles. "I like that idea. There are some boys I hopes don't listen."

"That's not nice, Mikey."

"Nice or not, it gives me some really good thoughts."

"So, will you be my business partner, Mikey?"

"What? Business?"

"Well, someone has to collect those coppers. Do you think I have time every day to pick them up? I'll give you one penny in fifteen."

Mikey's expression changes. "One in ten," she snaps back in automatic negotiation mode. As that is what I wanted to give her in the first place, I agree and shake her hand to bind our partnership. More on, I fully intend to use every cent I make to upgrade things to make it nicer for them.

"Couple of things, though, Mikey. If a girl can't come up with that penny one night or two, don't worry. Let her in anyway. I don't mean someone who is a true deadbeat, but I won't turn away a girl down on her luck. Don't become a tyrant, or I'll find someone new."

"Yes, ma'am."

"We also can't start until my building is finished. Call it three weeks from now. Also, we can have some chores for the girls to make a few pennies. I'm sure the ladies staying here would be more than happy to have someone to do their laundry, clean their rooms, or fetch groceries."

Mikey just sits there looking at me for a few breaths. "Why are you doing all this, Miss Stella? It makes me nervous that you is so good to us."

She does have a good question. "So, I had no father, and my mother wasn't a stellar parent, even though I didn't want for material things. That being said, I doubt I'll ever have a child," which brings back to my conscious mind the partially forgotten fact of my demonic heritage. "Why not at least try to give some of that love that I missed out on, and that protection that even my cold mother gave me, to someone else. Add to that, you all have been very good to me, and you have a winning combination."

Mikey nods. I'm not sure I've convinced her, but I've allayed any suspicions she might have.

"With that in mind, why don't you stay here tonight? Tomorrow is going to be busy, and we can get a fresh start early."

"I'm OK with that if you are, miss. I don't wanna impose."

"Not a problem. There is enough room in this suite to have a bullfight. But, I am going to impose on you."

"What's that, Stella?"

"I am so hungry I could eat a whole pear tree," I moan. Mikey giggles. "I imagine you haven't had anything to eat either. So, I want you to go down to the Bell in Hand, just a few blocks away. Get Michaeleen to put us together two trenchers and a jug of cider and bring it back."

"Stella, I don't mind going, but you can get fancy food from the hotel."

"Maybe, but it won't be as good."

14—Tuesday, May 15, 1888

Morning arrives, and I find myself lying on top of the covers, fully dressed. A head of bright red hair uses my shoulder as a pillow. Mikey lies next to me, also still in her utilitarian garb and holding her empty cup. While Xena assures me that I likely may never be a mother, I can still be motherly. I gently comb my fingers through her hair.

Last night had been a nice meal and deep, sharing chat about our families. She revealed that her two younger siblings died during Ireland's Great Famine. Her parents scraped together what they could and bought their way here on a tramp steamer. Her mother, Marsha Byrne, died of the pox on the ship. I hadn't known her surname until last night. Her dad, Brian, died a year later in a steel mill accident. No one wanted to take in a young girl. It left her to fend for herself.

The revelations brought tears and a young girl's recriminations on herself that she hadn't been able to save even one of them. The self-loathing surprises me from the normally self-assured Mikey. Her reactions had been so strong that I surreptitiously spiked her cider from a flask of whiskey I carry in my purse. I guessed right that the young lady hadn't had much experience with hard spirits. She dropped off in no time. I have a feeling the strong Mikey will be back the moment she wakes.

My back throbs a bit, and my bladder could use to be emptied, but neither are insistent enough to make me want to disturb my young friend. This, unfortunately, leaves me with my own thoughts, or perhaps better put, it leaves me with an emotional hole in my heart and nothing but time to agonize over it.

I'd been running on sheer grit not to let my life fall in on me. I hadn't had the opportunity to take out my grief and examine it. The pain makes the knifing I received seem like a scratch. Worse, I knew I could salve this wound at any time just by showing up at her door.

There was a time before witches when the word of God was only a myth, a story passed down from generation to generation. A sinner only worried about the truth of the word. I almost envy those who didn't know for certain. They could close their eyes and choose not to believe. For me, giving in to temptation would lead to the loss of my immortal soul. Endure the pain of living within reach of my love, or undergo infinite suffering for all eternity in hell. The choice seems so obvious, but tell that to the emptiness in my middle.

Mikey opens her eyes and starts upright. "I'm sorry, miss. I didn't mean to fall asleep on you. Oh, that hurts," she says, cradling her head in her hands.

Upon seeing the condition of my errand girl, I remind myself, *One thing at a time, Stella.* If only the world would slow down and let me deal with one thing at a time. "Hold on. I'll get you some water. That's the best thing for it." I get up and pour her a glass from the pitcher at hand. "That and some potatoes."

Handing Mikey the drink, I stick my head out the door. One of my bodyguards, Milton, if I remember correctly, stands up from a chair as I do. "Anything wrong, mum?"

"No. I just need some breakfast. Can you get the floor steward to send us up three breakfasts? Two eggs over medium, bacon, hash browns, and a big stack of pancakes with syrup and jam for each." I hand him a dollar coin. "Give this to him. It will get it here sooner rather than later."

"Yes, ma'am."

Mikey is standing up, squinting. As I come back into the bedroom, she says, quiet as one might speak in a library, "I'm sorry, Miss Stella. I shouldn't have fallen asleep on your shoulder. I shouldn'ta burdened you with my problems. I'm truly sorry."

"You have nothing to be sorry for, Mikey," I reply with equal care in the volume. "I asked, and I shared, too. It was a rough night for both of us.

"Now, go into the bathroom and wash up. Drink some more water. But don't dally. I have food on the way, and I also need to micturate."

"Micturate?" she asks on the way to do as I say.

"Water my nag."

She grins from ear to ear. "Oh, you need to piddle. I understand. I won't be long."

Getting my chance in the en suite lavatory, as the room description called it, makes me feel more refreshed. I eye the bathing tub and want to dive in, but breakfast is on the way. I choose a bracing sponge bath instead. Before buttoning up my blouse, I call out, "Could you take a look at my back, Mikey? I need someone to tell me if the stab wound is healing well."

"Sure, miss, if'n it's OK with you."

I use my connection with the metal around my body to open up the back. Temporarily it doubles its thickness at the front to expose my skin and underpinnings. At one time, its movement made me shudder like I had a spider crawling across me. Now, I don't even notice.

"Making the iron move like that be quite amazing, Miss Stella. Could I learn to do that?"

"We can check to see if you have the talent, Mikey. Not many do. If your parents aren't witches, then it's likely you aren't either. Please don't get your hopes up."

"I won't, Stella. I just wanna be my own person."

"You don't need to be a witch for that. I'd say you are there already."

"I just does what people tells me to."

"Most people do. Yet, you manage to boss a group of kids, some much older and bigger. You are stronger than many, many I know. Be proud of that." I reach back to unhook my brassiere, but my back just won't allow my arm to reach the junction. "Could you undo my hooks, Mikey?"

"No need, Stella. I can see the wound without it."

It figures because I haven't felt the straps rubbing against it. "What's it look like?"

"There ain't no blood or puss or nothing. It be kinda pink to red in color."

"No bulging?"

"No, miss."

"Is it feverish?"

"You want me to touch your skin? Is that OK, Stella?"

"Why would that bother you?"

"I never want nobody to touch my body," she says with a shudder.

"It's OK, Mikey. I just need to know if it is hot. Use the back of your knuckle."

She announces after the briefest of touches, "Nope. Not hot, Stella."

I encourage my iron girdle to rewrap but then order it off of me. I decide that I'll spend the day here in the hotel and won't need its protection. I form it into a block and set it into the closet. I button up my blouse just in time to receive a knock at the door. As silly as it seems, the lack of the weight of my armor makes me feel naked. "Food." As I finish with my last button, I say, "Let him in."

"Your breakfast, ma'am," I hear someone say.

"I ain't no ma'am," Mikey replies.

"You are if you are a guest at the Parker House, ma'am," says a bellhop, wearing a white and gold Parker's uniform. He rolls in a table with covered dishes.

"Thank you, Robbie," I say, reading his nametag. I hand him a quarter. He ducks his head and walks away, closing the door behind him.

"Mikey, go fetch Milton in here for breakfast."

"Ma'am?"

"Oh, don't 'ma'am' me. If I have to have someone hanging around, I don't want him or her faint with hunger."

I set chairs up around the table as Mikey retrieves my bodyguard.

"Ma'am, I don't be needin' any vittles," Milton objects as he comes in. His body language screams his discomfort.

"Sit, both of you." Mikey winces at my strident tone. I moderate my volume but not the firmness in my voice. "Milton, you can tell the folks that you are trading off with that if I have to drag you all around on my coattails, then you will take what I offer, or you can all go pound sand."

"Yes, mum."

I pull off the covers of breakfast to steaming wonderfulness. From the tantalizing smells, I doubt we could have gotten better. Milton's eyes go wide with greed. "Dig in," I assure him. He grabs a serving spoon and starts scooping in food like it might run away.

Mikey, on the other hand, holds her middle and clenches her jaw. I address my next comment to her, "I know it may make you queasy right now, but trust me that after a couple of bites, it will go away. You'll thank me." She picks at the hash browns. "Try the pancakes. They will soak up that sour stomach in no time."

I also have a severe hunger. I need to replenish the white repairs done to my back and bolster my natural healing. In the past, I've also found it padding against dark thoughts, like the ones that continue to creep around the edges of my thoughts.

Mikey is finally tucking in, making a similar destructive swath across her plate as Milton and I. I take the time to clear my mouth before asking, "Mikey, can you read and write?"

"Some, Stella," she says hastily, swallowing a mouthful of pancake with a gulp of milk. "I knows my letters and numbers. My mam taught me. I can't spell good-none, but if you show me a word, I usually can tell what it is."

I reach over to the writing-table and pick up some paper and a pencil. "Good," I say, handing them to her. "I've got a list of chores for you today. It will be a busy day as I have decided to stay here and let my back heal. That should make your job easier, Milton." He just nods and continues his assault on a breakfast that I would have sworn would feed three of him. The plate is belying my thoughts, as it is nearly empty.

"If'n I might have an opinion, I think that is a good idea," Mikey says.

"Unless I say otherwise, I always want your opinion, Mikey. Just because I'm your boss doesn't mean that I have all the answers."

"Thank you, Stella. Too many bosses think they got the corner on all things to do with smarts."

"Youse can say that again. And most of the time, they is more stupid than a brick," Milton adds, punctuating it with a belch and a blush. "'Scuse me."

"That's why I want you both to keep me on my toes."

A knock on the door interrupts me. I get up, but Milton puts up his hand. "Then learn, miss. Youse stay outta sight whiles I answer it. It could be anybody comin' to hurt ya."

Briefly, I wonder if I've made a mistake telling them that I'm willing to listen but wave him forward.

"Whatcha want?"

"I have a message for Madam Stella Ochoa. Is she here?" The words are delivered in a crispness that I recognize as instilled in his majesty's navy.

"Give it here, and I'll deliver it."

"I have orders to place it in her hand."

"Ma'am, are you expecting something from the orangies?" Like the British term limey, the American navy had become known as orangies for their own choice of fruit to ward off sickness in the crew.

"Yes, Milton. Let him in."

Milton follows in a naval cadet who is resplendent in his pressed and creased blues. "Are you Mrs. Ochoa?" he asks.

"Yes, I am."

"Here is a message for you." I reach for a tip out of my bag, for it couldn't have been easy to find me. "I'm sorry, ma'am, but I'm not allowed to accept any gratuities."

I give him the warmest smile I can muster. "Thank you, sir. You have performed your task admirably."

"Mr. Murphy says that I should remain for your reply."

"Well then, I should read it." I rip open the message and read it.

Naval Dispatch
From: Collin Murphy, Dockmaster, Royal Naval Yard, Boston
To: Mrs. Stella Ochoa

Mrs. Ochoa,

Per our agreement of Thursday, May 10, we will be requiring your services at 2 PM on Thursday, May 17, and again on Saturday, May 19, at 3 PM.

Please RSVP with the courier.

(s) Collin Murphy, Senior Engineer

"Please inform Mr. Murphy that I will be happy to attend him at the two times he requests."

"Yes, ma'am." He nods before leaving.

It is money in the bank, or maybe I should say money to pay off my debt. It does make me wonder if it makes sense to make extra payments on my loan. Milton catches me at my woolgathering. "Mum, thank you for the feast this morning. I ain't had nothing like it. May not need to eat for a fortnight. But I should get back to guarding the door."

"You are quite welcome, Milton. You can go. And thank you for keeping me safe." He beams back at me as he leaves to resume his post. "Now, where was I?"

"Giving me chores, Stella. 'Cause, you is being smart and staying here to get yourself better."

"Right." I spend the next fifteen minutes calling out things that need to be done and in what order. They range from getting introduction cards made for my new address at the Brick Factory to fetching any number of people to visit me here. I write a number of letters for her to deliver amongst the tasks, not to mention giving her a moderate amount of money. In all, I must have given her sixty-odd things to do.

"You got all that?"

"I thinks so." She repeats my orders almost in my own words.

"Good. Head all better now?"

"Yes, Stella, thank you. You are right that those 'taters seemed to be just what I needed."

"Every time," I say. "Now off with you. I don't expect to see you until tomorrow morning at nine." *Please don't come earlier because I have a date with a bathtub full of hot water up to my chin.*

# # #

A long, hot soak in a tub, clean underthings, and a fresh, satin dress in pale teal put me in a much better mood to receive my first guest. I'm assuming Mikey has been successful as there a knock on the suite door.

Mrs. Otto Krieg, a plump dumpling of a woman, proves to be wonderful and warm. In her way, she reminds me of Adrianna. The similarity rips open the very hasty emotional bandage I've placed over that wound.

Mrs. Krieg's weighty accent takes a bit of getting used to. Still, once I get it, we spend a delightful ninety minutes going over fabrics, colors, tile, rugs, and catalogs of bathtubs and other fixtures. Her knowledge of home finishes proves invaluable, not only in color and texture but also in details I've never considered, like price, durability, and ease of cleaning. Her experience steers me clear of folly in some of my more silly choices.

Bolstered by Mrs. Krieg's professionalism, the joy of designing my dream home overcomes what had been a dread of the necessity to make a million-and-a-half niggling little decisions. She even reminds me that I need to purchase furniture.

A change in bodyguards shows Aria on duty as she snaps to attention when I escort Mrs. Krieg out with a smile and a hug. As soon as my visitor has entered the lift, I turn toward my protector. "Aria, I'm not the queen or Mother Mary. You don't need to genuflect just because I move."

"Yes, ma'am."

"And it's Stella, not ma'am. I'm a person, not a feudal lady."

"Yes, Stella."

"That's much better. Now, can you get the floor steward here, please?" I ask.

"Yes'm, but before I do, a message arrived for you whilst you were talking to the German lady." I wander inside while unfolding it to find Henry's neat script.

Stella,

I'd be more than happy to do an installation on the Brick Factory. I'll charge you exactly $1 (one dollar). We will start this afternoon and work hand-in-glove with Mr. Krieg.

Henry

I give a sigh as I sit down in my overstuffed chair. I'll let Henry go forward and fight with him later about the bill. There is a knock on the door.

"Come in."

"Miss Ochoa, you sent for me?" asks a man in a uniform at least twice as ornate as that of the bellboy.

"Yes, Cantor," I say, pulling the name from the embroidery on his uniform. "I have two requests. I'd like to get some lunch, just whatever soup the cook has on the stove and maybe a grilled cheese."

"Easy enough. What else can I help you with?"

"Who supplies your furnishings?"

The man stands still, staring like one of limited mental capacity asked to do long division. For a moment, I think he is going to drool all over himself. "May I ask madam why?" The delivery of the question is dry, almost accusatory.

"Because I like it. I am about to furnish my first home. I would like to at least consider the craftsmen who made this."

I can see the relief on his face. "Well, in that case, the maker of almost every piece of furniture is the Paine Furniture Company of Boston."

"Thank you for your help, sir, but call it a woman's curiosity…I have to wonder what you were concerned about."

"Sometimes our competitors try to sniff out our suppliers and make exclusive contracts with them. We then can't get matching replacements. The hotelier business is quite cutthroat."

"I see. And how did you know I was telling the truth when I answered?"

"As I know you are somewhat famous, I have to assume that you wouldn't lend your name to such a shady endeavor. The question was more than a formality as I didn't expect someone of your known integrity would lie."

"Well, I will be honest. My home will be a long-term boardinghouse. I will be needing quite a good amount of furniture. But, I don't think you have anything to worry about in competition to the Parker House or that I might entice your builder into some contract that would leave you in the lurch."

"I appreciate your candor, Mrs. Ochoa. Now, if you have no other questions, I'll return to my duties."

"May you have an excellent day, sir."

"I'll place your order for food immediately."

"Thank you."

I spend the time waiting for my lunch reading the *Boston Herald*. George Covington aboard MacBeth II wins the Kentucky Derby in 2:38.00. More ominously is that France and England announce the formation of the English Channel Accords, nominally to cement their financial partnership. Buried within the fine print is that one would come to the aid of another in the event of a formal declaration of war.

It seems to me that America is sailing straight into war with England, as much as Spain is with France. Am I the only one that can see it and the cost that it will have?

# # #

The crispy, sweet rye bread is almost better than the gooey center of the tastiest grilled cheese sandwiches I've ever eaten. Lingering over my plate is interrupted by a knock at the door. Mikey seems to be batting one thousand. That being said, this interview is the one I fear and doubt the most.

"Stella, there is a woman here named Yolanda Simmons. She says you invited her."

"I did, Aria. Please let her in."

Closer to crone than mother, a woman with a drawn face and sallow complexion hesitates at the threshold before shuffling in. Her dress has more repairs than cloth. Her shoes, once high-quality and sturdy, now sport sole repairs and damaged spots on the uppers. I can see a warring on her face from two extreme emotions—one that wants to rip me limb from limb and another that is already half-buried in grief.

"Come in and have a seat, Mrs. Simmons. Would you like some tea? Or maybe some lunch?"

She doesn't waste any time with pleasantries or even sitting. "Youse was the woman with my 'Manda when she done got kilt."

"I was," I admit.

"And they was trying to kill youse." They aren't questions.

"Yes."

She pulls a kitchen knife out of her baggy dress and waves it at me. "Why don't I kill youse right here for getting her dead?" The torture on her face screams out. She wants an excuse to not take out her pain on me. I sit still. I don't try to defend myself in any way.

"Because I didn't cause your pain. Because I may be able to find the person who really did. Because I may give you a reason to keep living. But mostly because it won't bring back your Amanda."

She slams the knife, point down, burying it into the table next to me. I trust I didn't flinch. "Bitch!" She collapses onto the settee, burying her face into her hands, crying. I get up and sit next to her, wrapping my arm around her. As she leans into me, I fold myself around her frail body as well, letting her sob against me. My pain seems insignificant compared to what she has born, both literally and figuratively. I hold her close and just empathize, nothing more or less.

Time doesn't exist in this communion, but I'm sure more than an hour passes as we hold one another. She finally regains some composure. "Thank youse, Mrs. Ochoa."

"I do regret my part in your loss. You deserve better."

"Youse be a compassionate lady."

"Not as much as you might think, Mrs. Simmons. I have a situation brewing, nothing to do with killing, I assure you, which I am not sure I can handle on my own." I can see beneath the grief at least a spark of curiosity. "I may have overextended that empathy you just mentioned. In the near future, I will be opening a boardinghouse for ladies. I'm not sure how many we will have, but the number will be less than ten. However, in the same building, but not under the same contractual obligations, I'll be letting a large number of homeless girls live off the street."

"Youse a tambourine lady?"

"No, ma'am, nor am I do-gooder by nature. But the plight of these girls pulls at me. It will cost me nothing to let them sleep in the unfinished portions of my home."

"Why youse be telling me?"

"I understand you've lost all your children through no fault of your own." She just nods as a black veil crosses her face. "I also understand you are widowed." She nods again. "Then I tell you because I'd like to offer you a chance to be a mother again. I want you to come work for me as a housekeeper and mother-like figure to a slew of kids that will need a firm but loving hand."

"But youse don't know me, none. I could be a bad mother."

"You grieve for your losses. That tells me more than most. And, I've had a couple of those same said kids checking up on you without you knowing. They say you are a good cook, your house is clean, and you are a fair hand with the children that run rampant on your street."

"And what do I get outa helpin' you with your passel of kids and huge house?"

"Why don't you tell me what you want? I think we can come to an agreement."

# # #

The final guest I have invited is announced by Kid near the evening meal. "Stella, a Miss Karie Taylor is wanting in."

"Show her in, Kid."

I've spent every spare moment of the day wallowing in self-pity at the loss of Adrianna. Even though I am a lucky woman, with much going for me, my own pain at the loss of my short-lived relationship rears its ugly head whenever I'm not dealing with a crisis or other people's pain. Part of me longs to hear the two bells of the Mission Church calling me out to put away a demon. At least then I'd be doing, not thinking.

To salve my own grief, I had Mikey take a note to Karie. It had said only that I needed her desperately but gave no incriminating details. I hope it hasn't been inconvenient for her to get away.

Normally, I'd be very interested in what my friend and sometimes mistress wears or doesn't wear. Instead, I just need her compassion, her advice, and her acerbic tongue to pull me up short.

My face must tell its own story as she rushes over and wraps me into as much of a bear hug as her slight frame can give. After a good long time, she pulls back and gives me a peck on the cheek. Disengaging, she looks around. "This brings back memories. I'm sure glad these walls can't talk." In a rapid change of subject, she drops onto the settee and says, "So tell me all about it. What went wrong?"

I sit demurely into my chair and begin my tale, starting with her previous advice. I am quite detailed, sharing Adrianna and I sleeping (and not sleeping) together.

"That sounds like a win so why are you in a hotel?"

"I'm getting there," I reply with some testiness. I continue my story with our mutual realization of love, the viscountess and I. When I get to my confession to Father Juan, Karie stops me.

"Stella, darling, sometimes you are the biggest idiot I've ever known." A friend has to know when to tell another friend they are wrong. The other half of that story is the other friend forgiving the manner of the telling.

"Go on," I force out of my mouth.

"You haven't even told me his response, and I can already tell you what he said. In short, you are a vile, adulterous woman who will go to hell for all eternity unless you mend your ways."

"Similar but essentially correct."

"Sweetheart, the priesthood has only two functions. To comfort you when you have lost, and to make you stop doing what is breaking society." I just sit here with my mouth open. "Did you think he would welcome you with open arms and tell you to go keep eating seafood on your married partner?" She scoffs with a sound that rattles the chandelier.

"It's more than that."

"Stella, we've not talked about religion much. I believe in a god as much as the Catholics that live on either side of me. What I don't believe is that stupid book of rules they call the Bible. Oh, most of it is good enough for tribal nomads, but for a modern society, they are woefully out of date and mostly made for the privileged few.

"Before you get all bent out of shape, I respect that you believe differently, and because of your belief, I can't understand how you didn't see this coming. You are at loggerheads with your own values. I honestly thought that years ago you'd given that up for Lent if you will forgive the pun."

It's hard for me to admit it, but she is right. I've trampled upon my own moral code. The pain that is there is for something I've no right to. Covet not thy neighbor's wife. It is the same thing Father Juan has told me.

"But, if you can get your feet out of the track where you must follow this age-old set of laws and customs, I don't see that what you have done with Adrianna is a crime, a sin, or has hurt anyone. In short, my dear, you have to choose the letter of the law or the spirit of the law."

Her analysis just makes my nerves feel like strings on a harp, taut and ripe to be plucked.

15—Wednesday, May 16, 1888

Asleep, Karie spoons behind me in bed, keeping my back warm. Last night, I tried to instigate something more, but my heart wasn't in it. Each time I touched her, I thought of Adrianna. My amorous attempts were on the order of a wet newspaper being used to lift an anvil. She did hold me through a couple of crying jags. I'm not strong enough to simply put my love behind me and march forward into an empty new world.

Oh, I thought and still think about giving up my need to follow the letter of my faith in order to follow my heart, but in that I find my core beliefs too unyielding—one of the corners of my person.

I keep thinking that my situation is unfair. Each time I do, I realize that I'm unworthy of God's love. It is a tenet of faith that we are all unworthy, but I feel especially unclean as I can't erase the heresy from my thoughts.

This doesn't bring on another bout of tears, but a sadness settles in over me like a thick fog on a warm spring morning. At the same time, as oxymoronic as it seems, I feel that I've passed some threshold with my grief over Adrianna. This lets me get on with the other troubles I'm dealing with, like Carlson, Jasperson, and Meier.

It looks like in the future, I may be costing my karma by removing their filth from the earth. If that is my destiny, then I shall try to endure the retribution as close to the way Jesus did nailed to the cross for his beliefs.

Looking at the clock on the dresser, I realize I need to get ready for my morning meeting with Mikey. I'm looking forward to it as it has the potential to set many things in motion. I disengage from Karie's cuddle. She barely stirs. Karie's idea of an early morning ranks right up there with luncheon in bed.

I visit the en suite and deal with my morning tinkle and wash. I look longingly at the tub, but that will have to wait.

Fresh underthings feel nice against my skin. I'm pleased to feel my back isn't hurting nearly as often as I get ready. I fasten my brassiere with only the slightest twinge of pain. With that reminder of at least a few of the people wanting my death, I put on my metal corset after yesterday's respite. The weight is beginning to feel comforting rather than a nuisance.

Out in the bedroom, I ponder my closet. Mikey has done an exceptional job of organizing my clothes. As a working woman, I've never had so many choices. I think about what would happen to any of these beautiful dresses during a demon escape. Well, that is why I had my seamstress put together that heavy-duty dress. In fact, looking at it hanging there, I take it down and fold it up into the carpetbag I use as my purse. I nod to myself at the forethought. That still leaves me with what to wear today. I choose a crisp white dress with a bright blue ornamental belt and matching wide collar. The skirts are long and pleated, not requiring a petticoat. I ensure the fit and cut of my outfit in the free-standing mirror—conservative and classy. I smile at myself. My fundament usually eliminates the need for a bustle, and this dress is no different.

I enter the sitting room of my suite, pulling the door closed to muffle any morning noise I might make. My dear friend needs her rest as she'd done much to heal my spirit yesterday. She deserves any consideration I can give her.

My tummy rumbles. *I need to stoke my inner demon*, I think sardonically. I pop my head out the door to order some food. I find Mikey chatting with Aston. The pair of them jump up like someone had shot a cannon near their head.

"Yes, Stella?" Mikey asks before Aston can get his mouth open. He seems more focused on his lap. His clothes are too floppy for me to get an absolute read, but I wonder if Aston might have a crush on my Girl Friday.

"No rush, you two can finish your talk. I can wait."

"No, ma'am, we was just chewing the fat waiting for the time for yours and Mikey's meeting. We's didn't wanna disturb you none as you had a guest." I stifle a chuckle.

"OK, then, could you see if the floor steward can rustle me up some potato pancakes, two scrambled eggs, a slab of ham, and some coffee for breakfast. Make it three servings of everything. You both can come in and share."

"Yes, mum!" Aston says, racing down the hall.

"C'mon in, Mikey. I'm dying to hear how yesterday went."

"Yes, Stella," as we come in and sit down. "You know that you are spoiling us?"

"Maybe. But you are all worth it. Where would I be without each of you? Dead and buried, in all likelihood. I can afford to show gratitude for not only the deed but the continuing efforts."

"As you will, miss. Do you want me to share now or wait until after breakfast?"

"Start now and pause when we get food. I want you to eat it warm, not cold."

"OK. This is the easiest one." She hands me an introduction card. It is a sample. In brilliant blue ink on a cream-colored, heavy stock with raised edges, it reads:

Stella Ochoa—Mistress Earth Witch
The Brick Factory
45 Irving Street
Boston, Mass, Monarchy of America

"This is excellent work and so quick."

"You did ask for it to be rushed, ma'am. I sat while he set the type and made that sample. I'm supposed to bring your approval back to him as quick as I can this morning so he can make the lot. He does say he can make it perdier if'n you want it, Stella."

"Nope. Just the facts. A fancy card doesn't make a fancy person. I always thought that it made me less likely to trust the person handing something gaudy to me like they can't be interesting enough without the frills."

"If'n youse says so, Stella. As you can think, I don't need them much."

"That may change, Mikey so don't get rid of my advice. That reminds me, we are partners now, right?"

"Yes, Stella."

"What's your real name? I can't imagine your mother saddling you with Mikey."

This got a smile out of my young friend. "No, she didn't. I used Mikey so everyone would think I was a boy. That and some dirt and baggy clothes and it done worked, too. My momma named me Michelle, Michelle Byrne. I don't know that I likes it anymore. Not sure it fits me none."

I think back about Aston's reaction in the hall. "Don't get rid of it entirely. You may find you want it back.

"What's next?"

"I visited Inspector Guizzetti last thing yesterday, like you said. He shore is perdy, ain't he?"

"Yes, and about twice your age, Mikey."

"I know, but I's just lookin'."

"Just don't let him catch you at it. I'd feel like I'd sold my daughter to a brothel if I found you two together."

"Yes, Stella. Anyway, the inspector told me that Mark Carlton tried to keep his hole shut until they started talking about attempted murder charges by the crown. Then he were willing to talk."

I'm sure he is, I think with some sarcasm. The royal prisons aren't a place you want to visit, much less call your address for the royal post.

"Carlton says he were ordered to do it by Heinrick Meier, the new head of security at the coal place. Him also says that he heard Meier and someone else talking about the pope's visit. He don't know what they said. The 'spector told me that Carlton may be holding that out to make the deal official.

"In the meantime, they are getting a piece of paper to let them search Meier's home.

"Miss Stella, can't they just break into his house? Why do they need a paper?"

"Well, the constables can do quite a bit. Never cross them." Mikey nods. "There are limits that the king puts on them so we can all be safe. Otherwise, they could do whatever they want."

"Huh. I never knew."

"I don't say that they always listen to what the king tells them so keep that in mind, Mikey."

"Yes, Stella. I mostly stay on the right side o'the rules. Here, the inspector said to give this to you." She hands me a wax-sealed note. I break it open and read almost exactly the same things Mikey just gave me, just less laden with her colorful way of speaking. I make a mental note to reassure the good inspector that Mikey carried the message accurately.

"Good. Now, what do the kids say about Heinrick?"

"I'm sorry, Miss Stella, but we lost track of him. He went into the coal building but didn't come out any of the ways we knowed about."

"I assume he didn't go back home."

"No, Stella. We found six different ways in and out of the coal place that we didn't know about. Surprised us. We are now watching all of 'em."

"OK, spread the word around that I'll pay six bits to know where he is."

"You'll have every bummer in the city beating the bushes for him."

"So much the better. Make sure that you pass the warning about how dangerous he is along with it. I will pay just to know where he is. I don't want heroics."

"I'll make sure the message be passed clear, Stella."

There is a knock on the door, and Aston pokes his head in the door. "Breakfast, Miss Stella."

"Bring it and your appetite in here."

The smells preceding him and a server rolling in the table full of food make my stomach rumble again. I fetch a tip. Mikey and Aston are just sitting there. "Don't wait on me, you two. Dig in."

"Thanks for the service," I say to the bellhop.

"OK, now I do plan to stir myself today," I say, sitting down and carving off a piece of ham. "We'll be heading to the Brick Factory and then shopping for furniture. Do either of you know where the Paine furniture factory is?"

"Ain't that the one over across from the south freight depot?" Aston says around a bit of pancake.

"Near the Point Channel," Mikey confirms after finishing a sip of coffee.

"So Harrison Street?" I ask.

"Two blocks toward the seawall," Mikey offers. "I need to learn more street names if'n I'm going to be doing more stuff with you, Stella. Normally, I wouldn't even bother. We kids have places we know, like the steel mill and the fish market. We just uses them to gets close. I'll start watching out for them, Stella."

"Good."

The door to the bedroom opened. Karie slinks out wearing a loose dressing gown over her satiny underthings. Both of the kids stare with mouths open, and in Aston's case, even with food still in it. "That smells wonderful," Karie says, planting a kiss on my cheek and pulling up a chair next to me.

"Jesus, Mary, and Joseph," I say to her. "Couldn't you have put on some clothes, first? Can't you see you shocked these kids?"

"Should we be leaving, miss?"

"Nonsense," Karie interjects. "Eat, you two. And to you, little miss perfect," she says, pointing at me, "I don't want it to get cold. Now feed me, woman."

I take my coffee cup off the saucer and scoop some of my food onto it. I hand it and a fork to my corrupting friend. "Here. Feed yourself."

"Mum, t'is your food. I don't need as much," Mikey says, trying to offer me her plate.

"Don't worry, Mikey. I could probably use losing the weight the food I gave her represents. Aston! G'dang it, close your mouth, and chew. I think you broke him, Karie."

"Saved him a nickel to see it in the circus tent."

"I think it is a dime," I correct.

"Even better. 'Sides, he is old enough to have seen a woman."

"Not quite so brazenly, perhaps."

"I...I ain't seen no woman in her uh...underthings," Aston stammers.

"Then you will have plenty to tell your friends later today," Karie says after she clears her mouth with some of my coffee.

All in all, this is small potatoes compared to the rest of the stuff on my emotional plate. I roll my eyes and sigh.

# # #

Wrangling the poderabile with a newly acquired wound isn't for the faint of heart. I stop by the apothecary and get a tincture of willow bark. I pop the cork and take a swig. I already had Karie smear some arnica cream on the bruising around the wound. That worthy pronounced me well enough in physical and emotional health to soldier on by myself. After exacting a charge of one kiss in the hallway that shocked Aston, she took a cab back home. Fortunately for the collective morals of Boston, she did so after getting dressed.

I barely recognize the Brick Factory as I pull up. A coat of sunflower yellow paint on the outside has made it look less like a rock collection and more like a home. There are at least sixteen wagons on the street. Workers are going in the big bay doors and the front door in a steady stream. A cacophony of sawing, hammering, and even the chuffing of a steam engine issues from the doors and windows.

"Ma'am, if'n you wanna go inside youse need a leather hat," Aston, half a step behind me, says. "Mr. Krieg says they save folk from bad hits to the head. Ya get one over here." He leads me to the back of a wagon where there are stacks of them. I pick one that will fit my head and slip it on, despite the stink of sweat and the musty odor of leather. Donning one as well, Aston leads me inside. Mr. Krieg explains something to a worker up on the floor of what will be my room. There are only bare wood sticks upright from the platform to the ceiling. In another place, I see another of my kids nailing thin boards to those sticks so they can plaster.

"Mrs. Ochoa," my builder calls down upon seeing me. "I'll be right down." He says something more to the man he is with, clapping him on the back. He then skips down to the main floor on some stairs that weren't there a couple of days ago. "Mrs. Ochoa, it is good to see you. Frau Krieg and I prayed for you. Terrible vhat some people vill do."

"It is at that. We should all spread God's love, not hate."

"*Ja.* I am glad you come. I tell you that we find things when we work. I haf found two thinks. First, you haf a leak in your roof. It is on the side, away from the rest of the house. You could ignore it."

"No, sir. I have need of that space. Please fix it."

"Another forty dollars?"

"Agreed. And the second thing."

"This be more important. Your cistern isn't lined. So the water isn't fit to drink. I could get it lined in copper for seventy dollars."

"Do it," I say without quibbling over an amount of money that would have given me apoplexy just a week ago.

"Excellent. I bring more workers and not even take longer."

"Thank you, Mr. Krieg. I came to get some measurements of how the rooms are shaping up so I can order furniture."

Otto reaches down into a leather pouch at his waist and pulls out a scratchpad. He makes several rectangles and scratches numbers next to each. Pointing to each in turn, he says, "Parlor, diner room, kitchen, bedrooms—eight of them—your room, bathrooms. I let you in, but it can be dangerous."

"Will my room be ready to move into tomorrow?"

"*Ja.* Done and dry tomorrow lunchtime."

"Thank you, Otto. You've given me hope that I'll have a home soon."

# # #

Paine Family Furniture, or so the sign says, sits on Hudson Street. It is a factory, not really a showroom. As I've never purchased furniture, I had guessed that it will be filled with all sorts of finished goods that I just load and take away with me. This apparently is my mistake. I ignore the huge bay doors that show numerous pieces in all stages of assembly and the raucous sounds similar to the construction going on at the Brick Factory. Instead, I enter the door marked "Office." It is quiet as a library. One stout fellow is working figures in a ledger, a garter holding his sleeve back from the inked paper.

"Good day, madam," he says, standing up. He gives a slight bow. His precise diction matches his impeccable manners.

"And to you, sir. I'm here to buy furniture."

"Excellent. For what hotel?"

I pause for a moment. "I'm not buying for a hotel."

"I'm sorry, madam, but there seems to be a mistake. Paine Furnishings only sells large orders to hotels and retailers. For single sales, I can give you a referral to Thompson's Furniture within the Quincy Market."

He's been unfailingly polite so I let him finish. "I actually need to purchase at least nine, probably ten sets."

"I'm sorry?"

"While I'm not a hotel, I am opening a new boardinghouse, and my stay at the Parker House has made me desire your quality goods." Flattery rarely goes astray in any negotiation.

"Well, that is different completely, madam. My name is Vernon Paine. Can I show you some samples?"

Three hours later, I realize just how little I know about things outside demon hunting and witchcraft. Didn't Confucius say, "True wisdom is knowing what you don't know?" My brain can't even remember all the topics Vernon talked about.

"So we will deliver one complete bedroom set tomorrow to your home at three in the afternoon." I manage to fall in love with a bedroom set, and they have one in stock, which they were frankly glad to be rid of, if I read my salesman's face correctly. I won't have to get the kids to schlep my old furnishings up the stairs only to have to move them again. "The remaining bedrooms, dining room, and parlor furniture will be delivered two weeks hence."

"Thank you for your professionalism, Mr. Paine. I'll have the balance ready for you when your driver delivers tomorrow."

"That will be more than fine, and thank you for your patronage, Mrs. Ochoa."

I left wondering how some chairs and sundry cost me as much as all of the remodeling. I haven't even approached my seamstress about draperies, but I'm exhausted.

Recovering from any serious injury is not to be toyed with. I've had multiple of them in the last ten days. Grit pushed me through the first one. I just can't muster the energy to do more today. "Milton," they had swapped the duty at the Brick Factory, "what would you say to a beer and a trencher of whatever they have on the stove at the Bell in Hand?"

"That would suit me right down to the ground, Miss Stella."

# # #

"Look what the cat dragged in," Menaj offers as she strokes the belly of an opossum in her lap.

"Stella!" Maxwell squeaks. "We thought you might have been killed."

"I'm dying of hunger but not dead. Why would you think I was deceased?"

"Well, we did at first when you didn't respond to the bells," Carlos says from the far end of the booth.

"Bells? What bells?" Have I let my team down with my dalliance with the viscountess or maybe my funk about losing her? I remonstrate myself for about half a second until Carlos continues.

"Sunday evening there was a demon escape in Cambridge."

"I was—"

"Yes, we learned from Tommy that you'd been stabbed and were likely recovering. We managed with just the five of us. Are you OK?"

"A witchdoctor patched me up," I said, hedging just a bit. The padre may not want it widely known that he has powers. "I'm glad you managed without me."

"Who's your big sidekick?" Bea asks.

"Forgive my manners. This is Milton, one of my self-appointed bodyguards. Milton, this is my team, starting with the big man himself, Carlos. The squeaky mouse is Max." Max flips me a universal hand gesture that can start fights in most bars. "The critter collector is Menaj. Donny is the one with the fire on his head, and the young lady to your right is Bea."

"Is you the *Dos Campanas*?"

"That's us," Donny says with one of his baby-faced grins. "And anyone that can keep that witch out of trouble is a friend of ours."

"Yes. Good luck with that," Menaj jokes. I flick my teeth back at her in a motion almost as known as the one Max gave me with his middle finger. "You're not my type, Stella. Not enough fur."

The table chuckles. "Michaeleen!" I bellow at a clatter I hear in the kitchen. "I'm dying out here."

I hear a yell out from that direction, "You know where the taps are, you little slitch. Get it yourself."

"Well, I can do that, but we also need two of whatever poison you are cooking up back there." I slip behind the bar and draw two steins of house dark.

"You won't starve in the next minute. Just sit down, and I'll bring it to you."

I motion to Milton to pull up a pair of chairs. He offers me one as any gentleman should but so rarely does in these permissive days. "Thank you, Milton. Here," I say, shoving one of the handled cups at him.

"So tell us all about it. We only got a sketch from Tommy."

I give them the full tale up to Milton and his friends stepping in, omitting the talk with my confessor about Adrianna. "And then Milton here, and his friends, came up before the *pendajo* could figure out just to slit my throat. He can probably tell it better than I can."

All the eyes turn to my protector. He blushes just a bit. He takes a swig of his beer before saying, "Twernt nothin'. We was following him 'cause we heard him talkin' 'bout killin' somebody. When he attacked Stella, we jumped him, and we decided not to let him up again. That was until the round-hats showed up and kept us from making shore he never kilt no one ever again."

"You know that the constables are taking credit for saving Stella?" Donny says. I want to smack him.

"Yeah, but Stella done explained that if we insist, then we might go into the hack. We don't like it none for doin' the right thing."

"And I appreciate it more than anything, Milton. You'll never hear me give anyone but you boys credit."

"And that there is what matters," Milton says with no little smugness.

"Well, I don't remember anything else until morning."

Michaeleen comes out of the back with two wooden platers, each bearing a big slab of shepherd's pie that oozes gravy and meat out the bottom. "You need to learn to duck, Stella," he says, obviously following the conversation from the kitchen.

"I don't know about ducking, but I'm going to tuck into that pie." After a mounded spoonful of the potato, cheese, veggie, and meaty mess, I say, "Now it's your turn. Tell me what happened Sunday night."

A story that wouldn't have earned ten lines in a newspaper takes half an hour as they fill me in on so many details that wouldn't interest anyone but another hellfighter.

# # #

"Should I be getting her back?"

"Can you drive her infernal machine?"

"Naw."

"Got money for a cab?"

"Then let her sleep. I won't hurt her. She'll get just as much rest in that chair as in a bed."

"Yeah, besides, if you take her away, we won't be able to make fun of her."

With my eyes still closed, I'm awake enough to say, "You know I can hear you, right?"

Milton says, "I's sorry, Stella. I didn't mean to wake you."

"Milton, only three things wake me when I'm asleep: the two bells, being rested, or the second coming. Nothing to be sorry for. I just was more tired than I thought. And achy," I say as I stretch my back.

"You want me to look at that?" Maxwell asks.

"I think this is just the leftovers, Max. Healing magicks can only go so far. What I really need is to get back to my bed for more rest. Tomorrow is going to be a hellacious day."

"Why is that?" Carlos asks.

"I'm moving into the Brick Factory. I'm over on Irving Street, off of Cambridge. Drop in if you want to be roped into work or you want to get wrapped up into a construction zone."

16—Thursday, May 17, 1888

I really need to ask Father Juan to make moving a mortal sin. Even with thirty kids, the furniture delivery folks, and the occasional help of construction workers, I've sweated through all three layers of clothing. My underpinnings stick to me like a second skin. I'm worried that my iron underwear is going to rust. All this just for my room.

A handful of kids have gone to my old garage to collect my things from there. Others have brought a whole cartful of clothes from the Parker House. When did I become a princess with a different dress for each day of the fortnight? The furniture delivery men tote up my new wardrobe and eighty-seven, or so it seems, more pieces up the stairs, where they assemble everything.

Through it all, Mikey choreographs each person like a play's director. Kids, shippers, roughnecks, and even Otto Krieg are doing her bidding. Miss Byrne is already a force to be reckoned with. I hope that she blossoms into even more and doesn't settle for being just another housewife.

My work seems to be limited to pointing where I want things. Every time I pick up so much as a pair of bloomers to put them in my new dresser, Mikey directs someone to do that chore. Nevertheless, I still end up doing more than my recovering body seems to be able to manage. And the tasks seem never-ending. I belatedly realize I don't have linens or blankest to go on my new bigger bed. I send Aria down to Alameda Fine Fabrics to get some. I give her strict instructions. I don't yet have curtains. Millions of details just to be able to sleep here tonight.

Inspector Guzzetti finds me taping newspaper over the windows in lieu of curtains. "That is an interesting look," he offers without any intent to help.

"Unless you can summon up curtains and rods, I'd advise you to keep your damned-all opinions to yourself."

"Sorry," he remonstrated. "I actually came to get your advice, and I seem to have started off by making you upset. I do apologize."

I climb down off the chair I'd been standing on. "Tell it to the birds. What do you need?"

"We searched ex-constable Meier's homes—"

"Homes? Plural?"

"Yes, he both had a room with his mother and another slum apartment above a fish cannery down by the docks in the red light district, right at the end of Lewis Warf." I made a mental note to share this with my kids. "His mother's house had little in it except a change of clothes, a copy of *Blood Crimes*, and some homemade glass witch cuffs."

"Blood Crimes" is a vile fictional story that tells of a young warlock who comes to believe his power is evil. He kills a number of other witches before committing suicide, all on the advice of his close friends. It has been an NPP propaganda piece for as long as I can remember.

"His own flat turned out to be much more interesting. We found NPP fliers, and six of your toy demon sweepers, and a train ticket to Philadelphia and another to Biloxi, Mississippi."

Biloxi is a thriving town, as it is the monarchy's gateway to the Freeport of Baton Rouge. "Really? Now that is interesting, but it still leaves four of those wicked mechanical sweepers out there." He just shrugs his shoulders.

"We also found two marked-up maps, one of Boston and one of Philadelphia. Each had three stars on it, all near the wharfs the newspapers have announced as the docking locations for the pope."

"'I am the Light of the World. Whoever follows Me will not walk in darkness, but will have the light of life.'"

"John 8:12, if I'm not mistaken." My surprise must be written on my face. "You don't need to be a hellfighter to have memorized the Bible."

I compose myself and offer him a chair, one of MY chairs. "So he intends to make a scene of the pope's arrival, in one place or the other, or maybe both. Even if we successfully reinter those demons, the embarrassment to the crown would be enormous."

"That's the way we read it as well. Put down the devices and then run. When he gets to the Freeport, where we can't touch him, he laughs as witches become, at best, second-class citizens, and demon power is outlawed."

I agree with his assessment so there is no reason to bring it up. The best course is to prevent it. "Have you compared the marked locations against Lord Helms's upgrades?"

"Way ahead of you, Stella. Helms tells me that the locations in question are all installed by one of his competitors, who wouldn't sell out or put containments around the demons. Likely Meier just bought the information from some employee in that company."

"So what did you need me for? Sounds like you've got this wired for telegraphing now."

"Well, first, we can't find Meier. I wondered if you had any ideas with your pack of wild children running around."

"If I did, I'd be knocking at your door instead of the other way 'round."

"Fair enough. The other thing that I want to run by you is what we've done and are doing so far and see if you can think of any way around it."

"Shoot." I think about that sentiment before saying, "If you don't mind, don't. Just tell me."

Antonio laughs. It takes him several seconds to stop. "Well, we have a ship standing by to direct the pope's vessel to a different dock. However, if that interception fails, Lord Helms has gotten the Duchess of Massachusetts to issue a highly unusual warrant to the three business owners to allow him to upgrade their holdings with enclosures. Helms is like a man possessed. He says he'll have the enclosures complete before the night is out. He has also found one other installation within a quarter-mile of there that hasn't been completed and added it to the list to be done in the next two days."

"How about Philadelphia?"

"We telegrammed the constabulary there with our suspicions. I received word from a colleague that the Royal Guards have changed the arrival dock to across town nearer the castle and mandating that all demon installations are enclosed no later than three days prior to the pope's arrival. They are also looking for some kind of accomplice as there is no way Meier could have scouted those locations himself." I nod. "Mark Carlton is under lock and key. Heinrick will be as soon as he is found, here or in Philadelphia. The king has issued a Detriment to the Crown order for his arrest." I've only heard of three DtCs in my entire lifetime. King Frederick must be serious.

"What else?"

"That's about it."

"I'd park a hellfighter team at the dock on each arrival, just in case," I offer in the way of payment for all the information he's shared.

"Good idea. You don't know anyone that might volunteer, do you?"

"I just might," I say with a smirk. "In Philadelphia, I could recommend either the Acorns or the Poly covens. Also, if you don't catch him in Boston, you might leave those installations alone in the capital and instead stake them out. If he goes there, you nab him. Obviously, keep the new arrival spot a secret."

"Thank you, Stella. I still say you should be in the constabulary."

# # #

Chuffing down Chelsea Street in the poderabile, I'm sweaty and tired from all of the work to move in. Even though still recovering from my exertions, I've got my first day on a new job. Mentally I'm selling myself on this. *Just go, empty the slip and go back home to sleep.* The little voice in my head doubts my optimism.

As if on cue, I notice that the entire street is lined with parked traps, buggies, and other conveyances. Not only that, but the avenue itself is jammed with more horse-drawn traffic at a standstill. I stand up in the cab to see if it is opening up in front, but all I see is a continuous track of vehicles. Worse, ahead, I see people getting out and tethering their horses to nearby parked carts and buggies. This behavior rolls back toward me. "*¡Madre Dios!*" I curse under my breath. People behind me are similarly dismounting. I reach back and turn off the air before climbing out myself. It is only another six blocks so I'll employ shank's mare.

As a family, dressed in their Sunday best, walks past, I ask, "What is going on?"

"Oh, we are here to watch a witch cast spells. She is going to lower the entire ocean," the father says.

"Don't lollygag," the mother says, with one hand on two of her six children. "You don't want to miss it."

"I won't," I mutter under my breath.

I feel a pain in my head forming. I turn and look back the way I've come to find dozens of people streaming toward the Naval Yard. There are too many parked buggies, dog-carts, and such blocking an escape with the poderabile. I think long and hard about slinking away and ignoring this employment. I didn't sign up to be a circus performer. Unfortunately, my own sense of honor won't let me turn away no matter how much I want to. I agreed to do a job. I may never do another one, but I must at least do this one.

With a growing headache, I trudge off in the direction of the slip. As I get within a block, I can see bleachers on either side of the vessel, stretching up to the height of a three-story building. People are packed shoulder to shoulder, with more spilling out around on the ground. Others stand on nearby parked wagons. A couple of aggressive types actually sit on the backs of the draft animals.

"Keep a lane clear," I hear a naval cadet call. "Stand aside so we can get workers through. Keep a lane clear." In the places where people don't keep at least a three-foot pathway through, he gives a rude shove with his shoulder to the amazed squawk of the recipient. I take the opportunity to get into the empty space. I don't like the idea of pushing through that packed assembly. It reminds me of the main causeway of the circus without the continuous movement.

"Ma'am, I have to ask you to keep this aisle clear for our workers," the plebe says, interposing his body as I use the corridor.

"I am one of your workers," I retort with no lack of venom in my tongue. "Now, step aside before I move you."

I can see the mental decision-making going across his face. It is unheard of for a smaller woman to question his moral superiority, especially as he outweighs me by at least double and has six or more inches of height on me. The choices are clear on his face. I'm either making the most egregious bluff of all time with no setup, or I am who I say I am. Like most, he decides to pass the buck.

"Yes, ma'am," he says as he moves aside.

I repeat this little scene four more times. Each military student makes the same correct decision, until I come to a waist-high wall keeping people outside a fifty-yard perimeter around the docking slip.

This wall is guarded by an actual military man in a naval working uniform carrying a rifle. From the grim look on his face, I hope it isn't loaded.

"Excuse me, but I need to get in."

"And you are?"

"I guess I'm the main attraction," I offer with no little sarcasm.

He doesn't react to my prod. "Name?" I hand him one of my newly printed cards. "Hey, Chief, I got someone here claiming to be Stella Ochoa."

A gray-haired man wearing a white naval uniform and the manner of someone who has worn both longer than I've been alive answers, "Let her through." The junior man opens the gate just enough to let me slide through. "Miss Ochoa, I apologize for the delay. We weren't expecting this crowd, and we were dragged out here out of sheer desperation." His torso is like a triangle on its point—broad shoulders, arms that look like they can crush me even through my armor, and a waist that would have put most women in the tightest corsets to shame.

"Can you tell me what is going on?"

"A few of the powers-that-be decided to make this a dog-and-pony show for some of the brass." He points to a narrow band of people on one side of the bleachers that contains a disproportionate number of starched white uniforms and fancy women's hats.

"I would say it has gotten a tad out of control."

"I'd say so, ma'am. I'd bet that some of the workers told their families, who told their friends, who told..." he trails off.

"Yeah, I see that. Well, can you point me to—"

"Dockmaster Murphy is over near those yellow bitts."

"Excuse me? Bitts?"

"Those two yellow posts next to each other that look like mushrooms. They are used to moor the ship to the dock."

"Thank you, Chief..."

"Senior Chief Wells, madam."

"Thank you, Senior Chief. I appreciate the warmth and information." I give him the brightest smile I can muster.

"My pleasure, Mistress Witch Ochoa."

I still want to turn around and go back into the anonymity of the crowd, but instead, I march forward. There is much pointing in my direction and some cheering that starts low and builds. The dockmaster looks around and sees me. He runs toward me.

"Stella, I am so sorry. I didn't mean for this to happen. I just invited a few of the naval brass to witness how this is going to improve our throughput. Instead, it seems to have turned into a circus." I just look at him with my hands on my hips, my brows raised, and tapping my boot against the cobblestones. He pauses, shifting from one foot to the other. He takes off his horn-rimmed glasses and cleans them with his handkerchief. "The most important part of any apology is an honest attempt to ensure that it never happens again. Our work will remain a naval secret for all future engagements."

"Thank you, Mr. Murphy. I accept your apology."

"In the nature of my contrition, I will reschedule your Saturday engagement as it has gotten out through many folks." I pose my mouth into a stern frown but nod as he is doing the right thing.

"Let's get on with this. I'm tired and grumpy, due in no little part to being turned into a freak show attraction."

"Thank you, ma'am. We've even come up with a box screen so you can take off your boots and stocking out of the view of the public."

"That's good. I'm not a floozy to be showing off my ankles to everyone in the city."

"Where would you like it? Is right there amidships acceptable?"

"That's fine." He shoos off a crew who stood ready to move a cute, knee-high screen of wood painted in naval white with a royal blue acorn blazoned on the side. I lean into him and whisper, "Would it help you if I make this a big splash? Pun intended."

He whispers back into my ear. "It wouldn't do any harm, Mistress Witch Ochoa."

"Then move everyone back. I'll see what I can do to make it a spectacular event."

I strut over to the screen. They've placed a chair next to it where I sit and dangle my feet behind the screen. I take off my footwear to several catcalls from the audience, even though they can't possibly see anything.

I stand up in the open box and hold up one hand. In my most penetrating voice, just short of yelling, "I..." the crowd falls all but silent. "I didn't plan on providing a show today." I slowly turn to speak at people around the entire perimeter. "I was hired only to empty all of the water out of the slip to help facilitate faster refits for our great navy. But I'll try to give you something a bit showier than I might normally use because I have an audience. With that in mind, I suggest everyone back up a bit."

To my surprise, people try to push closer. *So be it,* I say to myself.

I close my eyes and ears to the crowd, erasing their distraction. I speak to the earth and form the image in my head. The ground agrees. I feel it moving beneath me like the hiss of snake scales across the grass. Over minutes, I use one hand to lift the imaginary bowl in my mind, careful to form it around the bottom of the ship. The mental projection is like molding clay rather than the rock that it really is. Fully lifted, my bowl cradles the ship and the thousands of gallons of water.

I open my eyes to see that, in fact, I've formed a soup dish that stretches up so I can only see the tallest mast of the ship above the rim.

The crowds are clapping and cheering with abandon. There are whistles of appreciation. Now for the drama. I chuckle to myself.

I draw sand from the nearby beach, moving it in to replace the rock of the bowl walls. As it reaches a critical point, the entire structure collapses in a rain of sand and a cascade of tons of water in all directions. Before the leading wave can hit me, I roll myself, and that thoughtful screen, into a ball of stone.

I count ten Mississippis before I open my protective cocoon to even more cheers. I'm standing in about half an inch of water. The crowd on the ground is wet up to some level between their feet and waist. The folks in the front two rows of bleachers are dripping wet. I take a bow as I lower the stone down to its normal resting place in the bottom of the slip, save for the bands supporting the vessel.

Those in the stands are on their feet applauding. The crowds, minus a few who are indignantly wet, are screaming for more. I, on the other hand, have gone beyond my endurance. I am weaving on my feet. I feel a strong pair of hands on my waist, holding me upright. "*Cuidada, Señora Ochoa*," says a familiar voice. I turn to find myself face to face with Manuel Gomez y Ruiz.

"Thank you, *señor*." Part of me wants to drag him back to my unfinished home to sleep with him. The thought of a pair of strong arms holding me while I fall asleep is appealing, with or without something more strenuous to follow.

My moral sense wakes up and chastises me. *You'll have slept with three different people in four nights. What is wrong with you? Fickle? Puta?* I have to wonder.

Mr. Murphy comes over and unintentionally interrupts the moment. Manuel releases his support. "Mrs. Ochoa, you've done an exceptional job. I thank you again. Now, if you don't mind, there are some people who want to meet you."

My head swims. "Mr. Murphy...Collin, could you please tender my regrets. I don't know if you knew this, but I was injured on Sunday, and I'm not yet fully well. This event has taken the rest of my strength. I don't wish to dodge the people you wish me to meet, but I'm knackered beyond endurance. As a suggestion, you could hold a small soiree maybe this weekend?"

"Capital idea, Stella. I'll do that and relay your regrets."

"And by small, I do mean less than five thousand," I say, looking around at the crowds slowly drifting out of the Naval Yard.

Mr. Murphy laughs. "I do understand. I'll send you an invitation by messenger."

"Thank you."

I turn to say something to Manuel, but he has snuck off while my attention was elsewhere.

That kind of inattentiveness is exactly why sleep can't come soon enough.

17—Friday, May 18, 1888

As much as I need sleep, it is broken up on the reefs, *un buque naufragado*. I have vicious nightmares about being smothered in a sweet-acrid smell. It reminds me of the one time I actually have been in a hospital. That image folds into a kaleidoscopic dream of stars and cold and red fires, all while being bounced around. I envision red-hooded squirrels with spears circling around me speaking in tongues.

An explosion of pain in the middle finger of my right hand blasts anything resembling sleep from my head. I try to move my arms but find them fastened above my head. I'm lying flat on a slab of something. My ankles are bound tightly enough to threaten the circulation of my feet.

It is a dark night with a fire burning near me, keeping at least half of me warm as I'm only in my nightgown.

Another cacophony of pain is driven under the middle fingernail of my left hand. "What's going on? Why am I—"

"Shut up, witch. It is your time to meet your just desserts," says a familiar voice. The pain in my head, which rivals that of my fingers, is keeping me from identifying it. Men stand next to me with staves topped with crucifixes. They wear red robes and matching hoods that reach high above their heads to end in a point—*the NPP*.

I can deal with this. I just need to summon some earth or metal to me. I close my eyes and send out my senses, but they can't escape my physical body. It is an unnerving feeling, like being blinded or unable to hear.

"There is no need to try your devil tricks, woman. We have you bound in witch cuffs." Another spear of pain pierces the end of my fingers and makes me scream. I look up to see them driving wood slivers under my fingernails.

Witch cuffs are glass forms that contain many different essentials. They are not only solid because they contain many elements; they are impervious to all witchcraft. I can't manipulate fire or water, yet they all form part of the cuffs, nor will they allow witchcraft to flow without. I am well and truly bound.

"And once we are certain your claws have been pulled so to speak, by shoving wood under your fingernails, we intend to send you back to your master in a fiery pyre. It will be a short-lived agony to have your body burned alive. But when you return to your lord, the devil, your soul can burn in hell for all eternity."

Would "Killed by Myths" be carved on my tombstone? Wood under the fingernails only makes it harder to concentrate, thus nigh on to impossible to work with the elements. We no more make pacts with the devil than demons. And being burned alive is another myth that, along with drowning, doesn't do anything but kill a witch in great agony. It doesn't prevent her from using her connection with an element, but it makes it harder to make it clear what you wish to happen.

"*Señora,* do you have anything to say for yourself before we send you to your eternal punishment?" The syrupy Spanish word makes it clear who it is behind the mask—Manuel Gomez y Ruiz! So many things fall into place.

I look at him, even if his face is covered. "You are the one who released the demon at the circus."

"*Si.*"

"And told Heinrick Meier when and where I'd be at the Helms Estate."

"*Si.* And made sure he shot me to allay any suspicions."

"A dedicated warrior, you are. Dating a witch."

"I sacrifice what I must *por mi Dios.* I am God's warrior to remove the unnatural filth from this world."

Another burst of pain fires up my fingers, followed by another and another. I can barely remember my name. It feels like my fingers have been turned into hamburger and thrown into a vat of acid. I don't even try to hold back my screams.

When the tears have slowed enough for my brain to function again, I manage to say, with pauses between each word, "But why the notes and the assassination attempts both?"

The other shorter, wider figure speaks in a Germanic accent. I have to assume it is Meier. "The NPP just wanted to scare you off. But you've made some powerful enemies who wanted you dead. So eventually, we compromised in removing you completely."

"No nails through the hands and the feet? I thought you were purists."

"We are ignorant of all of the powers Satan gives his minions so we decided not to give a possible weapon to you. Rope will hold you until after you are nothing but a charred corpse," Manuel says.

"It's a shame Carlton couldn't be here to witness this," Meier says.

"I'm right here," says another hooded figure, this one with a golden cross embroidered onto the forehead.

"You're late," Meier snaps. "We thought you were going to miss this."

"You think I'd miss this filthy trollop's demise? Not for all the gold on the planet. Lift her up," Mark Carlton orders.

Figures I can't see pull a rope taut that tilts me. The support I'm on is lifted up at my head end. It is now that I find that I'm on a wooden cross. The foot end settles into a hole in the middle of a cone of firewood the size of my old apartment. The bitter smell of kerosene wafts up from the wood. They are serious. I wonder what they will do when I don't burn. This gives me an idea. It will require some acting, but I just might walk away alive.

"*Señora*, I would say I'm sorry or even that it has been a pleasure, but I feel dirty just being near you. We will not mourn you," Manuel says as he throws the first torch into the kindling. It is followed by eight other brands.

"I will actually rejoice," Carlton says. "To be rid of a witch and a woman who doesn't know her place is a service to all mankind."

There is some chanting in Latin as the bonfire starts in earnest.

"No. I'll repent. Please don't burn me!" I cry out. I try to make myself sound as desperate as possible. "Nooo." The fire wicks up my nightgown, wreathing me in flames. "Pleeeeeeeease! I'll do anything." I punctuate this with a scream. It isn't difficult with the pain radiating through my hands. Actually, I'm enjoying the warmth and protection from the chill night air. I'm worried about looking burned. I'm hoping the char of my nightdress will mask the fact that I'm not being damaged.

The lesser members pile a few more logs up against me, I'm sure, to ensure a complete cremation of my body. The flames start licking up the new fuel creating a pyre, an epic blaze that I'm sure can be seen for several miles.

"Goodbye, witch," Manuel says as the group turns around and walks away.

I offer some whimpers. "Nooooo. Come back. Save me!" I give another scream. They are well out of my sight, being blinded by the light of the fire. I think I hear horses taking off, but with the crackling of the wood and the flames, I can't be sure. Without knowing where the NPP is, I need to continue my ruse. I wouldn't put it past Carlton to be watching for the sheer sadistic pleasure of watching me suffer. I put in random screams for a few minutes. Actually, the hardest part is getting enough breath. It's like the hot air isn't air at all. I'm breathing like I'm a horse that's been running for a full day. I'm dizzy with all the panting. I drop the screams and go to moaning. It uses up less breath.

Meanwhile, I worry the thinner rope, which holds my arms above my head, back and forth. I need to get them loose to be able to do anything at all. Thankfully, the more slender rope burns through against one of the fuel-soaked logs they laid against me. Bringing my hands down in front of me, I see the glass-like material used to seal the magic of a witch within her. Now to see if my plan is going to work.

Acting again, I slump over at the waist. The ropes holding my middle are much heavier and looped around many times. Leaning forward, I put my cuffs right at the hottest part of the fire, the tops of the yellow flames. As an added bonus, those nasty wood bits under my fingernails are burning as well. Maybe they will get out altogether.

I've seen misshapen glass in fires more than once. The one I'm in the center of is much hotter than an ordinary campfire. I twist and wiggle my wrists, and after what seems like hours, I feel the cuffs stretch a little. Working them back and forth, I pull them, stringing them out. Then a little more until, finally, I'm able to prize my left hand out—all of this I do while bending over and moving as little as possible. If Carlton or Meier has remained, perhaps with a gun, and he sees me moving, I'm done for. With one hand free, getting the right hand free takes not more than seconds before I prize my wrist out.

With my mind, I reach out to the earth, which sings me a song of my absence. First, to protect me, I pull a bubble of dirt around me with all of the speed and strength I can muster. It snaps the top of the burning cross off like a child might bite off a candy cane on Christmas morning.

The fire continues to burn around me as I've left some air holes for it and me. I summon up the form of a stone knife to saw the remaining bindings off my body. It takes several minutes to do as there is a limit to how sharp I can make the granite. I lie there quietly among the coals rubbing the pins and needles out of my ankles. My middle, having been bent in half for hours, takes the opportunity to unknot.

I've been so sure of my superiority and that I could handle anything that comes my way—I've blinded myself. How easy it is to take down a witch. A bit of ether or chloroform on a rag, and I'm helpless. I wonder what happened to my bodyguards. I don't blame them—quite the contrary. I only hope they aren't hurt. Many things go through my head; but first, I have to get away. I'm safe now, but if I open the dome, I can be shot, stabbed, or any other number of things. If nothing else, just pile enough people on me and I'm powerless.

"Why don't I take the protection with me?" I ask aloud to myself. "And why alert anyone to my movements?" I mentally gear up for something I've never tried before. I reform the dome into a granite bubble around my seated figure, ejecting the fire and the coals. I sink my vessel down about ten feet under the ground before moving myself horizontally. Even without seeing outside, I can tell it isn't fast, maybe that of a slow walk. I know I'm not going west or southwest as I can sense no significant breaks of the earth in that direction that would indicate water. I keep at it for an hour or more. With nothing to see, it is hard to judge.

I feel I'm well out of range of anyone who might, at an outside chance, be looking for me. Nevertheless, I need to know which direction to go so I ease up to the surface. I poke my head above the plowed field I emerge from.

After the absolute darkness of being buried alive, a quarter moon casts silvery illumination plenty enough to see only fields around me. There is no evidence of people or pursuit. In the general direction I am traveling, I can see the illumination of a city in the distance. It doesn't take a witch to realize that I'd been toted west of Boston for my sacrifice. I must be out near Chestnut Hill. That's a two-hour walk back to town, nude. Everything I was wearing is now nothing but soot.

Los Lobos! I think. They are a hellfighter team that lives only an hour away in the Fens. I'm sure I can coax something to wear from them. I'd love to make my way there underground to cover my nudity, but it is just too far to creep along at the speed of a worm. Also, navigating would be an issue.

So, I make a path for a water spring to leak into the soil near me. I mix the fertile dirt with the water to make some mud. My mother scolded me when I was little for making mud pies. She told me to concentrate on more serious endeavors. I chuckle as I take the goopy stuff and smear it all over me. It's cold, but that just makes me work faster. In minutes I'm covered from horn to hoof. OK, I leave my face unblackened—almost time to move.

I kneel onto the earth and lift my head up to the heavens. "Dear Lord, I thank you for delivering me from that evil. You must still want me for some purpose in your kingdom. I will endeavor to fulfill the requirements you have for me.

"And if I might, I want to thank my unknown ancestress who bred with a demon. Had it not been for her, I would be nothing but ash. Thank you, Grandmother.

"Amen."

# # #

It takes me two hours to get to the Fens. I have to jump behind a bush, tree, or even flatten to the ground every time I hear a noise. Being nude in the dark of night gives you hearing that would rival that of an owl. One time, I dive for cover because a mouse scurries across my path.

As usual, the Lobos, in their longhouses, have a fire burning outside. I find Cora Leaping Fish, a water witch, tending the fire and keeping a general lookout.

"Pssst. Cora," I hiss from a nearby bush.

"Oh, it's you, Stella. I wondered if and when you'd announce yourself. I heard you sneaking around out there fifteen minutes ago."

"I wasn't trying to sneak."

"Then why are you still in the bushes?"

"I don't want you or me to be embarrassed. I'm nude."

"Interesting choice for so early in the year," she says in response.

"It wasn't a choice. It would take too long to explain. The short version is that I was kidnapped and my clothes destroyed."

"You aren't hurt, are you?" her voice says, taking on the tenor of concern.

"Some, but I'll live, thank the good Lord."

"So you escaped."

"Yes, in a way. Is there any chance I can borrow a robe or blanket or something? It's chilly out here, and I need to wash off this mud."

She goes over and pulls a bearskin off the wall. "This has dried long enough. Use this for now, and I'll go in and get you one of my deerskin skirts and a blouse." *Los Lobos* follow the ways of the American Indians, as it is the tenets of their leader, Red Hawk.

I take the skin and traipse over to the slough nearby. I'd love to have a hot bath, but the cold water here is all I'm going to get. I plunge in and start scrubbing off the black mud. The moon has long since set so I'm doing it in the dark. Who knows how successful I am. Once I start shivering, I climb out and wrap the hide around me and scamper to the fireside.

"Careful not to get too close, Stella," Cora says, handing me a bundle of clothing. I don't tell her that I've been more than intimate with a fire already tonight. "I gave you an old pair of bloomers as well. They're clean. My best pair of moccasins may fit your feet. I don't have any breast bands that would come close to fitting you."

"Trust me, these will be wonderful. I'll have them laundered and returned to you as soon as possible."

"No rush. Thy need is greater than mine. Oh, and here are a few dollars for a cab."

"You don't need to do that!"

"Stella, we spend so little money in this way of life that we have it to burn. Use what you need and then pay it back to the needy."

"You are a wonder."

"It is part of our beliefs," Red Hawk says before Cora can answer. He steps out of the shadows into the firelight.

"When did you get here?" I say as I pull the bearskin closer to me.

"You already know the answer to that, Stella."

"So you've been here the whole time."

"How couldn't I when I hear this herd of buffalo crashing through the brush up to our home."

"I am not that loud." Red Hawk just stands mute. "OK, I wasn't stealthy. So you heard everything?"

"Yes. And you fibbed. You are hurt," he says, pointing at my bloody fingers.

"I was going to go to a witchdoctor as soon as I returned."

"We now have a medicine man in our team. I will wake him."

I start to protest and then realize that no matter who I go to, I'll be waking someone. When Red Hawk leaves, I take the opportunity to slip out of the firelight to cover myself in more than a blanket. Getting into the clothes is another matter. With my fingers so damaged, every action elicits pain. Grab ahold of the waistband—pain. Try and tie the skirt—pain. Even tugging on ornate, soft leather slippers—pain. I am pleased when I finish, not only for being covered but because the agony from my hands can subside into a dull throb.

I come back to find a young boy, not more than fifteen, beside Red Hawk. The youth is wearing a loincloth and nothing else but a stylized blue tattoo of a thunderbird on his chest.

"I am Garth. You need healing?"

"And I am Stella. Yes, and I would be obliged if you could assist me," I say, holding out my fingers.

"Truly ugly people did this."

"I won't disagree."

"We must first get the remaining wood out. It will be painful. Red Hawk, bring some whiskey."

"Can't be any more painful than when it went in."

"I might disagree with that. I suggest several good slugs on that bottle before I start."

"Oh, why not. Getting drunk will be the least of my problems tonight."

18—Saturday, May 19, 1888

I wake up with the sound of birds chirping, the smell of cedar chips, and my loose hair tickling my nose. My fingers throb and ache. I remember last night and the eternal agony of having each long splinter dug out from underneath my fingernails. It had been like a preview of what hell might be like. Garth had been right. It had been worse with the wood spikes coming out, even with the booze masking much of my feeling.

I open my eyes and sit up, banging my head on a low log beam. "Son of a biscuit eater!"

"Noisy as an entire herd of buffalo," Red Hawk says from a cot nearby.

"Bloody hell. You let me sleep? I wanted to get home before anyone knew I was missing."

"I didn't let you do anything, Miss Stella," he says. "After a whole bottle of whiskey and half a bottle of rye, you just collapsed. I don't think you could have walked a straight line even had I woken you."

I'm surprised I don't have a hangover, but my mouth does taste like the floor of a trolley. I note that the bottle of rye is still next to the bed. I take a healthy swig of it and swirl it around in my mouth before swallowing to clear my palate.

"I really need to get back before anyone suspects I've been kidnapped."

"As you will, Stella Ochoa. You are always welcome in our lodge."

"Thanks to you and to your medicine man for taking good care of me. Oh, can we all just keep this between us? I don't know how I'm going to respond to this affront."

"Just remember the threefold law, Stella—whatever energy you put into the world, it comes back magnified by three. The universe doesn't give exemptions on vengeance."

"I understand, sir. I haven't forgotten the Rule of Three."

# # #

I find a cab outside the Mission Church, home of the signals of my *Dos Campanas*. I have him stop at Gibson's Fine Clothing, where I get a pair of gloves. I need to hide my hands until they heal. They are downright ugly at the moment.

With my hair braided into a ponytail down my back, olive skin, a beaded leather skirt with matching moccasins, and a white cotton blouse, I now look like an American Indian woman trying to fit into monarchy society. I should be unrecognizable to anyone who doesn't know about the scars on my neck and ear.

At my direction, my driver drops me a block from the back of the constabulary. While I may be incognito, I want to make sure that anyone Mikey's sent to watch for me fails.

"Sergeant," I hiss toward a man having a pipe on the back stoop.

"Yes, ma'am," he mouths around the stem.

"Could I sneak in through the back there to visit with Inspector First Guizzetti?"

"And why won't the front door be adequate, miss? Oh, it's you, Miss Stella. I didn't recognize you right away. That is a much different look for you. Anyway, front door, back door. It makes no nevermind. The inspector has left instructions that you may see him anytime you want."

He has, has he? I wonder to myself. *Are there ulterior motives here?* That is a question for another time. "Thank you, Sergeant."

"Interesting outfit, Stella," Inspector Guizzetti says after a double-take at my appearance.

"Hobson's choice, Inspector."

"By the by, are you reading my mind?"

I give him a quizzical look. "Not that I know of. But I am a good guesser. Like right now, I think you are going to tell me that you released Mark Carlton yesterday."

"You are reading my mind. What, did you see him on the street?"

"I think it was a field, actually." I pull off my gloves and show him the still healing damage to my fingers. Antonio recoils before coming in closer to look. "I was kidnapped by Meier, Carlton, and the rest of their NPP scum. This is what I got out of it."

"Carlton is NPP?" he says with his distaste showing on his face.

"Without a doubt. He was gloating over my demise."

"Demise? But you aren't dead."

"I escaped. But, they don't know I escaped, and I'd like to keep it that way for the time being."

Belatedly, Inspector Guizzetti pulls out a notebook and starts writing in it. "I can understand that. Was it only the two of them?"

"Not hardly, there were nine in total, but I didn't recognize any of the others," I say, knowing I'll have to do penance for the lie I just told.

"And how do you know they were NPP?"

"Red robes and pointed hoods, Latin chanting, and being tied to a cross and set out to burn in a pyre."

Antonio looks up from his notes. "Wait a minute; if they were wearing hoods, how did you identify them?"

"Carlton was introduced and told me as much. Meier I could tell by his shape, size, and accent. He also was friendly with Carlton during the encounter."

"That's surprising as Carlton is going to implicate Meier in not only murder for hire but plain out-and-out attempted murder for a much-reduced sentence."

"Meier might not know yet, or Carlton may recant."

"I'll investigate this, but you know what will happen as well as I do."

"They will have dozens of high-ranking, unimpeachable witnesses that prove that they couldn't have been anywhere near me all night."

"Right."

"Then use Carlton to nail Meier. Jail Carlton for what you can and let the NPP stuff go," I say, not intending to do any such thing myself.

"That's a very rational statement after having gone through this," he says, indicating the damage to my digits. It reminds me that they need not be on display any longer, and I pull the gloves back on.

"Oh, I'm not happy, not one bit. But I know their tactics. Besides, whoever casts false witness for them, is likely a member of their dirty brotherhood or at the very least a liar and sympathizer. It will give you names to keep an eye on."

"The Royal Guards do keep such a file. I'll add to it when I get those alibis. On a related topic, we've searched for Meier everywhere we can think of without success. We even served a warrant at both Jasperson's home and the Coal Syndicate, all to no avail."

"I'm not surprised. The Coal Syndicate has hundreds of properties all over the Boston area alone. They could have stashed him in a quiet little corner, and we'd never know it."

"True. But, as they are a publicly held company, we can get a list of all their properties and put it in front of a magistrate. Hopefully, he will allow us to look all of them over," the inspector says.

"That's a good deal of manpower."

"Stella, whether you like it or not, you are still a very popular figure. The powers-that-be have all but given me an unlimited letter of credit to investigate the multiple attempts of murder on your person."

"I don't want to be a public figure. I'm happy just being me."

"That ship has sailed, Stella. Live with it." I cross my arms and put on my best belligerent face. "Anyways, may I ask two questions?"

Still grumpy, I nod, saying, "That is one."

"Smart aleck. How did they catch you and keep you without you going all witchy on them?"

"Witchy? Isn't that a bit of a slur?"

"Sorry, but I couldn't think of any way else to say it."

"OK, you've earned enough friendship that I'll let it pass. I think I was chloroformed in my sleep."

"That would do it. We've been having a rash of attacks on women using that method. One minute they are asleep or sitting quietly in a bar, and the next, they are nude in a field with a man's seed in their belly. If we ever catch that perpetrator, I'll personally castrate him."

"I'll flip you for the privilege."

"We'll do it together," Antonio agrees. I know it is nothing more than talk. The inspector values the law too much to go vigilante. It is for this reason I keep Manuel's name from him. "Well, then how did you get away?"

"I'm going to keep those details a secret, Inspector. Let's just say I did 'something witchy.'"

"Touché, Stella. I'll get started on inquiries."

"If you can, imply that I'm dead. That should keep them from trying for me again in a different way. They have been too inventive."

"So you are finally going to hole up and let us do our job?" the inspector asks with not a little sarcasm.

"Do I have to answer that, Inspector?"

"That's enough of an answer. Where will you be so I can get in touch?"

"Tommy will know how to find me," I say.

"Not your young girl runner?"

"Her name is Mikey. And no, I want her to think I'm missing. She will continue tearing the city apart, trying to find me. Can you think of a better way to make everyone think I'm dead?"

"That's not a bad plan."

"Thank you, Inspector. Coming from someone as devious as yourself, yes, I'll take that as a compliment."

# # #

"Tommy," I say quietly, entering the Helms's stable. I'd waited around until his boss had gone to the house. "Are you alone?"

"Stella!"

"Shhhhh. Keep it quiet. I don't want anyone to know I'm here."

He waves me into one of the empty stalls where there are a couple of stools. He offers me one. "Yeah, I heard about you and the mistress. It's a dirty rotten shame. You would be good together."

His statement flicks an unhealed wound that I'd been able to forget about for other pressing matters. "Yes, but that's not the reason I don't want anyone to know I'm here. You see, I'm dead." Tommy raises one eyebrow at me. "I mean that I want people to think I'm dead." I give him the thumbnail sketch of what happened, less anything about Manuel.

A dark cloud comes across his face. "I's can kill 'em for ya, if'n ya want, Stella."

"No, Tommy. The law can take care of any of that for me. But I'd like to ask a favor of you."

"Anything, Miss Stella."

"It's nothing bad but might involve a bit of fibbing."

"I learned that before I could talk."

"I'm sure you did. What I need is to know if the kids have found Meier, and if so, where. I'd ask Mikey, but I want her to keep beating the bushes for me. She can play her part in this little charade better if she thinks I may be dead. See?"

"Yes, Miss Stella. But if'n the law is going to take care of it for ya, why do you need to know where he is?"

"I need some information from him. I think I can convince him to talk, but I have to find him first. The law hasn't been able to."

"I'd rather be horsewhipping him, but I'll see what I can do."

"And remember, not a word of this to either the viscount or his wife."

"Then I'd better wait until when my duties are done."

"That's fine," I say. "I'm not in that much of a hurry," I fib, just a little.

"So, where you gonna stay?"

"You know where the Fens are?" Tommy nods. "There are a group of witches there called *Los Lobos*."

"Yeah, we all know 'bout The Wolves. Little wonky that they lives like savages, but they is good folk."

"Well, I'll be staying with them. I'll let them know that you are coming so they don't scalp you." Tommy laughs nervously as if he isn't sure they would or wouldn't. "If I'm not there, leave the information with any of the team, and I'll pick it up later."

#

My feet complain, forming a few blisters, something I've not had since I gave up store-bought shoes. They have not formed a good working relationship with my borrowed moccasins. I've not walked this much since I got the poderabile. Two miles to the Helms Estate and now over three until I find a bench along the street outside the *Science of the Miraculous* building right as the Mission Bells toll four.

Settling into place to watch, out of a bag, I liberate a quesadilla that I bought at a street vendor along the way. My stomach complains that it is being neglected. I don't blame it. I hadn't had anything since the liquor last night. I take a big bite and savor the hot, tangy cheeses. I may be here for a while so I want to keep up the façade of being here for a legitimate reason. So, with my middle no longer sitting up and begging, I change my behavior to taking very small bites.

My mind churns over something that I still haven't decided—what to do with *Señor* Gomez y Ruiz. Not a little part of me wants to grind him to paste between two massive stone slabs, something well within my capabilities. This smacks more of vengeance than justice. I have to be careful of the threefold law that says whatever energy you bring into the world, good or bad, will come back to you multiplied by three. I must factor in both the negative of my colossal enmity to the man for what he has done and the fact that he can't and won't be punished by the law.

I still haven't settled on anything when I see Manuel walk out the front door just past six. He says something to a companion and then turns east alone. As I'm dead, at least in his mind, and I'm dressed and coiffured differently, he doesn't notice me. I drop my paper bag in a nearby trash receptacle and follow.

I'm very conscious of what is going on around me. It is quitting time for nearly the entire waterfront. The street is crowded with pipefitters, naval construction workers, accountants, and more. There is a swirl of people trying to get home to their evening meals, children, and spouses. In this chaos, I have zero chance of making a quick and quiet capture of my quarry.

I will detain and deal with Manuel, of that I am certain. This is no idle boast or brag. I have absolutely no fear or doubt at this moment. I'll admit that witches are vulnerable. The scars all over my body are a testament to that. Usually, this is the cause of inattentiveness or being caught off our guard. All that being said, Inspector Guizzetti is correct—a single practicing witch can and likely will destroy even ten men without even breathing hard. Thus, the reason for the Special Service Division of the Royal Artillery.

But tonight isn't about implementation. Tonight I'm scouting my target. *Pendejo* Gomez leads me to the Constitution Inn, a long-term hostel. I watch as he goes into their restaurant. This must be his lodgings. That is good enough for now. I'll be back.

# # #

The hack I hired drops me just outside the Fens. I slog through the brush around the well-beaten track. To my surprise, I find Tommy sitting eating stew and chatting with Patrick O'Donald, the ice witch of the Lobos.

"S'ella!" Tommy manages around his food.

"Perfect timing," I reply.

"I bribed him," Patrick says. "Not too many can turn down me Mulligan stew."

Tommy hastily empties his mouth, setting the wooden bowl down on the ground next to him. "I got what ya need, Miss Stella. The kids found him dossing in the barn of the Knapp Dairy. They says he been there fer days." It reminds me of the stenciling I saw on one of the NPP signs.

"Excellent," I mutter under my breath. *I just may be able to wrap this up in short order.* "Excellent," I say louder to Tommy. "Patrick, might I impose on the *Lobos* generosity for just a couple more dollars? I'll pay it back with interest the minute I get these vultures taken care of."

Without an answer, the young Irishman walks over to a bag hanging innocently on the side of the lodge. He reaches a hand in and comes out with a fist full of banknotes. He strolls back over and drops them into my lap. Tommy's eyes are the size of saucers. There must be a hundred dollars!

"This is way too much. I just—"

"Take what you need, Stella. Use the rest for good. We know you won't squander it."

"Thank you, Tommy," I say, handing him a five-dollar bill. "You did something I couldn't. You are a true friend."

"Then I ain't be needing paying. Friends help friends," he retorts, handing me back the money.

"And I am helping you. Save it for that one special gal," I say, pushing Tommy's hand back toward him. He gives me an odd look but pockets the money.

"Thanks."

"And friend, can I get you to do one more favor?"

"Sure, Stella."

I write a quick note. Without an envelope or sealing wax, I fold it four times for good measure. "Could you take this to the Bell in Hand for me? Give it to someone of my team and only someone from the *Dos Campanas.* And whatever you do, don't read it."

"On my way now, mum. Patrick, I'll be back for some more of your stew and a game of checkers later, if that is OK."

"That would suit me right down to the ground," Patrick says with a big smile.

"Well, I have to run again if I want to finish this off tomorrow."

"Don't leave without some food. Heck, take it with you if you are in that big of a rush. You'll need the fuel. It's going to be a cold night."

#

It is long after moonset and the night sky is brilliant with stars. Without a blanket of clouds, the temperature is enough to give me goosebumps as I wait behind a pile of unsplit firewood. I can barely see the wisps of my breath.

A blaze of light flares as the door to the bunkhouse opens. The illumination spilling out frames the unmistakable gorilla form that exits. I stay hunkered down behind my blind, watching Meier move to the barn without the aid of a candle. Other than some field mice in the corn crib and a restless mare in the paddock, nothing else moves.

I don't want to give Meier an opportunity to cry out. I emphasize to the earth that we must be quick. As the speediest of the options, some mud from the pigpen will move first. Heinrick turns the corner, where no one could see him from the workers' accommodations, even if it were daytime. I urge the earth to attack.

The mud engulfs the vermin's head, Meier, not the mice, before he can even realize why his legs feel wet. In a panic, he reaches up to strip the muck from his face, but not one sound escapes his hole. He does issue a series of grunts. At first, the stone lifts up like a bowl before creating a bubble around him, similar to what I'd made around myself in protection. It now imprisons rather than protects, and no more sounds come forth.

I pause, listening for any signs of discovery. No pelting feet answer my assault—no clang of an alarm bell as an intruder alert. I pad forward to the ball and urge it to roll on with a flick of my wrist. If someone were to see, it would look like a young girl rolling a barrel hoop along with a stick.

I had a fortunate find when I'd crept up to the Knapp Dairy workers' quarters tonight. Maybe a mile away, I came upon the burned-out remnants of my cremation location. If the NPP hadn't been worried about anyone hearing my screams there, I can be pretty sure I don't need to worry about Meier's.

Upon reaching the site, I spend a few minutes kindling a small fire so that I can see who I'm talking to and gauge his veracity. I release a portion of the sphere to form a cage rather than a solid sphere. Meier is prone inside, still clawing at the mud over his head. I call off my attacker.

"Hello there, Heinrick. I can call you, Heinrick, can't I? I feel that assassin and target should be on a given-name basis." While my tiny blaze provides only a limited color palette, even I can tell that his face drains pale. There are six or eight breaths before he summons up enough of his courage to bluster back.

"Let me go, you witch...you vile abomination...you harlot of Satan!"

"That kind of talk isn't going to win you much love, Heinrick."

"Filth! Release me this second, you devil spawn."

"Well, Heinrick, I'm sure you know I have no love for you."

"Stick it up your arse and holler fire!"

"Well, then this is so appropriate. I don't know if you recognize where we are, but this is where you tried and failed to kill me. Now I'm going to ask you a few questions. Answer right and I might just let you live."

"You wouldn't dare kill me. The threefold law, demon slut."

I think that his deprecation is probably closer than he could possibly know. *But I have a task. Don't get sidetracked,* I remonstrate myself. "Well, unfortunately for you, Heinrick, I've already lost my life a couple times over. Remember that the devil takes care of its own." There is no reason I can't use his own prejudices against him. "So here is what is going to happen. We are going to play a game. Every time you don't answer me, lie to me, or are obnoxious, I'm going to give you a taste of what will happen if you really make me angry. Ready to play?"

"Fuck you!"

"I guess you are ready then." I mentally shove the cage into the ground, thirty feet deep. Oh, there is still the open space and air to breathe in the middle for my victim, but no light. I sit down next to the firelight and pull out a book I borrowed from Patrick, *Portrait of a Lady.* I get through the first chapter and decide that my victim has had a strong enough first taste.

Working with the earth, I lift the cage back above ground. I can see the defiance still in Meier's face. This may take quite some time.

"Heinrick, let me give you a couple thoughts before I have to demonstrate again. I don't have to leave any space. I can fill up every cubic inch, including your lungs, with stone, gravel, or sand. But honestly, that is too good for you." He opens his mouth as if he is going to say something but holds his tongue.

"Also, there is nothing that says I have to bring you back. You could become permanently entombed under that soil. You'd have nothing to eat or drink, trying to decide whether you'll die from the cold, the dehydration, or the scavengers in the earth that could pick at your flesh with impunity. Nope, too quick," I add. "How about I push you down far enough so you are at the top of the water table. That way, you'd at least not die of thirst. In that way, I haven't even killed you and can confess with a clear heart."

I let my words sink in for a few moments. Meier doesn't say anything. "Silence is a bit rude, but it's better than your vile speech. OK, here is your first question. I want a complete list of names of the NPP."

I can see the defiance on his face. He is weighing his nonexistent options. "I'll make it a little easier on you. Remember that there is no evidence against them so they won't go to prison. I just want to know who I need to avoid." I offer him a pad of paper and a pencil. He hauls back and slaps them out of my hand.

"I guess that is an answer." With one hand, I reach out over the cage and shove it down. With the help of the ground beneath, I send it much deeper this time. I take him down to the top of the underground aquifer and maybe a few inches in.

I sit back down and bury myself back into my book. I can totally empathize with the main character, who doesn't want to get married.

I decide my charge has had enough for the moment and lift him back to the surface. He is shivering with the cold of the water. His clothes are soaked. There seems to be a bit more humility so I relent and move the cage closer to the fire so he can warm. "So, are we going to throw any more temper tantrums?" I ask. He shakes his head as he warms his hands through the stone bars.

I hand him the pencil and pad of paper. "Names and titles of all of the members."

His teeth are still chattering as he says, "Don't know all. Only know those of my *Turmae*, my Troop."

"Don't lie to me."

He doesn't say anything, only shakes his head. He writes fifteen names down on the paper, including Manuel. I only recognize one other, Chief Inspector Uther O'Hara, the same one that was part of the operation to take down John Quarrels. I point at the name. "O'Hara? Is this the truth?"

"Yes," he says, still shivering. I move the cage a little closer to the fire.

I tear that sheet off the tablet and put it into a small linen bag emblazoned with the slogan "General Mills Extra Fine Flour" on it. Cora gave it to me to carry my things.

"Where do you normally meet?"

"The Bitter. Bar in Boston proper."

I know the place. It's dark with private booths for less than savory business but too busy at all times for what I have planned. Too many witnesses.

"Is Bruce Jasperson involved?" He shakes his head. "Do you want me to believe he'd hire you as his chief of security just because of your experience as a policeman?"

"Carlton made him." I wrinkle my mouth. I'm having a hard time swallowing this, but barring dipping him again, I can't do anything about it. I will have to hold my suspicions about the president of the Coal Syndicate.

"Who is going to attack the pope in Philadelphia?"

"Don't know."

"Oh, Heinrick, I know you know. We have your map. So you just lied to me so it's back into the hole for you." I lift up my hands.

"Wait! I'll tell you. No more of that dark." Tears start dripping down his face. It seems I've broken him. I don't feel any pity. "Cushman and Gregory."

"Full names!" I bark.

"Victor Cushman and Winston Gregory. Manuel's plan."

"Good, now I have just one more task for you," I say, handing him back the tablet and paper. "I want you to write a letter to Manuel Gomez to meet you at the Evangeline Hotel in Biloxi, Mississippi, on June eighth."

"Bu—"

"Heinrick, if you do this one more thing, I'll let you live without burying you in a hole. It is better than you deserve, but I'm generous. Heck, if you tell the constables everything you've told me, you just might escape the noose.

"Oh, and keep me out of your confession, or I might just make your entire jail cell sink into the earth for the next thousand years."

19—Sunday, May 20, 1888

I wake up to the bitter smell of coffee and the sound of frying bacon. I really need to do something nice for the *Lobos*. They didn't hesitate to give me a soft cot, food, and even money.

Still wearing my clothes of yesterday, I climb out of bed, sliding into my slippers with care. I still have some blisters. The nice thing about the traditional native garb is that it doesn't wrinkle much. With my hair still in a ponytail, I don't even need to brush it. With a bit of sarcasm, I wonder if the Lobos need one overly scarred earth witch.

Patrick, the only member of his team around, is looking a bit worse for wear as he tends a fry pan that stretches a good four feet across. His eyes are bloodshot, and there are dark circles under each. Notwithstanding this, he has a sly grin on his face.

"Good morning, Pat."

"And a *bueños dias* to you as well, Stella."

"Where is everyone, not that I can't eat that whole pan of bacon and all of the eggs in that bowel, fried, of course?"

"That's good, Stella. We had a demon escape early this morning. The rest of the team is out dealing with it. I decided to hang around and rustle grub. I wanted everything ready for them when they got here. Dig in. I can always fry up some more. How many eggs do you want?"

"Scramble three, I'm hungry," I say with a reverse blow around a hot chunk of meat that I snatched from the pan.

"Yes. So any more hijinks today? You couldn't have gotten in much before three."

"And how would you know that, Master O'Donald?"

"You mean other than you being as loud as a bear in heat?"

"I don't think that would wake you, Patrick."

"It might. But I wasn't asleep. I was entertaining a young maiden."

"Ohhhh. I'm sorry."

"I'm not. Wish her parents were a bit less status-conscious so we could be open about our relationship. I would like to make her my wife."

"I bless you both."

"I don't think it will ever happen. I've inquired with her father. He won't even see me."

I see a potential way to pay back at least some of my debt. "Would the intercession of a genuine hero help?" His quizzical look tells me that he'd never considered it.

"It just might, Stella. Would you, please?"

"What is her name and her father's name?"

"She is Miss Fredericka Clark—"

"Wait a minute. I thought Tommy was sparking with her."

Patrick blushes here, but not earlier, about sharing his intimacy with the girl. "No, Stella. Tommy has been helping her get out to see me." What did I tell Tommy about not always believing gossip? Here it bites me. Patrick hands me a steaming plate heaped with fluffy eggs, bacon, and pan toast.

"Thanks, Pat. So that makes her father Earl Robert Clark the Third."

"Yes."

I wonder if I have bitten off more than I can chew. Earl Clark is known for his conservative bent, but I'll give it a try. The worst thing is that the poor kids are in the same spot they are in now. "I'll give it a whirl, Patrick."

"Thank you so much, Stella. On a completely different topic, did you hear that the pope's ship has been delayed by a storm?"

# # #

"Are you sure you want to do this, Stella?" Carlos asks softly as he stares into my eyes. "The cost could be horrific."

It's quiet in the Bell in Hand on Sunday morning. Most of the regular patrons are sleeping off their previous night's drinking or preparing for church. The *Dos Campanas* are six of the nine people in our watering hole. Maxwell yawns. Raquel's unruly hair is even more so this morning with what looks like a family of field mice peeking out from within the chaos.

I nod. "I'm sure. If you think you have another way, I'm all ears." Donny and Bea both shake their heads.

"I can't," Max squeaks. "Remember that the law is likely to be the least of your troubles."

"Oh, I haven't forgotten the witches' law of three. I just believe down deep that this is justice, not vengeance. I can't let him roam the streets."

"*Policía* will know nothing but that you siesta with us all day, *Señora* Stella," offers Bea, the newest of our group. Everyone else nods, including Michaeleen, who has come over to see what his best customers are talking about in such hushed tones.

"Agreed," Carlos declares. "Now, shall we get some of that siesta started?"

"Pints for everyone?"

"Definitely," Donny says.

Mick turns and then says, "Stella, I believe you have a visitor."

I turn back toward the door to see Mikey standing on the threshold of the doorway. *Cacafuego*, I think. I'd hoped to avoid this until after I got back from my morning adventure. "Come in, Mikey."

She comes up and stands next to me. Her face reminds me of a parent that needs to paddle her offspring but is inhibited by being in an upscale restaurant. The smoke coming out of her ears would have alerted an entire native population. I decide to treat her like the nanny, and I've just about reached my majority.

"I was kidnapped, Mikey. I didn't run away. I mean, just look at what I'm wearing."

A host of emotions play over her face. She starts to speak four or five times only to shut up. Finally, she offers, "I'm glad you are safe, Stella. It woulda been nice if you sent word to us. We've been very worried."

"I'm honored that you are worried about me, but I needed to do some things before I returned home."

"Yes, miss," she says, stressing the honorific. "Shall I fetch some clothes for you so you can continue your siesta?" Her tone flays skin off my body.

"No. I'll be home this afternoon for fresh clothes. In the meantime, I need you to go back and call off the search for me. And no kids watching over me here, either."

"Yes, miss."

# # #

Finding a cab on Sunday, especially downtown, is a challenge. Fortunately, I decide that shanks mare is the best way to get to Saint

Andrew's Church. Getting a cab would only add a witness that I don't need. Saint Andrew's is the only church within short walking distance of the Constitution Inn. I revel in my mission this morning. The half a pint of bitter I'd had in showing my face openly at the Bell in Hand won't affect my judgment or skills.

I need a clear head, for I've finally decided what Manuel's punishment...no...his atonement will be. I know he will never confess his sins to a real priest so I'll give out the penance. What he does with it is between him and the one true God.

I avoid Chelsea Street. Too many people there know me and might, even in my somewhat disguised state, recognize me. Warren to Winthrop and then up Lexington and onto Bunker Hill Road. I walk past the Constitution Inn before darting into one of the dark alleys that empties out of this main thoroughfare, the direct route for my quarry back to his lodgings. I crouch behind some metal bins and wait.

I'm nervous with anticipation, not fear. I have to keep myself from fidgeting, especially scratching my healing fingertips against the rough brick of the building. The first crush of the faithful leaving Saint Andrews Church streams by. Mostly young people who are anxious to get on with the frivolities of a day without work. The bulk of the people in their Sunday suits and frocks pass with no sign of my quarry. The people passing slows to a trickle.

Have I missed him? Have I guessed wrong? I lean forward out of my hiding place behind some trash bins and discarded crates to look up the street. On the steps of the church is Mr. Gomez in a smart walking suit talking to a priest. *Somewhat fitting that I was attacked just leaving church*, I muse. *There is symmetry in the universe. Karma is a constant.* I pull back into my web.

This delay actually helps me. By thinning out the crowds, I won't need to be quite so circumspect. The cobblestones hum under me with anticipation of their own. The bins themselves have value in my plans. There is also a tiny sliver of clay that I can use instead of crueler choices.

I hear the heels of his shoes making steady time toward my trap. He strolls into the mouth of the alley. The ground tilts underneath him, with the side toward me going significantly down. No one from the street is likely to see anything other than a man stumbling into a shadowed roadway.

It would only be a stumble if I hadn't set a berm for him to trip over. He calls out in alarm, reaching out for a garbage can to steady himself.

Instead, the metal bins flatten, resulting in Manuel falling face-first into the ground in a heap of rubbish. I don't wait. I order the metal trash cans. They slither across the land and wrap around the man like a boa constrictor. As the *señor* opens his mouth to call out, the clay launches out of the earth and into his maw. So quick. So easy.

I give the command, and the earth rolls my prisoner over on his back. A tiny trickle of blood oozes from his nose where he smashed it. His eyes go wide when he sees me, but he can't say a word. He tries his hardest to expel the clay, but the wriggling mass, with a life of its own, is having none of it.

"I don't want to hear from you, Manuel. I'm not attacking you for what you failed to do to me. That would be vengeance. But as you are so crafty, the law can't touch you for your crimes. So, I will judge you for releasing demons onto this world. Your penance is to travel to the world of chaos on which the demons themselves live. 'For whatsoever a man soweth, that shall he also reap.'"

He struggles and flails. He tries to scream. All of these have about the same impact as a little boy throwing rocks at a ship of war.

I grab the planes of existence, sensing the weaknesses. I struggle to align the frayed edges. The dizziness is mild as I know its source and what direction it is coming from.

Manuel Gomez y Ruiz thrashes his head from side to side, I'm assuming to indicate no. All it does is batter his head against the cobblestones.

As the holes line up under him, I say, "May someone take pity on your soul because where you are going, the local denizens won't." The metal of the trash bins unwinds, dropping him. Even the clay leaps from his mouth, allowing Manuel to scream for the brief moment that I hold the gate open.

The world is a better place as I close the portal.

As I walk away, I drop Meier's letter, with Manuel's Constitution Inn address on it, into a post box. None of my fingerprints are on the paper, as I've worn gloves the entire time.

# # #

The musicians of the day, a piano player, and his chanteuse warm up in the main room of the Bell in Hand. Michaeleen winks at me as I slip into the *Dos Campanas* booth. I sing along a bit too loudly to embed my presence into the other patrons' minds. I make several unnecessary trips to the privy, ensuring I bump into folks I know and apologize. I even yell to Michaeleen for another round of drinks for the table. The overacting may be corny, but it should keep me out of witches' prison.

I lose two *doubloons* playing poker with my team, my mind not at all focused on the game. Usually, such a stunning loss would disquiet me. Instead, I just chalk it up to my disguise. I worry as I wait for one specific patron to show up. I can't leave for mass until he shows—and I very much need to confess.

Antonio shows up right at the three o'clock bells. They say a magician creates many of his illusions by creating a plausible diversion. Heinrick will be mine.

"'Tonio," I say, slurring quite a bit more than the actual alcohol I've imbibed. "Glad ya made it. Ya might sen' somebody ta the dairy. My kids say tha' the black'ard is in tha barn."

"Huh?" Understanding Drunk is a skill that takes some warmup.

"Ya know—Meier. Holing up there."

His eyes go wide as he urges, "Which dairy?"

"Knapp...I think I need one of those. A nap that is."

"I'll get someone right on it." He dashes out to the police box down the street.

If he thinks I might, just might be involved with imprisoning Meier this morning, he won't look at me for the disappearance of one Manuel Gomez y Ruiz.

# # #

"Forgive me, Father, for I have sinned. It has been two weeks since my last confession."

"Yes, my daughter, please tell me your sins so they can be expelled from your soul."

"Father, I have two sins to confess. One you already know of...I performed adultery."

"My daughter, adultery is a mortal sin. Have you stopped and prevented it from happening again?"

"The person in question and I have mutually agreed that it is against the tenets of God. We have agreed that it will happen no more."

"But do you wish it? Wanting it is a sin, as well, my daughter."

"I can't falsify myself by saying that I don't desire to be her partner. I do want it but only under the auspices of the church and my Lord, Jesus Christ. I can't lie with her without that."

"Good. What else do you have to confess?"

"I am guilty of the sin of pride. I judged a man when that right belongs only to God."

"We all sometimes judge others—"

"No, Father, you have to understand. I didn't just think he was evil. I actively judged and defined penance for his sins. Had there been any other way, I might not have, but I did."

Father Juan is quiet for some time. "Daughter, only the Lord of hosts can see what is in the heart of any man. You must remember that."

"Yes, Father."

"Daughter, do you repent of your sins?"

"I do, Father. I shouldn't have done either of those things."

"Then say fifty Hail Marys. Go forth and sin no more. I absolve you of your sin."

20—Monday, May 21, 1888

Knowing that my assassin and his key conspirators are dealt with and having guards on my door, and Stella-created stone bars on my windows allows me to sleep soundly in my own bed. I wake with a stretch and a smile on my face. On the whole, I feel right with the world. There are still sore spots, but I no longer feel like a blind duck in a shooting gallery.

I get up and manage to relieve my bladder in a very temporary chamber pot. I'll be happy when Mr. Krieg finishes and I have the comfort of indoor plumbing. Living in a construction zone isn't for me. The hammering and other intrusive sounds of the ongoing project have already started, and the sun is barely peeking above the horizon. I treat myself to a sponge bath while watching in the mirror. I'm able to clean up some of the soot, dirt, and mud I missed with the impromptu bath in the fens.

Clean, I pull on fresh underpinnings. Thinking about my metal corset, I pause. I do still have some people out in the world who would like to do me harm. I don't really notice the additional weight or restrictions. "Why not," I say, wrapping it around me, enticing it to grapple its own ends. It tightens to just a friendly pressure, like the hug of a friend. I choose my green satin dress with the ruffled sleeves and a white and green lace ruche over my chest.

I step out the door and am assaulted with even more noise. "Good morning," I say to Milton and Aria, who guard my door. Mikey bounds up the steps even before they can reply.

"Good morning, Stella," the pair says almost in unison.

Aria continues with, "We are so sorry for failing you Friday night!"

"Piffle," I snap with as much contempt as I can muster.

"But—"

"Jesus, Mary, and Joseph, how could you know they would scale up the wall and take me out through the window? Preposterous. Now stuff all that guilt into a sack and toss it into the ocean."

I can see the forlorn look on their faces like a pair of chastened coon dogs. I catch the tiny shake of Mikey's head in their direction before she says, "So what can we do this morning for you, Miss Stella?"

"Quit being so damned formal. Now, you three, ready for some breakfast? I hear Goldies, just a block over, serves some good lobster fritters."

"We are at your mercy, Stella," Aria said, her eyes showing her hunger.

"Well then, let's get moving. My stomach is talking to my backbone." We take my private stairs down outside the chaos of construction only to run into Inspector Guizzetti walking in our direction.

"Good morning, Stella," he offers in greeting.

"And to you, Inspector. To what do I owe this visit? Walk with us. We are on our way to something that will break our fast."

"Certainly. I came by to let you know we captured Heinrick Meier yesterday afternoon, right where you told us. Oddly, he was imprisoned already in a stone cage with no door or lock."

"Really? That does seem odd." Butter wouldn't melt in my mouth.

"Yes, it took us nearly two hours to chisel him out."

"Sounds like the work of an earth witch," I continue with my play. "Funny that he angered more than one."

"Yes, funny that," Antonio says with enough sarcasm to smother anyone within earshot. "You wouldn't have had anything to do with that?"

"Perish the thought, Inspector," I say, not quite lying.

"Hmmm. Well, you will be happy to hear that he immediately asked for a deal. He is singing like those little yellow birds people keep as pets."

"Canary?" I offer.

"Yes."

"Has he implicated anyone worthwhile?"

"A number of NPP members, including the men who are to release demons in Philadelphia. We are in the process of getting magistrate warrants for those local to our jurisdiction. We probably won't get them excepting those directly involved in your kidnapping."

"What a shame you can't imprison them all."

"Agreed. But my main reason to be here is to warn you that your friend Manuel Gomez y Ruiz is one of those implicated."

"Really?" Now I try to put genuine concern into my voice. "Are you sure?"

"Almost one hundred percent, Stella. We found a letter posted to him from Meier indicating that Gomez is on his way to the Freeport. So it is unlikely you are in any danger but keep your watch up."

As we reach the door of Goldies, I say, "I will. Join us, Inspector? I'd feel safer with you at my side—no deprecations to my guardians here."

"With pleasure."

21—Tuesday, May 22, 1888

Around sixteen million people cheer as *God's Gift*, the pope's private vessel, glides up to the dock. I have to admit to being one of the throng beside the rest of the *Dos Campanas*. Since the story about the plots broke in the newspapers, we are here more for show and our own purposes than any prevention of a demon disaster. All of the key players have been apprehended and in hack, except Manuel Gomez y Ruiz, who has a Detriment to the Crown telegraphed to every duchy in the country and every Spanish province in the new world. The Swiss Guard, the King's Own, and the Boston Constabulary all have a significant presence both as a barrier to the crowd and mingling within it.

Archbishop Mendel Mrak is on the pier, looking uncomfortable. I can't tell if it is from the unseasonal heat and sun or the likely consequences of how he's flaunted the pope's authority.

Extra-loud cheering, applauding, and whistling goes up when the pope, resplendent in white, shows on the deck of his ship. He holds up one hand until minutes later, he receives some level of quiet.

"*In nomine patris, et filli, et spirtus sancti, amen.*" He then continues in accented English, "I am proud to grace this land of God and his son Jesus Christ for the first time..."

22—Saturday, May 26, 1888

My new overstuffed chair is nearly as comfortable as my bed. I can see future nights of falling asleep while reading a book here. I lounge in little more than a dressing gown looking over the *Boston Herald* that Mikey slid under my door.

Two headlines have split the front page. "Archbishop Mrak Returns to Vatican City for Moral Guidance." "Pope names Dennis O'Leary Archbishop of Boston." The pope couldn't have made a stronger statement if he'd burned it into the skin of every parishioner—Irish are people. Treat them as you would any neighbor.

Also on the front page, under the fold, I read, "Are You a Witch? Come Join His Majesty's Forces to Save the Monarchy from Tyranny." If his majesty's government is recruiting this blatantly, I wonder just how much longer before hostilities break out.

In remembrance, I look at the newly mounted picture of my husband on the wall. It stirs a bittersweet longing within me.

I get up and sit at my writing desk, folding the gown underneath me. I have correspondence to write this morning, some of it nearly as painful as the loss of my husband.

Dear Adrianna,

I appreciate your generous offer to host me for luncheon today. However, I believe it is best if we mingle as little as possible until proper behavior can be assured on both sides. I know that isn't possible on mine at this time.

With enduring respect,

(s)Stella Ochoa

I manage not to cry as I seal it into an envelope, but there is a tightness in my chest and a hollowness in my belly. I almost wish the bitter coffee in front of me were absinthe.

As much as it pains me, I realize my own carnal desires are reaching a crisis point. I've put them out of mind to remain faithful to my feelings for Adrianna. However, I don't know how much longer I can fend off the balloon of need forming in my pelvis. Worse, I'll be having dinner with Karie tonight. I don't know if I will be able to keep my hands to myself, knowing she is ready, willing, and desirous every minute of the day and night. With no ability to have a relationship with the viscountess, am I torturing myself for no reason?

Pushing that out of my mind, I turn to other more pleasurable thoughts. I write each of the following notes with a perverse amount of sadism, but not toward the addressees.

Dear Susan Montrose,

I recall you fondly from my time at Chapman's Boarding House. I am opening my own boardinghouse and thought you might be interested in knowing about it. I want to give you the first opportunity to secure a place before opening it up for new tenants.

The rent for the Brick Factory is the same as you are currently paying, and our amenities are significantly more than your current situation. The Brick Factory boasts oversized rooms, new fittings from the makers that furnished the Parker House, and indoor plumbing that includes a water closet with bathtub, basin, and toilet.

As I'm nothing of a cook, I've hired an exceptional one to provide meals that are tasty, wholesome, and of the best ingredients.

Most of all, I have no interest in prying into your personal affairs. And what use you have for your room as long as it is not commercial or troublesome to our other guests, is your own business (this includes the opportunity to entertain).

I invite you to witness the construction and some preliminary furnishings on Friday next, June 1st, at six in the evening. We will provide supper as well so bring your questions and your appetite.

Please RSVP.

Yours faithfully,

(s) Stella Ochoa

P.S. I'm also purchasing an upright piano for the parlor that will be available for your pleasure.

There are similar letters for Carmen Rodriguez, Pamela Atwell, Isabella and Felicia Wolfe, and Janice Potsdam, all tenants of Chapman's Boarding House. Each of the notes gets a homey postscript that will appeal to that person. It is with a good deal of pleasure that I seal the last of them into an envelope. I'm assuming Chapman will learn about my ploy and die of apoplexy.

I crack the door open and call down the stairs, "Mikey!"

The worthy young lady shows up at my door in short order.

"Mikey, this one is for the Viscountess Helms. All the rest of these are for the women at Chapman's Boarding House. Their names are on the envelopes. I'd send them by post, but they almost certainly would go astray. Give them only to the lady in question. Do not give them to Mrs. Chapmen. After you've delivered them, that's all I have for you on this day."

"Yes, Stella," Mikey says, snatching the letters up in one hand and the rest of her fritter in the other. She dashes out like Hermes with the speed of the wind to deliver messages of pain and retribution.

I contemplate getting dressed for whatever adventure awaits.

Author's Note

I've never had such a problematic time titling a book. In the past, I've always had the name well before I pen more than a few lines of the outline, much less start writing the story.

In the case of *Courting Witchcraft*, I went through several iterations, none of which stuck. I had *Witching the Hour*, *Supping with the Demon*, *Power Plays*, and many more. I tossed two dozen possible titles out to my wife who vetoed the lot. Heck, I'd already written half of the current novel before narrowing the title to one of two choices. I had most of the first draft done before settling on *Courting Witchcraft*. This is probably why there has been a delay in releasing the cover image because I wanted to know what should be there. I was well into the writing of the trial of Quarrels before I have even commissioned.

I guess these are just some of the trials and tribulations of being a creator. Things don't come in a nice steady flow. Art isn't an assembly line. It flows from the heart, not the head. The head can plan for the bumps along that path but can't flatten it out.

On another topic entirely, I have a word for those who have opined that I'm drawing an analogy between demons and nuclear power—

balderdash and other stronger words. OK, don't get me wrong, I can see where readers might have gotten that idea—massive death and destruction if either one goes awry. However, I've stated many times in my author's notes that I am not making political or social commentary. I write for entertainment—full stop.

Now onto the regular feature of my author's notes. Where did I get my idea? The question crossed my mind, "What would Stella do when confronted by an impossible moral dilemma?" I wasn't satisfied throwing only the burgeoning lust and love for Viscountess Helms at her. I also chucked in what to do in the case where the law can't bring the guilty to justice, and she could.

At the same time, I wondered what loathing might witches stir up? Thus, I developed the NPP—*Non Patiatur Phythonissam*—Latin for "Suffer not a witch." There will always be a hate group around focused on anyone different. This is especially true if they can do things others can't (e.g., have some perceived or actual privilege or power). It only makes sense that something like the NPP would exist in Stella's universe.

Add to the above an impending visit by the pope. Sprinkle all of this liberally with Stella's unconventional sexual mores, her religious nature, and those who find her exotic/loving, and you have a recipe for *Courting Witchcraft*.

While I make no commitment, I've already fleshed out the outline of The Monarchy of America's book #3. Does this mean I'll be writing book three immediately? Likely. I am enjoying this book series and the characters within a great deal. Given nothing but my own whims, I'd probably write the next Stella book. But I have fans who are waiting for the end of the Toy World series. I have other fans looking for more CorpGov Chronicles. I even have one very loyal fan that would like to see a sequel to Wayward School (although I have no plans in this area). Needless to say, more books are coming. Thank you for supporting my efforts to bring you the sick visions from my head.

Note: I briefly quote the song "Away with Rum" in this book. I wanted a drinking song and came across this temperance work and thought it would be ironic if it were sung in a pub. Apparently, this is one of those songs that everyone in history seemingly has added verses to. Its true origins are buried in the dust of history. I want to acknowledge mudcat. org for the information I have on this song. They provided me lyrics and made it clear that the song is in the public domain. I want to thank them for the work they put in for me! If you want the full song, visit the thread: https://mudcat.org/thread.cfm?threadid=108622&messages=93

Translations (and other odd terms)

<Alphabetically>

absolutamente—absolutely

aether—a parallel universe touching but not seen by our world; mythical and theoretical only

amante—lover

amiga—female friend; not girlfriend

amigos—friends

amor—love

arroz—rice

arroz a la marinera—seafood over rice

diablo—devil or demon

bebés—babies

bien—good

borracha (fem) or borracho (masc)—drunk or drunkard

brujo—warlock

buenos—good

buenos dias—good morning or good day

buenos noches—good night or good evening

buque naufragado—shipwreck

cabrón—stubborn goat

cabrones—fuckers

cacafuego—shit fire or also braggart

campana—bell

capullo/capulla—like *gilipollas* but with a certain amount of evil intentions, aka wanker

cariño—sweetheart

casa—house

cocina—kitchen

concha—literally shell, but sometimes used by higher society woman for vagina

chimpancés—chimpanzees

chocho/chocha—senile person, also cunt

cicatriz—scar

como se dice—how do you say

coqueto—flirtatious

cuidada—careful

de—of

de nada—you're welcome; literally "of nothing"

descongelando el bistec—defrosting the beefsteak, a Spanish euphemism for a woman's menstrual cycle

dias—days

dios—god

¡Dios Mío!—Oh my God!

disculpe—excuse me

Don—master of a household of distinction

Doña—female version of Don

dos—two

dubloon—old Spanish currency that equals sixty-four reale or approximately eight dollars

dulce—sweet

duro—a five peseta coin where four pesetas equal one dollar

el—the male form of "the"

en sotto voce—in a soft voice meant to be overheard

flan—a custard dessert, usually with a crust of caramel on the top

fopdoodle—dumbass

fuego—fire

genial—brilliant

gilipollas—jerk, or stupid in their own right, often through social ineptitude

gracias—thank you

Gracias a Dios—Thank God

hija—daughter

¡Hijo de la chingada!—son of a bitch

hinchado—inflated, puffery

hostia—literally wafer, specifically communion wafer. When used as an exclamation it means the same as "God damn"

idiota—idiot, fool, moron

infierno—hell, inferno, underworld, Hades

jefe—boss or chief

joda—pain in the ass

¡Joder!—to fuck or colloquially just "Fuck!"

jodete—conjugated form of joder meaning to "go fuck yourself"

la—the feminine form of "the"

la perra—the bitch

lo siento—I'm sorry

madre—mother

Madre Dios / Madre de Dios—Mother of God

maldito—cursed, damned, fucking

mantilla—a lightweight ornamental veil or shawl worn over the head
    and shoulders

marinera—sailor

me disculpe—I'm sorry, or I apologize

merienda—snack or afternoon tea

mi—my

mi amor—my love

mierda de toros—bullshit

modista—designer, couturier

mujer—woman

murió—died

muy—very

niñita—little girl

no les importará—they won't care

noches—night

novia—sweetheart

Okeus—Powhatan American Indian god of war

pan—bread

pan dulce—similar to American doughnuts

papas—potatoes

peinetas—Spanish hair comb

pendejo—fool, idiot, asshole

perra—bitch

peseta—Spanish coin equal to a quarter

pinche—fucking

policía—police

por supesto—of course

porras—literally truncheons but are sweet pastries thicker and chewier than a churro

professora—a female professor

puta—whore

qué—what

que estafa—what a scam

querida—dearest or mistress

reale—old currency where eight reale equals one dollar

salchicha—sausage

scoth—excellent (Irish)

se folla un pez—literally fucks a fish—idiomatically, is screwed up

secreto del la corona—secrets of the crown

semana—week

señor—Mr.

señora—Mrs. without the implication of marriage, a mature woman

señorita—Miss

serpiente—serpent or snake or demon

si—yes

sopa de picadillo—minced meat soup—despite the name it is stew of mostly tomato puree and minced meat and vegetables

tardes—afternoon/evening

¡Tócate los cojones!—What a surprise!

tortilla—flatbread

trasera—ass, butt, bottom (feminine)

turmae—troop

un buque naufragado—a wrecked ship

vdo—widow

veinte—twenty

vete a la mierda—literally "to go to shit" translates as "go fuck yourself"

viuda—widowed

xièxiè—thank you

y—and

zounderkite—idiot

The Alternative History of the Monarchy of America

Like all good alternative histories, there has to be some event or events that have drifted this world away from our own past. In the case of the Monarchy of America series, there are several. If you haven't picked it up from the writing itself, let me share.

Napoleon brings the battle of Waterloo to a draw but is severely wounded, becoming a broken man. France continues to be a thorn in the world's side. Still, without Bonaparte as a driving force, it no longer threatens world domination.

Germanic tribes wrest themselves free of the French grasp but never become a world power.

Spain, with the aid of the Catholic pope, holds sway throughout a good deal of the world and never leaves her golden age. Charles II has several heirs who continue the line, maintaining a strong and united Iberian peninsula. Charles III and IV never seek any world conquest ambitions but rather domination by exploration.

England, with her smaller, more widely diverse empire, is forced to play a much more aggressive and smarter world view game rather than the massive hammer it was in our world. As a result, there are many clashes with the powerful Spanish. Most of these end with a bloody nose for the English. The Brits choose to bide their time.

In the mid-seventeen hundreds, King George decides to honor the troubled American colony's desire for representation. He appoints his son, Frederick, as hereditary Prince of America.

In 1843 Queen Victoria wants to replace Frederick with her son Edward as Prince of America. Frederick and the Americans take exception to this and declare America a monarchy of its own.

Over the following forty-plus years, tensions between England and America are at the point of war. Spain has declared that it will side with this new country if England intervenes. The pope himself presided over

Frederick's coronation as the first King of America, which includes what we know of as Canada as well.

England bides its time but seethes at the humiliations it has had to endure. It continues to find ways to incite incidents with Spain, and America while looking for allies.

Because of the smoother overall political landscape, the Industrial Revolution kicks off earlier. There is no fight for states' rights (there are no states, only duchies of similar shape and size) so no Civil War. In an ironic twist to previous policies, the King of America declares slavery to be an abomination, and all African Americans are forcibly shipped to Cuba.

The "Louisiana Purchase" becomes the "Caledonia Purchase" from Spain. Later, after Lewis and Clark's fateful trip, America and Spain enter into the "New Cadiz Purchase." It includes modern-day Oregon, Washington, Idaho, Montana, Wyoming, and parts of British Columbia, giving America her ports on the Pacific Coast. By that time, the Bonapartes in France have grown powerful again and are threatening to take back the Germanic countries, which are a Spanish protectorate. Spain does this transaction not only to be a good ally and to bolster America's ability to withstand the English aggression but also the New Cadiz sale helps Spain with the finances it needs to blunt French hostility.

By fiat, America annexes northern Canada and all of modern-day Alaska.

Native Americans are not kicked off their lands or slaughtered but rather convinced to relocate into the Oklahoma territories. They are given this land "until the sun grows cold." For once, a deal with the natives is kept. Eventually, the Native Americans ask to become colonies of the crown as the region Ysa, named after the Shoshone creation god.

Catholic Irish are persecuted by the Protestant English. They eventually plead to Spain and the pope himself for aid. In 1877 the Spanish publicly condemn the English for their meddling in Irish affairs and order them to withdraw from Ireland entirely.

Queen Victoria has the Spanish ambassador beheaded, returning the head in a gilt box as a response.

Spain can ill afford a war on two fronts so it beseeches King Frederick II to send their army to Ireland. In America's first flex of her fledgling might, she lands thousands of troops, and tons of supplies, weapons, and ammunition in Galway, Ireland, sparking off the War of

Irish Independence, June 14, 1878. Many more soldiers would cross the Atlantic, and tens of thousands of Americans would be buried in Irish soil.

By November of 1884, the remains of the English army, outnumbered by the Irish Nationalists and their American allies, are forced out of Ireland. The native Irish rejoice for a few short months. But, before Ireland can even get organized as a country, the Potato Famine strikes (forty-one years later than in our world). Many flee to America, as their ally in the war, and others to Spain.

England eyes the weakened country a mere twelve miles away, but knows to pounce would likely cause a world war. Victoria bides her time and lies about for allies.

In 1888, the date of our first book, there is growing tension between England and America. Spain and France are on the verge of war.

As with most steampunk, petroleum products just never take off. From a scientific point of view, I've made the assumption that it has approximately a quarter of the chemical potential energy of what it has in our world.

Thus coal-heated steam is the power of choice. It is relatively cheap, mobile, and an infrastructure exists for it. But coal has a new rival. As the education of magicks has increased, a fusion between technology and magic has led to captive demons coming into their own as a power source. They are summoned to a fixed location where their inhuman bodies heat boilers providing the steam to run homes and industry. No one has been able to hold a demon on a mobile platform.

Other Works Published by TANSTAAFL Press

Novels by Tom Gondolfi

Of Demons and Coal

As a witch, widow Stella Ochoa makes her living at the soul-grinding job of spelling coal dust out of the air. But infrequently, she and her team of Hellfighters are called on to do the dangerous task of capturing an escaped demon.

Now, years after demons have been put to use as power in steam engines, they are getting loose at an alarming rate. Each one kills and causes massive destruction of property. For king, God, and country, Stella investigates the increase only to unravel a plot only humans themselves could devise.

An Eighty Percent Solution – CorpGov Chronicles: Book One

In a world where corporations suborn governments as a part of good business practice and unregistered humans can be killed without penalty, Tony Sammis, a midlevel corporate functionary, finds himself unwittingly a pawn in a guerilla war between a powerful cabal of business leaders and an elusive but deadly underground movement. His final solution to the biological terror unleashed mirrors Tony's own twisted sense of justice.

Thinking Outside the Box – CorpGov Chronicles: Book Two

Winning one war doesn't seem to be enough. Tony Sammis and the Green Action Militia are once again thrust into the center of a conflict that will change the lives of everyone in the solar system. This time they are allies with the fledgling CorpGov and even the United States government against the ravages of the corrupt Metropolitan Police Force. The GAM and their allies are fighting a losing war with few soldiers and even fewer weapons. Behind the scenes, a humble and unsuspected power block lurks with its own axe to grind.

Self-interest, romance, freedom, and a lust for power simmer together in this chaotic soup of tension, intrigue, assassination, and war.

The Bleeding Edge – CorpGov Chronicles: Book Three

Tony Sammis and Nanogate lead a patchwork alliance that includes the nascent CorpGov, Green Action Militia, the president of the United States, the Pacific Northwest Mob, most of the megacorps and the United Brotherhood of Bodyguards. The war the CorpGov alliance knows they can't win has begun, but they are no longer fighting to win. Tony and

Nanogate know they may not survive, but they intend to deliver the most grievous wounds they can. The most dangerous animal is one with no hope.

Window of Opportunity – CorpGov Chronicles: Book Four

Window of Opportunity offers short stories from the CorpGov Chronicles universe. They give backstories of familiar characters, provide foreshadowing for upcoming novels, and paint color onto what makes the CorpGov universe unique. "Life Cycle" fills in some background on how a young Christine becomes the sociopath that we know and love. A corporate-sponsored final solution to an ongoing brush war in South America can be found in "Lose-Lose.""Come to Jesus Moment" tells us more about Michael Beckman-Ford (son of Nanogate) and how he finally makes his first mark on the world. Interpol uncovers prophetic corruption in the church in "Pain Point" and continues into the story "Kick into the Long Grass." Grandma Ice must deal with a hate crime against her family in "Cradle to Grave.""Negative Growth" shows the impact of overpopulation on something as normal as the birth of a child. One man's unique solution to a corporation changing its retirement criteria is investigated in "Exit Strategy." And MANY more! Twenty-eight tales of the trials, victories, and failures in the dark future.

Toy Wars

Flung to a remote world, a semi-sentient group of robotic mining factories arrive with their programming hashed. They can only create animated toys instead of normal mining and fighting machines. One of these factories, pushed to the edge of extinction by the fratricidal conflict, attempts a desperate gamble. Infusing one of its toys with the power of sentience begins the quest of a 2-meter-tall purple teddy bear and his pink polka-dotted elephant companion. They must cross an alien world to find and enlist the aid of mortal enemies to end the genocide before Toy Wars claims their family—all while asking the immortal question, "Why am I?"

Toy Reservations

For years the living toys of Rigel-3 live in the peace that their president for life, Don Quixote, fought so hard to achieve. Their former masters, the Factories, watch on in silence as President Quixote leads his people through many of the growing pains of a new society. On the anniversary of their tenth year of peace, the exiled and mentally unbalanced Isp returns at the head of a massive new Army of the Humans. He openly announces his intent to replace President Quixote's democracy with a theocracy, either peacefully or by force.

Wayward School

After a media blitz that surpassed the Rodney King riots, the Patty Hearst trial, and the acquittal of OJ Simpson combined, Elizabeth sits on Alcatraz's high-tech, death row awaiting execution at the age of thirty. A Catholic priest convinces Elizabeth to tell her story as a warning to other young women who might find themselves in similar circumstances. Elizabeth shares how as a teen she is barely tolerated in an abusive family. When the private shame of her rape becomes an unwanted pregnancy, her father coldly sends her away to a school for wayward girls. At the School, Elizabeth trades her naiveté for a home and family of sorts. Out of her unique position and her nightmarish start to adulthood, Elizabeth goes on to save tens of thousands of lives, for which a jury of her peers condemns her to die.

Novels by Bruce Graw

Demon Holiday

Torval, Demon Third Class, Layer Four Hundred Twelve of the Eighth Circle of Hell, has been in the business of chastising sinners longer than he can remember. Delivering punishment is the only job he's ever known—the only job he's ever wanted. After Torval witnesses something unexpected, his demonic Overseer demands that he take time off to resolve this personal crisis. And so, Torval, the demon, finds himself sent on vacation . . . to Earth, the proving ground of souls!

Demon Ascendant

Torval, Demon Third Class, Layer Four Hundred Twelve of the Eighth Circle of Hell, on vacation to Earth has managed to find another demon, dated a woman and inadvertently explored some of the sins of humankind: greed, gluttony, and lust. Through all this, his biggest struggle involves deciding if he wants his holiday to end or to continue forever.

Lady Hornet

Elizabeth Fontaine is a lonely, ordinary young woman in a world where superheroes struggle daily against evil. To fill the empty void within her soul, she becomes a hero fangirl, following every super's event, subscribing to multiple fanzines, and never missing the daily superhero talk shows . . . until one day, fate grants her the opportunity to leave behind her boring, dreary life and become what she's always dreamed of . . . a superheroine!

Elizabeth learns the hard way the meaning of the phrase "Caveat Emptor!"—let the buyer beware!

Faerie of Central Park

The last of her kind in New York City, Tillianita tends the land and beasts as best she can, reluctantly obeying her departed father's warning to avoid humans at all costs. A freak accident casts her out of the relative safety of Central Park. Lost and alone with a broken wing, she wonders if she'll ever see her home again.

On his own for the first time in his life, college freshman Dave Thompson isn't sure he'll ever fit in. When he stumbles upon an extremely realistic fairy doll, he thinks perhaps it might make a good present for a future date until he discovers that it's not a doll at all. His find turns not only his life upside down but also expands his narrow view of the world.

Anthologies by TANSTAAFL Press

Witches, Warriors, and Wyverns
Enter the Apocalypse
Enter the Aftermath
Enter the Rebirth

www.ingramcontent.com/pod-product-compliance
Lightning Source LLC
Chambersburg PA
CBHW051329020726
47501CB00007B/1996